TRANSFUSION

BY

STEPHANIE HUDSON

Transfusion
The Transfusion Saga #1
Copyright © 2020 Stephanie Hudson
Published by Hudson Indie Ink
www.hudsonindieink.com

Transfusion/Stephanie Hudson – 2nd ed.
ISBN-13 - 978-1-913769-36-9

I dedicate this book to all the wonderful fathers out there like my own, who is and always will be, the foundations of our home and the light in our storm, that life sometimes throws in our way.
This is for you Robert Hudson...my Dad.

Being a Dad.
He welcomes you to the world and vows to protect,
Holds on to your tiny hand and will never forget,
How it feels to be a dad as you call his name,
You've gifted him with a new one, forever he will claim.
He rocks you to sleep and lays you down in your bed,
And the knowledge that you will leave, fills him with dread,
For you will have grown but a constant will remain,
For his love for you will always be there and the same,
Because you're his little girl, or his big boy calling,
The sweetest of things, when a dad catches you falling,
Because he will always be there, no matter your age,
A dad is for life and that will never change.
So, no matter if they aren't with us forever,
For in our hearts they will leave us never.

Love you Dad, Steph x

WARNING

This book contains explicit sexual content, some graphic language and a highly additive dominate Vampire King.

This book has been written by an UK Author with a mad sense of humour. Which means the following story contains a mixture of Northern English slang, dialect, regional colloquialisms and other quirky spellings that have been intentionally included to make the story and dialogue more realistic for modern day characters.

Thanks for reading x

CHAPTER ONE

HOLDING BACK THE YEARS

Closing my eyes, I listened to the beautiful and meaningful words of Simply Red, doubting they had any clue when picking out the name of the song they would know that there was at least one girl in the world that only thought of blood in the name.

Okay, so I know that sounded weird, but I guess in my world weird was actually considered the norm. Well, it *had been,* I should say as I had walked away from it all years ago. Which was another reason why this song was one I had on nearly every playlist I made.

'Holding Back the Years' just seemed to say it all for me and with lyrics like 'chance for me to escape from all I know' and 'holding back the tears, cause, nothing here had grown', then let's just say it was like listening to my inner secrets singing back to me and telling me to still hold on, no matter how much I didn't want to. Because I felt like I had in fact, wasted so many tears, and so many years holding on to a fantasy that would never come true.

And it all started with one name, one I would never let pass my lips no matter what my dreams of him begged of me to do…

Lucius.

Gods, I hated the name, but not as much as I hated the one who it belonged to!

No! I wasn't going to go back there, not again, not today of all days. Seriously though, was there ever going to be a day when I didn't do this to myself?

"Right, you curly-redhead singer, time for something else," I said aloud as I pulled my phone from my pocket and tapped on another playlist, one I'd named 'Badass'. Oh, and a playlist that just so happened to be one that didn't include one single song that would remind me of a certain someone. No, instead it made me feel as if I could be an empowered bitch that could walk straight into that damn club of his with a sexy swagger… *one that didn't just look like my ass cheeks were chewing on my underwear.*

No, I would be wearing kick ass heels I wouldn't fall over on and some sexy little black dress minus the usual food stains a clumsy person had no choice but to wear like a badge of honour (Thanks for that one, Mum!)

Then, I would watch as his mouth dropped open in shock before I simply slapped that cunning and ridiculously handsome smirk from his face before walking back out again with one of my own.

Okay, so I admit, it was a far-fetched fantasy, especially seeing as I swore to myself that I wouldn't ever, and I mean EVER, step foot in his Gods' forsaken nightclub again! That and I usually became a bumbling idiot around him anyway, which trust me, didn't exactly go hand in hand with the badass picture I had painted in my mind.

I released a sigh as I pushed up my square, black rimmed glasses that I'd bought as a buy one, get one free at Specsavers.

But like most people who wore glasses on a daily basis, and I am not talking about the 'part timers', but instead the type that if they didn't then they were likely to get run over by some mad cyclist (as London had many to spare, trust me on that). Then for those blind enough to rely on the use of touch and blurred colours to locate them, no matter the free pair, we usually got attached to one and felt the connection was like being given an extra limb…*or was that just me?*

Well, either way, it was the reason I had a pair sat in my desk as a back-up, just waiting for my next disastrous calamity. Like when I unintentionally dropped them down the loo, then had to fish them out of my own urine before they slipped from my hand and I accidently stepped on them as they were the same colour as the tiles. I swear I was my own worst nightmare, as Demons had nothing on me!

But now to get back to my task at hand I thought, pushing my replacement glasses back up my nose as I carefully handled the Canopic jars, lifting them from the wooden canopic chest of Gua. I couldn't help but marvel at the fact I was handling something from the 12th dynasty, as I always did when touching something from the past. These were discovered in Deir el-Bersha, which is a Coptic village in Middle Egypt. A place that was located on the east bank of the Nile in the Minya Governorate and yet another place in the world, no doubt, that I would never get to see, I thought with a bitter taste of my own past.

I shook my head not thinking about it and concentrated on my job. As the museum's chief specialist restorer and one of the curators in the Department of Ancient Egypt and Sudan, I was used to dealing with rare artifacts. Which really was a fancy way of saying I was like an ancient cleaning lady, my friend Wendy had said once, making me nearly choke on my Pina Colada at the time.

Even now I allowed a small giggle to escape my lips when replaying the comment. But, glancing down at the soft brush in my hand and then a quick look up at all the crates of artifacts still to be prepared, then my argument of 'it's a bit more than that' was looking weaker by the minute.

Which meant here I was on cleaning duty for the new exhibition that was coming up and with weeks of work staring me in the face. So, I cranked up the music and the sound of Bryan Adams singing about the summer of 69, making me wonder if I shouldn't have learnt how to play guitar instead of always having my head stuck in a book?

But then I smiled to myself as I carefully picked each of the four jars from their divided compartments in the old box, knowing that this was my life. And no matter how my mad imagination was suddenly conjuring up images of me on stage rocking it out in leather and leopard print, in this little workshop at the lowest levels of the British Museum in London was exactly where I was meant to be in life.

I momentarily studied the exterior of the box, noting that it had faded blue paint along its edges as well as its lid. Then I started to decipher the carved hieroglyphic inscriptions that were on each side that also ran in a T shape, with two lines of text crossing at the top. The four calcite canopic jars had painted wooden stoppers, and each was in the form of a human headed deity. Pale beige faces with black details and blue-painted wigs decorated each of the jars that varied in shape from narrow to wide shouldered.

Canopic jars were used when a person was mummified, as their internal organs were placed in these jars and were said to be guarded by four different gods. These were the Jackal headed god, Duamutef, who guarded the stomach of the deceased in his jar and who represented the East. Then there was the Human jar that the liver was placed into and was guarded by the god Imsetys, who had a human head and represented the South.

There was also one the lungs were stored in, guarded by the Baboon headed god named Hapi, representing the North. But out of the four it was the Falcon jar that was my personal favorite, with the falcon headed god Qebehsenuef, who was protector of the intestines. He was one of the four sons of Horus, like the others in Egyptian mythology, but he was known as the god of protection and represented the West.

I don't know why he was my favorite, but maybe it was due to my love of birds, which was also another passion of mine. I just loved nothing more on my days off than exploring the British countryside and finding myself at some grand manor house owned by the National Trust. I would then sit in the immaculately pruned and trimmed gardens with a good book or more often than not, bird watching and trying to take pictures of them with my phone.

Now I know that these weren't exactly the exciting pastimes of someone in their twenties. Even more surprisingly, I will have you know, that even with these old fashioned, solitary hobbies of mine, it didn't mean that I didn't have friends. Because if you hadn't already gathered by now, I wasn't just a mega geek, I was also a mega nerd right alongside it.

However, even though my nature tended to side with a good book or admittedly, a weekend filled with constant reruns of The Next Generation (As I was a closet Trekkie and proud of it…well, *in private that was*), it didn't mean that I also didn't enjoy the occasional night out or the Gods' forbid, even going out on a date. Which was how I sort of ended up with a boyfriend in the first place and therefore having no choice but to give up my 'swearing off all men' vow.

Of course, I blamed Wendy for that as she was determined

to play matchmaker yet again. And speaking of the demons she had no clue really existed…

"Yo Smock, whatcha cleaning this time?!" The second I heard her voice being shouted so close to my ear, one loud enough to penetrate through the sound of Fall Out Boys' 'Centuries', I nearly jumped out of my skin. I screamed and in doing so dropped the Canopic jar I had been working on. It was as if the world had suddenly been put on slow motion as I watched the jar filled with four-thousand-year-old intestines falling from my hand, first yelling in fright and then in horror the second it started to make its final destination to the floor.

I ended up sucking in a sharp, shocked breath the second I saw her hand snatch out and catch it just before it could hit the floor, saving about four thousand slices of my bacon!

"Holy shit!" I shouted in shock after yanking the headphones from my ears and staring at the jar in her hand. Then she started making a 'Thank God for that chuckle' before saying,

"Phew, well that was lucky because no offence, Emmie, but you would have never caught that!" And yeah, she was right because being as clumsy as I was, then I needed to come with my own proximity warning. Because if you got too close then chances were, I was gonna fall into you…once again, thanks for that one, mum, I thought with a wry smirk.

"Amen to that," I commented dryly, making her raise one strawberry blonde eyebrow at me, one that matched the colour of her short pixie cut. She was a pretty girl, with cute round features that lifted when she smiled and a pair of green eyes that always seemed to sparkle with mischief. She was also shorter than my 5 feet and 5 inches, but you wouldn't have guessed it unless you were looking at her feet, as she still seemed to tower over me with the ridiculous heels she always wore. And today was no different in a pair of Irregular Choice shoes named Trixy.

I only knew this because I had been with her at the time she had bought them. I had actually laughed thinking she was joking when she had asked me if I liked them. But then I saw she was actually serious about the blue and gold damask covered shoe that had a shiny gold unicorn's head as its heel. My reply had been the most natural in the world,

"Oh yeah, they're great…in fact I know someone back home who would openly drool over them," I told her with a smile, as I couldn't help but grin whenever I thought of my green haired aunty, who wasn't related by blood but definitely by the heart. I remembered Wendy's shock when I had said this as it was rare for me to talk about anyone from where I grew up, let alone my family.

Oh, she had asked me about them plenty of times, but I always remained vague. Which, thinking back, must have killed her curious nature, but one look at my sombre face and she knew not to ask. Don't get me wrong, I loved my family dearly and missed them on a daily basis, speaking to them as often as I could, but they lived in a different world to me…

A world, heartbreakingly, I just didn't fit in to.

Those had been the words he had used that night and to say that they had cut deep would be an understatement. Because they hadn't just cut me, *they had destroyed me.* They had destroyed every hope and dream I'd had first as a child and naive teenager, then finally as the young girl turning twenty. Well, that was seven years ago and yet the pain he'd inflicted felt like only yesterday.

"Hey, earth to space cadet, you gonna make me hold this creepy thing all day or what?" Wendy asked before she popped her pink gum she was addicted to chewing. She said it made for the perfect accessory to her Rockabilly style… me, I just think that she was addicted to sugar and bubble gum flavored things.

"It's not creepy, its beautiful," I told her, rolling my eyes at her lack of appreciation for anything she classed as 'old as dirt'.

"Yeah, then what's inside it, huh?" she asked with another pop of her gum and a hand on her hip as she wrapped her fingers against her cherry covered blue swing skirt. One she had matched with a red buttoned cardigan that also had a cherry pin. Personally, I didn't think it matched the shoes but when did it ever, I thought with a smirk.

"Intestines, that look like four-thousand-year-old beef jerky," I told her with a hidden smile as I turned back to the desk and placed it gently back in the box for safe keeping. After all, it had been safe in there for this long and seemed a better choice than in my hands, that was for sure. In fact, thinking about it, I was surprised considering how clumsy I was that I hadn't yet broken anything in the last two years I had been doing this job, well other than a few cups and a muffin basket once from the cafeteria. But in my defense, they had hidden the biggest chocolate muffins in the bottom and it needed a good tug to get one out. The cups, however, there was no excuse for as my number was currently up to five casualties. But hey, just one more and that would make it a full set I thought with an inward groan at myself.

"Right, in that case remind me to email Tim Burton and ask him for ideas on what to get you for your birthday this year," she replied sarcastically to my 'beautiful not creepy' comment, making me giggle.

"No need, I have an Amazon wish list I can send you," I told her with a wink, this time making her chuckle.

"Bird books and brush sets are not my idea of presents, so unless it's got a pair of shoes and at least two handbags on it, then don't bother, as I will just guess." I rolled my eyes again, this time for her to see and said,

"You do get the concept of giving gifts is not to buy the person something *you* want, just so you can 'permanently borrow' the item…right?" I asked knowing her too well by now that I was a Christmas present away from asking for the receipts with all my gifts.

"Now, where's the fun in that?" she asked grinning like a Cheshire Cat that was one step away from cute and becoming evil.

"And anyway, what are you doing here this time…and seriously, how do you even keep getting down here without a security card?" I asked in astonishment. Her guilty face said it all and I held out my hand and said,

"Come on, hand it over," now knowing she had nicked my security card yet again. I swear if she ever got bored of being a journalist then international jewel thief would be right up her alley, because she could pickpocket, crack locks and do the most basic James Bond stuff I have ever seen! Half the time when she wrote her articles I had to wonder if she hadn't broken into some bigwig's house just get the scoop on what dodgy deal he was doing with foreign nationals.

"Hey, you would be thanking my ass if I had just popped by and saved you from being kidnapped by the guy who had this shit stolen from him." Oh, and did I happen to mention that her imagination was almost as crazy as mine was.

"It's the British museum, Kirky, and I'm working on some dead guy's dried up organs in a jar, not the crown jewels," I told her making good use of the nickname I had christened her.

"Yeah, and just how much is a collection of around 8 million objects worth on the black market these days, huh…? Just one of these bad boys would fetch a pretty price to some bored billionaire Godfather wannabe, who suddenly feels like he needs something that screams cultural class to match his hungry traitor eating sharks in his basement." I laughed and said,

"You seriously need to stop watching old Bond movies and drinking coffee at three in the morning...but I guess point made," I told her, snatching my missing card that I had lost over a week ago from her palm.

"You´re damn right, point made, Smock," she replied using my own nickname, the result of a drunken night watching Star Trek movies and trying to merge our names with our favorite characters after consuming a bottle of wine and eight shots of caramel flavored vodka each. The result had been a hangover that had lasted three days and two nicknames that had lasted four years.

"So, come on fess up, what was so important you couldn't have waited until tonight to tell me...oh wait, oh hell no, you can't do this to me, Kirky!" I shouted the second I saw her face grimace as if she had just been busted. She held her hands up and said,

"Sorry honey, but it can't be helped."

"But you promised to be my date at tonight's gala," I said knowing my tone was whiney and needy.

"Yeah, but look it's time to be honest with you, I am kind of bored of acting like your lesbian lover and pretending to be interested in old shit." I groaned out loud and let my head fall into my hands, knowing I had no choice but to attend alone, something I hated doing. Tonight was a gala to try to raise money for a new archaeological dig to be funded and the best way to do that was to show off to all the rich people, what had already been found during these efforts.

To be honest, it was the part of the job I hated the most as I much preferred doing my job down here, surrounded by eternally quiet mummies, than explaining to rich snobby bankers and investors what exactly my job entailed. And doing so all the while ignoring the way they were talking to my breasts or giving me cheesy lines like, 'So how did such a pretty girl like you end up digging up bones for a living?'

Hence, why I came up with the cunning plan of inventing a 'girlfriend' which funnily enough tended to make men feel quite uncomfortable when introducing Wendy to them. Stranger still, it also seemed to make them feel more charitable, as they always ended up writing bigger cheques for me after this. It was as if it was a way of making sure their awkward actions weren't being shown enough to offend and cause reason for a discriminating lawsuit. I smiled at the thought, which quickly died when I realized this time I had no choice but to go 'mission solo'.

"Now what am I gonna do?" I whined.

"Um, call a sicky?" she suggested, making me give her my best 'are you serious' glare before banging my head on the table and groaning.

"Oh, I know, why not just take your actual boyfriend... what's his name again, Patrick something or..."

"Peter, jeez Kirky, you're the one who set me up with the guy!" I scolded.

"Yeah, but I only met him the once and that was at a coffee shop after he picked up my mocha instead of his latte." I swear, on hearing this I felt my eyes start to bulge!

"Please tell me you're kidding?!"

"Relax, I am joking...it was a cappuccino...anyway my point is, he is technically your boyfriend and therefore the shmuck that convention states you drag along to these types of things, so go ask him." I rolled my eyes again (something I seemed to do a lot around my friend, which was a term I used in the loosest sense right now due to my utter disappointment).

"I can't do that."

"Why not?" she asked popping her gum again and leaning on my desk, making the two jars I was yet to put back inside the box, wobble. I reached out and grabbed them both to steady them and shot her a sideways, reprimanding glare, one she deliberately ignored.

"Because that would give him the wrong impression," I argued making her snort a laugh.

"Like what, that you like him, because newsflash honey, dating someone kind of already says that."

"No, I know that!" I snapped before carrying on.

"I mean it would make him think this was more serious that it is and it's not."

"It's not?" she repeated.

"No, it's not...look, I like the guy."

"Patrick?"

"No, Peter! Bloody Hell, Wendy, can you focus here, I mean you can remember my pin number from watching me at an ATM three years ago, but you can't remember the name of the guy you set me up with only six weeks ago?!" I complained.

"It's a cash machine."

"What?!"

"It's a cash machine not an ATM, that's American talk, and your little britches are in the UK and land of the midnight Kebab, Friday night Indian curry takeaways and pavements, high streets and our wonderful use of the letter U in words you guys choose to ignore," she said looking at her manicured nails as if they held the key to her next British Journalism Award.

"Well, excuse me little Miss 'I got a problem with calling my knickers, panties'! Anyway, I am half English, so I resent that," I argued making her laugh.

"Yes, well your English panties aren't going to do shit for you tonight considering you don't have a date."

"Yes, and whose fault is that, um?" I threw back at her.

"Gods?" I laughed at her reply and said,

"Doubtful Kirky, very doubtful."

"Well, he and the powers that be, made me this way so whatever…but getting back to real life problems, *as in yours not mine,* what're you going to do?" she asked after her dramatic explanation, or should I say *excuse* to 'her being made this way'.

"Well, I think praying for a handsome stranger is off the cards, don't you?" I said throwing my hands up dramatically before banging my elbows back to the desk so that I could use my hands once more to cover my face. But then I let the unusual silence wash over me before looking back up at Kirky to see why it was she was so quiet. I frowned the second I saw her gaping mouth hanging open in shock before she slammed it shut and whispered,

"Uh Emmie, I think it's time to thank God, because it seems he just answered your prayers." I snapped my head around to see what she was staring at and sucked in a startled breath when I did. Then, as I took in the last sight I ever expected to see, I released it back again on a whoosh of emotions.

The dark and handsome features were ones I had grown up seeing daily, but for an outsider, I tried to put myself in Wendy's shoes when seeing him for the first time. A tall and wide build of someone that one would only assume was achieved by dedicating long hours to the gym. Midnight black hair that matched my own in colour, was cut just shy of his massive shoulders and pushed back. This done, no doubt, through endless times of frustration when he gave in to his habit of running a large hand through it.

Tanned, olive skin and dark eyes framed by equally dark long lashes were features I had also inherited, something my friend had not yet realized, due to the effect he had on most of the female population.

13

I grimaced at the thought.

"I hear you're in need of a date," he said in that velvet way of his, a tone that he reserved for getting what he wanted.

"Hell, I know I am," Wendy said making me hold the bridge of my nose in frustration and add a groan for good measure as this was the last thing I wanted to witness. Besides, her comment about Hell was more apt in ways than she could ever even imagine.

Well, before she could make this even weirder with another sexual comment, I decided to get this over with and drop my family sized bombshell by asking,

"What are you doing here…" then I paused, releasing a sigh before continuing with letting my friend know just who this handsome stranger was before she started to drool, and shit could get even weirder…

"…Dad?"

CHAPTER TWO

FAMILY CONNECTIONS

"**D**ad!?" Wendy screeched making me wince. I turned to her and said,

"Yeah, pretty much," before turning back to my dad, trying to ignore my friend when she hissed,

"What, was he like twelve when he did the deed?" I chuckled when my dad replied,

"I can assure you, young lady, I am older than I look." I shook my head and stopped myself from commenting drily, 'yeah, I'll say' with a scoffed sound to match it. That's when I noticed Wendy blushing, something I hadn't seen achieved in the whole time I had known her. Seriously, was there anyone with ovaries my dad didn't affect, I thought in disgust, the way any daughter would when thinking of her parents having sex. Or in this instance, obviously showcasing in every one of my friend's sexual fantasies from now on for the next decade at least. Now forget a jar of intestines, that thought right there was creepy enough, I admitted with a shiver and a grimace.

"Wow, he just called me young lady," she said, a breath away from swooning.

"Stood right here, Kirky…" I muttered before I turned my attention back to my father.

"…So, like I said, what are you doing here, dad?" I said in a curt tone as me and my father hadn't exactly parted on the best of terms when he heard of my decision to move away seven years ago. But of course, I had seen him since then. As my mother would have hunted my ass down and dragged me back home every Christmas, no matter if I had been hiding somewhere in the Amazon and getting eaten alive by mosquitoes the size of gorgon leeches.

Oh, and she would have done it with my Aunty Sophia, my Aunty Pip and my Aunty Ari as her backing singers as they all broke out into Guns N Roses, 'Welcome to the Jungle'.

I swear when you got them all together they were as thick as thieves and could take on a bloody army in Hell if they were let loose long enough. In fact, most of the stories I had heard growing up, I didn't know whether to believe them or class them as just elaborate fairy tales you tell a child. Only in this instance just switching out the names to people you know to make it more fun. But as an adult, then thinking back to most of them, now I wasn't so sure as they were certainly capable of getting into that much trouble and surviving.

The fact I was certain on though was that when they got together I think it was the only thing my father did fear…that and my mother's wrath. But on the whole, as the only daughter of the King of the Supernatural world and a mother who was half Vampire, quarter Demon/Angel mix and quarter Human, I was brought up in a relatively normal and happy household. If, of course, you could call an old castle style mansion on the edge of a cliffside normal that was… oh and one which just so happened to be the small town of Evergreen

Falls' gothic Nightclub of choice (as in there wasn't any choice and we were the only ones to provide that brand of gothic crazy to the locals). Then, yep it was normal. Or at least my mother and father's variety of normal. Which, granted, wasn't much to go on seeing as everything I had just mentioned in that list.

So, what the heck, it wasn't the suburban upbringing that most kids in my school had, but one thing was for sure, living in the town's creepiest and coolest of places meant that I was the very last target for a bully, not when they believed that the ghost of my ancestors would rise up from the grave to haunt them. The funny thing about that was that I didn't have any ancestors to speak of, not considering my father and his siblings, my Aunty Sophia and my Uncle Vincent, were thousands of years old.

My father gave me a warm and amused grin before answering my question on why he was here,

"Can't a father surprise his beautiful daughter with a visit?"

"Aww that's so sweet…what, all I get from my dad is a grunt and half assed wave…oh and a head nod if it's Christmas," Wendy said defensively when I shot her a silencing look.

"Yes, but he's a recovering alcoholic that smokes fifty a day and half the time can't see you through the cigarette fog," I reminded her, making her giggle instead of her taking any offensive, as let's just say there wasn't much love lost between them.

"Very true, damn you, but it looks like you won the parent lottery with that sexy piece of DNA right there," she muttered quietly, not knowing that of course my father could hear her just fine. It was at this point that I lowered my head and slapped my forehead the second my dad sounded like he was coughing back his laugh.

"What…too much?" Wendy asked me in response to my reaction.

"Yeah, just a tad." She laughed once, slapped me on the back and said,

"I am gonna take a wild stab in the dark here and guess that I should probably give you two some alone time." I grinned back at her and agreed,

"That's probably best, yes."

"Right, well it was nice meeting you, Mr…"

"Draven, my name is Draven, but you can call me Dominic." I swear if my dad carried on like this he would soon be catching her, she was that close to swooning.

"Wendy, this is usually the part when you say bye," I reminded her after she just started smiling at him like a loon or someone high on drugs, whichever suited.

"Oh yeah, right…okay well nice to meet you like I said and Smock, call me later," she said giving me wide eyes as if silently telling me she will be eagerly waiting with her phone in hand for me to call her and give her all my family gossip. And well, considering I'd never said anything before about my ridiculously handsome parentage, then it probably meant it was going to be a long phone call.

After this she left and the second we heard the door close behind her my father asked,

"Smock?"

"They call me Emmie here…you know, short for Amelia and well Wendy thought it was funny to combine it with…"

"Spock," my father said smirking as he knew all about my obsession with Star Trek growing up, as he was the poor sap I had to drag with me to all the conventions. In the end it turned out that Spock was his favorite as well. Or at least he said it was after I also made my parents sit through the original series, along with all the spin offs they made. Like I said, they were good parents, but even the best kind have their flaws and my dad's were…well let's just say that they were *suffocating*.

"My dear Amelia, give this old man a break and come here, sweetheart," my father said with such a tender tone I could never have refused him, no matter the distance that had grown between us since the day I left home to make it on my own.

"Oh dad!" I said as I made the first steps towards him before I threw myself into my father's arms. I hugged onto him as he lifted me up as he always did when I was a kid. He also did so with my mother, who was quite a bit shorter than him and also me by two inches.

"I missed you, little one," he told me as he lowered my feet back to the floor and ended the sweet statement with a kiss to my forehead.

"How's mum, is she here?" I asked hoping that she was but with a small shake of his head he told me that she wasn't.

"Let me guess, she doesn't know you're here, does she?" I asked. He actually looked sheepish because if there was one single person in the world that could render my father speechless and squirming it was my wonderful mother, Keira.

She was his kryptonite and Achilles heel all wrapped into one. As it was a clear and constant reminder living with them both that true love wasn't only real, but it could also be fated and blessed by the very Gods themselves. Love was a gift and one I had been hoping to find in a man who I had been dreaming about most of my life in one way or another…but, boy had I been wrong!

But my parents knew nothing of this or that he was the reason I had walked away and turned my back on the same life my parents had chosen. Now, maybe it would have been different had I been like them, but the sobering truth for them and for me was that I wasn't like them. As in… Not. At. All.

Because I wasn't supernatural…*I was human.*

"No, she doesn't know but no doubt will by the time I get back," he admitted making me chuckle before nudging his arm with my shoulder and saying,

"Yeah, well good luck with that one, Pops." He smirked at my teasing knowing that it was only me and my mother that could ever get away with it and it was fun at that. But my dad was a good sport and amazingly still managed to uphold that same level of authority he always did, even when in the past he had a toddler on his knee pulling his nose or making him blow raspberries in my face. He simply sat at his council table most nights and obliged me and my silliness until it was time for my bed, more often than not leaving it to my mother to discipline me, as he found that he just couldn't bring himself to tell me off.

However, the one thing that he would not do, under any circumstances, was go against my mother's wishes as he always backed her up and declared that her say was final and decreed law. Of course, when you're five and told to go to bed sooner than you would like or being denied dessert after not eating all your dinner, these all seemed pretty end of the world things to a child. But let's just say that I learned early on who the softies of the household were and that was pretty much anyone who wasn't my mother.

In fact, in the end, I felt so sorry for my poor mum that I would often choose to be good just to give her a break in having to explain to a table full of clueless Supernaturals the importance of a child's routine, or the value of not being hyped up on sugar before bed.

Because, no matter how much my mum had to play the bad cop in my upbringing, the simple fact remained that I utterly adored her. She may have been the one to tell me 'No', 'Not yet' and 'Don't touch', but the rest of the time she was so much fun I would find my days filled with more laughter than I could possible count and tears that could be counted on one hand. They were, without a shadow of a doubt, the best parents any child could have ever hoped for, but then something awful happened and that was what most parents have to face…

I became a teenager.

So, no matter how much my dad used to dote on me, the second I started to grow up and know my own mind was when he found the list of things he couldn't give me was starting to mount and one of those was what I craved for the most…

Freedom.

You see, I was stuck smack bang in the middle of two worlds and in neither one of them did it feel like I truly belonged. I was human in the supernatural world I was brought up in, but the longer I was in school surrounding myself with my own kind, the more I longed to belong in their world. But, like I said before, this didn't mean I didn't adore my family and included in that were those who weren't related by blood like my Aunty Pip and Uncle Adam. But they all had their place within their world, whereas I wasn't even allowed to go on a simple shopping trip to Evergreen Falls' Mall without having a tank sized bodyguard named Ragnar watching my every move. Even if he was another person I considered as an Uncle, it still didn't stop the fact that he was a scary ass Viking the size of a house!

But it wasn't just the unfair restrictions my parents laid down for me as I knew it was only done for my safety, it was also where they wanted my life to go. The way my dad wanted me to play it nice and safe and work in Afterlife, in whatever area I could that would make me happy. But what made me happy was living out my dreams in a museum somewhere. Or even being out in the field discovering the world's unknown hidden treasures of our history and being the first one to lay eyes on something that had not been seen for a millennium.

This was where my father and I started to disagree, and it quickly became the first time that my dad could no longer give me everything I wanted, being the one to say the word NO to me in place of my mother.

Hence our tense relationship ever since. Not that we argued much or were vocal about it. It was just that my overbearing father and his need to constantly protect me was starting to sound like a dictatorship of my life rather than friendly advice on where he thought my life should lead. Which was why I decided to move to London to first study and then get a job straight after in the British Museum.

It also didn't help that my family was insanely rich, which not to sound like an ungrateful bitch here, but it also meant that my dad wanted to pay for everything and ensure it was the best. Whereas, I wanted to learn the value of hard work and the ways of the world with it like my mother had taught me.

That was where they clashed on my upbringing the most. But I sided with my mum, which was why I lived in a small modest flat on the outskirts of London that I bought cheap. And was why I caught the bus into the city every day for work. Okay, so it was also why I didn't go home much as I couldn't afford my living expenses and flights back to Portland as they weren't exactly cheap. But I refused to ask my dad for money or for the use of one of their private jets, as that would have been against the point I was trying to make.

In truth, I simply wanted to make it on my own. Which was why, like most people, I bought my clothes not from the many designer shops on Bond Street, like my Aunty Sophia would have liked. But instead in Oxford Street and from the places most people did on the high street. And I was honestly okay with that. In fact, I enjoyed finding my sale bargains just as much as the next person, determined that my parents' wealth would not influence my nature as a human being and instead make me a better person for learning to value what I have earned. And I did, especially when setting up my first home by myself and going to the British Heart Foundation for my second-hand furniture to fill my flat with.

I remember my mum's face when she saw it for the first time and how proud she was, nudging my father's side and prompting him to say the same. I wanted to laugh now as I remembered the way he looked down at my shabby sofa as if any minute rats were going to break free from the springs and attack him. In truth, my dad was a bit of a snob at times and I remembered laughing when my mum told me stories of when they had first started dating. At how he acted when she took him into places like Burger King and Poundland. At the time, I'd had tears in my eyes at just the thought of it.

But then again, my dad had never known anything other than his extreme power and wealth, spending thousands of years as a King, then really…who could blame him? All I could hope was that in time he would come to understand my decisions and come to respect them as my mother did.

But then again, with one look at my dad now, then I knew today was not that day. He was here because of something else and if he was here without my mother knowing, then my guess… it wasn't anything good.

"You're looking well and more grown up every time I see you," my father said, running the back of his hand affectionately down my cheek and giving me a tender look. I knew that my dad struggled watching me growing from his little girl into an independent woman, as no doubt most fathers did. And even if I couldn't have seen it clearly myself, my mother spoke about it often enough, no doubt trying to get me to understand his reasons for being the way he was.

In fact, every time we spoke for our weekly catch up phone calls and I would ask how he was, she would laugh in her light hearted and teasing way before telling me, 'struggling as always'. Half of me felt guilty for my decision to leave but then I would stretch out on my little sofa, look around at my own little slice of heaven that I had worked for and know that I had done the right thing. And like I said, one day hopefully he would see it too.

Which was why knowing that he was a long way off that yet, I took a step back, folded my arms over my chest and asked him,

"Yeah, well that's what happens when you're twenty-seven, dad... now come on, spill...why are you here?" I asked getting down to business and knowing taking a family trip down daddy and daughter good old times lane, wasn't going to do me any favours in trying to get my dad to see me as an adult. He gave me a knowing look but obviously thought better of whatever it was he wanted to say and instead replied with the actual reason he was here.

"I have something for you," he said after releasing a big sigh that showed only of his frustration. So, deciding to opt for less tension, I gave him a big grin and hopped up onto the nearest table, thankfully the one without the four-thousand-year-old Egyptian artifacts upon it and said,

"Alright, let's have a look." Then I rubbed my hands together like I always did out of habit when something exciting was possibly coming my way. I knew with the warm look my dad gave me, that he was reminiscing back to every Christmas and Birthday when I would do the same thing before being handed a present to open. What can I say, I loved receiving gifts and still acted like a kid when being surprised with one.

"This box was found hidden behind one of the walls in a building I recently acquired," my dad said picking up an aluminum case that I only just noticed was sat on the floor next to him. It was like the ones you would have seen in any action movie where the hero is trying to stop a case full of nuclear uranium from getting into the hands of terrorists. Of course, it always does get into the hands of terrorists, where a bomb gets made that threatens the city and the hero is essentially left at the end contemplating in the five seconds remaining which wire to cut. And, of course, they cut the right one with mere seconds to spare. Even after knowing nothing about nuclear bombs yet still managing to save the day anyway and along with it the love interest that they just happened to pick up half way through the story line.

But enough about the box and my runaway imagination along with it, as it was what was inside the box that interested me the most and I very much doubted that it was anything radioactive.

"Wow, now that's certainly different," I said the second he ran a hand over the other-worldly locks, ones no human could ever hope to crack before flipping back the lid. Inside sat an intricate wooden rectangle that was no bigger than a regular sized shoe box. It had raised panels on each side which in turn held three framed squares and each were painted with different symbols at their centres.

"It's shaped like some kind of miniature sarcophagus, although definitely not of the Egyptian kind, yet there are some hieroglyphs here...but wait, that's strange as these are Demotic script...and look here, this looks like Ancient Greek..." I looked back up at my dad as I had been spinning it around in my hands for he and I both to see, when I stopped, gifting him with a look of utter astonishment.

"But that's...well that's..."

"Surprising?" my dad said finishing off my sentence with a word I wouldn't have used... no astonishing, unbelievable, amazing...those words I would have used!

"Where did you say you found this again?" I asked as I

picked it up gently and turned it around again, this time looking at it in more detail and already trying to make out some of the markings I knew.

"New Haven, Connecticut," he said making me raise a brow at him.

"And what wmy feelings for Lucius, as let's face it, that was one canere you doing at Yale University, umm? Decided you needed yet another doctorate to add to the collection?" I teased, knowing the university would have been his sole interest there. He gave me one of those 'you're too clever for your own good' type of looks that made me chuckle.

"Can you decipher it?" he asked ignoring my question in place of one of his own. My eyes went wide in surprise when I replied,

"You can't?" This shocked me because if there was an ancient language out there that my dad couldn't read then it really must be an even bigger mystery than I first thought.

"No, hence why I rushed over here to the one person I knew that could…eventually," he said adding this last part as a tease. I smirked, taking on the challenge as he knew I would and looked at the box again.

"One of the only other artifacts found with all three texts is the Rosetta Stone, which has been here in the museum since 1802… you know it's how they ended up deciphering Egyptian hieroglyphs." I told my dad even though I didn't know why I bothered considering there was very little my dad didn't know about important world history and he confirmed this when he said,

"I remember seeing it the day it was first put on display for the world to see, although ever since its rediscovery, I believe the stone has been the focus of nationalist rivalries. Which include the debate of its transfer from French to British possession during the Napoleonic Wars, thanks to a long-running dispute over the relative value of both Thomas Young, and Jean-François Champollion's contributions to its decipherment." I whistled and nudged him with my elbow,

"Impressive…you know mum is right…"

"Oh?" he enquired as I knew he would considering I had mentioned his biggest weakness, *my mum*.

"It must be like living with the intelligent superhero…no wonder mum calls you 'Google Man'." I said in a deep 'man voice' and making a stance like a superhero with my hands on my hips and my feet apart. My dad rolled his eyes at me and my playful banter as he always did before muttering,

"Too much like your mother."

"Well, they may have wanted it in France but since 2003 there have been demands for its return to Egypt," I told him, getting back to the reason he was here.

"Well, I don't see that happening anytime soon, not when it's one of the museum's biggest attractions that has been sat on display behind its walls for over two hundred years," my father commented.

"So, what's inside?" I asked nodding back to the box after seeing for myself there was no way inside but knowing that from the weight of it then an educated guess would tell me it definitely had its secrets at its core.

"I don't know." I frowned at this at the same time jerking my head back in shock.

"What do you mean you don't know, surely you have just willed it to open before now?" I said, knowing object manipulation was just one of my father's many supernatural gifts.

"I have tried but to no avail."

"You're telling me that it's protected against supernatural means?" I asked in utter astonishment but was soon to learn that

27

this wasn't the most shocking part of all. No, it was when my father told me,

"There might be one with enough power to open it, for his exertion over people's will far exceeds my own." I had a bad feeling about this as I felt the shiver creeping down my spine, only knowing the deeper reason for it the second he said his name.

"Who?" I still asked as if compelled to do so. However, the second I stared at the box that wouldn't open I knew just by asking, that the question was opening a far more dangerous one for me.

One not named Pandora's box, but one named...

"Lucius."

CHAPTER THREE

PUZZLES

Shortly after my father spoke his name I quickly swallowed down the gasp I knew wanted to break free and schooled my features the best I could, just as I had trained myself to do around my family. The very last thing I wanted was for them to know of any feelings I may have had for the Vampire King. Of course, it hadn't helped that not only had he once been my father's enemy but to make matters worse, all had been forgiven and he was now one of the many Kings that sat at my father's council table.

Thankfully, I no longer had to endure these yearly meetings at Afterlife or having to explain my absence on account of no longer living there. Something that had happened a little time before I left for good and let's just say that the excuse of a headache didn't really cut it in our family.

But, surprisingly, my parents were still in the dark when it came to Lucius and the callous heartbreak he had inflicted that night, which was precisely how I preferred it. For starters I didn't know if the King of the Supernatural world could suffer from a heart attack, but I am sure that if there was ever an occasion for that to be tested, then my dad finding out about Lucius would have been it.

My first thought would have been that my dad would have simply killed Lucius or at least tried to, seeing as it was whispered that Lucius was in fact my father's only equal in power and strength. I didn't know how true this was, but I knew enough of some of the Kings of the Seven Realms that they were all pretty equal in power, which included my Uncle Vincent who mainly ruled over the rogue Angels in the world, along with my father.

But then it was rumored that if Lucius, being the King of all Vampires, was ever to find his ultimate demise and the unbelievable happened, like his death, then he would also take with him all other Vampires to his grave. Which, terrifyingly, also meant my mother being on that unfortunate list, seeing as he was her Sire. I didn't know all of the details of this story as certain things were, according to my parents, better left in the past. I hadn't given much thought to this growing up until the truth of it was used against me.

I shook my head and with it ridding myself of the sticky residue of pain that would latch itself to me unwittingly whenever his name was mentioned.

"Then why not take it straight to him?" I had asked my dad, turning my back and busying myself with putting away some of my tools just so that I could hide the bitterness I felt in saying that sentence. I could just imagine my dad's single raised brow at me from behind, but I ignored the temptation to look, knowing I was too close to giving away my feelings if I did.

"Because I know how you like puzzles and I first thought to let you look at it in case it holds some greater meaning to our world." It was at this point that I had wanted to correct him and say, *'don't you mean your world'*.

But in the end, I remained silent so as not to upset him when hearing this as I remembered the look of hurt the last time I threw it at him. It was just before I left for university and he pleaded with me not to go, telling me that I had a responsibility as his daughter and therefore strictly speaking also as a princess to a King that I called father. But the second he called me this I heard it being said as an insult by another and therefore lashed out venomously, feeling guilty then for the entire flight to London.

Which was why I was currently sat on the bus with the box inside my large handbag, clutching it on my lap as I made my way home. I had wrapped the puzzle box up in bubble wrap and decided it was best not to speak of it to anyone, hoping I wouldn't get stopped for a random search at the end of my working day.

Of course, it would have been easy to prove that it was mine considering it wasn't catalogued as being in the museum's possession and neither had it been catalogued as due in on any of their shipment manifests. But proving it to be mine would have been a lengthy process, for which I didn't have the time, that was if I was to make it home and get myself ready for this gala, then every spare minute counted.

Well, at least two things had come out of my father's visit as he was right, I did love a good puzzle…that, and I finally had a date for the gala as my dad promised he wouldn't let me go there alone. So, after the fifteen-minute walk to Oxford Circus, I caught my usual bus to where I lived in Twickenham. All in all, it usually took me just over an hour to get home with both the walk and bus journey combined. But I didn't mind as I liked the bus. I liked being able to just sit back and watch the busy world go by, wondering at each person I saw what their story was. Where they were on their way to, where they had just come from and who it was they were going to meet. I had always been curious by nature but today I had to admit that my thoughts were most definitely elsewhere.

I remembered back to when I first came to find a place to live in London, getting lost more times than I could count. I also thought back to when I spent a ridiculous amount of time stood staring at the multicolored lines of the Underground map, asking myself if people needed to first pass some unknown test just to navigate their way around the city. A test no one had told me about.

Then I remembered when a kind and uniquely fashionable older lady in her seventies came to stand next to me and ended up explaining the whole system to me. She had asked where it was I trying to get to and in the end, when hearing that it was the museum, thought it best to tag along and ended up spending the day with me.

Her name had been Queeney (to her friends anyway, as I never found out her real name). She had also been the one to recommend the flat I now lived in, telling me that a friend of hers was trying to move quickly and would soon be putting it up for sale at a steal of the usual price. Hence, how I ended up being the proud owner of a small one bedroom flat in Twickenham in a sweet and well-kept block of flats overlooking a small park.

So, just as I approached where I usually got off, which just so happened to be only a minute's walk from where I lived, I pressed the button to let the driver know that this was my stop. Then I heaved the bag over my shoulder remembering to take care considering what I carried inside it. I then smiled at the bus driver in thanks before stepping off onto the curb. Hitching up my bag once more, I made my way back home on foot, getting there in just over a minute. I could literally see my building's door from the bus stop. Which meant I could have that extra sleep on work days, as I wasn't exactly a morning person.

In fact, to all who knew me well, I was a morning monster and could rival Hell's wrath if woken up before I absolutely had to. Which made getting me up in the morning for school a bit of a challenge for my parents. But, since then I liked to think that I had matured in this department and therefore no longer growled like a bear at people should they wish me good morning.

However, I wasn't yet above cursing loudly when hearing the annoying ringtone of my phone's alarm in the morning. I especially loathed getting up out of bed if it was still dark outside. It was true, I was a complete bed monster and could basically sleep through most things, which was why I loved my days off, only rolling from my comfy crypt no earlier than ten.

"Happy Friday, Mrs Benton," I said wishing one of my neighbours a good day, who was reaching out of the kitchen window of her ground floor flat, watering her herbs that sat neatly inside a hanging window box. She smiled at me and tore out a handful of basil, passing it to me as I passed.

"I recommend pasta tonight," she said as way of hello and I thanked her before entering the passcode to gain access to my building, now with one handful of fresh herbs. My building was filled with high tech gadgets and a top of the range security system as it seemed that the owner was somewhat paranoid of break-ins. This had been one of the features Queeney had pointed out at the time she had first shown me around her friend's flat. I just remembered thinking that at least my father would be happy to hear this, as my safety had been one of his biggest issues with me moving away. I had just turned a corner after navigating up the first flight of stairs when I saw a familiar face speckled with paint.

"Hey Ben, how's life treating you on this fine Friday evening?" I asked this of my neighbor who lived in the flat directly opposite mine and who was currently painting his front door an array of geometric shapes in mad colours. Not surprisingly, he was an artist, and this had been the second time I had seen him painting his front door this year and it was only March.

"Oh, just fine, fine, fine... although Owen is away again would you believe?" Ben said waving around his blue soaked brush in an overly dramatic way as was his personality. I gave him a sympathetic smile knowing that he hated it when his partner Owen was away. Which he tended to do a lot these days, making me wonder if their relationship was as strong as it had been when they first met last summer.

Ben had lived here longer than I had and from what I could gather had paid a lot more for his place than I had for mine. But I was wise enough to keep quiet on the matter as money was usually a sore spot with him.

I had met him the first day I had moved in as he saw me struggling with my boxes. He had grabbed the door for me and minutes later helped me move the rest of my things in, that had been shipped across from Portland. After that I had treated him to takeout sat on the floor and using a box for a table and we had been friends ever since. He was about my height, a little podgy around the belly area from his love of baking, which I actually think suited him better as the extra weight also gave him a rounder face to match his big blue eyes and dark blonde hair. He always seemed to be flushed having a redness to his cheeks and when he smiled it was so big that it transformed his face and made his eyes sparkle. He was like a cute teddy bear that made you want to hug him even when just saying hello. Which I would have done now if I hadn't had a handful of herbs, a heavy bag full to the brim of ancient wood and eyeing up all the paint stuck to his work shirt and ripped jeans.

"I would say let's get into our PJ's, crack open a bottle of Zinfandel and stick a movie on but I have that stupid gala thing tonight," I said groaning at the end.

"Oh, poor you, a glamourous night ahead surrounded by handsome rich people…just however will you cope?" he said, being bitchy in a joking way. I rolled my eyes as I did with Wendy and said,

"Yeah, well it's not exactly my ideal Friday night as you know."

"Seriously girl, you have this so backward," he told me making me frown as I unlocked my door.

"Yeah, in what way?" I asked over my shoulder at him.

"Because usually people feel depressed when they *don't* have something to do on a Friday night other than sit at home only wishing that they had the excuse to wear a cute dress, killer heels and an actual reason to paint their nails…you on the other hand seem to wish for Netflix and pizza on the nights you have something awesome to do." I released a sigh knowing he was right.

"Yeah, well you are more than welcome to take my place since Wendy let me down and ended our fake lesbian relationship," I told him making him laugh.

"Ha, can you imagine me trying to talk seriously about shriveled up dead things with the same passion you do…*perleeease* Geekgirl, I would just be there for the free champagne, hors d'oeuvres and the potentially rich and handsome husband I might find," he said dragging out his 'please' and rolling his hand in the air.

"And what about Owen, huh?" He gave me a pointed look that told me I had been right; their relationship was on the brink of coming to an end.

"So, what time do you want me to come round and do your hair?" he asked changing the subject. I gave him a surprised look prompting him to say,

"Oh, come on, you know you're shit at it, no offence but if its more than giving it a quick blow dry and stuffing it up in a messy bun or a half assed plait then you're shit at it," he reminded me, calling me out on something I already knew to be true.

"Fine, give me an hour to get showered and changed before knocking…oh and don't you dare turn up here without that bottle of wine I know you have hiding in your fridge from last movie night." He gave me a salute when taking back up his brush, so he could finish his last blue shape.

I walked into my flat and breathed a sigh of relief that I could finally rid myself of my weighty burden. Hell, I was half tempted to just let the thing drop to the floor the second the door closed behind me. But then I remembered the thing was thousands of years old and did deserve a little more of my respect and professionalism. So, I carefully placed my bag down on the kitchen table and proceeded to carry out my daily ritual of kicking off my shoes, shrugging out of my jacket and clicking the kettle on all at the same time.

Then, by the time the water had boiled, I was out of my work clothes into comfy PJ bottoms and was pulling one of my funny T shirts over my head. I kind of started collecting them after my Aunty Pip suggested it and therefore now received at least one from people I knew as gifts every year on both my birthday and Christmas. Today's choice had been from my Uncle Zagan, who was married to my father's sister, my awesome Aunty Sophia. It read,

> 'Guns don't Kill People,
> UNCLES
> who have pretty
> Nieces DO!'

Needless to say, all the men in my family had loved this one. I, on the other hand, saved it for 'inside wear only' as let's face it, I might have made a 'no men' vow, but I didn't want to be single for the rest of my life. Which made me think about Peter and when I had planned to see him next. I decided to put it out of my head, making myself a cup of green tea. Which would have been much to my mother's disgust who was herself addicted to a more basic 'English Breakfast' variety, declaring all other tea's as the work of the devil. I always giggled at this and the sight of her nose wrinkling in disgust whenever I ordered my 'Devil tea' when we were out.

Then I plonked myself down at the small kitchen table I'd picked up from Gumtree, the online second-hand site that lets you find hidden gems cheap that people were selling and wanted gone. So, it had a wonky leg I had to glue every few months but so what, it was mine and I loved it, chipped paint and all.

I reached into my bag and carefully removed the puzzle box my dad had given me so that I could finally examine it in more detail. I hadn't had much time to do so by the time my father had left, seeing as I needed to catch my bus home. But now, here under the hanging light I had got in the bargain section in IKEA for missing a few screws in its packaging, I could now see that it held so much more than I originally thought.

I soon began to understand why it was my dad couldn't read its ancient text as it wasn't your straightforward hieroglyphs. In fact, it was starting to look more like its Egyptian symbols had been morphed with other known Glyphs used in many forms of ancient texts and language. It had been very cleverly made that was for sure, as you would turn it one way and it would look like Cuneiform, the writing of the Sumerians. Then you could look at it upside down and Cretan hieroglyphs could just be made out.

In fact, the whole box was covered in text, with three main scripts and the two languages being Egyptian entwined with ancient Greek. None of it made any sense as the time frames were all off. I decided to take pictures of each side with my phone so that I could print them out later and then circle each symbol as I deciphered it. I usually did this when studying a new object, that way I could easily make notes and break down each element as it came to me.

I set the thing down and picked up my mug, drinking the hot tea and letting it soothe my ragged nerves, just knowing who could soon be holding this box if I couldn't crack its code first and get it open myself. A part of me wanted to fail, just so that I had the excuse to pass it onto him. But the better part of me, the rational side that screamed at me on a daily basis that I hated him, wanted to stick two fingers up and crack it without needing his help. So, I set my mug down and continued to take pictures of it until I was sure every inch had been documented.

Okay, so I know what you're thinking. Why, given my family's background, would I choose to study ancient artifacts and the ancient Egyptians? Why not something like demonology, seeing as I pretty much knew all there was to know on the subject. And, considering I was probably one of the only humans on earth to know exactly what was fact and what was fiction, then something like that might have been handy for the rest of the population...or so I thought.

But I would have been wrong.

Because unless the human world really knew the truth about what secrets lay in plain sight, then what use was I, the know it all on the subject? No, there was good reason why the supernatural side was kept hidden to them, as was part of my father's job. I mean look at what damage can be done in the name of religion. How man throughout history has twisted their beliefs and the beliefs of others to start wars only for their own gain of power, land and another man's riches.

So, the answer was simple, there weren't too many jobs out

there for such a person and especially not in the work place of my dreams, that being the British Museum. A place I visited on a school trip once when I bravely snuck out and forged my parents' signatures just so that I could fulfil my wish of seeing London with the rest of my school friends.

But from the very first moment I stepped inside the amazing place, I knew that it had been fate and I would have done anything in my academic power to get a job there. Even if I started at the very bottom and had to clean toilets to get it.

Okay, so I wasn't exactly cleaning toilets, but cleaning artifacts was what I did most days. However, I still loved it. I fell in love with history pretty much from day one when I first learned to read. And well, in truth, when you are brought up with a father who had lived through most of it, then each one of his amazing stories of his past just stuck with me and I couldn't get enough. I wanted to learn all about the ancient cultures my dad had lived through, learning more about his past as I did. I also inherited this passion for history from my mum, who studied it at college.

Well, admittedly it was that and my love for watching the Indiana Jones movies, quickly deciding when I was only six that this was what I wanted to become. Okay, so it's true that the booby trapped, cave hunting, out running crashing boulders, pit of snake diving, high flying and death-defying adventures had yet to happen, but I still had my fingers crossed that one day something exciting would finally find me. And seeing as my mother and father were the King and Queen of the Supernatural world, then you would have thought that by the age of twenty-seven it would have happened by now.

But, in short, my life was pretty ordinary. Then again, since I made the decision to leave home and basically live life like the human I was, then what did I really expect? I guess it shouldn't have been that surprising that my life was as it was, like most people's lives, the most exciting things to happen were falling in love, marriage and babies. Oh, and the occasional accident that might mean a long wait in an A & E department.

Well, I had already done the falling in love part and stupidly let it then dictate my life by swearing off all men for the rest of eternity. Okay, so that's not strictly true as I was sort of seeing someone, but how far it was going to go was anyone's guess, as we hadn't even slept together yet. And let's just say that when it did finally happen for me, I had a feeling that Peter was the turn the lights off kind of guy.

Not that there was anything wrong with that but for me, it definitely seemed overshadowed by my ideals of how someone's first time should go… especially when I had my traitorous fantasies and dreams to plague me of a certain Vampire King. And I can safely say that my ideals and imagination tend to lead me down a much darker and taboo path when thinking about what Lucius would be like in the bedroom. Chains, ropes, distinct teeth marks and red palmed skin tended to come to mind, as it was definitely more the red room from Fifty Shades, than the tame kissing on your wedding day from Pride and Prejudice in a horse drawn carriage.

But Peter was a sweet, kind and gentle man and most of all he was safe, which no doubt my father would like most about him. Although, thankfully that day was far, far away from happening, no matter how much my mother thought it funny to tease him about it.

Ha, well there wouldn't have been any teasing if either of them knew about my feelings for Lucius, and let's face it, that was one can of demonic worms nobody wanted to open…as in EVER! Especially not what I knew now and how that bastard had taken great joy in telling me back when I had a fragile naive heart, one he stepped on and decided to break for nothing more than what seemed like his amusement. Even if the bastard had saved my life that day, it didn't matter, because for long years after, the backlash of his actions had often made me wish that he hadn't.

Man, how foolish I had been back then, I couldn't help but shake my head when just thinking back to it. No man was worth my life, that was the lesson I had learnt, and no man would ever love me as much as my father.

Or so I thought.

But offering my love to a man like Lucius, then really what had I been thinking? For how could a man, as cold and hard as he is, ever love anyone? I had often wondered this but then again, I knew the heartbreaking truth now, didn't I? Because there had been one woman the Vampire King had fallen in love with and it most certainly hadn't been me.

No, I learned the truth of that the hardest way anyone could learn it. From the very lips I wished would spend long hours kissing my own and teaching my body what it felt like to have the determined touch of a dominant hand.

I heard it from the cruel lips of who I once believed to be my Chosen One. The only person he told me that he had ever loved had been none other than my own...

Mother.

CHAPTER FOUR

ETERNALLY LOVED

"Okay, so what about this one?" I asked holding up yet another dress from my closet, wondering why I had even agreed to let Ben in my bedroom, let alone to help me pick out what to wear. Well, maybe help wasn't exactly the right word to use…no, maybe to boss me around and basically make me feel like I had a collection of dustbin bags or shabby outdated hand me downs from eighty-year-old ladies in mourning! Yeah, that was it.

I swear that he was the most over critical gay man I had ever met…okay, so he was the only gay man I knew but still, he was worse than Wendy on her period!

"Oh, that's fine…" he finally replied.

"That's great…" I sighed in relief which turned out to be premature as he quickly added,

"…If you're going to a funeral." I let my head fall back and silently asked the Gods for patience, knowing there must be at least one up there who specialized in the field.

"Fine, then what would you pick?!" I snapped, making him smirk.

"You gonna wear it if I do?" he tested in a sneaky tone. I shrugged my shoulders, moved aside and said,

"Have at it, Skippy," I said, naming him this as he was always nicking my peanut butter, which just so happened to be the best brand EVER in all the history of buttery goodness. Well, it was my favorite anyway and I really would have to love someone to share it, considering my mum would send it in her monthly packages, which also included some of my other American favorites. However, my fellow Americans were really missing out not having crumpets to smother it on as, if you asked me, it was a match made in heaven.

"Alright, but you have to pinky swear you will wear what I choose."

"What are we, six?" I asked with a frown, making him chuckle before holding out his little finger and replying,

"If it gets the job done, then yeah, now put it there Emmie girl!" I rolled my eyes, which admittedly was a habit of mine, and gave him my pinky swear, knowing there wasn't much to worry about seeing as it was a closet full of my own clothes that I would be seen dead in… and living for that matter.

"And this job that needs to get done, is what exactly?" I asked after plonking myself down on the bed. Ben started rummaging through my closet with a concentration that almost looked painful or that he was close to needing a bowel movement. I would have laughed had he not answered my question at that moment.

"It's called cherry popping and usually happens well before you're in your late twenties." I swear I nearly choked.

"And what makes you think I am still a virgin, huh?" I asked in a high-pitched voice that should have sounded way cooler if what he just said was as false as my question claimed.

"I have lived opposite you for years and not once seen you bring a man back to your flat."

"So? Who's to say we don't just do it at his place?" I argued making him chuckle.

"His? Oh honey, I doubt you have even seen another man's bedroom other than mine," he replied making me suddenly blush crimson and that was because he was wrong. I had been in another man's bedroom and the memory made me want to squirm. Just like I had done that night under a pair of steel grey eyes that had the ability to undress me without even touching me. I couldn't help but close my eyes for a second as I felt a shiver penetrate the base of my spine.

"Now, that look tells me all I need to know, so come on, spill, who is he and what's his name?" Ben asked me sounding excited and clapping his hands, making my eyes snap open the second he did. I swear it was as if the memory of Lucius had just been real for a moment and the end of it had been him clicking his fingers in front of my face to get me to snap out of it.

"He is a no one...*not anymore,*" I told him allowing my tone to say all it needed to, and Ben was a good enough friend to let it drop, but not until after giving me a small sympathetic smile in return.

"Alright, it wasn't easy, but I would say we have found a winner," he said after another moment of rummaging through my closet. Then he cast aside a shopping bag I didn't recognize making me frown, wondering where it had come from? But this question died in place of another one, when Ben held up what he expected me to wear.

"Oh, hell no! No way, no how, just no," I said making him adopt the bitchy, I am not impressed look that consisted of a hand to the hip and a pout that could have rivaled any supermodel on the runway.

"You pinky promised me," he reminded me, making me shake my head in denial.

"What is this, first grade?" I asked him, throwing my hands up in the air and being just as dramatic as a first grader.

"No, but it will look like it when you see how bad my man paddy can get, so just do me a favour and suck it up and put it on." I released a sigh and said,

"You get that I am supposed to look professional at these things...right?" I said in my defense to the sexy garment he had hold of.

"Oh, I am sorry, I thought the point of it was to get rich men to open up their wallets and fund yet another pointless dig in the desert just by getting an eyeful of your feminine bounty."

"Hey! They are not pointless! And really...feminine bounty, what are you this time a gay pirate?" I said making him chuckle and smirk as he held up his hands to make a box with his fingers. Then he looked at me through the finger made small screen like a director would do and said,

"Perfect! Now just say that again only wearing this and you could make a mint for the next discovery of some dried-up dead guy who didn't know immortality really meant having his crusty carcass displayed behind a glass case for the rest of eternity," Ben said making me first try and scold him for taking the piss out of my work, only for me to end up in a fit of laughter.

"Come on Emmie, just try it on...for me, yeah?" Ben asked now trying with the pleading route, knowing I was a sucker for doing what people asked of me. The word 'no' was usually one that just stuck in an invisible speech bubble over my head, just waiting there for me to get the guts to pop it and make good use of the word. Of course, this never happened, and I usually just ended up going with the word 'yes' instead.

"Fine, but I can guarantee it will not suit me," I said getting up and grabbing the dress with a humpf, one that lacked the impetus of being pissed off.

"I very much doubt that, as you would look hot wrapped up in toilet rolls, trick or treating in the rain." I laughed once before needing to ask,

"And I would do that because?"

"Because your parents had no money at the time of Halloween and toilet rolls were on offer and forced you to be a mummy, whereas half an hour later you came home covered in white mush thanks to the rain…I think I blocked the drains for a whole week after that," Ben told me making me howl with laughter at the idea before giving him a kiss on the cheek, telling him,

"Aww, I bet you still looked cute though." He rolled his eyes and replied,

"Yeah, yeah, go get your sexy ass in that dress already before I tell you about the time they dressed me up as wolfman." I smirked, as I grabbed the dress and went into the bathroom.

"Let me guess, you were allergic to the costume and broke out in hives?" I asked through my bathroom door.

"No, think tights, glue and a bucket of hair clippings collected from our local hairdresser's and you will have a small idea of the nightmare that was my upbringing." I laughed again and shook my head just trying to picture it.

"Hey, I bet wolfman was rocking all those different colours and streaks!" I said making him chuckle. I loved hearing stories of Ben growing up, always making me laugh, no matter how bad my day had been. I also happened to know for a fact that Ben adored his parents and visited with them often, but it still didn't stop him from joking about them.

I listened to Ben as he continued to make me laugh and chuckle through the ordeal of dressing in something so revealing, it was making me fidget just thinking about walking out of the bathroom wearing it. Don't get me wrong, it wasn't as if I'd never dressed up or wore tight clothes before. It was just that I had grown up with an overly protective family that consisted of a lot of dominant males who still viewed me as a little girl. I wore dresses and even went to prom, but I think my father would have locked me away in his Scottish castle had he seen me wearing something this low cut.

Which gave me an idea. Had that been half the problem? The fact that my dad had never been given the opportunity to see me as a grown woman instead of his little girl? I had to wonder then that if he saw me wearing this tonight would that be enough to change his view of me?

Well, maybe it was worth a shot, as what was the worst-case scenario here, he gets pissed off and demands me to march back home and change? Well, yeah, that did sound a bit embarrassing, but it didn't mean that I would have to do it.

I looked at myself in the mirror and turned to the sides trying to take it all in. Ben had already done my hair in a classic soft up-do that was a cascade of soft curls gathered to one side and resting across one shoulder. He had also helped with my makeup, making me wonder if he'd taught himself or learned off a 'how to' You Tube video or something, as he was certainly skilled. I even told him that if he ever wanted to branch out from the world of art, then he could get paid a lot of money to do this professionally. I think I even made him blush. But it was more than worth the compliment I gave him as he had created a smoky effect that would go with any black dress I had picked, or more like he had picked, the sneaky bugger! It wasn't that I couldn't do my own make-up, as I did daily, still finding myself with the skin of a hormonal teenager whenever I was due my period. But doing my make-up dramatic, was something new for me.

And now, the more I looked at myself, seeing most of my legs on show, the more I thought why the hell not. I was a grown woman and it was time I started dressing more like one and less like a teenager. Yes, I had professional clothes for work, where I would wear black trousers and some smart knitted jumper, or a shirt and blazer, if we had anyone important in that day that needed to be impressed with our work. But never once had I worn something like this to an event. Making me now wonder about the smart business wear I usually reserved for these occasions and seeing it in a different light. Had I always been too conservative?

Well, now I vowed to change and the first chance I got after tonight, I was going shopping and this time, I was thinking sexy! And why not, as it wasn't as if I was hideous or anything. My legs were slim, if not a little short, but a pair of black heels would usually do the job nicely.

I also had been blessed with a flattish tummy, no matter how many donuts I ate, and one that tonight, because of the style of dress, gave me an hourglass figure. This was thanks to the band of black material that pulled my waist in before the skirt part flared out due to the hidden pleats and added under layer.

The length of the skirt came well above my knee and dipped longer at the back, so at the very least, I wasn't self-conscious of showing my ass cheeks all night. But it wasn't really this part that worried me the most, as the top was the main foundation of my concern. It was black beaded lace, cut in a halter neck style that dipped low at the front and showed a revealing amount of cleavage.

It cupped my decent C cup sized breasts and pulled them in, creating a bountiful show of pale skin. This was yet another thing I had inherited from my mother. That, as well as my blue eyes, only mine were less grey than my mum's and I had unusual flecks of violet running through mine that brightened when in sunlight and darkened when I was upset and crying. This, combined with my dark midnight black hair I had obviously inherited from my father, was said to make for a startling combination and made for some cute baby pictures...Or so my aunty Pip thought anyway, and she should know considering she still had a collage of them on her and my uncle Adam's wall. These were framed in fluffy fairy lights, cut out glitter paper hearts that we made together when I was five. Oh, and not forgetting my favorite part, our painted hand prints from when I was three and she had lifted me up onto my uncle Adam's shoulders so that I could slap my rainbow hands everywhere.

But even with my pale skin and blue/violet eyes, I still looked more like my dad than my mum. For one, I wasn't as curvy and also didn't have the same shaped face as my mother. Some even said that I looked more like my Aunty Sophia, due to having the same coloured hair and shape to my eyes. Eyes that I had decided to frame not with glasses this time, but with contact lenses I rarely wore. Not unless I was going swimming, or it was an unusually bright sunny day out and therefore sunglasses were needed.

I ran my hands down the taffeta skirt, liking the small strip of deep red satin that could be seen peeking out of the bottom from the underskirt. Also meaning that it went well with the ruby red lipstick Ben had painted on my full, heart shaped lips.

I looked like a completely different version of myself and I was starting to like it. It was time to show both of my worlds that I wasn't the unsure, awkward geek or the over-protected princess, a certain someone had accused me of being once upon a dark time. I was my own person and made my own decisions based on my own happiness, so if wearing a sexy dress for a party was what I wanted to do, then so be it. I nodded to myself in the mirror and stepped out to face my first judgement, which I knew the second I heard the wolf whistle, that it wouldn't be a judgement at all but more like a blessing.

"Wow…just wow, Emmie," Ben said after he had finished making a dramatic fuss and causing me to blush, which was something I rarely had occasion to do. But then again, when was it that I ever had reason to blush? I used to watch my father manage to do it on a daily basis to my mother and now that I was older, I absolutely did not want to know what it was he was whispering in her ear to achieve the reaction he did…because as sweet as it was to witness such a loving relationship between my parents, what they did behind closed doors will always be… well, quite frankly… *eww.*

But when I had been a child and thought his actions as nothing but playful, then I had always asked what it was he had said. Most of the time it was something one of them would make up, 'Oh, he thinks my dress is pretty' or 'He thinks we should tickle you', sweet endearing things like that. But now as an adult I knew better. But, unbeknown to me at the time, just how much witnessing my parents love for each other would end up shaping my views when it came to finding my own 'true love' were now forever rooted in my soul. And, as nice as Peter was, I knew that it would never be him.

Love was, after all…

Eternal.

CHAPTER FIVE

INVITED

An hour later I found myself walking from my flat wearing my old faithful black heels that seemed to go with every dressy outfit I owned. Amazingly, they were also what I classed as the holy grail of shoes, as they lasted the whole night and were a definite ten on the comfort scale, so needless to say, they had been re-heeled twice.

Ben had demanded that I do a selfie photoshoot with him, even if it was only for his own Facebook page as my parents hadn't thought it wise to partake in social media and announce to the world where I was living. And in this I had to agree, thinking that this time my parents' worries were a solid base for concern. Because, no matter how much my father was obeyed as King in his world, it didn't mean that there weren't those out there who opposed his rule, meaning my father had his fair share of enemies which essentially made me a target.

So, not being stupid over my move to another country and away from my parent's protection, I conceded in accepting some ground rules for my own good of course. Which meant that I basically only used my phone for what it had been first invented for, making calls and sending text messages. But other than doing the occasional internet shopping on my break times or taking pictures and playing Bubble Witch, that was pretty much the extent of my phone's use.

I would often catch people glued to their phones scrolling through the lives of other people and seeing what it was they were up to, which I thought was a great platform for keeping in touch with the outside world. But I had to wonder how much of their own lives they missed by always looking down at a small screen in their hands instead of the world right in front of them.

I had been tempted to ask Ben this as he was taking pictures of us both in my kitchen doing peace signs and performing our best 'Blue Steel' Zoolander poses.

"There, posted!" he declared after a few taps on his phone. I frowned, wondering if that was still classed as a bad idea, but then I shook it off as being paranoid considering it wasn't as though he could tag me in the picture.

Well, that had been just before I received a text message telling me a car was outside waiting for me. I texted back,

'Thanks Dad x'

'You're welcome.'

I then frowned back down at my phone, wondering where my return kiss was. But then again, knowing my dad, he was getting used to a new phone as he was forever taking his frustrations out on it, breaking them without thinking. Actually, this made sense considering the number had flashed up as unknown, not registered as my dad's number under my contacts.

Then, just as I opened the front door of my building, I noticed a black van with blacked out windows parked on double yellow lines across the street. It had a small logo on the side advertising it as a plumbing business which I suspected was a magnetic sign that could have easily been peeled off. I frowned, thinking there was something not right about it, as the van itself looked an expensive one and if you were a plumber making enough money to buy a van like that, then why wouldn't you go the extra mile and get the whole thing covered to advertise an obviously booming business?

Maybe I was over analyzing it as I usually did. But it was just the finer details always screamed out at me like that. However, I didn't know whether half the time I could put it down to instinct or just paranoia. For starters, the company could have just contracted out the job in this area and had removable signs for when those type of jobs occurred.

In the end, I shrugged my shoulders, fastened up my smart, woolen jacket, one I reserved for nights out, and walked towards the car my father had sent for me. I couldn't tell from here what make it was, but it was luxurious enough to be a Maybach, which knowing my father, it most likely was. Well, it sure beat the bus whatever it was.

"Good evening, Miss Draven," the driver said opening the door for me and tipping his cap in a gentlemanly fashion. I smiled back at him before lowering myself into the seat, being mindful not to catch my skirt in the car door (something that had happened twice before now).

I was surprised to find myself alone in the back, wondering where my dad was, so as soon as the driver started to pull away, I pressed on the intercom to ask.

"Are we picking up my…Umpf." My sentence was cut off as another driver cut in front of us unexpectedly, meaning we had to brake suddenly, jarring me forward in my seat.

"I apologize, Miss," he said in response to his actions and no doubt the muttered curse he let slip.

"That's fine, there is no accounting for idiots on the road," I told him to put him at ease and at the same time bending down to pick up my handbag, struggling to do so in such a tight dress. Well, I was just glad I hadn't overdone it this week on the doughnuts as they were my weakness in life.

"In answer to your question, Miss, I believe my instructions were to take you straight there where he will be with you shortly." I nodded in thanks and relaxed back in the ultimate level of comfort, thinking that there were some perks to being rich. But for me, who had been brought up with it, I just viewed it as unnecessary. Yes, it was nice not having to count the pennies when you wanted something and being able to travel and come and go as you pleased. But I thought there was something more freeing by paying my own way in the world than if I had just accepted my father's credit card he'd tried to give me, telling me there was no limit on it.

At first, I had outright refused, turning my back in frustration and telling him that he just didn't understand. But in the end, we came to a compromise whereas I promised to take it and keep it solely for emergencies. Seven years later I still hadn't spent one penny on it. In fact, it remained in a shoe box hidden beneath a broken section in the floor boards I'd found once when moving my room around. It was in the center of my bedroom, now concealed by a rag rug I'd made with extra cut offs I had from when I made my own curtains. Did I mention how much I loved crafts, having filled the space under my bed and half my closet with material, paint, sewing gadgets, wool, scrap book stuff and a shoe box full of glue sticks?

However, I should also mention that I couldn't paint an actual picture for toffee. Not like my mum, who was a great artist. I used to sit on a swivel chair in the studio my dad had made for her, just spinning around and getting lost in the movement of colours around me from all the artwork she had displayed on the walls.

It seemed like no time at all before the driver was pulling

the car up alongside the imposing black and gold tipped gates of the British Museum. They had been opened wide to allow cars inside so that the rich wouldn't have to walk the distance of the vast courtyard to reach its main doors.

The grand entrance was primarily designed in the Greek Revival façade, which was an architectural movement of the late 18th and early 19th centuries. This was a style predominantly found in Northern Europe and the United States and in this case, suited the grandeur that was the British Museum. The entrance was made up of forty-four grand looking columns that reached forty-five feet high, making you believe yourself to be stepping back in time to Ancient Greece.

I couldn't help but look at the building as I had done that same day when I first laid eyes on it. I remembered it like it was yesterday at the naive age of only sixteen. It had been my first school trip and with the rest of my class, I turned a corner and walked through the gates for the first time in stunned silence. I even remember the way I faltered a step when looking up and seeing the past stood there in front of me.

I couldn't help but look down at my feet, half expecting to find myself stood there in someone else's shoes, as if this was all part of some dream. I had heard rumors of something called the Janus Gate that was said to hold a gateway to the past. But every time I had asked about it growing up, it just seemed to be a taboo subject that people shrugged off. So, needless to say, if it did exist I had never seen it.

But, in that single moment, it was like being hit with a vision of my future, something inside the root of my soul beseeching me to take this leap of faith. To take the initial steps as to what would be the first of many steps to come. And I had done it. I had achieved my dream of working here and finding my place within its walls. And it had not been a difficult choice, for the second I wandered up to the upper level and into the first

Egyptian room which was named 'Death and the Afterlife', I knew it had been the place for me.

The very first moment I saw the mummy of Cleopatra I was hooked! To the point that my teacher had a job finding me again as the first chance I got, I broke away from the group and spent all of my time in those six Egyptian rooms.

Which is precisely why, whenever I found myself at its grand entrance, I couldn't help but look up at those tall columns and smile to myself before entering. Something I did once more right after the door was opened for me and I got out of the car. I thanked the driver before walking up the steps to lead me inside.

The rest of the museum was closed for the night, which meant it was something quite marvelous when there weren't hundreds of bodies crowding around in each of the rooms, moving like cattle. No, now there was only the gentle hum of life from within the vast and famous space of the great court.

The great court has what was called a tessellated glass roof which consisted of 6100m2 of glazed triangular panes creating a unique shape and making it the largest covered square in Europe. The entire court then surrounded the original circular British Museum Reading Room at its centre. Which, although it remained the same structure having been refurbished, it unfortunately no longer housed any books as it once did. Because in 1997 the British Library moved to its own specially constructed building next to St Pancras Station and all the books and shelving were removed from the museum's reading room.

However, it didn't mean that the space wasn't put to good use as throughout the years it has been used to house the world's most spectacular exhibitions, such as 'The First Emperor: China's Terracotta Army' and is used as a stage for temporary exhibitions, like the one I was currently working on.

Tonight however, it was the great court that was to be the grand venue for the gala and what better place seeing as the court acted as a central linking point for the museum, similar to the Louvre Pyramid in Paris.

The sound of the harp being played as the guests all walked in echoed around the vast space. This, combined with the night sky above and the flickering lights of hundreds of candles situated in modern chrome candelabras, well let's just say that it created a sheer delight for the senses. They had really outdone themselves this year I thought as I took off my jacket to hand to the attendant who was waiting to take it from me. I thanked him and swallowed hard at the admiring look he gave me, hoping it wasn't because of how revealing my dress was.

Then, as graceful as my natural abilities would allow, I walked further into the large space dotted around with London's elite. I recognized a few faces from previous events, one of whom spotted me and was currently making his way over to me, grabbing an extra champagne flute from a nearby waitress. I sighed inwardly, wishing Wendy was next to me or at least my father, who I couldn't yet see anywhere, and it wasn't exactly as though he was the type of man you would miss.

Not like the man who was on his way over as though he could smell fresh meat. He was a businessman in something or other that I held no interest in the last time he told me, so it was no wonder I hadn't retained the information. All I remembered was him asking me what I had planned after the event, which at the time had been another fundraiser.

It wasn't that he was bad looking per se, if not a lot older than me, but it was the air of self-importance he portrayed that made me want to groan aloud the second he made it to my side. He was wearing a tailored tux and reminded me of a younger Sean Connery about ten years after he did Bond. He looked me up and down, displaying a smirk as if openly gawking at someone was totally acceptable and I suddenly was starting to curse this dress.

Well, if I didn't want to get stared at then maybe next time I should stick to the good old faithful pencil skirted dress that looked more suited to a boardroom than a Gala. And anyway, it only took a quick glance around the place to see that there were others dressed in smaller, tighter dresses than I was. But the one startling difference was that none of them were alone and dateless as I was. Then he opened his mouth and began his conversation with a compliment. At the same time, he held out the spare glass in his hand for me to take, something I didn't do for fear he would see it as a green light to chat me up. Damn you, Wendy! I shouted in my head, knowing this had been so much easier last time when I could just reply,

'Oh later, well me and my girlfriend are going to get a kebab on the way home'…yeah, that had stopped him in his tracks.

"May I say that you're looking exceptionally beautiful tonight, Miss Draven." I opened my mouth to reply but promptly found the 'thank you' stuck in my throat the second I heard another voice coming from behind me,

"No, you may not!" was the stern reply given before I myself could utter more than a muted gasp of shock. I then found myself frowning as I quickly convinced myself that I must have been hearing things. But this was easier said than done when I had to ignore the way a strange shiver shot down my spine at the sound of the man's voice.

"And you are?" The Sean Connery lookalike in front of me asked and doing so in a haughty tone, obviously not appreciating the frankness of the man's reply behind me.

Then two things happened at once. The first was that another glass of champagne was swiftly held in front of me, therefore rendering the first offered glass obsolete, as this one came from the mystery man who was still standing behind me.

And the second was his firm reply…

"Her date." The deep and authoritative voice replied decidedly, this time making me audibly gasp the moment I recognized who it belonged to.

But no… it couldn't be…*could it?*

Well, there was only one way to find out, so I held my breath and turned to face the man who claimed to be 'my date' after so many years ago vowing never to be one. The man who had broken my heart and who I hadn't seen in years. The man whose name I couldn't help but let slip from my blood red lips in what sounded like a breathy plea for sanity to be restored…

"Lucius."

CHAPTER SIX

UNLIKELY DATE

"*Lucius.*" The second I uttered his name I saw his harsh gaze that had once been centered on the man behind me, shift to my own. It then softened for a mere second before they snapped back into his usual steely composure. This in turn made me also snap out of my dreamlike state and I frowned up at him, quickly remembering how much I hated him. So, I took a step back and folded my arms across my chest, telling him first without words, that I was not impressed with him being here. It was then I decided to trust my voice and say with a mild waver in its tone,

"Wh...what are...are you doing here?" The second I asked this the bastard actually smirked down at me. This made me so mad that the next time I spoke, I couldn't help the bite that came with it, even if that bite came out as an intimidated whisper,

"Looking smug is not an answer." His lips twitched with his amusement as he still looked down at me. I suddenly felt that being under his intense gaze was as though I was being studied

by a predator, so that he could find my weaknesses and abuse them as he wished. The only thing that broke his connection was the sound of a voice being cleared behind me, reminding us both that we weren't alone.

"Leave us...*now.*" Lucius' demand came with a bite of power that told me this wasn't just an order but more a control of the man's mind, rendering his will useless...something Lucius just so happened to be a master at. And when I say master, what I really mean is the most powerful being alive at it!

Instantly the man left with no complaints and no doubt doing so with no memory of why he had walked over to me in the first place, or quite possibly even of me to begin with. Well, a girl could hope as that might save me at the next gala.

I don't know why but the second I felt myself alone with him, I suddenly wished the man hadn't been made to leave. As now it left me feeling open and exposed, with only the reminder of the worst mistake of my life standing opposite me. And even in a room full of people, I couldn't shake the feeling that we were the only two beings stood at the centre of a private storm fueled by my emotions and battling it out in our silent standoff.

I felt like running away as fast as my legs could carry me, knowing the power he held over me. I hated to admit it...no, I *loathed* to admit it, but it was the truth no matter how I pretended otherwise. I couldn't lie to myself, but I would be damned if I let him believe anything other than my utter indifference towards him.

I was no longer that unsure girl who once shook with nervousness and stuttered with uncertainty around him. But even as I told myself this, I couldn't help but nearly choke on the silent plea for him to allow space between us. For the second I took a step away from him, he simply took one closer to me. Then he took my hand in his, causing intense sparks to flutter in my heart the second he made the contact with my skin. I watched as he raised it up and placed the champagne flute he had held out to me into my shaky hand. Damn my traitorous body and the way it gave evidence to the way he still affected me.

"Here, drink this, as it will help settle your nerves," he told me in an impassive way, looking over my head due to our height difference and moving his interest towards the rest of the room. I wanted to growl at him the way I would often hear other Supernaturals do in anger, but I knew it would have been wasted on such a man. Instead, I took the glass just so that I could get away from his touch, unable to stop my eyes taking in his gloved left hand.

I never knew why he kept it hidden and every time I had asked someone about it, all they told me was that it was a price once he paid to save us all. To say that this vague answer had been a frustrating one would be an understatement. But when it came to the history between Lucius, my dad and my mum, then let's just say vague was the nature of the only beast they would let out of the cage.

Hence, why I didn't know what he had hidden behind that black leather but from the look of things, it didn't exactly render him handicapped as he used it just fine. However, I could tell he didn't like it being stared at or mentioned in any way. I had made that mistake once when I reached out to touch it, only to regret it instantly the second I received his snarled response.

In short, Lucius was and always had been, an enigma to me. I couldn't make him out and with regards to his feelings, then as ever I was at an utter loss. But what did it matter now? No, all that did matter was why he was here right now, which I was determined to get to the bottom of. That was if I could take my eyes off him long enough to form a coherent thought.

Unfortunately, Lucius looked as though he was the bad boy

at a wedding who refused to conform but thought that you should just be grateful that he turned up at all.

He was wearing a suit that looked more like you'd expect to see at the end of a night out than the beginning of one, for he was minus a tie and his top two buttons were undone. This, unfortunately for me, was showing the length of his corded neck and just the hint of his extensive muscles you just knew were hidden beneath the white shirt. This, of course, making my mouth feel dry enough so that I quickly found myself downing my champagne until not a drop was left. I also ignored his handsome, smug face as he watched me do this, one that sported a knowing grin I could just feel was there.

His darker blonde hair had been tamed back, giving him a severe edge to his usual stern gaze as he looked upon the space with annoyance, no doubt asking himself why he was even here at all. Which still begged the question to be asked once more.

"So, are you going to explain to me what it is you are doing here or am I left to guess?" I said, hoping my haughty tone wasn't lost on him. Well, I don't know if it was or not because he didn't even grace me with a look when he answered me.

"And why should I not be here, considering a museum is usually obligated to willingly grant admittance to the general public," was his sarcastic reply. I rolled my eyes and finally found my bravery when I replied with a slice of sarcasm of my own,

"Does this look like the type of party where everyone is welcome…there are more designer shoes and handbags in this room than Bond Street…now cut the bullshit, Lucius, and tell me why you're really here?" I snapped this last part after first ridding myself of my empty glass thanks to a passing waitress and folding my arms once more across my chest. Unfortunately, for me though, I had forgotten about the deep and low cut of my dress and only remembered it again when I saw Lucius' perfect lips form a cunning smile when eyeing up my cleavage.

I released a pissed off 'humpf' sound as I dropped my arms quickly, hating that he knew how much he had just affected me.

"If you wish to know my reasons for being here then I suggest you had better ask daddy, for he requested my attendance in his place." I frowned, knowing now the reasons why he was here and hating the way Lucius always referred to my father as the childish 'daddy' he always did around me. Acting as if I was still the young girl that foolishly cared what he thought of me.

I decided not to answer him, instead getting ready to call my father himself so that he could explain to me why he thought to have Lucius come here, when he hadn't even given me chance to open the box. But then, as if on cue, Lucius' phone started to ring, and he pulled it calmly from his suit jacket with ease.

"As instructed," was his cool answer to the obvious question my father had asked, which would have been, 'Are you with my daughter?' or some other version of that.

"Very well...he wishes to speak to you," Lucius told me as he handed me his phone.

"Dad?" I said in question. He could also tell with my tone that I was less than pleased.

"Sweetheart, I am sorry but business at home prevented me from being there and as I knew that Lucius was in the city, I thought that you could..."

"Kill two Gorgon leeches with one arrow?" I said cutting in and trying to ignore the raised brow Lucius gave me.

"Yeah, I get it... but you could have waited and given me more time," I told my father trying not to sound as whiny as I felt like I was being.

"Well, when you said you needed a date..." I groaned aloud, cutting in and hissing with embarrassment,

"I didn't say that I *needed* a date."

"No? Because the way I heard it, was that you hated attending those events alone." my father argued back in a calm tone. This then made me wonder who my dad would have sent instead, had he known what my true feelings had been towards Lucius years ago and was in fact, one of the reasons I hardly ever came home in fear that Lucius would be there.

I released a sigh and muttered,

"Yeah, but not that much." Of course, he heard this and chuckled, obviously finding my reluctance to be around his old enemy both reassuring and amusing. Lucius, on the other hand was outright frowning at me and I had to question the reason why? Because let's face it, what else did he expect? But more importantly, why would he even care?

"Then think of this as a good time to show him the box I gave you and he can soon be on his way," my dad said, obviously believing that I had left it at work and not taken it home with me. I suddenly wanted to curse myself knowing that this wasn't going to be a quick and flying visit, both Lucius and my dad had obviously believed it would be. I decided it was wise not to correct him and instead just agreed noncommittedly,

"I will see what I can do."

"That's my girl." He praised, making me subtly wince and close my eyes longer than I needed to, meaning that the second I opened them again, I found Lucius studying me in a quizzical way. I ignored this, not daring to think too much into it and instead concentrated my time in saying goodbye to my dad and asking him to give my love to my mum, who he was no doubt eager to get back to. Then I handed Lucius back his phone, annoyed that my dad had unknowingly put me in this situation.

"But of course." I heard Lucius say in response to whatever request my dad was asking of him this time. This was why I hated being the only mortal in my family sometimes, knowing how handy having super senses was in situations like this. Especially when you wanted to hear both sides of the conversation and only got the brief and curt end of one.

But the only 'gift', if you could call it that, was that I could choose whether or not to see a Supernatural in their true form. Most of the time I just didn't bother as it wasn't exactly needed, and I had grown up seeing those around me for who they really were and let's just say that it affected me more when I saw a spider the size of my thumbnail than a demon stood next to me. Spiders were the ones that received the petrified screams, whereas most demons didn't even see me flinch.

However, the only one who I couldn't see in his true form and never had, was Lucius. Oh, I had come close that night when he saved my life but what I had seen had been too close to the shadows to fully make out.

Normally I could have just conjured up the sight with a mere thought but for some reason this wasn't the case with Lucius. As that night I had only seen what he had allowed me to see, along with the others that had attacked me. But even stranger still, was that I wasn't the only one afflicted with these restraints around him, as it seemed Lucius had some of his own around me.

Shockingly, I was the only one who was immune to Lucius' mighty control over other people's will. Meaning he couldn't make me do a damn thing he wanted unless of course it was by force. And well, considering the size difference in not just height but also given his immense bulk, then that wouldn't have exactly been too hard to accomplish for him. Lucius was almost the same size as my father, who was a large and imposing figure of a man.

Lucius's broad shoulders did look fit for swinging an axe in the woods somewhere or more fitting, the huge sword I knew he had used in battle, if my father's stories were to be believed… which there was little reason for them not to be.

But Lucius was certainly an intimidating man to behold, even in a suit and I doubt he would have had much trouble getting my earlier admirer to go away, even without his use of mind control. Being taller and bigger than most men kind of did that. Damn him and his abundance of hot, sexy muscles!

"Ah, Miss Draven, there you are, you sweet thing, you!" A voice I recognized as the Chairman of The Board of Trustees, and who was essentially my boss, appeared at my side looking slightly flustered. He was a middle-aged gentleman with slightly greying hair at the sides and laughter lines around a pair of brown eyes, and he was dressed in a tux.

His name was Sir Nelson Allerton and he was the one Trustee appointed by Her Majesty, in accordance with the British Museum Act of 1963 and the Museums and Galleries Act of 1992. He had also been appointed Chairman by the Board from its members, so needless to say, he was well liked.

"Sir Allerton, a pleasure seeing you as always," I replied smiling and I don't know why but I could instantly feel the air around me becoming statically charged. I refrained from frowning in question and shooting Lucius a strange look, as I had a feeling that it was coming straight from him.

"You are looking beautiful this evening as no doubt your girlfriend has already told you this…speaking of whom, was she not able to accompany you this time?" he asked making me suddenly want to blush scarlet, especially when I heard Lucius cough back a laugh at my side. I saw the unimpressed look the chairman gave him in response and I quickly decided that I needed to speak now. Especially before Lucius managed to put his foot in it by doing something stupid, like asking me outright if I was a lesbian as I let my colleagues believe.

"No, Wendy had other plans tonight but asked me to give

you her regards for she was truly disappointed not to be able to do so herself," I said lying through my teeth and imagining her sniggering the second I told her what I was forced to say. Well, she wouldn't be sniggering if she could see who was stood next to me right now, that was for damn sure! She had a weakness for sexy, eye candy.

"Ah, but of course, news never sleeps in the city…and your replacement, will you not introduce me?" he said, smirking playfully which I doubted Lucius appreciated.

"I am her…" I just knew that Lucius was about to really confuse matters and with it, my sexual preferences, by declaring himself as my date, so thought it wise to interrupt him quickly…

"Cousin!" I said a bit too loudly and I knew this when Sir Allerton jerked back a little because of it. Then he looked from Lucius and back to me, obviously trying to find any family resemblance at all, which was a pointless endeavor.

"On my mother's German side," I added with a whisper, once again making Lucius scoff next to me. Then I remembered my manners and introduced my boss to Lucius, letting him know in my tone how important he was in my world and therefore to behave himself.

"Cousin, this is Sir Nelson Allerton, who is Chairman of the board." I said trying to ignore the disapproving glare he gave me when I started that sentence out with calling him my cousin for the second time.

"It is very nice meeting you Mr…?" He let that nameless question hang in the air along with his hand for Lucius to shake and waiting for him to complete the sentence. Which after a pleading look from me up at him, he finally did.

"Septimius, Lucius Septimius," he replied taking his hand and giving it a strong shake, something that clearly took Sir

Allerton off guard as I noticed him rubbing his hand discreetly once Lucius let it go.

"Ah, an unusual name to be sure, and I will wager your father was a fan of Ancient Roman literature, as if I recall the name being one you share with an assassin of Pompey the Great in 48 BC." Sir Allerton, I should have mentioned was also a historian of high esteem. But one look at Lucius' face and the cunning smile he had upon it, no doubt at being referred to as an assassin, told me that he seemed most pleased.

But knowing Lucius and his arrogance I was surprised that he didn't say something crazy like, 'Oh those were the good old, ancient days', because if the rumors were to be believed then Lucius had in fact once served as my father's own personal assassin.

Thankfully though he went with something less creepy and definitely less threatening, when he said in a self-confident tone,

"I believe the Roman emperor, Lucius Septimius Severus Augustus was more in mind at the time." Sir Allerton grinned back at him as if he had just found the one person in the room who had the same interests in Roman History as he did. Even though we were currently in one of the largest museums in the world and there were no doubt plenty enthusiasts to spare.

"Ah yes, correct me if I am wrong but Severus seized power after the death of Emperor Pertinax in 193 during the Year of the Five Emperors, did he not?" I looked at Lucius once again in a wary way, begging him with my eyes not to say anything like 'Yes I did', giving freedom for Sir Allerton to then think I had brought a crazy family member to this gala.

Of course, the second I discovered that it was true, that Lucius had once been a Roman Emperor, then not only did this bombard my historical mind with a bucket load of questions, but it also plagued me with about a years' worth of fantasies too. Wendy had wondered at the time why I was on a mission to watch every movie and tv series that was based in Ancient Rome. Something which only ended up adding fuel to the raging fire that was imagining Lucius dressed as a Roman Emperor, fighting general or heck, even as a gladiator in nothing more than a helmet and leather tasseled skirt. My imagination had been endless for many nights alone, keeping me company and my hands shamefully busy.

"He did indeed," was Lucius' curt reply and I released a secret sigh of relief before deciding to change the subject.

"I trust, Sir Allerton, that the gala is looking to be a successful one?" I asked, taking a look around and seeing that there were definitely more people than last time.

"Oh yes, which reminds me of what I wanted to ask of you."

"Oh?"

"Would you be so kind as to show a few of our guests along room four, and you know, give them a little taste and insight to your knowledge, for you have better people skills than Duncan, and a prettier face to be sure," he said jovially, making me laugh. Duncan was a nice guy, once you got to know him that was, as he worked in the same department as I did. But Sir Allerton wasn't exaggerating as Duncan's people skills were more than lacking as he most definitely preferred the company of people that had been dead for thousands of years.

"But of course, it would be my pleasure," I replied knowing this was really what I was here for. To woo the rich with my easy manner and extensive knowledge. Which was why after this, Sir Allerton clapped his hands, declaring 'excellent' and reminding me silently of Mr Burns from the Simpsons, only with a lot more hair and minus the ass kissing sidekick, Mr Smithers.

"In that case I will gather those who inquired after the

private tour and have them meet you in room 4 in ten minutes, should give you time for another champagne to calm any nerves." I gave him a nod and watched as he left, making him the second person of the night to suggest I drink to ease any stress. Well, in that case, if Lucius stuck around any longer then I would no doubt be an alcoholic by the end of the night!

However, this thought didn't sway me enough to stop me from taking another glass from the waiter, gaining a sound of disapproval from Lucius for my actions.

"I...I'm not expecting you to stay," I told him, trying once again to steady my voice now I was alone with him.

"Why did you tell him that I was your cousin?" he asked, flatly ignoring my comment.

"Well, I could hardly say you were my date, and besides, we would make unlikely friends considering we don't even like each other," I replied being honest, but from the look of his face, it was clear I had shocked him.

"Why do you think that?" Okay, so his question definitely threw me off my guard, and my face must have said as much. In return he took a step closer to me, then in a blink, took hold of my forearm the second he saw I was about to retreat. Then he took that last step into me until I had no option but to bend my neck back just so that I could maintain eye contact. Something I wasn't sure I wanted to do, let alone thought as a wise decision, not with those dangerous eyes of his.

However, it was as if he had me captured with my body and mind having no choice but to obey him. This was the danger of being around a man like Lucius. He knew the effect he had on me and the bastard used it to his advantage, for he may not have had the power of will over me, but he certainly had other means to exploit. Primarily those which were named my foolish feelings for him.

This was why I needed to increase my efforts in making him

believe that there were no longer any feelings there, even if it was the biggest lie I would ever tell.

"You believe me to be indifferent to your beauty because we aren't friends as you call it, and therefore I could never be classed as a date in your eyes?" he asked, and I swear my mouth fell open, no doubt rendering me much further down that 'beauty scale'. But I didn't care because my shock overrode any good sense I had not to show it. Worse still my mouth confirmed this when I couldn't stop myself from uttering the incredible hushed words,

"You think I am beautiful?" The utter shock in my tone softened his gaze when he looked at me just like he had when I first whispered his name not fifteen minutes ago. It was as if he found my surprised response endearing in some way. He showed this through the tender emotion in his stunning eyes, eyes that turned to amber shades in a heartbeat, making me wonder if it had been a trick of light or his demon side breaking through. My father's eyes would often do this, especially around me and my mother, when they would turn from their dark blackish brown to a vibrant deep purple tone.

But then, as if some invisible cord had just been snapped, he let me go and took a step back, replying sarcastically,

"Do I look blind to you, Princess." The use of this royal title was one I utterly loathed to hear. Especially coming from him and the way he always managed to say it as though I was the spoilt child he had accused me of being all those years ago. I gave him a glare in return and muttered a lame,

"I told you, don't call me that." Which in the end was said through gritted teeth over my champagne glass and with me looking at the rest of the room, wishing I could just ignore his presence until he was gone. Because this was the dangerous thing with Lucius: one second, he could look at you as if you were the only girl in the world. The way he would draw you in

with every gentle yet owning touch, captivating you and making you fall into that hopeful place you dreamed would be real.

But then the inevitable would follow where he would cut you down by mentally snapping his fingers in front of you, waking you up to the reality that was him.

The cruel and stern truth, that Lucius Septimius was a King...

Without a heart to give.

CHAPTER SEVEN

ALONE IN PASSION

Ten minutes later I found myself stood in room four with a much larger audience than Sir Allerton first led me to believe. So, now stood in the wonderful gallery of Egyptian sculpture, I started at one end and began to work my way down the space that included some of the world's finest depictions of kings, deities and symbolic objects ever found. These ranged from the time of the Old Kingdom right through to the middle of the Roman Period. There were also some grand architectural pieces from temples and tombs that I had the pleasure of showing them.

The room itself was a large painted white space, framed with columns either side, creating an almost serene quality to the colourful Egyptian history. With its tall, square cut ceiling and its wall of tall windows that were usually flooding the place with natural light, then it was the most perfect place to display them in all their glory. Especially like this, when it was silent and still, being without the hustle of cram packed tourists, it was one of my most favorite places to be. However, being as it was one of the most popular parts of the museum, being so close to its entrance and situated next to the great court, it was rarely seen like this by anyone but the museum's staff.

But no matter how much I loved it, I had never once been forced to share it with the likes of Lucius, who was currently making my job very hard indeed. From the very first moment he followed me into the gallery, he stood in the background, watching my tour like the master of his own universe. He was totally at ease being surrounded by the godly figures of Egypt and considering how old he was, then I could sort of understand why.

After all, most of what we saw now, being housed as a way for modern day society to view these small snippets of the past, he himself had most likely seen in its original form. Then, no wonder a room like this would be underwhelming to a man like Lucius, compared to seeing these mighty statues stood proud where they were always intended to be. Statues not broken and weathered through the whirling sandstorm of time.

So, maybe it was this reason that, unlike the others who seemed to be listening to me with great intent, he wasn't looking at the ancient treasures I had been referring to. No, instead, the whole time he had solely been looking at me talking about them and no doubt hearing the way my voice wavered slightly whenever I caught sight of him staring at me.

I tried not to look at him, I really did, but when such a powerful figure was in the room, standing out just as much as if one of these ancient kings had come back to life, then it was very near impossible.

I felt as though I was being studied by Lucius, and surprisingly, not necessarily in a scrutinizing way. But still studied all the same. At first when I started speaking he would raise his brow at me when my voice faltered slightly with my nerves and in a way, it never had done before when talking to people about my work.

So, eventually I had no choice but to act as though he wasn't there, which like I said, was near impossible to do considering it was as if I could feel every one of his movements. As though in some way I was connected to him on a deeper level.

At one point during the start of the tour I even found myself having to shake my head a little after he had simply placed his palm at the lower part of my back, so that he could lead me into a space I knew well. I didn't know why he did this, but I knew two things…one was that his actions felt more driven by a possessive side of him. And the second was that unfortunately there was no way that he could have missed the audible gasp I had created by sucking air back through my lips in genuine surprise.

But then I started speaking and addressing about twenty people with a slice of history that felt as though it was rooted to my very bones.

"In the first section of the gallery we are greeted with Egyptian monuments that give you a sense of kingship ideology and both Egyptian religion and their magnificent art," I told them coming to stand in front of the first of two matching statues.

"This here, ladies and gentlemen, is Amenhotep III, a king who ruled in Egypt in the 14th century. But don't be fooled into believing this a likeness of his image as kings were rarely replicated as such," I told them ignoring the way Lucius held two fingers casually over his lips as if concealing a smirk underneath those large pale digits.

"What do you mean, didn't he look like that?" A woman asked, who was clearly surprised as she walked over to the largest of the two and looked up at him. It was a statue that was extremely well preserved given its age, but that was most likely down to the hard, dark stone it was carved from named granodiorite.

"As you can see here in the largest of the statues, which I think you will agree is the best preserved of the two, it is a perfect summary of what an Egyptian king was supposed to be thought to look like by his people." I told her and the others, as I walked over to the statue, noticing how Lucius was the only one not to move with the rest of the group. But then again, why would he, as he could see everything just fine from his advantage of being six foot four and a head above most people.

In fact, I hadn't failed to notice the admiring looks he had already received from the ladies in the room. This had been the case since he first escorted me in here and even now was no different. But this hadn't surprised me, for what female in their right mind *wouldn't* look. However, what was shocking was every time he had ignored these appreciating glances. Because, unsurprisingly, there were more than a few pretty women here and a few of which that were now occupying the space around him. One in particular who had also been the one to ask me the question about the king's appearance.

"And that was?" Someone else asked me in reference to what an Egyptian king should be portrayed as.

"Well, essentially he was thought to be half human and half divine, which is why he is therefore made to look eternally young and his features are very idealized. So, although not at all a true portrait of the king, it was like most people who preferred to hold on to their youthful days and was most undoubtedly a representation he would have approved of." I said making a few people laugh and more unbelievably, it also managed to make Lucius smile. Had he just found me funny? Well if he had, then that old saying, 'A first for everything' certainly suited.

"And how do you know he's a king and not just an

interpretation of a God?" A man asked me with a skeptical tone I was about to crush with fact.

"There are a few different ways that soon become obvious, for example, can you see that he is wearing a pleated head cloth with the cobra on his forehead?" I pointed up and each of them followed my direction.

"Can anyone tell me what they think the cobra meant?" I asked deciding to involve the group more, seeing as it was obvious with their questioning that they wanted to get involved. But in the end, my answer came from the most unlikely source and not someone I would ever have classed as a team player.

"It's the symbol of divine protection," Lucius said in a controlled tone that gave none of his thoughts or feelings away.

"I uh...well, yes, that's right," I said in a flustered way, making me wonder if this hadn't been his intent all along.

"Unfortunately, though, the cobra is rather damaged, as well as a piece of the king himself, as he would have originally had a long beard...these are both ways of telling us the statue is one of a king," I told them and before another question could be asked, I provided them with more concrete proof.

"But even if these had been too damaged to see, then if you look on his belt there is a small inscription that presents his official name, as is the beauty of hieroglyphics and the extensive abundance of information they tell us." I went on after this to explain about a 'Cartouche' which were formerly only worn by pharaohs and the oval surrounding their name was meant to protect them.

"Protect them from what?" Another of the guests asked and I couldn't help but glance at Lucius when I answered,

"From evil spirits in both the living and in the Afterlife." Lucius gave me a wry grin at this and I wondered then if he knew the hidden meaning that I was referring to. This was him being one of my own personal evil spirits that I seemed to be forced to live with, at first in Afterlife and now here, in my new life. His coy look certainly told me that it hadn't been lost on him.

"The cartouche has become a symbol representing good luck and protection from evil. And as a hieroglyph, it is used to represent the Egyptian language word for "name" which therefore tells us his name as being Amenhotep III. And even more interesting still is what you can see in between his legs," I said pausing for the laugh I knew would come from everyone. Again, a single glance at Lucius granted me a questioning and amused look, which included that sexy raised brow. One he combined with just the hint of a playful smirk, therefore I couldn't help but blush in return.

"Is he exaggerated as a divine entity down there as well," one of the gentlemen joked, making the rest of us laugh, all except who I supposed to be his wife, who smacked his arm in reprimand.

"What you say is not far from the truth as in between his legs you can in fact see the ceremonial bull's tail which an Egyptian king would typically wear at official occasions."

"Why in God's name would he do that?" An older lady asked in mortification. I wanted to laugh out loud for if she knew only half of what the ancient world used to do, then she would be doing more than just blushing. It had often been strange to me when reading these unusual customs of lost cities and civilizations that were born with nothing but a river and vast sands of the harsh desert. It made me think about my father and the ancient world he knew. But not only that, it made me think of Lucius' own past as well. Which was why I looked at him now, in his tailored suit, swapping it in my mind for what he would have worn back in those times. Had he visited Egypt back then? Had he seen these magnificent cities in all their glory? Oh, what I wouldn't have given just then to excuse myself and beg upon him to tell me everything he had seen throughout the ages.

However, his questioning stare was one I knew was trying to read what I was thinking and again I was asking myself why would he be bothered enough to want to know?

"Miss Draven?" The second I heard my name I shook away my thoughts like the cobwebs they were, for they had clung to my mind for much longer than today.

"Because the bull is a strong animal that represents the king in both strength and power. Now, moving on from here, we have two truly magnificent statues from the same reign as our king, Amenhotep III, over there." I said as I approached the two resting lions carved from red granite. I explained about their relaxed state being something quite rare seeing as they also represented the king.

"But they're lions…how would that represent a king?" A haughty and rude woman asked, who up until now had looked quite bored, well with me anyway, with Lucius, not so much.

She was in a sparkling blue dress that was tight enough, I half imagined her to have at least four people all grabbing a quarter of her hem and giving it a good tug down.

I would have said she was most likely in her late fifties and not doing so with grace as she'd had so much Botox she couldn't have smiled even if she had wanted to. But it soon became clear where her distaste for me arose, for she had been one of the women eyeing up Lucius like he had been a piece of man candy she wanted to lick to the bone. And well, it was becoming very apparent that his eyes were locked onto only one sight and that was me.

She even went as far as to walk over to one of the lions that Lucius was stood close to and ran her fingers along its back seductively. And even though I was tempted to remind her not to touch the exhibits, I had to remember that we needed money from these people, and her clueless husband was wearing Armani.

However, Lucius merely spared her an unimpressed glance of indifference and it was obvious that from this, I wasn't the only one that thought her to be rude and obnoxious.

"It is true that the human headed lion, which is better known to you all as the Sphinx, is a very familiar motif in Egyptian art. And for those of you that don't already know, these Egyptian sphinxes as a rule usually represented the kings as powerful creatures. So, in this instance to see the king completely depicted as a lion and one so relaxed, it makes them both quite rare." I then couldn't help but think of Lucius, seeing him as another king depicted as a lion, one hidden in plain sight and right now surrounded by the unsuspecting cattle of humanity...*me included.*

"You can see here on the inscription that it identifies the king as 'A lion among rulers'," I told them after swallowing hard and knowing where my eyes would rest upon after it was spoken. Seeing as I had included it solely for his benefit, telling him this was how I viewed him. The look he gave me in return came with the slight tilt of his head as if voicing the question in his mind and trying to silently connect with me. For in that single moment, one that lasted only seconds, it felt as though we were suddenly the only two people in the room. The only two communicating so much, yet none of it something we could trust, for not a single word was uttered between us.

"Right, let's continue should we...?" I said holding out my arm and leading them to the next part of the tour, wondering how I had managed not to crumble by now under Lucius' intense gaze. But then I looked back and saw the woman in the sparkling blue dress linger by the lions until he walked past her... or at least, he tried to. Because this was when the woman boldly approached him, and I had to give it to her, she was brave. That much needed to be said for there wasn't many people that would have intruded on such a stern looking man.

It wasn't just the air of authority that clung to him like a man of great power and strength. But it was that otherworldly element that shrouded him in a cloak of deception and mystery. Like the shadows under your bed, not knowing what could be lurking there ready to snatch you from your world at any second you got too close.

Well, that was Lucius, an unknown depth of fear that held you locked to the nightmares he wanted you to see. Never seeing the buried layers that meant he *could* care, as they lay hidden deep beneath the surface of one of the most frightening men in the Supernatural world.

Oh yeah, she was brave alright, I thought trying not to look but finding myself unable to find the strength not to.

In the end I was glad I did, otherwise I might have missed his reaction to her stepping up to him and running that same finger she had down the lion, now down his chest. His hand snapped out as quick as a venomous snake bite and combined with this lightening quick response, came one on the other end of the spectrum. The way he bent his neck slightly in such a calm, cool manner, so that he could whisper something down at her. Once more I was damning my inability to hear like a Supernatural being, because the second I saw her snatch her hand away I was desperate to know what he had said to her. Especially as now she was looking both mortified and *scared* as she quickly made her escape back to her husband, who had been more interested in the next artifact I was to talk about.

I saw her saunter past me, giving me an evil glare as she did and making me wonder even more what it was that had been said to her? Well, whatever it was, then I doubted it had been anything good because now she looked murderous and actually left the gallery, after first muttering something to her husband about needing the rest room.

It was at this time that I decided it was best not to let him see that I had witnessed the exchange for fear of what my expression would confess for me. My constantly looking at him was doing enough damage already, of that I was sure. But then again, it wasn't as if I was the only one looking. And surely my response to his staring would have been the same as any others, which primarily was a natural response to simply stare back?

Someone cleared their throat, once more telling me to get on with my job. Something which I decided was best to do right now, before I got too lost in my own thoughts and I ended up burying myself under all the questions I was asking myself in regard to his strange behavior.

"So, moving on into the gallery after our introduction to concepts of kingship, we enter the first period of great Egyptian history, the Old Kingdom. This is the 25th century and this great monument here that looks like a doorway is from part of a tomb created around 2400 BC. It was part of a chapel that remained permanently accessible to the living, where they could bring offerings to the dead," I said motioning to the reddish stone wall that did in fact look like a doorway.

It was covered in rows of hieroglyphics down each side with a larger column running horizontally along the top, depicting the image of the high priest it was created for. I went on to explain about the piece as I had done with the others and like before, Lucius continued to stand masterfully in the background and watch me like a hawk.

It became so unnerving that I often found myself stuttering my words or getting lost in them, whether it was saying very little or way too much about one of the exhibits. Sometimes Lucius would look amused by this. But then there were other times when he would give me such an intense look of what I could only hope was the respect I read it to be, that it was in these moments that he simply took my breath away.

"And this, who is this handsome fellow?" One of the gentlemen asked, who had been making comments throughout and getting closer to me with each one made. This, in turn, would make Lucius scowl as his displeasure deepened, making me question why? Once again, I had to shake off this question and answer another one rather than trying to guess the answers to my own.

"Ah, this is one of the museum's most renowned pieces. This large bust represents Rameses II, another great ruler of Egypt who ruled no fewer than 67 years, which I think you will agree is a feat in itself." They each agreed in unison, nodding as they gathered around one of the museum's most popular pieces. It was also one that each and every one of the curators was most proud of as it alone brought in thousands of people from all around the world just to see it.

"Now it gives me great pleasure to end our little tour with the museum's most famous exhibit, the Rosetta Stone," I said coming to stand in front of the large glass box it was sat inside, looking upon it now with fresh eyes considering it was only earlier today that I had been discussing it with my father.

Everyone else stood at its sides, giving me the space directly opposite it so that I could explain what the signs would have told you, like the rest of the pieces in the gallery. But the one person I could no longer see was Lucius. However, I didn't want to look around and make it obvious to the others who it was I was looking for.

"The stone you see now is but a fragment of a larger stela, which for those of you who don't know is a word used in archaeology as an upright stone slab or column, one typically bearing a commemorative inscription of sorts," I told them after receiving a few questioning looks and remembering that not everyone knew the different terms that were used in describing our artifacts.

"Were any of the other pieces ever found?" A lady asked that had been the same one to ask me why the first statue wasn't made to look exactly like the current king, letting me know that she truly had a passion for history, unlike most of the others who actually pretended to.

"Unfortunately not and as you can see, because of its damaged state, none of the three texts is absolute, which is a shame as we won't ever truly know what it would have looked like or what else it could have told us." It was at this point that I had another glance around looking for Lucius but once again, I couldn't see him. Which meant I was unable to prevent the disappointment from setting in, knowing that in all likelihood he had hit his limit on babysitting me and left as I had told him he could. I let my shoulders slump without thinking of my audience and in that moment the man, who continued to comment and annoy Lucius, stepped up to me. He then placed a hand upon my shoulder before saying,

"It must be a great frustration to such a passionate young woman who clearly wishes she could simply step back in time and see these types of things complete once more?" I frowned up at him, now seeing him as if for the first time and being struck by his choice of words.

He was a handsome man and one of those where age agreed with him and the added years only ended up enhancing his good looks. He reminded me a little of Pierce Brosnan with dark grey hair and a groomed beard and mustache to match. His eyes were a startling green and ones that seemed to have the ability of staring directly into your soul, which was unnerving to say the least.

I was about to answer him, not sure how I felt about him touching me or the way his fingers tensed, digging in slightly as if he was trying to relay something private to me without the use of words. But then something strange happened as his eyes seemed to glaze over a moment and he looked away from me, focusing on something else. Then his fingers twitched once before releasing me with a snap, as if something invisible had broken them backwards. I winced for him for his own reaction was that of someone in a trance and had no knowledge of what he was doing.

"I have to go now," he said in an almost robotic voice that reminded me of someone reaching out to a dead person. Then he simply left without anyone else but me taking notice of his strange behavior which itself was odd.

"Why is it called the Rosetta Stone…Miss…Miss Draven?" Someone asked, saying my name when I hadn't responded in time.

"It's named after the site of discovery in Rosetta or pronounced Rashid in Arabic," I answered looking at it now and still finding myself fascinated by what secrets the scholars had unraveled. I couldn't help but wonder what else could have been learned from it, should it have been found intact. Which led me to continue my explanation of why it was so important to the museum and to people like me that had dedicated my adult life to Egyptian research and would continue to do so for the foreseeable future.

"What is remarkable about the Rosetta Stone is that it contains text in three different scripts, not three different languages like you would think at first glance." I took a step closer and held out my hand, running it just shy of the glass to indicate the top lines of script.

"At the top as you can see we have the hieroglyphics script, which was mainly reserved for monuments, temples, sculptures and tomb walls, which makes sense seeing as it is most certainly the more decorative of the two. Which brings me on to the next lines of script in the middle." I then lowered my arms, indicating to the middle of the stela.

"Now here we have the demotic script which was used as a more everyday kind of text by literate Egyptians who could read and write. But it is the script on the bottom that was the key to unlocking the hieroglyphics, as it is ancient Greek. Which of course scholars had already mastered by the time the stone was discovered in 1799, during which was Napoleon's attempt to invade and conquer Egypt," I told them, now taking a step back so that they themselves may look upon the stone more closely.

During the day and the peak times that tourists were at the museum I would often walk by and notice that unless you wished to wait your turn, then this piece was often crowded by many people. All of which were either taking pictures or reading what their guide books told them about the piece.

"What does it all mean?" The same inquisitive lady asked and her husband, not one to be left out, agreed with her question and also asked,

"Yes, that's what I wanted to know, what is actually translated?" I chuckled once and said,

"It's a recipe for a very nice ancient chicken soup." I then waited for them all to gasp in surprise and each give me their own version of a sheer look of incredibility before I laughed once more.

"But of course, I am teasing." They all started laughing with me at my own private joke and once they had composed themselves I continued.

"Now, what it actually refers to and this is thanks to the Greek section of the tablet, is that we are actually dealing with a decree issued at Memphis, Egypt in 196 BC during the Ptolemaic dynasty. It was in honour of King Ptolemy V as he came to the throne and it was erected after the coronation," I told them then swiftly going on to explain about King Ptolemy and the immense weight that must have been bestowed upon his shoulders given his tender young age.

"Now, the interesting thing about this king was that he was known as the Boy King, inheriting the throne at only five years old, and under a series of regents, the kingdom was paralyzed. The Rosetta Stone however, was produced during his reign as an adult and the text actually documents benefits bestowed by the King to the priesthood of Egypt. In return the priests' decree was one that established the divine cult of the new ruler, declaring him King," I said unable to help myself from smiling when I saw the keen interest that was clearly visible in their eyes.

"And this, ladies and gentlemen, concludes our tour and just in time it seems as I believe the Chairman will be making his speech soon. So, if you would please make your way back to the great court which is through this exit here," I told them knowing that I should have really shown them the way back myself but found that I needed a moment alone after all that. Well, being totally honest with myself, it was more the fact that since talking about the Rosetta stone Lucius had disappeared, affecting me far more than I would care to show and also, care to admit to myself.

I smiled and nodded to each of them that thanked me and praised me for both my knowledge and the manner in which I presented the tour. I then waited until the last person had left before letting out a big sigh. I was tired, both emotionally and physically and each reason I could put down to seeing Lucius again. It was like he physically sucked the energy out of me and one that had been solely used to help me restrain myself around him. I needed to be constantly on guard and in turn he simply seemed with little effort to be able to grind those protective barriers to pulp, rendering them useless.

I walked closer to the glass and stared at the stone not seeing any of its texts as my mind couldn't help but focus on only one thing. I closed my eyes and silently cursed myself for not being strong enough to conquer this like I had convinced myself that I would, should we ever have to meet again. After all, given his connections to my father's world then I guess it was inevitable, but all those times dreaming of such a meeting and you would have thought I would have handled it better.

But yet here I was, in this vast room, feeling as though I was being buried alive once more by the weight of my emotions. I wanted to hate him just as much as I already knew I loved him. It was the cruelest of realities to face as I couldn't help but replay those honest words he had thrown at me like a slap across my face.

'How could I ever love you?' That was what he had said to me, for I could never forget it. Never forget the moment as if those very words had been branded against my heart, before slamming the vault door and walking away from my damaged soul. It sounded dramatic but that was how deep the pain cut for there was no other way to describe what he had done to me.

I swallowed hard as I pushed those words back down, deep into the abyss of forgetful thought where I only wished they would stay for eternity. Then I opened my eyes and the second I did, my palm flew to the glass so as to steady me. For now, I was no longer looking at the stone but instead the reflection of Lucius' face staring back at me.

He had something to say and the second it was heard that damn abyss started to flood with hope, for what else was there for me to think when he simply stated…

"Alone at last."

CHAPTER EIGHT

HOT AND COLD

"*Alone at last.*"

The second his words were uttered I seemed frozen to the spot. I watched in the reflection of the glass as he stepped closer towards me from behind and where he had remained hidden in the shadows. I felt him getting closer until surely any second he would stop. But stop he didn't, not until his chest must have been a mere inch from my back.

He brought his arm around me from behind and I sucked in a sharp breath and held it captive as he placed his gloved left hand flat on the glass in front of us, so that it was situated next to mine. Then I felt him lean down, getting closer to my neck, causing my questioning panic to double. What was he doing? He had never voluntarily put himself this close to me before. What did it mean?

Well, I was soon to find out.

He was currently looking down the front of me from behind, and I could see, thanks to his reflection in the glass, that he was grinning. Then I felt the fingers from his free hand come to rest at my neck, his touch as gentle as a bird's feather. He skimmed the delicate skin there, travelling its length and brushing back the few loose hairs that had come free from Ben's creation of gathered hair on the other side. Then once he was done teasing my overheated skin, one that felt closer and closer to being burned by his touch, he whispered directly over my ear,

"I suggest you breathe for me, Princess, before I let you fall." The second he uttered these condescending words I released my held breath and took in another one quickly after it. Then, at the same time, I ducked out of his hold. I needed the space as he was once again getting inside my head and playing games with me.

"I told you not to call me that!" I snapped in defiance, only it was backed up with nothing more than the steps between us and me unable to look him in the eye.

"But that is exactly what you are," he replied in a contemptuous way that had me clenching my teeth.

"No, not anymore I'm not," I said with determination coating my words, but the bastard just laughed at me.

"Then you are as foolish as you were that day," he replied, making me visibly jerk back, aghast in sheer disbelief, something he didn't miss. He looked ready to add something more when I held up my hand stopping him with a single worded warning,

"Don't." The tone in which I said this must have made him realise that even for him he had gone too far, so instead he released a heavy weighted sigh, as if this was all very taxing for a being such as he. As if he was thinking about the unfortunate task that had brought him here and the annoyance that once again forced him to deal with me. The spoilt little princess he had declared I was and nothing more than a minor aggravation in his world.

"If you believe it that easy to walk away from the world in

which you were born into, then your intelligence is back to being in question and thus shadowing your little endearing show of intellect," he said, motioning with his arm down the gallery where I had started my tour. I swear for once I heard myself growl in response and it felt good but not half as good as when I shouted at him,

"Why you…you…" I stuttered to find the right words and in the end it was the second his smug eyebrow went up in question that I finally finished my sentence,

"…Nasty bastard!" I had my fists clenched at my sides as if any minute now I would let rip and punch him! He looked down a moment to take note of my anger before stepping up to me so quickly I had nowhere else to go but being backed up against the glass of the Rosetta stone. Then he looked down at me with burning eyes the colour of hot molten lava before telling me with what sounded like an odd mixture of pure venom and lust,

"Nasty? Oh Sweetheart, *you have no fucking idea.*" After this I let my impulses kick in and before I could stop them I found my hand rising just before I pulled it back. Then I let it swing into action, that being in the direction of his face, to deliver my slap. But it never made it that far. As the second before it made contact with his cheek, it ended up making contact with something else instead.

He grabbed hold of my wrist, capturing it in his tight and unyielding grasp before using his hold on me to yank me forward. I fell a step into him and he in turn bent lower, getting in my face and coming just a hairsbreadth away from my lips before he spoke,

"Try that again and see where it gets you, my little Šemšā," he threatened, calling me something I had never heard before. It certainly wasn't from any language I knew and thanks to my dad I knew quite a few.

I swallowed hard, losing some of my bravery in sight of this locked battle we currently had going on. And it wasn't exactly hard to see who was winning, not considering Lucius was definitely the more intimidating of the two. But still, my stubbornness wouldn't let me fail just yet, so I pushed.

"And where will it get me, Lucius?" I challenged tipping my chin up and showing him a slice of who I *could* be. His eyes seemed to burn just that little bit brighter and the hopeful side of me could have sworn it was the tiniest show of respect for how I stood up to him. That was until he told me exactly where it would get me, leaving me utterly dumbfounded.

"Bare, bound and across my knee ready for my palm if this childish behavior continues and you dare push me again," he warned making my mouth hang open in shock, so much so that I couldn't even think of a single comeback or response to that. I was too flabbergasted to even fully comprehend his words right now. Thankfully, he must have thought it wise to give me space as I swear I wasn't far from kicking him in the nuts and making a run for it.

"Now, I think it best to get this fucking night over with and you show me this box your father gave you before I do something I regret," he stated whilst casually pulling down on one of his cuffs through his suit jacket and twisting the cufflink that I now noticed was a small demonic symbol of some kind. However, short of grabbing his hand and bringing it closer to my face, then I doubted I would ever know.

I quickly replayed his harsh words, wondering what in the world would a man like Lucius ever regret when it came to me? Did he mean he would regret hurting me physically, for he certainly didn't give a shit enough about my feelings for fear of hurting them. The proof of that was crystal clear considering he had already done that...ten times over in fact.

So, unless he did mean to hurt me physically, which even

that I doubted. Because even though he had just threatened to bend me over his knee like a naughty brat and spank me, deep down I knew he wouldn't dare touch me. No, he cared too much about my parents to do something like that. Which, let's face it, was the real reason he was here…because my father had asked him to.

I was so stupid I wanted to look myself in the nearest mirror and call myself a fool before slapping myself silly!

"Amelia." The sound of him saying my name yanked me out of my mental scolding as it was a sound I rarely heard. No, it was usually princess or some other childish and patronizing name he used when referring to me. Which was why the second he said it, I wanted to take hold of the memory and keep it safe, reserving it for my dreams, wherein this meeting would have gone quite differently. But nevertheless, him saying it was enough to jar me in to action.

"I don't have it here," I uttered in annoyance, knowing that because of my decision to take it home I now had unknowingly extended this painful experience.

"Excuse me?" Lucius said in a disbelieving tone because even though I had merely whispered it, I knew that his supernatural hearing wouldn't have missed it.

"I said I don't have it here," I repeated louder this time making him look at me sternly.

"Then where is it?"

"I took it home with me," I told him, unable to ignore the roll of his eyes as if he were dealing with a simpleton.

"Why in the Devil would you have done that?" he asked almost growling the question at me and making me fold my arms across my chest in response.

"And why not? I wanted to make sure it was safe!" I snapped back making him look around the large space and as if to prove his point he said,

"And what, you believed your little flat in Twickenham to be a safer place than the Fort Knox you work in?" he asked with a sarcastic tone making me feel foolish. But then I thought about what he'd just said and couldn't help myself.

"How do you know where I live?" I questioned, catching him off guard. I could tell this by the way he frowned at me and paused a second as if deciding how best to answer that. When in the end he said,

"Your father told me… now why is it in your flat and not here?" he asked again making me groan before throwing my hands up in frustration.

"No one even knows about it, Lucius, so I don't see what your problem is?" I said as part of my argument which from the look at his face, I would say wasn't a good one.

"And what if someone did know about it and furthermore, wanted to get it… tell me, Princess, just how well do you think you would fare when they turned up at your door and you were without the museum's security to call, or do you think they would simply wait for daddy to show up and save the fucking day?!" he snapped back suddenly in outrage, making me flinch back at the sight of his rage. I didn't know where it had come from and why he even cared so much, but the only thing I could put it down to was his worry over this box. Which meant only one thing, he must have known about it longer than he was letting on.

"You know what, screw you, Lucius! I don't need this shit!" I barked at him before storming off to retrieve my purse from where I had left it at the start of the tour. I didn't think it would matter too much as it wasn't like there were many people wandering around in here as no one had set foot inside.

However, I didn't get far as a few seconds after a frustrated sound came from Lucius, I was suddenly gripped from behind and whipped back around to face him. I was about to protest as

I was suddenly pushed up against the red granite statue of one of the lions I had been talking about earlier. Suddenly, I realized that I may have had the symbol for a relaxed king at my back, but the king I had in front of me now couldn't have been further from the relaxed cat but was more of a snarling lion showing his teeth.

"Word of warning, Princess, it's not wise to turn your back on a Vampire...*ever.*" The last part of this threat was backed up with a hiss through gritted teeth and a pair of fangs that were lengthening dangerously.

"Yyy...you know, I am...am really getting tired of you threatening me," I told him trying to keep my voice as steady as I could in the face of such a beast, but from the very first second it had started to waver, he seemed pleased and a cocky smirk appeared at the corner of his lips showcasing more of one deadly fang.

"Then I suggest they start to sink in quickly before the use of another one is needed...now do I make myself clear?" he said in a stern tone that demanded my submission. I swallowed hard at the sheer depth of authority he held in his voice and the subtle action wasn't lost on him. He homed in on my neck and watched me with a grin after seeing the visible effect he was having on me and well...the bastard looked like he enjoyed it. This then provoked me to respond.

"Why do you enjoy playing with me?" I bravely asked in a barely heard whisper. At this, his grin deepened, and it was both pure evil and bad to the bone. Then he lowered his face and I froze, too frightened to even move for fear of what he was planning to do next. At first, I even thought that the impossible was going to happen and he was going to kiss me. But then he shifted his weight a little and ended up placing his lips against my cheek, speaking directly over the heated skin I could feel hot against his cooler lips.

"Oh Sweetheart, I haven't even started playing with you yet," he whispered back before giving me a sweet and soft kiss, that only ended up cementing his words as a dark and menacing promise. Then, as I was still trying to catch my breath, he was suddenly gone at an impossible speed I should have been used to seeing by now.

I merely managed a breathy gasp in surprise as my hand was in his and he was yanking me upright. But then, just as I was about to fall into him from the speed, he spun me and placed a steadying hand at my hip so that my back was to him but in the direction of the exit.

"Now, let's go," he ordered giving me a squeeze of my side in a possessive manner before letting me go.

I swear…

I felt like running.

CHAPTER NINE

PETER WHO?

After this moment I had no clue what to think as my nerves, along with my fragile mind, were all over the place. I kept questioning his actions and quickly got nowhere. At first, I could put most things down to the fact he obviously wanted to see the box and was annoyed that it wasn't a simple case of me showing it to him right here and now. But then, if this was true, why had he walked back into the great court with me on his arm and spent the rest of the evening pretending to be my date?

I had expected when he said, 'let's go', that he meant to leave the gala completely. But all he had meant was to leave the gallery. Something that had most definitely been for the best considering being alone with him right now was clearly dangerous for my mental state of mind.

I swore that after tonight I was seriously considering taking up yoga or something equally as Zen because all this shit was going to send me packing to the nearest crazy house! Which also meant that if I wasn't careful then I would end up in a padded room decorated with his name on the walls and with bald patches on my head after trying to spell Lucius with my hair... once they finally took all stationery away from me, of course.

Okay, so that was farfetched even for my overexuberant imagination, but still, it couldn't be denied that the man was making me crazy! Every time someone would come over to speak to me I would feel him take a step closer. Then he would wrap an arm around my back, rest his hand at my waist with his fingers flexing at my side almost as if on impulse. Then, I would find myself without the power of speech and only able to nod like a muted dog on a dashboard. One that had come back in popularity a few years ago and was classed as retro, making my mum complain about feeling old.

Well, at least she would never need wrinkle cream as an immortal as my complaint back to her was always the same,

"Well, at least you don't look the same age as your mother and will one day soon start to look older." Because that was what I had in store for me in my future. And yes, to the rest of the human world, she had aged and looked like a beautiful woman in her late forties/ early fifties, along with how my father did.

But this was just a smoke screen, as it was with the rest of my family. Because if my mum wanted to keep her human family in her life for as long as she possibly could, then this was a necessary evil that had to be thought of. A lie to save the people she loved.

I knew it wasn't easy for her, but what was harder was knowing the inevitable would one day happen when it came to watching her own daughter getting old. Because I wasn't like them. I wasn't blessed with immortal life like the rest of them were.

Which meant that unless I dated an immortal and had sex with them on a regular basis, then I was investing in anti-wrinkle cream no matter if I wanted to or not. And I know what you're thinking, why not just find me a sex buddy that didn't mind getting his rocks off whilst taking care of my pesky little aging problem for me. But unfortunately, it didn't work like that. Because one of the biggest rules my dad had to enforce in his world was the utterly forbidden relationship between supernaturals and humans. So, unless it was fated by the Gods and decreed to be part of some almighty prophesied story written in the stars type of gig, then it was a big fat NO.

But this was something I had learned to come to terms with long ago, even if my parents had yet to follow me down that realistic path. Don't get me wrong, I can only imagine how hard it must be for them knowing that one day I wouldn't be here and they would still have to face eternity without me. So, let's just say that because of this, it was one subject I wisely stayed away from.

It soon became time for us to leave and Lucius masterfully steered me towards where our jackets had been taken, and as I fished out my ticket I noticed something was wrong. Of course, Lucius noticed my hesitation as there wasn't much he didn't notice.

"What is it this time?" he asked in exasperation that instantly got my back up, but I decided to ignore it and told him,

"It's nothing." Then I started to stretch my arm out to give the man my ticket when Lucius took it off me and handed it to the man himself, making me frown in question.

Why he did that I had no clue but the second he received my jacket he took me by my elbow and walked me through the exit. The cold hit me and just as I started to shiver I felt my jacket being placed over my shoulders. I swear the sight of Lucius acting like a gentleman was nearly as startling as he was handsome, which managed to easily take my breath away. With the backdrop of the night sky and roman columns behind him it suddenly felt as though we could have been stood, back in time, just the two of us waiting for our one moment.

"Thank…"

"What is missing from your purse?" he asked me, letting my softly spoken thanks trail off into the night, getting lost right along with my wishful thoughts.

"Does it matter?" I snapped pushing my arms through my jacket and walking down the steps. He followed me and was in front of me in a heartbeat.

"Where do you think you are going?" he asked in an incredulous tone as if surprised that I wouldn't answer his question before walking away from him. Was this the reason he believed me to be a spoilt princess? Because I wouldn't obey him? For sure there weren't many in his world he could place in that category?

"What does it look like, I am going to try and catch a cab," I said trying to walk around him, but he sidestepped to stop me, scoffing as he did,

"You are most certainly not getting a cab home." I gave him a sarcastic grin back and agreed,

"No, you're right." Then before he could comment arrogantly as I knew he would have, I pulled my coat together and added,

"I'm getting the bus…Goodnight, Lucius." I walked past him making my way down the courtyard to the sound of his exasperation behind me. Then I heard him speak and it took me a moment to realise it wasn't to me.

"How long?" he snapped and a quick glance over my shoulder told me he was speaking to someone on his phone.

"Make it two," he replied in a masterful tone and then promptly canceled the call. Once again, he was in front of me.

"There is no way I am allowing you to get the bus," he informed me, folding his arms and no doubt trying to intimidate me, which as usual was working.

"Lucius, I catch the bus every day," I argued softly.

"Yes, and if you place emphasis on the word 'day', then you should see the point which I am making," he replied.

"Which is?" I asked now folding my own arms and looking about as intimidating as a kitten showing the big cat her claws.

"Your father would not allow it," he said as if this would be a better argument as to the real reason he didn't want me catching the bus home…*was he worried about me?*

"Whatever. Look, I catch the bus all the time, day and night and nothing has happened to me yet." Okay, even to my own ears this was a lame argument and now, well he was starting to look pretty angry.

"You catch the bus home at night?" he asked in a dangerous low tone that told me I had better tread carefully here. But once again, it merely made me question his reasons for being annoyed.

"Look around you, Lucius, and tell me what you see," I asked him, this time trying for reason. He gave me a sexually slow look up and down and quickly blew me away with his answer.

"A beautiful target." I coughed back my shock and had to clear my throat after hearing Lucius calling me beautiful for only the third time in my life and two of them had been said tonight. The other, however, hadn't counted at the time for it was back when he was breaking my heart and combining it with an insult.

"It's the city that never sleeps, Lucius, I will be fine." At this he rolled his eyes and said,

"Yes and do you know who resides in that city that also never sleeps... thieves, rapists, the psycologically unhinged and lastly people willing to murder you for the contents of your purse... therefore, it is over my fucking knee that you will do as you're told and wait before I embarrass you in front of your colleagues who will soon be joining us out here as they leave." This threat caused my mouth to drop and take a whole minute before I found I could actually answer him.

"You wouldn't dare!" I hissed making him grin sadistically down at me and then he glanced over my head when he heard the sound of a car pulling in through the gates.

"Just try me, Princess, as there is only one sure way to find out," he warned me, looking back to the crowd of people now all coming from the exit as if to put emphasis on his threat.

"Now get in the fucking car," he snapped the second it stopped next to us and he opened the door before the driver even had time to get out to do so. I groaned aloud once before snapping,

"Fine!"

I then tried to fold myself into the car as graceful as possible repeating my usual mantra of 'don't slip, don't slip, don't slip' in my mind, but doing so in an angry inner voice because, well... I was still pissed off! Well, at least I hadn't fallen once tonight, so I guessed I deserved some brownie points for that one.

I shifted over to the far side and sat there in your typical sulky girl fashion, which I think was totally lost on Lucius. It was becoming clear that there was no way he had ever had a girlfriend before or if he had then they were the super compliant, bimbo, 'I just want a sugar daddy' type. Eww, the thought repulsed me, and I barely suppressed a shiver.

"Now, you can tell me what was missing from your bag,"

Lucius asked once we were well on our way out of the main part of the city.

"My lipstick," I replied making him chuckle and shake his head.

"What?" I questioned unable to help myself.

"Your lying is as shit as your mother's." The second I heard him talking about my mum everything inside of me turned to ice and I swear he must have felt the sudden chill in the car, because he turned to look at me and I swore I could see the hint of regret there.

"Amelia, I…" he said my name in a way that I suddenly hated and just to save myself the humiliation I quickly said in a dead tone,

"My keys, I have lost my keys." He frowned at this, so before he could come to the worse possible reason I quickly added,

"It's not a problem as my neighbor has a spare set."

"Then for your sake I hope she's home on a Friday night." I rolled my eyes at the window.

"He will be."

"He? You're telling me that another man is entrusted with the keys to your apartment and can come and go as he pleases." I swear the way he worded it sounded like I had stood outside the block one day, held up my keys and said, 'here, here, come and get 'em, who wants access to my flat 24/7?!'

"Yes, that's right Lucius, my very good and loyal *gay friend* has a spare set of keys to my flat, in case I do something stupid like walk out without having them on me," I said, making sure he didn't miss the part about me saying he was gay and therefore possessed no threat to my prized womanhood…geez, but he was certainly going overkill on protecting me and doing my father a favour.

Lucius visibly relaxed so I would say for certain that he hadn't missed the gay friend bit.

"Find yourself doing that often do you?" he asked after another long moment of silence.

"Well, it comes with the clumsy territory I am afraid," I replied thinking this was the longest most civil conversation we'd had so far. That was until I saw his face and decided to beat him to voicing his opinion.

"Yes, I know, *just like my mother.*" My tone said it all. He looked as if he was about to say something else, but the sound of my phone ringing stopped him. I rummaged through my purse and saw who it was, so answered it in a way that I knew Lucius would question.

"Why hello there, my lesbian lover." Oh yeah, now that got me a look, especially when Wendy replied,

"What's happening my favorite pussy cat?" I laughed once, not at her reply but more at Lucius' confused face...it was priceless!

"So, did you go to that stuffy gala thing in the end or what?" she asked finishing off her question with the sound of popping gum I was used to.

"Yeah and no thanks to you bailing on me."

"What, I thought you had hot daddy dearest to take you?" she asked.

"I did, but what do you know, must be my day for people bailing out on me," I told her just as Lucius was answering his driver by telling him where we were heading. Of course, Wendy didn't miss the sound of a male voice, especially not one as sexy as Lucius' deep and masterful one.

"Oh, you sly puppy, you! You asked Peter, didn't you?!" she shouted, screeching down the phone at me. And of course, not only did I hear it, along with a boatload of dogs within a ten-mile radius of her, but Lucius did as well.

I knew this the second I heard a growl of one pissed off male next to me and quick to follow it was the threatening tone of Lucius' snarled question…

"Who the fuck is Peter?!"

CHAPTER TEN

UNTIL TOMORROW

"Oops, not Peter then?" Wendy said referring to the sound of the now angry male sat next to me who was demanding to know who my boyfriend was.

"That would be a no," I muttered in a dry tone that secretly said, 'thanks for putting your foot in it but I have to go now and try and explain to an overbearing Vampire asshole that my personal life is none of his business…but hey, thanks for that'. Okay, so my tone didn't exactly say *all* of those things, but it said a lot…and the main one was the 'oh shit' moment she knew she'd caused. I knew this when she then said,

"Right, well call me when the man storm has blown over… laters Lessy Bessy," she said using code for her not really lesbian bestie.

"I am still waiting," he said in a tone that made me both want to shove him and recoil from him all at the same confusing time.

"Well, then I guess you'd better get used to the feeling because you're going to be waiting a long time, as who I date is none of your business," I told him and doing so with sweaty palms as I was now worried that he would tell my parents and the next people I had to say these things to, would be them.

My mum would be hurt, and my dad would be furious. Not the fact that I was dating per se but more the fact I didn't tell them first so that my dad could have flown here, whilst doing a back-ground check on the plane, arriving in time for the interview/interrogation to start after he had his men set it up with the poor unsuspecting Peter.

Lucius, on the other hand, just looked outright enraged and ready to commit murder, a fate far worse than an intimidating talk with my dad. But the question was always the same with Lucius and that was…

Why?

Why would he even care, as surely he wouldn't go as far as to be outraged on my dad's behalf, would he? Well, sure as shit something was obviously wrong with him as he looked ready to tear the bloody car door off and throw it at some poor innocent pedestrian in anger. You could see him fighting with himself for what looked like all the reasons he shouldn't say something and also all the reasons that he should. The latter ended up winning in the end as he snarled at me,

"It is the business of your family and as I am here in your father's place then therefore, I have every right to know why it is you choose a lesser being that obviously cares so little for you as to let his woman go alone to a gala." My mouth dropped before I hissed,

"Now just you wait a…"

"And what's more, a cretin that expects her to get the fucking bus home! Pray tell me, just how would you have gotten here had I not sent my car to pick you up?" Lucius asked, after interrupting me and doing so by growling the words at me in a barely contained demonic side that sounded close to rattling the answer from me. But to be honest there had been so much in that one sentence that I hardly knew where to start!

"You sent that car for me?" I asked going with the less important of the two. He raised a brow at me and answered me the way you would an aggravating child that had asked the same question one hundred million times.

"Yes."

"But I got a text from…"

"Me," he said interrupting yet again and making me frown.

"But I sent one back saying, thanks dad."

"And?" he asked making me shake my head a little…I mean was he for real?

"And…well don't you think you could have said something," I said dragging out the 'and' in a condescending way.

"Like what?" he snapped.

"Oh, I don't know, maybe something like 'Hey, its Lucius here, not your dad and you're welcome for the car, see you soon, as FYI, I am going to be your date for the evening'. Maybe that kind of something." I said flicking my hand out at the end unable to help being slightly dramatic. Needless to say, he looked down at my hand and didn't look impressed with the fact I nearly just hit him with it by mistake. Therefore, he grabbed it and placed it back in my lap as though this would be a safer place for it. I, on the other hand, just felt myself blush because of it.

"Would it have changed the outcome?" he asked me, and I decided to be honest thinking that I would have surprised him… I was wrong, as he was counting on it.

"Yes." I said knowing that I wouldn't have gone if I had known he would be there.

"Then that's why… now tell me who this Peter is," he said finishing this off with a firm order. I released a frustrated sigh and rubbed my forehead like my father sometimes did when my mother was giving him a hard time or putting him in his place as she often did.

"Seriously, Lucius, why do you even care?" He looked taken back a moment and opened his mouth as if ready to say something but then stopped, obviously thinking better of it.

"I don't." he replied, and it was as simple as that. However, what wasn't simple was how much hearing those two small words affected me. But the saying, 'the truth hurts' was created for a reason and now…well, now there seemed like no better time for it to be true.

"Good, then leave it be," I said after swallowing down what I really wanted to say and having to look out the window for a second to compose myself. But of course, this was Lucius we were talking about here, the man utterly incapable of letting anything…well…*be*.

"I would have thought your taste in men to be better than that." It was at this point I turned in my seat to look at him as my mind tried to ask itself had that really been what he had said? Which is when my mind came up with a deciding yes, as I had heard him right, which unsurprisingly made me snap back,

"Oh, I can assure you, my tastes in men have *greatly improved.*" The meaning definitely wasn't lost on him, not with the venomous tone in which it had been said. The second I finished I saw his eyes flash once more, only this time in anger as they burned crimson a second too long, as was just enough to portray his annoyance.

"I doubt that!" he snapped back, which is when I decided to inform him,

"Look, not that it is any of your business, but the truth is that I was the one who didn't invite Peter, so he had no idea about this Gala because I was taking my friend Wendy, who usually comes with me to these things, so now you can just get off his back because Peter is a good, kind hearted man and you have no right to..." The sound of his laughter suddenly cut me off.

"What is so funny?" I asked managing to get at least one hand on my hip even though I was sat down.

"You just described someone who only fucks in the dark," he replied crassly, shocking me to stutter on my next words,

"Sss...so! What the hell is wrong with that?" I asked in outrage, even though I myself had thought the same thing only earlier that day and I couldn't remember...had I viewed it as a bad thing at the time? Well, if I hadn't then, I did seconds later after Lucius gave me his reply.

"It's wrong because when you finally possess beauty, two things happen, you do so as often as you possibly can, and you do so with her body illuminated, so that you can burn the image to your mind for all the times that you can't," he answered, and it seriously made my heart suddenly start pounding in my chest. Was this how he really thought about being with a beautiful woman? Just that question alone made me think about all the women Lucius must have been with in all his time upon the earth and I swear that pounding in my chest quickly started to turn into a painful ache. Which also meant that I had no come back to this other than a very lame murmur, which was aimed at the window,

"Well, not everyone thinks like you."

Thankfully, after that he said no more about it, obviously appeased enough now he knew that the man I was dating hadn't just let me loose on the town unchaperoned. But to be honest, one look at Lucius' reflection in the window and I had no idea what he was thinking. Well, that was until he cut the silence with another question and this time it ended up cutting the tension too, as it made me chuckle.

"Why do you pretend to have a lesbian lover as your date?"

"Ah, well, before Peter came along I never had anyone to take with me, so I asked my friend Wendy to come, then one thing led to another and…" I stopped the second I heard him drawing in a startled breath, realizing he had the wrong idea.

"No, not that type of idea, what I mean is that when chatting to the guests some of them would hit on me…you know, ask me out or even ask me what I was doing after the event," I said making him once more look annoyed, only at least this time he hid it slightly better than before, this time only frowning and clenching his fists until his knuckles turned white.

"So, in the end Wendy came to my rescue and pretended to be my lover, and well that soon developed into my 'partner' as more people found out and then pretty soon I found myself being asked at work how my girlfriend was. Then, before I knew it, bam! I was suddenly in a relationship with Wendy." At this he chuckled, and I don't think that up until then I had ever heard the sound. I liked the idea that he found me funny, so I tried to carry it on by nudging him slightly and telling him,

"And as it turns out, that once you have been in a fictional lesbian relationship, it's actually quite difficult to get yourself out of one, as it's not like I can just go into work one day and shout surprise everybody, Wendy's gone and I'm not gay anymore…" Again, he chuckled, and it was such a lighthearted sound I nudged him again and added,

"Although, you turning up tonight has kind of put a spanner in the lesbian works." Once I had finished he gave me a heart stopping grin that again, was another first for me, for this time it wasn't the usual 'bad boy, I am plotting evil things grin' I was used to. No, it was the blindingly handsome, breathtaking type of smile that had you admitting to yourself that if that was the last sight you ever saw, then you would die a happy woman.

By the Gods, he was beautiful.

"I am surprised they believed it in the first place," he

replied, now making this the longest conversation we had ever had about anything that wasn't done so in anger.

"Why do you say that?" I asked, desperate to keep this easy manner going.

"Because you're about as lesbian as I am gay," he replied, this time making me laugh as that was one thing I could never have said about Lucius.

Men were obviously not his preferred flavour of willing victims and there was only one person he had looked at tonight with lust…

The willing victim sat next to him now…

Me.

Before long we were at my building as it was only a thirty-minute drive, especially at this time of night when there was minimal amount of traffic on the roads. I turned in my seat and said,

"Thanks for the…*lift.*" I ended up letting the last word trail into a whisper as Lucius was already exiting the car. Now as to why, I was yet to find out. My door opened, and a hand was held out to me that definitely didn't belong to the driver.

Wow, it looked like he was getting an easy night tonight as Lucius was obviously determined to do half his job for him. Not that I was complaining as it gave me a wonderful excuse once more to place my hand in his. The tingles that bombarded my senses the second our skin made contact was almost as though someone had flipped a switch, instantly making me flex my fingers in his hold, telling him without words that his touch affected me. In return his grip on me tightened and in that moment something unspoken passed between us. But as quickly as it had arisen it was gone again the second he let me go.

He then took a step back and held out his arm to indicate that I should precede him which I did, happy to be ahead of him just so that I could hide my reddened cheeks and the effects of how his touch still lingered. But had I been the only one? I guess I would never know unless I asked him and even then, how could I ever trust in his words, for so far, he wasn't just an enigma, he was also turning out to be a contradiction. He would act as if he was duty bound in being here but then in the next instance he would go above the realms of obligation. Like now for example, walking me to my door instead of just sitting in his car and making sure that I made it home in one piece. There, job done and dusted with a clap of his hands and then congratulating himself on being rid of me at least for the rest of the evening.

But this hadn't happened.

Which was why I questioned his reasons all the way to the front door and beyond when he still stood next to me as if waiting for something. So, I turned towards him, feeling suddenly shy and tucking some loose hair behind my ear as I fumbled for my words,

"I…I guess I should say…"

"Open the door, Amelia," he said interrupting me with a purring of my name and I looked up at him in confusion for a moment until he strangely cleared his throat and nodded to the control panel, trying to jar me into action.

"Oh…right." I muttered with a little shake of my head turning around to hide my shame and trying to stop my hands from shaking. I don't know why it felt so different now, almost as though we had entered a more intimate place of the evening and I wondered if it was the stigma that surrounded the end of a date. The quiet and almost expectant moment when your date walks you to your door and you spend those turbulent moments hoping that he liked you enough to kiss you. But I needed to remember that this was Lucius we were talking about and there was only one reason why he would be walking me to my door.

His duty.

Because if there was one thing I knew about Lucius, it was if he wanted something he was the type of man to just reach out and take it, caring little about the consequences.

Which is why this thought developed into the most obvious other reason why he held the main door to my building open for me and now I felt utterly stupid. In fact, I continued to chastise myself all the way to my door with him keeping a safe distance behind me. So, before I could make an even bigger fool of myself, I turned around to face him and was about to discuss him seeing the box when I faltered.

By the Gods, how had he gotten so close to me without me even feeling it? Out of instinct I took a step back and felt my back hit the door and I swear the sound of it echoed all the way down the staircase we'd just walked up. I bravely looked up at him and the second I did his gloved hand snapped out and gripped onto my door frame. I didn't know what caused this reaction only that for what seemed like long silent moments we were trapped in this strange space in time, and it kept us both captured until finally he broke through it. At first when he started to raise his other hand, I thought it was to touch me in some way but then I heard the door unlocking and it all started to snap into place.

The third reason that he had followed me up here...*I had no keys.* He obviously wanted to make sure that I could get into my flat in case Ben hadn't been home. Damn myself and my wayward imagination! This had been what had gotten me into trouble in the first place all those years ago. Suddenly, I felt a shame like no other as he had been right...I hadn't changed from that young, naive runaway mind of a girl simply full of unrealistic hopes and dreams.

Which was why I let my head drop and I looked down at the floor in a vain attempt to hide the extent of my shame. In fact, I was getting so lost in it, that when I felt his touch under my chin

I was startled enough to nearly jerk out of his hold. So, instead of letting me go, he held on to my chin with his thumb and forefinger, lifting my face up so that he could hold my gaze with the intense one of his own.

"You did well tonight," he told me, and I could feel the questioning line appear in between my brows, asking myself what he meant by that. However, if he saw it, then he ignored it because he said nothing further on the matter. No, instead he nodded to the door once and said,

"Now run along, little one." I swallowed the sexual lump I had stuck there that had inhibited my ability to speak.

"You're not coming inside?" I asked and the second he raised a brow at me in a way that told me he was getting the wrong idea, which meant I flustered and quickly carried on,

"I mean…well, you know, to see the box…which is why you're here…right?" This was when the smirk came back and damn him if it didn't make him even sexier than before. It left me wondering if he knew it and kept it in his sexual arsenal, reserving it for times like this?

Then he surprised me as he looked over my head at the closed door as if he was actually taking the time to think about it. But then he closed his eyes for a second longer than just a blink and opened them again by looking down at me. This was when he really shocked me as the next thing for him to say sounded like pained honesty,

"I don't think pushing my limits is a wise endeavor at the best of times." I wanted to ask what he meant by that but before I could he spoke again, and I had the impression that it was done on purpose so that I couldn't ask.

"Bring the box to the museum tomorrow and I will be there to view it." In the end I was left with no other choice but to agree with a slight nod of my head. Then he reached past me, turned the handle, brushing against my side as he did and making me weak enough to close my eyes at the contact. I knew by doing this that I was giving away my feelings towards him, but it couldn't have been helped.

My body wasn't my own around him.

The door at my back was gone and my exit from this contact felt like an abyss behind me. One he was expecting me to walk into and say goodbye. It had been such a turbulent night that I felt almost exhausted just from battling my emotions in his presence. And now was no different as I simply nodded my head and took that painful first step away from him. But then I swear I heard the sound of wood splitting and just as my head snapped up, homing in to the source of the sound, I only just caught the sight of cracked wood forging itself back together again under his palm.

Now why had that happened I wonder?

"I…" I only said that single lettered word, but it was enough for Lucius to know what I was going to say, for he got in there first before I had chance to say it myself. It was almost as if he couldn't bear hearing it…

"You're welcome…*Amelia.*" I don't know why he paused a second too long before whispering my first name, as if it had been a promise unspoken. I couldn't help but bring a finger up to my lips and bite at the end which was a nervous habit of mine. His eyes homed in on the sight and the quickest flash of hot amber seeped into his eyes, giving me a glimpse of his feelings.

However, what exactly those feelings were, I didn't know as it felt as if there was a million words left unsaid in just that single look alone. It felt like the weight of this connection we had also had the power to fill the canyon between us, one he himself had put us on either side. So, there I was, desperate for him to merely say the word so as to fill the chasm of space and end my misery.

But that only happened in my dreams and right now, his intense gaze told me that I was not only awake, but I was dangerously close to slipping into a living nightmare. For one painful word from him was all it would have taken to drag me there.

But in the end, I only received two words from him and thankfully, neither were painful. His actions however were painfully confusing as he took my fingers in his own, pulling slightly so I had no choice but to let them go from being bitten.

Then shockingly he raised them to his own lips and I sucked in a startled breath the second he placed the tips of my fingers against his mouth and kissed directly over where my own lips had not long been. I swear he would have been able to taste me, as they were still wet from where my tongue had teased the end.

And what, in that moment, had the last two words from him been. The sounds of a promise, for they were ones I had no power to stop from settling in my heart and holding on to the comfort of them like a lifeline,

A lifeline from a King of Death spoken…

"Until tomorrow."

CHAPTER ELEVEN

THE GREAT MUFFIN LOSS

The second the door closed in front of Lucius, I turned around and let my body slide down it. I then let my head fall back and closed my eyes, placing a hand over my pounding heart in the hope that it would eventually calm down. What had that man done to me once again? I needed to get a grip and move the hell on and in doing so, as far away as I could get. Because the reality of my problem was a simple one, Lucius was far too dangerous to be around, and it had nothing to do with being a Vampire, but everything to do with the fragile heart he owned.

I couldn't fall for him again…*I just couldn't.*

Oh, who was I kidding, of course I was falling for him again. Hell, the bastard had been the one to push me!

The sound of my phone ringing jolted me from my thoughts and I answered it without looking, already knowing who it would be.

"Hello, Kirky."

"Oh my God! Tell me everything, you lying hussy, you!" Wendy squealed down the phone in her excitement.

"You know, he could have still been here, in which case your phone call would have been most inconvenient," I told her, only wishing this had been the case. She snorted and said,

"Whatever, Emmie. Look, Ben already told me that he's left, so just get on with the juicy gossip already." I frowned at the floor and said,

"And how did Ben know when to look out for me and my…?"

"Date? Yeah, kept that one quiet didn't you...?" she quipped.

"Kirky!" I said her name for her to get on with it, which thankfully she got the hint that I wasn't in the mood.

"I told him of course," she informed me in a way that was just short of the 'duh' at the end. I rolled my eyes at no one and let my head bang back against the door in exasperation.

"Why would you do that, now he will want to know…?" The sudden sound of someone at the door knocking had me yelping in surprise.

"Who's that?" she asked and again I rolled my eyes out of habit.

"Who do you think, you called him after all?" I said then I opened the door, speaking as I did so,

"Ben what are you…*doing here?*" My voice suddenly trailed off into a barely heard whisper the second I saw that it wasn't Ben after all…

It was Lucius.

My heart once more started to hammer in my chest, and I swear it was so loud to my own ears, he must have been able to hear it too. In fact, I was so shocked that I let the phone slip from my hand and it would have crashed down on the floor had Lucius not saved it with his lightening quick reflex.

"So, not Ben then?" I heard Wendy say in a small voice from down in his palm. Lucius simply raised the phone to his ear and replied in a cool, deep voice,

"No, not Ben. Goodnight Wendy." Then he pressed the red phone icon and ended the call.

"Wh…what are you…?" The broken start of my question ended by Lucius cutting me off with a pissed off growl.

"What do you think…?" he said taking what would seem to anyone else was a threatening step towards me.

"I…I…um." I mumbled having no idea until he decided to growl his reason at me.

"I am waiting for you to lock your *fucking door!*" he snapped making me frown in confusion and mumble some more.

"I…I…" Lucius' eyes flashed crimson once, emphasising the first word of his next sentence as well as the snarl that joined it.

"You need to be more careful and *you* can start by locking your door the second you're inside and not opening it again to any fucker that could be on the other side, without looking," he said nodding behind me, so I turned to see that he was indicating towards the peephole that any smart person would have used. But I was still questioning why he was so angry?

"But it's a secure building and I…well, the door is…" At this he once again cut me off with only a single look and it was *deadly.*

"The code to your door is 2277."

"Uh, how do you know that?"

"Because it is a simple four-digit code that anyone could remember after only walking past the second someone was trying to get inside," he told me as if he had already accomplished this and it was as easy as eating pie.

"But the chances are…" He quickly cut me off by taking

another step closer to me and carried on with his point in an even more intimidating manner.

"You have twenty-four people occupying this building which gives anyone who wants to get inside *twenty fucking four* opportunities to get inside, knock on this door, be *fucking welcomed in* the second you open it and then rob you, rape you and potentially kill you, all because…" he paused to lean in close and snarl his next words in my face…

"You wouldn't first take a fucking second to look to see who it was!" Oh boy, yep he was angry. In fact, scrap angry, he was bloody furious! So definitely not how I saw the night ending, as in…*At. All.*

I didn't realise but at the sight of his anger I had unconsciously been trying to get away from the terrifying sight of Lucius beyond pissed off and in doing so I had been taking small frightened steps back inside my flat. He also followed me a step inside and without taking his eyes off me he issued me one last demand,

"Now lock your fucking door!" Then he slammed the door shut so that it rattled on its hinges and the second it was closed I ran to it and clicked both the latch and added the chain that was eye level so that he could hear me doing this. I swear I even heard the great sigh of frustration he let out before I heard the sound of his steps walking away. However, I only stopped shaking seconds later after those steps were making their way firmly down the stairs. I continued to listen until there was silence only then releasing a whoosh of air through my trembling lips, asking myself what had just happened?

I had seen Lucius angry before, but furious beyond all composure was a new one for me because usually, no matter how turbulent or powerful Lucius' emotions were, he was renowned for his deadly calm and imperturbable exterior. An incredibly powerful being that kept a level head no matter whether that was in battle or scaring the living shit out of someone before torturing them. One fact always remained… Lucius always kept his cool.

So, what had that been about?

I suddenly heard something vibrating and I jumped, not realising that he must have dropped my phone on a small sideboard by the door that I usually kept my keys and mail on. I picked it up and didn't recognise the number but knew who it was from the second I read the last order…

'Walk away from the door and go to bed, Princess.'

"AAHHH!" I growled out loud, cursing myself for only being able to do it now when the big overbearing ass wasn't here to hear it! I don't know who he thought he was or what right he had to boss me around, but it irked me to the point that I suddenly needed a drink.

So, I walked into my small, compact kitchen and grabbed the open bottle of rosé that still had a good two glasses worth in there. Then I poured myself a large one and toasted the door and said,

"To overbearing assholes that I clearly piss off!" Then I took a big gulp of my wine, nearly choking in the process and this was what Wendy heard when she rang me for the second time.

"Christ, I'm not sure I want to know what you're choking on?!" I cleared my throat the best I could and told her,

"That's disgusting!" Which in turn made her laugh.

"So, I guess the mysterious man came back, who, it has to be said, officially has the sexiest voice I had ever heard." I rolled my eyes as I slumped down on my cute little shabby sofa that was a miss match of chintzy cushions that I had lovingly made, thanks to the old ones having holes and stains adorning them.

I had picked it up for free, but only if I arranged to get it out of his house as soon as possible, acting like the whole thing had been condemned or something. Well, I just hoped no one had died on it or anything because, other than it being old and smelling a bit musty, it was in great condition. So, the dated brown velvet fabric was well beyond being called retro or even classic but the shape of it was great. It was one of those that had the sides held up in place with a tasseled curtain tie wrapped around two wooden posts. The great thing about it was that if you unraveled the red tasseled rope then the sides went flat and the whole thing became a long thin bed, one Wendy had passed out on many a time.

The back section had been tricky to cover in the cream fabric I found on good old eBay, but with some help from Wendy, and her industrial strength staple gun, we managed it. I had decided to re-cover each of the three bottom cushions in a different chintzy pattern, two of which were flowers and the center one was light pink and dark pink pinstripe reminding me of a candy cane at the fair.

It was by far my favorite piece, which was why whenever I was near it with any food or drink, I covered the bottom with a light grey throw that was usually folded over the back just so that I couldn't spill anything on it. I'd learned the hard way when I realized that nothing gets Chicken Tikka out of a cream rug or the Sag Aloo that quickly followed as a result of my surprise.

The rest of my flat was done in a girly yet country style that mirrored my bedroom back home. But this was me we were talking about, so it also had its geeky side. Like the Star Trek framed posters I'd had signed by the wonderful Leonard Nimoy. Or my precious shelf that was dedicated to all things Sci-Fi, complete with toy movie figures, some still in their original packaging.

Other things in my flat included a whitewashed and shabby

chic coffee table that had chunky fat legs. A new rug, that was swirls of cream and pinks underneath the table, which had replaced the old one and its ugly splotches of toxic looking orange and yellow. Then there was a small window and next to that, opposite the sofa, was a cute armchair with a low back that was in a scalloped arch shape. It was covered in the lightest creamy pink tones and was decorated with a small cushion that was a pink Star Trek Starfleet badge framed by bright pink piping. It had also been a house warming gift from my aunty Pip, along with a Trailing Rat Tail cactus named George. Or so aunty Pip had lovingly informed me.

Unfortunately though, George had died due to unforeseen circumstances and was no longer with us. But I assured my aunt that he went to a better place and not just at the bottom of a bin bag after he shriveled up and died thanks to forgetting about him needing sunlight for half a year. But hey, he looked pretty in my bathroom for that time. However, me and plants were a no go. I don't know why but I just couldn't seem to keep the things alive! Okay, so that's not strictly true as I knew why and as Wendy was always telling me, 'just think, if it's living then it needs shit to grow' and her version of that shit, had been your usual water and sunlight. She even went as far as buying me another plant and testing me to see if I could keep it alive for longer than six months. I had thought I had done pretty well, that was up until I noticed it was getting a bit dusty and on closer examination realised the reason I had done so well was that it had been artificial.

Wendy didn't know what she found funnier, the fact that I had occasionally been watering this thing, and I had been really happy it was still alive and proud of myself, or that I hadn't even noticed it had been fake. Needless to say, it was the first thing to get cut up one Halloween when I was without a costume. It was when I decided to go as Poison Ivy, just because I had a horrible green dress I stupidly bought on sale and a plant I was permanently pissed off with. The costume had looked great though and was still in a bag at the bottom of my wardrobe.

But getting back to my little flat, now I know what you're thinking, I am a girly girl who loves pink and killing plants… right? Well, the truth is that I just wanted a feminine space to call my own and was as far away from the Gothic antique look as you could get and well, pink and flowers just seemed like the easiest way to achieve that.

Hence all the pink.

Now, if you asked me if I owned a single item of pink clothing then other than maybe a sneaky pair of panties that had been part of a set, then yeah on the panties but every day wearing clothes that people could see…then that was a big, firm no.

"I guess his voice is kinda nice," I admitted getting back to my call and making her scoff,

"Kinda nice…kinda nice? I am seriously worried about your hearing if you think that a man's voice that deep and sexy is just 'kinda nice'…he sounded fucking gorgeous, so please…oh please, oh please put me out of my misery and tell me he's just as sexy in real life as I have made him out to be in my head." I sighed and was forced to admit,

"I can pretty much guarantee it's better." She released a groan as if she was eating chocolate and was in her own private heaven.

"So, come on, dish up the good stuff, how did you meet him, was it at the gala…did you fall in love over a thousand-year-old dead body…come on your killin' me here." I laughed before telling her,

"Gods woman, your imagination is worse than mine!"

"I swear if you don't start talking, Smock, then I am going

to get a cab over there in my Hello Kitty PJ's!" The funny thing was I knew this wasn't an idle threat as knowing her she most likely would. Oh, and she also had a thing for Hello Kitty, but she assured me 'not in a weird way'…her words, not mine.

"Don't get too excited as he's just a family friend my dad asked to show up in his place…it seems it was my day for being date dumped," I said drily making her laugh. Then of course, she asked the million-dollar question…

"So, family friend or not, do you like him?" I decided to play dumb at first,

"Uh yeah, I mean he's alright." This of course, *sooo* didn't work.

"Oh, come on, you know what I mean, do you fancy the pants off him and want to have his babies?" she then asked after first making a dramatic exasperated sound. Stupidly, at the time she asked this, I was taking a much-needed sip of my wine, which I ended up spluttering out and nearly choking on,

"What? No! Geez, look there's nothing in it okay, we are just friends…well kind of, I mean he's friends with my dad… well, maybe not my dad per se, maybe more my mum's, but not really…oh I don't know, just no okay!" I said and at every turn did it all sound so wrong I got so frustrated that I ended up nearly begging her,

"Can we just change the subject please?"

"Okay, okay but can I just ask one thing…?" I released a deep sigh, held the top of my nose with my thumb and finger before fanning out my fingers and motioning for her to ask, even though she couldn't see me, therefore I muttered halfheartedly,

"What is it, Kirky?"

"Did you guys have sex or what?"

Oh, by the Gods… *it was going to be a long night.*

The next day I found myself sat on the bus with the box wrapped up once more and tucked away in my oversized handbag, barely able to function. I could put this down to a combination of things. Firstly, I had finished the rest of the wine last night, swiftly finding myself unsatisfied, so therefore ended up opening a bottle of prosecco. One I *had* been saving for when this exhibition was finished as a way to congratulate myself on a job well done.

Alright, so I hadn't finished the bottle at least, but I was definitely swaying as I made my way into the bathroom before bed. I had also woken up this morning looking like a girl panda that was ready for a night on the town wearing a wig that had been back brushed. To say that going to sleep, or more like passing out, without taking your makeup off and taking the pins out your hair hadn't been one of my better moments was an understatement.

The next disaster to happen had been to find I had run out of toilet roll, forgetting them on my last shop and only realizing my mistake when I found no replacements in my cupboard, so therefore being forced to pee in the shower with my legs wide open like a cowboy missing his horse! Not one of my finer moments I had to admit. Needless to say, that after that my lady garden got a good watering after that golden rain shower...*eeew*.

Then, after that I stubbed my toe before realising my milk was off so couldn't have a cup of tea and on the way out the door realised my traitorous bitch of a bra was trying to stab me in the heart with the underwire. Hence, why I ended up running for the bus and smacking my hand on the doors just as they were starting to close. And who did I blame for all this...

Lucius.

Lucius, that damn sexy Vampire who had made me lose all sensible thought process so that I could function like a normal human being in society. Okay, so he couldn't exactly be blamed for most of it, but he could most definitely be blamed for my hangover and driving me to drink my thoughts of him away. He was like a plague on my mind, for all I could think about was him, replaying every second of the night before. The way he had looked at me in my tight revealing dress, as though seeing me for the very first time.

But it had been the way his intense eyes had stayed on me during the whole time I was giving my tour. Both shamefully and admittedly, even though I had been there to put on a show for those rich people and essentially get them ready to open up their wallets for the next big archeological discovery, what I had really been doing was putting on a show just for him.

I didn't know at the time whether he could tell this or not, as I let my passion and knowledge merge into one, whether he could hear it in my voice or not. But as the private tour had come to an end I had been unsure as to why he was still there. Had my father asked him to watch over me for the whole night? I put it down to this being the case as there was no other reason, but then I thought back to how it had ended. Starting with the rollercoaster ride of emotions he had summoned from me. But it wasn't just his actions at the museum that confused me but more like his action afterwards.

Like how had he known it had been Wendy on the phone, unless of course he had been listening to my conversation from behind the door, as he had been impatiently waiting for me to flip the locks. But more importantly, why had he cared so much? Why had he got so angry at the idea that I could get hurt just opening the door to anyone? I couldn't understand it and the whole thing left me frustrated at being left in the dark.

However, stranger still had been when I sent my dad a

drunken text message after first saving Lucius' number in my phone as 'The Overbearing Asshole'.

It had been a simple question,

'Dad, why did you tell Lucius where I lived?'

His reply however, had been far less simple even though it was only two words…

'I didn't.'

Which meant Lucius had lied to me when I asked him how he knew where I lived. So, the even bigger question after that had been not why he lied but more importantly, how did he know where I lived? Had he been keeping tabs on me? I suppose it was possible that he would do this for my father, whenever Lucius found himself in London of course, but then if that was the case why not just say so…why lie about it?

I didn't have any of the answers, but whatever it was he was keeping it from me for a reason and that reason was one that I intended to find out. Now, all I had to do was put this barely thought out plan of mine into action and I was good to go.

I arrived at the museum out of breath after the ten-minute walk of lugging this box around in my bag, annoyed at myself that I had taken it home for nothing. Well, I hadn't exactly expected a big brooding Vampire to turn up and demand that I work on a Saturday, also thinking that I would have the weekend to examine the box in more detail.

It annoyed me that my dad had turned up with this thing and then called Lucius in anyway, without giving me any time to even try and get the thing opened. And I don't know why but I had a nagging feeling in the back of my mind that I wasn't being told everything here.

Well, there was only one way to find out I thought, going straight to the cafeteria once inside and rectifying the biggest problem I had faced this morning…*no tea and no breakfast.*

I was one of those people who could barely function as a

human being in the morning if I hadn't had my breakfast and a cup of tea, and this morning I had been without both. So, I grabbed a cup to go after making small talk with the usual ladies behind the counter and after waiting in a queue for what seemed like forever.

I couldn't believe how busy it could get, especially on a weekend. But that would teach me for getting here an hour after it had opened. I also grabbed a blueberry muffin and a bag of chips, or how they said it over here in England, a bag of crisps. It was strange when I first came here because even though I had been brought up in the states, I already knew a lot of English slang and terminology thanks to my mum and her Northern ways. Which also meant that the human side of my family was also mainly English, along with my Aunty Libby. My cousin Ella and her dad, my Uncle Frank, however were American.

I grew up with my Cousin Ella as she was only a few years older than me and we even spent time at the same school at one point. We were really close, still are in fact and video call each other often. But unfortunately, we don't get as much time to see each other these days, considering her job keeps her busy where she lives in Canada.

It was clear at a young age her passion was for animals, so it wasn't a huge surprise when she went into animal conservation. But her story was a whole can of supernatural worms I wasn't going to get into. Especially when it looked like my own was about to unfold and today was possibly the start of that.

I stuffed my bag of chips in my bag for later before grabbing my cup and muffin bag. I was just glad I was wearing my sturdy tan suede boots that were laced up to my calf and were thick soled. They also had a cream brushed wool lining that kept my feet warm, which was something I was always complaining about. The rest of my outfit was stretchy navy-blue jeans that tucked into my boots and a dark grey sweater with the silhouette of a few blackbirds flying across my chest that were knitted into the design in a black glittery wool. Underneath this I had a light blue shirt and you could see the collar, cuffs and bottom peeking out under the grey.

I thought it was one of my cuter outfits, one that was ruined however by the practical navy-blue parker jacket I wore over it, thanks to it raining outside. At least the large faux fur rimmed hood had kept my high pony tail dry and also kept my daily make-up from dripping down my face. I didn't wear much to be honest, not like I had last night. But just a bit of foundation, sweep of powder and blusher so that I didn't look like death warmed up, pale pink lip balm that made my lips nice and soft thanks to aloe vera, or Hello Vera, as Wendy calls it.

A light dusting of pale pink eyeshadow and I was done because thankfully, I had been blessed with thick black lashes that curled up on their own. Which meant that I didn't really need mascara or more like an extra reason to make a fool out of myself in the rain, as it usually turned to black tears streaming down my face that I wouldn't notice I had until faced with someone kind enough to mention it...this, needless to say, had happened twice before. Therefore, as a general rule, I left out the extra hassle and saved mascara for nights out, ones that included regular trips to the toilet just to be sure.

I swiped my card in the security panel and entered in the code that I knew we were going to have to get changed as it was clear that if Wendy knew it, then it was time to get another one. Then I skillfully (for clumsy me anyway) held on to my tea, tucked my muffin bag under my chin and dropped the card back in my bag with the keys I had found on my kitchen counter. Something in itself that had been a conundrum, considering I was so sure that I had locked up and put the keys in my purse last night.

The door buzzed open and I slipped inside making sure not

to drop my breakfast. Then I dropped my bag on the table I knew was nearby so that I could fumble for the lights. Then the second I switched them on I turned around to face the room, screaming in fright the second I did. And I did this because I was not as alone as I thought I was going to be. Also, in the process I dropped both my tea and my muffin making me curse out loud the second I did.

"Son of a bitch!"

The three men dressed in black and basically looking like every other thug you would have seen in any action movie, all looked at me as though they were dealing with someone crazy. And who knows, maybe they were right. As I am sure the right response to have when facing three thugs was to grab my bag and scream for help as I high tailed it outta there.

But instead I just looked down at my precious goods on the floor and said…

"Oh damn it, there goes my breakfast."

CHAPTER TWELVE

ATTACK OF THE KILLER BOX

The second I shouted about the loss of my breakfast instead of screaming in fear really must have thrown them, as they each looked at one another in confusion. Well, they were about to find out why as let's just say that thanks to my upbringing, I didn't exactly scare easily.

"Sorry fellas, but if you're looking for dinosaurs then you're in the wrong place, try the National History Museum to fulfil those boyhood dreams of yours," I told them sarcastically as I shrugged out of my jacket, now getting ready for what I had an idea was soon to happen. Now, if only I could get away with doing some stretches and lunges, my muscles might survive this later. But then again, wouldn't that have been too obvious?

The three guys frowned, and one guy even cracked his knuckles making me roll my eyes at the cliché.

"Can we hurt this bitch yet?" the knuckle cracker asked the guy in the middle who shook his head slightly.

"We are here for the box, now hand it over and you won't

get hurt." The one who was clearly in charge said, making me scoff back a little laugh. He was taller than the rest, but still wearing all black like the other two. He also looked slightly older, maybe in his late forties, compared to the Beavis and Butthead that looked a similar age to me, if not younger.

All three were fairly large, fit guys but compared to the men in my life that I was used to, then it was like a couple of gymnasts or fit cyclists going up against heavy weight champions merged with the world's strongest men competition. Needless to say, I wasn't intimidated.

"Or you could just leave now, and *you* won't get hurt," I countered making them laugh as they clearly got the wrong idea of why I was acting so cocky.

"If you think your Vampire will be coming to save you, then think again Girl, we dealt with him and gave him a nice little diversion," the middle man said, who I gathered had started to go grey early as he looked as though he had racing stripes down the side of his hair…I wondered if it made him run faster? Well, maybe I would find out when he realized that assumption was the mother from where all mistakes are born…thanks for that one daddy, I thought with a grin.

But what he said had managed to throw me slightly off balance as not only did they know about Vampires, which for humans was unusual, but I wondered what they had done to Lucius as a diversion? Not that I was worried that he could be hurt, because let's face it, unless he was up against a God, then like my dad, he was pretty indestructible.

"Oh well…looks like he will miss the show, he will be pissed as he loves a good fight," I taunted causing the middle one to make an incredulous sound as if he couldn't believe the gall of my bravery. I knew this when he said,

"I gotta give it to you lady, you got balls…shame though, you were a pretty little thing too…" Then he nodded towards me and the one on his right came at me first, storming down the center of the room, one framed either side with a line of examining desks, with magnifying lamps and metal stools. It looked a little like a classroom with a library of artifacts at the end laid in drawers. Which meant that I had to keep this from getting as messy as possible because I would never forgive myself if something got damaged because of these three goons.

I shrugged my shoulders at his comment and the second the first thug got within striking distance I took him off guard by punching him first in the nose. Then, while he was still dazed and confused, I lashed out again and this time punched him in the throat, nearly crushing his windpipe. Then I grabbed him by the jacket and yanked him forcefully into my knee getting him in the testicles. I hit him so hard that I felt them recoil on impact, as if they themselves were screaming and echoing 'Nooooo!' as they knew what was coming…

Sickening pain, that's what!

He crumpled to the floor, landing hard on his knees and his hands didn't know what to hold on to first: his broken nose, his bruised throat that he couldn't breathe through or his tender nuts. Then he fell to the side and I grinned down at the man now lying sideways in a fetal position and cupping his balls.

"Good choice," I said with a smirk before looking back at the other two knowing what I would find…

Utter shock.

"You were saying something about my pretty face?" I said in an innocent little voice and chuckling as I looked at the guys blood on my knuckles, wiping it casually down my top. A move which I liked to think was threatening enough without being cliché, unlike the dickhead currently broken on the floor. But then he looked up at me through watery eyes and made his second mistake.

"Bitch!" he snarled through clenched teeth. I placed a hand on my chest and said,

"What, who me?" in an innocent voice. Then I twisted my body and dropped down, quickly delivering a hammer punch at his face, now knocking him unconscious. Then I stood back up, put a hand to my ear and said,

"You were saying, Dickhead?" Of course, I didn't receive an answer but asking him the sarcastic question felt good.

"Well, what do you know, I guess he doesn't feel like talking anymore," I said to the other two, making their features twist into angry glares. Then the one in charge nodded to the guy on his left telling him without words to go and have his try, who unlike the other one, wasn't taking any chances. He pulled out a large knife from behind his jacket and came towards me with it, twisting it round in his hand as he had no doubt practiced it in the mirror while convincing himself that he was a badass.

"Now you will pay for that!" he warned, trying to sound threatening.

"You know in some cultures they pay for things in teeth, let's try that should we?" I said making him roar at me before swinging out with the knife. I ducked once under the swing and popped back up quickly to his side and grabbed his forearm in a block with one hand. I then twisted his arm, yanked him hard and cracked him in the face with a swing of my elbow, catching him in the jaw and busting his lip. He staggered back but surprisingly managed to keep hold of his knife. Oh well, I will just have to try harder.

"YOU CUNT!" he screamed at me and again I shrugged my shoulders before he came at me again. Now it was time to get rid of the knife. So, this time when he lunged at me, trying to stab me straight on, I blocked the attack, swiping his arm to one side and breaking off the center line. Simultaneously, two things happened and the first was me bending my body back slightly, giving myself some distance from the threat of his blade. Then at the same time I grabbed his wrist, quickly bent it back on itself and took the knife from his hand, throwing it to the ground behind me.

"AHH, LET ME GO YOU WHORE!" he snarled pointlessly, because what did he expect after name calling, for me to say, 'Oh I'm terribly sorry dear chap, it was supposed to tickle?'

Douchebag, I thought with a shake of my head and sighing before putting him down for good. And I did this by still holding his arm in a lock, twisting it further back so that he had nowhere to go but down to the floor. I gave his body no other option but to bend further and at the same time I brought up my knee, connecting it with his face with a sickening crunch. It hurt me but not nearly as much as it hurt him when breaking his face.

Then, as he was still howling in pain, I made sure he wouldn't be using his arm any time soon, pleased to put that happy slasher move out of commission for good. So, I held out his arm straight and said,

"I hope you like hospital food," then I hammered my bent elbow down on his arm in just the right place, breaking the bone and feeling slightly sick when I felt it snap. Now he really howled in pain and funnily enough, there wasn't a single curse word uttered, as no doubt he was now worried that if he called me a whore again, I would kill him.

I then bent down and picked up the knife, all the time keeping the last guy in my sights, who was now looking slightly pale at the sight of what this little woman could do.

"What the...Who the hell are you lady?!" The guy stammered, and I was surprised that he hadn't ran yet. Oh well, more fool him. But it was rude not to give him an answer. So, I gave him one, smirking an evil little grin as I did…

"I'm a Draven." Then to drive my point home, giving him an idea of just what that meant, I flipped the knife once, caught it at the right angle before hurling it towards him, hitting its mark perfectly and embedding it in his shoulder. Well, I didn't want to kill him as after all, that would have been rather rude of me. He screamed, twisting his body side on after the impact threw his shoulder back, then he looked down at its hilt sticking out of his jacket as if wondering how it got there.

"You fucking stabbed me!" he shouted in astonishment and I shrugged my shoulders as if I was a little girl that had just been caught stealing cookies.

"You started it," I reminded him. See, that was the problem with taking one look at someone and assuming because people were small that they could easily be beaten. My father had been teaching me to fight ever since I could walk, knowing that I may have no supernatural powers, but there were other ways that I could protect myself. Alright, so I wouldn't have much of a chance going up against one of his own kind but in the human world at least I could defend myself. And surprisingly, I wasn't actually a violent person but knowing what I did, meant that I could face a situation like this with the confidence that I would walk away from it relatively unscathed.

But that was when the person had a blade or even a bat, knowing exactly what to do to block the hit before then disarming them. Then the next job was to break something important, like a leg so they wouldn't be getting up again anytime soon. Of course, knocking them unconscious helped too.

However, there was one thing that I couldn't fight against…*A gun.* Which was when he did something that I hadn't been expecting and with a determined look on his face he pulled a weapon from behind his trousers and aimed it at me.

"You should have just given us the box, Bitch." Then he cocked back the hammer and pulled the trigger.

And in that split second the only thing that managed to escape my lips just as the gun fired was...

"Ah shit."

CHAPTER THIRTEEN

HELLO HEX

A gun.

It just had to be a gun, didn't it.

I waited for the feel of the severe rush of pain as the bullets ripped their way through my body, but instead I felt something else entirely. In seconds it was as if my whole body was being spun around at a dizzying speed. Then I heard the gun fire five more times before I realised I was actually encased in someone's arms. It took me a moment longer, which was precisely when the arms left me, to realize that Lucius had got to me just in time. He had enveloped me in his arms and turned quickly enough so that he shielded me from the impact of the bullets, meaning they hit his back instead.

I turned around to the sound of a man screaming in terror as Lucius stalked towards him, throwing an actual desk out of his way as though it had been a bag of feathers. It crashed into the wall and I winced at the damage, thankfully taking stock of irreplaceable things that had broken, happy to see it was at zero.

Then I watched in utter fascination as the bullets that were embedded in his back started to re-emerge, first from beneath his skin and then from beneath his leather jacket, as his body rejected the metal. I knew that he could have mentally thrown up a veil of protection around his skin so that the bullets wouldn't have got that far. But I guess his first impulse had been to get to me and shield the human...*the very breakable human.*

"No! Nooo! Get away from me, Devil!" he begged as Lucius must have been letting his demonic features show, because now the man looked a heartbeat away from wetting himself and seeing Lucius this way, then I couldn't say that I blamed him. He was certainly a frightening sight to behold and if I hadn't been used to seeing badass demons, then I would have no doubt been joining the thug with peeing my pants.

But I had never seen Lucius like this. I didn't know what it was exactly about the sight of such controlled rage, but I found myself with a hand to my beating heart from fear I would pass out. He stalked the man who was heading closer towards the back row of artifacts and now I was starting to panic.

"NO!" I shouted running forward a little and Lucius whipped his head around and snarled at me, making me flinch back at the sight. By the Gods he was frightening! His eyes were two pools of crimson fire burning with blood lust. Black veins branched off around his forehead and his eyes, snaking down the sides of his face. It was thicker down his neck, looking as though an infection had risen from lower down his body and was creeping up under his skin like thin black snakes of venom.

I could tell that he thought I was trying to get him to stop before he killed the man and he obviously didn't appreciate the interruption.

"Don't damage the artifacts," I told him softly, then nodded to the back wall of drawers, letting him know that was all I cared about. He turned to look at what I was referring to and then looked back at me, this time with a grin that could only be described in one way…

It was prime evil.

Then he utterly shocked me by giving me a wink before turning his attention back to the man who was currently trying to escape through a locked back door. One that he didn't know only led to a storeroom filled with equipment. So, unless he intended to try and brush his way out to get away from the killer demonic vampire named Lucius, then it was pretty much a foregone conclusion that he was screwed.

I knew this the second Lucius appeared behind him and grabbed him so that he could throw him back across the room and opposite the wall of drawers that I was trying to protect. I couldn't help myself when I held up two thumbs for his actions in saving the precious artifacts, making Lucius shake his head slightly as if he was seeing things. Well, it was that or he clearly didn't know what to do with me.

The guy landed and skidded along the floor as if he had just been thrown out of a moving car. He was curled in on himself and just as he started to move out of his fetal state, Lucius was back on him. He hauled him up with a choking grasp on his neck and threw him against the nearest wall.

I gasped, making Lucius look back at me even as he had the guy suspended with his feet off the ground and being held there with just one arm. I quickly ran to the shelf he was next to and caught the large fossilized piece of a beehive that had been wobbling on its holder.

I let out a sigh of relief and then nodded to Lucius, saying,

"You may continue," making him smirk and shake his head to himself once again in what looked like wonderment.

"Fuck you, Bitch!" The guy stupidly said, making Lucius yank the goon's head closer to his face so that he could snarl at it, showing the lengthening of his fangs and this time the guy did piss himself.

"Now really, was that a smart thing to say, huh?" I said making him quickly shake his head saying no. But Lucius didn't care as he cracked his head once more back on the wall, this time choking the life from him.

"Wait!" Lucius didn't stop but he did at least look at me.

"What now?" he asked as if expecting me to say that the wall he was currently strangling someone up against was pissed on by Ramesses III and therefore also needed to be preserved.

"I don't know, shouldn't we at least interrogate him or something?" I asked, glancing in panic at the guy quickly turning purple at the end of his hand.

"Why? He tried to kill you, that's a good enough reason as any to end his life and I think your father would agree with me on this one," he added making me snort a short laugh and say,

"Well, yeah, that's a given but what I mean is, that there could be more of them and that would be kind of handy to know, don't you think?" Lucius rolled his eyes and said,

"Fine!" Then he let the guy go so that he dropped to the floor like a sack of turnips. He started gasping and spluttering the second he tried to breathe air through his burning lungs. Then, after a few more deep breaths, Lucius hauled him back up against the wall ready for our interrogation. So, I leant towards him, getting in his face and started to play bad cop...or were we both bad cops?

"Who do you work for?!" I shouted at him, making Lucius look down at me with a raised brow in question,

"What, it's one of the first things they ask in the movies," I said in my defense with a shrug of my shoulders, making him shake his head at me.

"Been to many interrogations, have you?" he asked drily.

"Nope, this is my first...you?" I asked unable to help myself. He looked down at me and replied in a dry tone,

"A few, yes." Telling me with his sarcasm that his real answer had been 'you have no idea'. Then Lucius turned his attention back to the task at hand.

"Well...answer her, asshole!" Lucius snapped when the half-strangled goon looked at him for guidance, as it was clear here who the biggest threat was.

"I...I...can't, th...th...ey will... kill me," he stuttered making my eyes widen in shock,

"Seriously, I mean you have a big angry Vampire about to snap your neck like a twig and you're worried about someone else killing you later on?" I asked him with disbelief at the sheer idiocy of the man.

"Now, tell us what it is you want with the box, starting with who sent you for it?" I asked again with a forceful tone. The second he didn't answer I nudged Lucius and said,

"Go on, show him," making him once again frown at me.

"Show him what?" Lucius asked, and I swear it was starting to look like a double act comedy show. Seriously, if we were ever going to do this again we would have to work on our communication.

"The fangs, show him the fangs again," I said with another nudge making him roll his eyes at me. But at least he went along with it and suddenly snapped his face around, this time with fully extended fangs that looked deadly enough they could have ripped half the guy's neck out. The man screamed in fear, turning his face away clearly terrified. Meanwhile, Lucius looked down at me to find me looking smug and I mouthed the words, 'Told you so' at him, making him again shake his head at me. But then my victory was short lived as the man started to beg instead of spilling the beans like I had thought he would.

"I...can't...I..."

"Enough of this!" Lucius snarled.

"AHHH!" The man's plea ended in a long wail of pain as Lucius sighed in annoyance before yanking out the blade still in his shoulder and then driving it into the other one, essentially pinning him to the wall with it. I glared at Lucius in response to his brutal actions, as it didn't exactly scream trust us with the information and we will let you live type of gig that I had been hoping for.

"What?" Lucius asked making me roll my eyes.

"Look, just tell us what we want to know, and we will let you go," I said making Lucius snap his gaze back to me and growl,

"No, we fucking won't!" I couldn't help but groan out loud and grit my teeth, before hissing,

"Yes, well he didn't know that, did he?"

"Ah, well in that case, we will let you live if you tell us what we want to know," Lucius said, this time making me smack my forehead.

"I think that ship has sailed, Lucius." Yeah and was half way across the Atlantic before it sank, I wanted to add but one pissed off look from a Vampire who was clearly losing his patience and I thought it best to restrain myself.

"Fuck this! Tell us what you know, or I will kill you and do it slowly, and when I say slowly, I mean one piece at a fucking time. Now, last chance, who do you work for?!" Lucius said in a threatening tone so deep I could have sworn his demon was trying to break free and take a bite. When the guy didn't answer quick enough, which in Lucius' mind was three seconds, he then placed emphasis on his threat by twisting the knife in his shoulder until blood spurted out from the wound, making him cry out again.

This was when the man found his breaking point and

opened his mouth to speak, only managing to say a number before he started to choke.

"Th...ree... tt...wo... two...AAAAHHHH!" He started to splutter out before it all ended in the most blood curdling screams.

"Lucius, what are you...?"

"It isn't me!" he shouted back after dropping the man and now we both watched as he started spitting out blood that looked contaminated with black chunks of thick congealed plasma. He started coughing even more violently and Lucius held a hand out across my chest and pushed me back a few steps as if he knew what was coming.

"What's happening...what's wrong with him!?" I asked in shock as it was as if he had just swallowed a bucket of acid and it was eating him from the inside out.

"Could it be a cyanide capsule?" I asked when Lucius hadn't answered me.

"No, this is nothing man made...this is a... *Death Hex,*" Lucius said pausing once to look at me with a dire expression before finally answering me with the last thing I ever expected to hear. Then I looked down in time to see the man's stomach cave in on itself making me want to gag. Instead, my instincts kicked in and I curled into Lucius' side, hiding my face against his leather jacket.

At first, he tensed at the contact and I was just about to pull away but then his arm wrapped around me, securing me to his side and warning me not to look yet. I waited until the sounds of gurgled death were finished before I peeked my head out from Lucius' hold. All that was left was what looked like a melted body on the floor minus anything structural to hold it upright...like its bones.

"Oh Gods, that's me never eating stew again," I said making

another gagging sound causing Lucius to give me a sideways glance and look briefly amused.

"What the hell could do something like that?"

"Someone extremely powerful, for the Hex was placed to stop him from…"

"Snitching on whoever he works for, yeah, yeah, I got that…what I mean is, what type of being could cast something like that?" I asked again interrupting him.

"Well, I think I already answered that bit, Prin…" He started to call me Princess and I lost it.

"Don't call me princess, Luc, or I swear I am going to start calling you Dracula," I threatened, making him smirk.

"You know I met him once," he said as he bent on a knee near the putrid blob of a corpse. I frowned and found myself asking,

"Who?"

"Vlad Țepeș, or better known as…"

"Vlad the Impaler!?" I interrupted again in shock. He didn't reply, so I gathered this was who he meant, seeing as I had just teased him about calling him Dracula.

"What was he like…and what are you doing?" I asked the second he started to sniff over the vile sight.

"Familiarising myself with the scent of the Hex so that I may track it should it arise again."

"Ah, okay, I didn't know you guys could do that," I commented before taking a sniff myself to see if I could pick anything up. Let's just say that I regretted it instantly as I all smelled was melted skin and hair, making me put a fist in my mouth to stop myself from gagging. Lucius looked back up at me over his shoulder and questioned drily…

"Us guys?"

"Yeah, you know what I mean," I said showing him my

non-existent fangs, with a wave of my hand making him grumble under his breath,

"Happily not." Then he rose back to his full height, once again making me feel like a short ass and said,

"He's misunderstood." I frowned now having no clue as to what he meant.

"Well yeah, sure he is, I mean he's dead for a start so I'm sure you couldn't get any more misunderstood than a dead guy," I commented dryly, making Lucius roll his eyes before correcting me.

"Not him." Then I watched as he walked towards the other casualties in the room.

"Who is?" I asked feeling as though we were having this conversation out of sync.

"Vlad is…now what happened here, did they turn on each other?" Lucius asked me, nodding down at the two men that were now both unconscious, one of which was still cupping his balls, the poor bastard.

"What, no…! I did that," I told him making him snap his head back at me and the look he gave me was priceless. Anyone would have thought he had turned to find me wearing my panties on my head and walking on my hands. I swear he was a second away from his mouth dropping open in that comical way. But instead of letting his utter shock get to embarrassing levels, he did something better with his mouth and unfortunately that wasn't kissing me senseless. No, instead he spoke in a tone that was clearly astonished.

"You did this?" he asked again, repeating my words in clear bewilderment that I found insulting. So, I crossed my arms over my chest, cocked my hip out a little and said,

"Yeah, Lucius, I did this." Then he looked back to the men again, this time taking a better look and obviously now calculating a list of their injuries. Something he confirmed when he turned back to face me and said again, only this time with even more amazement,

"You did this?"

"Yes, geez, what do you want me to do, film it next time as proof!"

"Next time? Are you planning on making this a hobby?" he said sounding surprised but from the mirth dancing in his eyes, I could tell he was also teasing me. Which was astounding in itself, as I didn't even know that Lucius had it in him to tease anyone, I had certainly never seen it before. Which, painfully, made me think of my mother and ask myself what had he been like with her?

I hated whenever my thoughts would spiral down this rabbit hole filled with nothing but a dark taboo of history I really didn't want to face. Because, no matter how much I loved and adored my mother, it was an inner battle I fought when feeling as though I would never be as good as her.

"Well, that depends," I replied trying not to let my dark thoughts seep into my words and coat them in bitterness.

"On?" he enquired,

"How often I am going to turn up to work and find thugs waiting for me." This answer didn't please Lucius, I could tell. He walked over to the one with the broken arm and hauled him up with a fist full of his jacket, doing so as though he weighed nothing at all. Then he twisted his wrist so that he could take in the unconscious man, once again assessing the damage.

"You broke his arm?" Lucius asked as it was clear he was still in disbelief.

"Well, he didn't do it when he fell that's for damn sure and I needed to force the knife out of his hand," I replied leaving out the fact that I got the knife off him without needing to break a limb...but hey ho, I thought that best to keep to myself. However, I couldn't help but get annoyed as he still didn't seem to believe it was me. He confirmed this when he dropped the man on the desk with an audible thud and asked,

"And just how did you accomplish that?" I groaned aloud first and said,

"You have met my father, right? How do you think I did it, by asking it nicely to break?" I said sarcastically, once again making his lips twitch.

"Your father taught you to fight?" he asked as if needing this confirmed, which I didn't exactly think was the best time to discuss how capable I was at beating a man's ass.

"Since I was three years old," I told him, making Lucius mumble under his breath,

"That explains a few things." I was about to ask him what he meant when suddenly the door was flung open and three security guards all piled in.

"Stop!" Lucius demanded making all three men freeze as if time had been paused.

"Oh shit, what are we going to do now?" I asked, however Lucius seemed unfazed by the fact it looked like we had just been caught at a murder scene, although I was not sure what to call that pile of human goo on the floor.

"Forget what you have seen since entering this room and go back to your posts," Lucius demanded with a flick of his wrist making them do as he commanded, leaving us alone once more.

After this he pulled out his phone making me notice what he was wearing and having to quickly prevent any drool from escaping the second that I did. He was wearing a pair of dark jeans the shade of charcoal that molded perfectly to his long strong legs to the point where I couldn't stop myself from staring at his ass. Then he wore a black leather jacket that zipped up his abs, had pockets at the sides I wished I could slip my hands into and a stiff belted standing collar that he wore open. Underneath, I could see the long-sleeved t-shirt in a ribbed light grey material that looked both lightweight and worn deliciously tight to his powerful body.

I also wanted to groan every time he bent his arm, making the leather around his large biceps tighten, groaning at the strain.

"I need you here at the museum," he said without so much as an 'hello' or 'how're you doing?' I guess Lucius was too important to bother with the formalities. It reminded me of the Spanish and the way they would answer their phones, saying 'Digame' which literally means, 'tell me' or basically, 'speak'. Which was sometimes how I had heard my dad answer the phone to one of his, should we say, 'subjects' for lack of a better word.

"Let's just say I found some new friends for Ruto to play with," Lucius replied to whoever it was on the other end and he did so with a knowing grin, one that made me want to shiver. Especially when one of the guys started to come round and the second he did, Lucius grabbed the back of his head and bashed it on the table so that his nose exploded, and he blacked out once more. And he did this without a single show of emotion on his face... I swear it didn't even twitch.

"Nice," I commented drily, making him grin at me. Then he listened to whoever was on the phone for a few seconds more who must have asked the question, 'will that be all?' because Lucius looked over his shoulder down his back as if remembering something.

"Bring me another jacket," then he ended the call after this demand that was snarled in annoyance. He then fed his phone into the back pocket of his jeans and unzipped his jacket before peeling it off his torso. I swear the lump in my throat became the size of a plum for I had to turn away from him just so that I could swallow it down without looking like an idiot. The sight of his tight T-shirt molded to his muscles was having the equivalent effect on me as if I had seen him emerging naked from some tropical waterfall, flicking his wet hair back like he was on some damn shampoo advert.

I had to clear my throat before I spoke again, hating the effect just the sight of him had over me.

"Umm…so, what about that…uh…mess on the floor, because no offence, but I don't think we can make everyone who comes in here ignore it forever," I told him giving my nose a rub as the stench of the man puddle was making its way across the room.

"Can you fix it?" I asked in a comical tone whilst holding my nose and after following Lucius closer to it, seconds later really wishing that I hadn't.

"No," was his simple answer, unfortunately for me though, it wasn't the one I wanted to hear.

"Well, you're going to have to do something because we can't leave him…*it*…there forever." The next thing I knew he clicked his fingers and like Hades himself, flames suddenly appeared, burning away all traces of the body and with it leaving behind a big black melted patch on the floor.

"And that?" I questioned, wondering how I was going to explain that too. This was when he finally looked down at me, grinned that bad boy grin of his and said…

"Now that I can fix."

CHAPTER
FOURTEEN

YOU WERE SAYING?

By the time Lucius indeed 'fixed' the floor, along with the rest of the room so that my boss wouldn't freak out, the other problem was taken care of. This was in the form of two of his men walking into the room and each of them removing the unconscious men. The strangest thing about this happening wasn't in the act itself but more because the second they both looked at me, Lucius snarled at them. I had no clue why he did this but the second he issued the animalistic warning they lowered their head in submission, continuing on with their jobs without a single glance my way.

"I am starting to see now why your father allows you to get the bus," Lucius had commented dryly as he watched the two broken men being carried from the room. I would have smiled at this comment if I hadn't been too concerned with how odd two unconscious bodies may have looked to the near twenty thousand visitors we get a day at the museum.

"They won't be seen," Lucius said as if he could hear my

thoughts. Most likely though he just saw me looking nervously at the door chewing on the end of one finger. Lucius homed in on the sight and the second I saw his eyes flash a deep and warm amber tone, I let my finger slip from my lips. He cleared his throat and for a second looked as though he was going to reach out and touch me. However, he didn't and instead fisted his hand by his side and commanded in what was a strained, stern tone,

"Now, show me the box." I walked past him towards my handbag muttering,

"Geez, bossy much." I knew that in all likelihood he had heard me, but I refused to turn my head to check. Instead, I did as I was told and pulled the box from my bag, unwrapping it from the bubble wrap I had rolled around it.

"So, you were saying something about Fort Knox," I said reminding him of his comment last night, saying it would be safer to have left it in the museum. Then I passed it to his waiting hand and couldn't miss the spark of mirth that ignited in his steel grey eyes that I only just noticed had flecks of ice blue in them.

"Point taken, sweet" Lucius said giving me a new nickname and it was one I would take over 'Princess' any day of the week.

"So, any ideas?" I asked after giving him a minute to examine the box on the table he was now leaning over. His eyes shot up to mine and he said,

"I thought you were the expert here." I couldn't help but roll my eyes at his comment.

"I'm not an expert at everything and besides, it's not as straight forward as you first think it is," I told him before taking the box from his hands, unconsciously making contact with both his bare fingers and the ones he always had encased in leather. The second we touched I felt that same bolt of sensations course through me as if I had tapped into something hidden deep within him. I couldn't understand it, as it was a feeling that only happened around Lucius. Years ago, it had been only one of the reasons I believed him to be my Chosen One…*seven foolish years ago.*

He suddenly stood up straight, pulling his fingers from beneath mine and cutting the cord on the electricity we created. It seemed, by his tense and strained look, that I wasn't the only one who had been affected. Or had it been because I had touched his gloved hand? I could tell that this was a big no-no with Lucius and I didn't fully understand why? I knew that it had something to do with a sacrifice he made to save the world, but I was never told the full story.

I swallowed hard and tried to act as though nothing had happened, clearing my throat before I spoke.

"You see it looks from first glance to hold Egyptian hieroglyphs, and then entwined is Demotic script. And then here is…"

"Ancient Greek… but then it is like the Rosetta Stone," Lucius quickly surmised, and I couldn't help teasing him,

"Looks like someone was paying attention in class." At this, I received a playful grin in return and in this moment, you could have almost forgotten the fact we didn't like each other.

"But there is more," I said, taking the box and showing him the only way I knew how. Which meant I had to walk around the table and stand close by his side. I tried to ignore the way he looked down at me as if curious by my behavior or the way my heart started beating erratically by being this close.

"Okay, so if you look at it head on, then you can clearly make out the three types of script in the raised squares, but then look what happens to the hieroglyphs when I turn it slightly this way." I angled the box so as to view it tilted and I watched as Lucius saw it for himself the moment he frowned.

"It's Sumerian," he stated in surprise.

"It's *Cuneiform Sumerian*, which means it is one of the earliest forms of writing, invented by the Sumerians, which begs the question as to why it has been hidden in Egyptian hieroglyphs?"

"Well, do they know which came first?" Lucius asked surprising me that he didn't know, but then again at only just over two thousand years old, then he was considered a baby next to my father's unknown age. Something I had tried to nag out of him since I had learned to say my own age. Let's just say the most I got was at least double the age of Lucius, if his account of historical events was anything to go by.

"Well, that's an ongoing debate and unfortunately without evidence to support either side, it's one that no one can agree on," I told him in answer to his question.

"But that is not the strangest part...do you see these hidden symbols here once it's turned this way." I did the same again and this time pointed to the few glyphs I'd missed the first time.

"This looks like Cretan hieroglyphs, which were used in the Bronze Age in Crete." Lucius looked even more surprised and asked,

"What does it mean?"

"Well, Cretan hieroglyphs are generally considered undeciphered and only found on very few artefact, so who knows. But the more important question is what on earth are they doing on this box along with the others?" I asked making him look down at me and it was in that moment that I realised just how close I still was to him. So, I set down the box and took a step back, now giving him the space to examine it himself. However, when he didn't touch it, I decided to prompt him.

"Maybe we will know more once we get inside it," I added nodding for him to do just that. However, he just gave me a quizzical look in return before saying,

"What?" I frowned thinking it was obvious...*wasn't it?*

"Err well, aren't you going to open it?" I asked, making him frown as if what he was about to say next he didn't want to.

"I can't," he said shocking me and making me realise this was what he hadn't wanted to admit...*failure.*

"But you haven't even tried yet...have you?" I said, changing this statement to an unsure question.

"I have been trying to open it since you revealed it to me," he confessed with a slight edge of irritation to his tone.

"You have?" I asked clearly shocked to hear this. He didn't answer me this time but instead gave me a pointed look that spoke volumes. He wasn't going to dignify himself with an answer that he felt he had already given me.

"But you haven't even touched it yet," I argued, thinking that surely that should at least be a requirement. This was when he must have decided to prove his point and seeing as this was Lucius we were talking about then he did it in his usual way...*intimidation.*

He took a step to the side just as I mistakenly turned to face him. Then he stepped into me and I took one back until I felt the rim of the desk digging into my lower back. Then he placed both hands either side of me, gripping on to the table and caging me in with his large frame. I held my breath, too scared to let go of it for fear of my breasts pressing against his own chest and making contact. For at that moment there was at least an inch between us and right now it could have been a set of steel bars and it still wouldn't have felt safe enough against this man.

He stayed like this for long enough that I couldn't help but start squirming as if I was the prey waiting for the final blow from the predator that had me dangling from the end of his claw. Talk about cat and mouse! I swear I was three seconds away from begging him to either let me go or kiss me.

Finally, he leant down close enough to my ear that I froze,

other than finding the table's edge myself and holding on with a death grip next to his own hands. Then I leant my body back as far as it would go. But with his height it still wasn't far enough for he reached my ear easily.

Then it was his time to prove a point…

"I find things bend to my will just fine without the need for my touch…now don't you agree, *my little puppet?"* he said purring yet another little pet name for me and making me want to growl back and then stamp on his foot as a way of throwing that point back in his face. But, for once, I stopped myself before I could and decided to fight fire with fire.

So, trying to take back a shred of control, I first tried to steady my breathing before then applying some pressure to the desk, forcing my body up closer to his own. This time he was the one who froze and the look in his eyes was one of shock. I bravely maintained eye contact so that I could deliver my come back with more backbone than usual.

This was when I finally whispered back in a strong and steady voice,

"But where is the fun in that?"

The second I had said it I knew that I had made a mistake as his reaction said as much. He jerked back as if he had been stung and the look he gave me spoke both of his displeasure and annoyance. So, before my shame could triple, I pushed my body out of his arms to break his hold on the table and subsequently freeing myself.

I felt like an idiot and vowed that I wouldn't do this to myself again. I wouldn't put myself or my confused heart in this situation again and that vow started right now. I hated him for doing this to me. For feeling as though he could sadistically play with my feelings and then act outraged when I allowed myself to be drawn in. This was when I realised he must have been a sadist, for it was clear he must enjoy doing this to me far too much to be able to stop himself.

Well, if he didn't have the strength to stop, then that only left me to take control and I would start by acting as if nothing was wrong. So, placing that professional veil back over my head and more importantly that cage back around my heart, I spoke,

"Well, I thank you for trying but if you don't mind, I have a lot of work to do, so if you will be so kind as to leave me to it, then I would be most grateful," I told him as I walked towards the door and held it open for him to take the hint. Then I finally braved a look at him, seeing him now looking completely different than just moments ago. No, now he looked as if he was trying to suppress a grin and what else was that in his eyes? Was it a hint of respect?

I watched as he took a step back and leant his weight back on the table behind him, doing so in a casual way that told me he wasn't going anywhere. So, this was when my professionalism went and took a flying leap out the window and I slammed the door and shouted,

"Oh, come on! Seriously Vampire, what are you still doing here?" This snap of anger was just proving how worn my patience was.

"Isn't it obvious… Professor?" he asked in a cool, calm tone that only managed to make me snap further,

"No actually, it's not… not even for a professor," I replied, nearly snarling his sarcastic comment. Then I took a deep breath and tried once again for calm.

"Look, you came to see the box like my father asked and found that even you couldn't open it, so job done, fini, fertig, terminado, you are therefore good to go," I said quoting the word for finished in French, German and Spanish, trying to make my point in an around the world kind of way and yeah, showing off a little whilst doing so.

I'd learned quite early on when growing up that if I wanted to know what was going on around me, then learning as many languages as I could was the key. So, not only was my head mostly in a book, it also meant that whenever it wasn't, it was framed by headphones as I listened to different professionals teaching me foreign languages. My parents used to find it funny to see me muttering different phrases to myself and my mum would always comment to my father, saying 'she is so your daughter.'

However, Lucius didn't look as though he found this little show of intellect as endearing as my parents had.

"I am not here to do your father's bidding, no matter what you have been led to believe." The second I heard this I swear my eyes started to bulge and I had to bite my bottom lip just to stop it from hanging open. Not in nervousness as was my mother's habit and something these days only my dad still managed to achieve. But Lucius didn't stop there, ignoring my reaction to this confusing and surprisingly honest sounding statement.

"Now this is what is going to happen. I am first going to take you home, check just how safe I have been assured that building you live in really is, and then I am going to take that box back to Germany with me where I will have my own people look into it." Okay so if I thought the first part of his admission was shocking, then the second part was downright astounding and quite frankly, bloody cheeky! The noise of disbelief slipped out of my lips in a combination of a scoff and snort that granted wasn't the most ladylike sound I had ever made.

"No, you're most certainly not!" I declared after grabbing the box off the table and clutching it to my chest. Lucius didn't look impressed and for a moment looked at the floor and shook his head. Then, as if coming to a decision, he pushed off the table he had been leaning against.

"Give it to me, Sweet" he ordered, now coming towards me and holding out his gloved hand.

"No," I stated firmly making him frown, fist his hand and then let it drop.

"You know I am just going to take it from you physically, so why fight when you know you cannot win?" he asked me.

"I may not be able to fight you but you're forgetting one thing."

"And what's that?" he asked with a smirk as he looked highly entertained by all of this verbal sparring.

"My father gave the box to me, not you," I stated, straightening my back and holding my head high.

"Is that so? Well, let's ask him then, shall we?" Lucius said in a knowing tone that gave me a bad vibe. He slipped his phone from his back pocket and called my father, now clouding my argument in doubt. Surely my dad wouldn't take it from me now?

"Dom, Salaam old friend," Lucius said as a way of a Persian greeting.

"She is well, if not a little angry," he then said after it was obvious my father had asked after me.

"In this case I believe it is with me, but that is unsurprising considering I am about to take possession of the box she is currently clutching to her chest," he said in an outright admission. One that was surprising enough for me to hold onto the box tighter as if any minute now he would pounce.

"He's not having it!" I shouted loud enough that I knew my father would hear it. I waited as it was obvious my dad was now asking what had happened to make Lucius think taking it was for the best. And this was when I knew that I was screwed.

"There has been a breach of her safety," Lucius told him making me gasp and knowing now exactly why he had called my father. I could hear his roar of anger from where I was stood, and Lucius even held the phone away from his ear for a second. Then I heard the one worded growl from my father after his initial outburst was over,

"Explain!" he snapped.

"Three men were waiting for her when she got to work with intent to take the box. I was detained by a decoy that caught my attention when I heard two others asking a member of staff which room she worked in. I got to her moments later to find all but one dealt with," Lucius told him, relaying all that happened in a composed tone, perhaps knowing it was the best way of dealing with my father. After all, once upon a time they used to be friends and worked side by side as Lucius had started demonic life as his right-hand man.

Lucius paused a second listening to my dad asking his next question and I only knew what it was when Lucius answered,

"Human." I could then imagine my father taking a large sigh of relief at this point as his greatest nightmare was me encountering something I couldn't handle...like a Supernatural.

"She did well, Dom..." Lucius told my father pausing to look at me and the look he gave me was this time most definitely one of respect. Was he proud of me for fighting back? I couldn't help but blush as I quickly looked down at my tan boots.

"However, I do not know how well she would have fared had I not got here in time and shielded her from the rain of bullets heading her way," Lucius added and when I glanced back he was still maintaining eye contact with me and making me wince at the memory. Because Lucius had saved my life yet again and now he was using that fact against me, knowing now that my father would, without a shred of doubt, side with him on this one.

"Calm yourself, Dom," Lucius said to my dad's obvious outrage that was being blasted down the phone.

"She is safe now and I intend it to stay that way and one way of doing this is by taking the object they desire out of her hands and therefore taking her out of harm's way." Lucius listened to whatever my father had to say, which turned out to be the last thing I wanted to hear.

"I knew you would agree," Lucius replied before agreeing to something my father asked, something that I only understood when he held out the phone to me,

"But of course... Your father wishes to speak to you." I felt like groaning aloud but instead stuffed the box under one arm as I took the phone from him.

"Are you alright?" This was my father's first question and the tense worry in his tone was easy to pick up on.

"Dad, I am fine...nothing I couldn't handle," I said making him growl back at me,

"And the gun? Handle that could you...?! By the Gods, Amelia, when I think of what could have happened!" My father's anger was mounting by the second and after closing my eyes a moment as the guilt washed over me, I then shot Lucius a dirty look. He didn't have to do this. However, it was a glare that seemed to be ineffective.

"Dad please, I am fine and..."

"Well, thank the Gods Lucius was there! Now you will give him the box and that is that," he said sternly.

"But that's not fair, you gave it to me to decipher and..." My dad quickly cut me off.

"Fair? Amelia Faith Draven, do you think it's fair knowing that I was the one who gave you a damn box to look at in the first place, one which ended up putting your life in danger!?"

My father asked me, and it was clear by the anger in his voice that he blamed himself.

"It wasn't your fault, Dad, you weren't to know," I told him, hating the idea of him feeling guilty.

"No, I wasn't but that is no excuse. At least now I may rectify that mistake…Give Lucius the box, Fae." My father told me in a tone that broke no argument and also using my family's nickname for me. Faith or Fae was what I usually went by and I was only ever called Amelia when I was in trouble. Which told me that right now, my dad was trying to be stern without pissing me off enough to argue back and damn him it was working!

The second I had come to England I had wanted a total change, which included giving people my first name when they asked, which surprisingly got changed to Emmie by my friends. No one here knew me as Faith or Fae and I had never even heard Lucius refer to me as anything but Princess or, on the very few and recent occasions, Amelia.

"Fine!" I said in defeat. Because I knew that deep down it was because I wasn't like my father and had no supernatural gifts. Well, other than being able to spot them, which was pretty useless in a fight.

So, it meant that without being like him or the other supernatural king that stood in front of me now, then I had no chance at getting them to trust that I was capable of keeping the box without getting hurt. And to be honest they were right. Because if Lucius hadn't walked in when he had then I would currently be bleeding out on the floor and my death would have all been in vain because they would have simply taken the box anyway and literally it would have been…

Over my dead body.

"Good girl." My dad said making me sigh, thinking that yeah, that was always the case wasn't it. I was always the good girl. Just that little teenager who did what she was told while secretly felt lost in a room full of people she didn't belong in.

When I didn't reply my dad decided something else needed to be said,

"Fae?"

"Yeah Dad?"

"I am proud of you, kiddo," he told me, no doubt referring to the human ass kicking I had issued the bastards that had tried to attack me.

"Yeah." This was my only response back and it was one that was said in a deflated way that spoke volumes as to how I was feeling. In the end I didn't say goodbye to my father as instead I just handed Lucius back the phone and slumped down onto one of the stools feeling as though all the fight had been zapped out of me. And Lucius never once took his eyes off me.

"The two I left alive are in my custody." Lucius answered my father's obvious question, no doubt demanding to know what was to become of the three men that had attacked me.

"What do you think, Dom, I'm going to host them a fucking tea party? Of course I am going to question them!" Lucius snapped, freeing a breath of that usual cool exterior momentarily. Then he went on to say,

"And trust me when I say it will be my own personal brand of torture, have no fear of that," Lucius snapped back, once again losing a slice of that famous, deadly, calm composure of his.

"The shooter is dead, and my only regret was that it wasn't by my hand," Lucius added again in response to another question asked by my dad.

"Someone cast a Hex upon him, for the second he started to speak his…" Lucius paused and glanced my way as if what he was to say next was both difficult to comprehend and so disturbing that he didn't want to say it in front of me. But then my father must have been getting impatient because I could hear him snap,

"What? Speak Luc!" Lucius released a sigh and then shocked us both when he finally told us the horrifying truth…

"…His soul began to rot."

CHAPTER FIFTEEN

SECOND NON-DATE

"**H**is soul began to rot."

I gasped when hearing this and stared at him in utter shock that something like that could even be done to a person. Okay, for a human such as myself or even a supernatural, then death only meant there was still a life left to be lived after this one…*The Afterlife*. Now whether that meant Heaven or Hell or the realms in between, it didn't matter, for your soul would live on in some way.

Of course, there were ways to destroy a soul, but this was usually a job left to the Gods to decide. So, to hear of a Hex that was powerful enough to eradicate a soul just like that was… well, it was basically unheard of or at least it was for me.

I don't know what my father's response to this was as I had been lost for a moment in my own thoughts, but managed to bring my mind back to the room just in time to hear Lucius assure my father in whatever it was they were now discussing,

"It will be done, Dom." Then just before he hung up he added,

"Until my next update then," as a way of goodbye. The second he ended the call he then held his hand out to me and I had no choice but to hand over the box.

"Alright, but will you at least let me know what you find?" I asked in a hopeful tone.

"I am sure your father will pass on all he wishes you to know." This was his arrogant reply making me glare at him in return and slap it into his hand with a little more force than what was needed.

"Well, if that's the way you want to be then fine, have a nice flight home and I hope none of the engines blow up on that private jet of yours," I responded dryly as I grabbed my bag and jacket and quickly left the room…or at least tried to. The door was wrenched out of my hand and slammed shut without Lucius so much as twitching a finger.

"You're acting like a child!" he accused, making me clench my teeth and coil a fist full of my jacket in anger.

"What? By going home because I am no longer needed…? What do you expect me to do, sit around and wait by the phone like a good little *Sweet*, hoping someone will call and include me in this…uh no, I don't think so!" I snapped making sure I snarled the word Sweet, now hating it almost as much as princess.

"Well, you could at least finish your working day like your boss would expect you to," he argued making me look utterly shocked.

"Are you being serious right now?" I said frowning and shaking my head a little. His only response however, was to fold his arms across that massive chest of his and raise a brow, hence giving me his 'serious' pose.

"So, let me get this straight, I have come in to work on my day off, I might add, only to find three men that were waiting for me in hopes of kicking my ass or even killing me for this damn box! Then having to defend myself before I was made to watch in horror as I was about to get shot!" I snapped but I was long from finished, even if he had started to open his mouth to say something.

"Then I was made to watch a man literally melt from the inside out, which is now officially top of my 'shit I want to forget and burn from my retinas' list, only then to be told that I have to hand over the box I just defended with my life," I said but again, I was far from done and paused long enough so that I could slam my handbag and my coat down on the table before shrugging my shoulders as I said,

"But hey, my father's proud of me so what should it matter and as for you... well, you don't even give a shit enough to grant me a quick phone call to tell me what you found...and this was all with a damn hangover, before a cup of tea because my bloody milk was off, putting on a bra that tried to stab me and before anything to eat because I lost my damn muffin on the floor thanks to those bastards! So, excuse me Lucius, Mr Almighty, if I just want to go home and try to forget this day ever happened!" I shouted slamming my hands down on the table as I let the rest of my frustrations and events of the day flow out of me. And what was Lucius' only response to this...

"How does someone's bra try to stab them?" I growled and snapped,

"Well, you're not a girl, so just add it to the list of shit you don't have to deal with and leave it at that!" This made Lucius' lips twitch as if he was fighting a grin, which only managed to make me even angrier to the point where I held up a hand giving him a warning,

"Don't you dare laugh." Needless to say, this wasn't one he took seriously but thankfully all he did was release a sigh before shocking me with what he did say next.

"Come on, I'll drive you home."

Now, not only did I find his response to this outburst surprising, but it was more what came directly after it that shocked me the most. Because Lucius grabbed my jacket, handed me my purse and then said…

"But after we've had lunch."

"Well…this is different," I said as I got out of the car along Hereford Road, that was opposite Leinster Square. It was a road framed either side with two rows of tall terraced buildings, that were mainly white. Each had three sets of large windows above the few shop fronts we now stood in front of. I don't know what surprised me more, the fact that it didn't look fancy or that Lucius would pick somewhere that wasn't fancy?

Like last night, Lucius helped me out of the car before the driver could and soon I was stood on the curb looking up at the brown restaurant with its canopy extended out and with the name of the place over it. It was called 'Hafez'.

"You brought me to a Persian restaurant?" I questioned the second I knew what it was. Lucius didn't answer me but instead opened the door and nodded for me to enter. So, I walked past the few tables and chairs it had outside under the canopy and stepped inside. Then I watched as Lucius approached a man who came rushing from behind the counter. We were the only ones there even though it was lunch time, so it was strange that the rest of the place was empty. Not that it would have taken a huge amount to fill it as there were only ten, maybe eleven tables in the whole place.

Shortly after Lucius had announced that he was taking me for lunch, I had found myself being led from the museum in a quiet and stunned state of mind. I was sure Lucius took this as an after effect of just being attacked and watching a man self-combust into a body boil by supernatural means. Which meant that before I knew it I was stood next to him outside the gates of the museum where he handed over the box to someone in exchange for a new leather jacket. I gathered it was someone who worked for him as they nodded respectfully when Lucius had issued his orders in another language, this time annoyingly, one I didn't know. Then his car pulled up and we were on our way.

"Salaam, old friend," Lucius said as he greeted the man in an openly warm way and was a new side of Lucius I hadn't seen before.

"Salaam, Mr Septimius, it is good to see you again and I see that you have finally brought a young lady friend with you," the man said nodding to me and looking pleased. I couldn't help but feel my heart flutter slightly at knowing I was the first girl he had brought here, not caring one bit how childish that feeling was.

I gave him a beaming smile in return and shook his hand,

"Hello, I am…" I was about to introduce myself when Lucius cut me off and he did this in two ways, one which was more shocking than the other. First, he wrapped an arm around my shoulders and pulled me closer to him whilst introducing me himself,

"This is my girlfriend, Amelia." The second the words were out of his mouth I had been forced to quickly act as if my heart wasn't trying to beat its way out of my chest. Then I also had to try to ignore the way my whole body froze by his side and try and focus on saying that simple greeting. Lucius even gave my side a squeeze as if to prompt me further which finally managed to do the job.

"Salaam," I said, knowing the word for peace and was what was most typically used as a greeting with the Iranians.

"And this is one of the restaurant's owners, Amir." Lucius said introducing him like you would an old friend.

"Salaam," he repeated the greeting back and then held out his arm and said,

"My old friend, you may have whichever table you wish, for today they are all yours." Lucius nodded his thanks and picked one in the corner by the window. Then, as I was shrugging out of my jacket, I felt Lucius' hands come to my shoulders and help me to remove it.

"Thanks," I muttered shyly turning to see Lucius had handed it, along with his own, over to Amir. He placed them both over the back of a nearby chair first so that he could get us settled into our seats.

I subtly glanced to one side as Amir was about to hold my chair back for me but with a slight shake of Lucius' head he stepped back. I then pretended not to notice how Lucius took his place and pulled back my chair making me fight a smirk.

I was beginning to think that Lucius had some kind of issue with people assisting me with things, because so far, he hadn't let the driver help me either. Or thinking back, even when the security guard I knew well had been about to open the door, Lucius had got there first, ushering me out of the exit with his hand on my lower back. To say that this was all a little confusing was a huge understatement, but that seemed to be the nature of the beast, for Lucius was nothing *but* confusing!

"You have been gone a long time, my friend, I feared you had forgotten us," Amir said smiling and obviously teasing him.

"I had little reason to bring me to London until now," Lucius answered carefully, and I suddenly felt guilty as it was obvious that I was that reason. Amir grinned down at me as Lucius took the seat opposite and replied,

"Ah, but now I see you have big reason to visit," he teased, obviously referring to me and for all the wrong reasons. Lucius looked directly at me as he answered him, this time in a teasing tone himself.

"No, no, she is still a little reason...don't you think?" And then he motioned with a flat hand up and down a little to indicate my height making Amir laugh, especially when I shot him a look of shock.

"Careful my friend, for I can see it in her eyes, this one has a fire in her belly just waiting to burn you if you continue with your wicked ways," Amir replied, and Lucius in response muttered,

"Yes… and burn she does." Meanwhile I was left wondering what it was he meant by that…or by any of this to be honest, for my head had felt like it had been spinning ever since I woke up this morning and it had nothing to do with my hangover and all to do with Lucius.

"Do you wish to see the menu this time or will you order your usual dishes enough for two?" Amir asked but my mind was too focused on what Lucius had meant by his reply to worry about what it was I was going to eat. So much so that I hadn't realised we were alone until Lucius turned his gaze back to me.

"Oh, did we order?" I asked wondering if he was coming back with the menus.

"I did." Lucius replied, obviously fighting a grin.

"And that was?" I asked not surprised that this was all the answer I received.

"You will have to wait and see," he replied, almost playfully. I released a sigh and gave up, instead turning my attention to the rest of the room. The restaurant was just a decent sized room, that had white walls decorated with different pictures here and there all in different styles. For example, directly next to us were eight pictures all the same size, all hung in a thin plain frame that each held a colourful abstract design. But then above the next set of tables was what looked like an antique painting set in a thick gold gilded frame, holding a scene of what looked like men all sat feasting around a small table set in ancient Persia.

On the opposite side of the room was a section of exposed brick with three lamps in between even more artwork and calligraphy paintings. The hardwood flooring had a lovely patina on it due to age and in the center of the room in a curved recess on the ceiling was a lovely chandelier that was a collection of teardrop shaped glass lamps.

A bar stood at one end with a cute light feature above. It ran the length of the bar horizontally in a long rectangle and was made up of dangling dessert spoons, dinner forks and teaspoons all fixed on a metal rim with lights at its center. It was a piece that was a beautiful example of utilizing discarded objects for a new purpose.

As for the table settings, they were classic and simple with not the usual overabundance of cutlery to choose from. And as we sat next to the window, our view offered us the picturesque sight of a typically busy London street at lunchtime. However, it was now that I noticed Amir had flipped the front door's sign so that it now said closed. I gave Lucius a questioning look, before asking him why.

"I like the privacy," was his response.

"Yes, but won't that be bad for business?" I asked, unable to let it go and not thinking it very fair on the poor owner to lose out on the lunch time rush. Lucius gifted me with a smile that I suspected meant that he found me endearing.

"Don't worry, Princess, I'll make sure he is well compensated." This was the part where I started frowning.

"Why do you have to call me that?" I hissed, unfolding my napkin just for something to do.

"Why do you hate it so much, it is after all, what you are," Lucius argued back, making me want to throw my fork at him and see if it stayed there, preferably embedded in his skin! I released a deep sigh and said,

"I walked away from that life for a reason and you being

here and calling me that just...well it just..." I said pausing as I struggled for my words.

"Just what?" he asked, trying to push the reason from me, which in the end I had no choice but to follow through with.

"It just stirs up bad memories, okay. Can we drop it now, along with calling me Princess?" I snapped making him look thoughtful a moment as if he wanted to explain something to me but instead thought better of it. So, in the end, he just shrugged his massive shoulders and said,

"Fair enough." After this we fell into a comfortable silence...well, for Lucius anyway, as for me it was pure hell. I swear I couldn't stop fidgeting and spent the whole time trying to suppress the urge not to bite the tips of my fingers off. In the end our drinks came, one I didn't order, so when a bottle of still water was placed down in front of me I frowned down at it... after thanking the waiter first of course.

"You're dehydrated, something that tends to happen when a human has a hangover...or so I believe," Was Lucius' sardonic response, that now made me shift my frown from the bottle directly to him.

"Yes, *us humans* do tend to get dehydrated with a hangover, but as I am an adult do you not think me capable enough to decide on whether or not I wanted water, um?" I asked, making him look bored as he gazed off to one side before telling me,

"I don't give a damn if it's what you want or don't want... it's what your body needs and that's what counts." I rolled my eyes and shook my head a little, thinking it was like being sat opposite a related control freak who thought it was his position in life to control me and my life. Which is when I couldn't help but mumble to myself,

"Seriously, what did I ever see in you?" Of course, he heard it and his response was almost as shocking as me saying it. He burst out laughing and I found myself utterly mesmerized by

the sight. I swear just the sight of his bare neck and I was almost drooling. In fact, he was still chuckling when he called Amir back over so that I could order myself a diet coke. Amir even looked at him as if he had never once heard the sound of Lucius' deep laughter before and I had to say that it made two of us.

"So…do you come here often?" I asked after his amusement had simmered down, however, the grin playing at the corner of his lips was telling me that it had far from passed. But then I wanted to slap my own forehead the second he pointed out something embarrassing.

"You know that sounds like a pick-up line you would hear in some seedy bar," Lucius commented, and he was right it totally did, but instead of admitting to that fact I retorted,

"Then no doubt it is one you have said often." This verbal sparring was obviously one he was starting to enjoy because once again he was smirking.

"Perhaps," was his one worded comment and I had to admit, it wasn't one I relished hearing, now only having images of Lucius picking up women or should I say unsuspecting victims in a bar.

"In answer to your question, I have been coming here for years as it serves the best Ghormeh Sabzi," Lucius said before the silence between us could linger too long.

"What's that?" Lucius looked surprised that I didn't know and the obvious reason for this was down to my dad's heritage.

"What, can you really see my dad cooking for us all in the kitchen?" I asked chuckling.

"Hell, I am sure he wouldn't even know where it was if it hadn't been for my mum's love of cooking, and trust me, Ghormeh Sabzi isn't her specialty." At this Lucius laughed again, only this time it wasn't the full head thrown back type. But it was cute all the same and gave a warmth to his face that was beyond handsome. In fact, it was one you could easily fall in love with. I found myself twisting the napkin in a fist on my lap just as if the thought had physically pummeled me in the chest.

"I am just surprised you have never tried Persian cuisine before," Lucius admitted with a shrug. I then thanked Amir for my coke and downed nearly half the glass making Lucius raise a brow at me.

"Alright, so maybe I was a little dehydrated," I admitted.

"Yes, well little good that artificial poison will do for you," Lucius commented dryly. I frowned before folding my arms and then nodding to his bottle as I said,

"Oh right, and that stuff popped straight up from a natural spring, did it?" He grabbed the bottle of beer and grinned at me as he took a long swig.

"Nope, but it tastes damn good though."

"Yeah, well right back at ya," I said, taking a sip of my own.

"What is that stuff anyway?" I asked, trying to read the label that he currently had hidden in his large hand.

"It's saffron beer." I pulled a face that said it all and Lucius grinned before tipping the bottle my way, saying,

"Here, try some."

"Oh, I don't think s…" I was cut off the second his right-hand closed round one of mine. The same electricity ignited the second our skin made contact and I swear he felt it too when his fingers flexed against my hand automatically. Then he placed the cold beer bottle in my hand and applied pressure on top of my fingers so that I would get the hint and take the bottle.

"Just one sip," he urged in a kind of hypnotic purr and he may have not had control over my will but that didn't mean he was without strong powers of manipulation. For I did indeed now feel like the puppet dangling on the end of his strings as he had mentioned not long ago.

So, with a nod of encouragement from him, I took a long swig, unable to care too much about the flavour as my mind was just thinking about the fact that I was placing my open mouth directly over where Lucius' lips had just been. Needless to say, it tasted delicious and again, I wasn't just talking about the beer.

"It's good." I said, trying to keep my voice steady and without giving away the inner meaning to that statement. I passed him back the beer and watched as he took a swig of his own, only this time without taking his eyes off me. It was as though he was daring me to say something. To comment on the fact that our lips had received but a small taste of each other and what I was desperately waiting for…

One kiss from a Vampire King.

A short time later and our Persian stew, Ghormeh Sabzi, was served along with aromatic basmati rice and a side of Tahdig, which turned out to be a crispy rice crust. Before this we had a quick starter of freshly baked Persian Lavash bread which was served warm and was a kind of thin flatbread. It was served with an assortment of dips and the only one I recognised was hummus. However, it wasn't just the fact it was delicious that was the reason it was my favorite course. No, that was because it was a meal we had to share and therefore there were more than a few occasions that our hands would touch when we were both reaching for the bread to tear a piece off.

Of course, the main was pretty good too as it turned out that Ghormeh Sabzi was a Persian stew that was a mixture of sautéed herbs, kidney beans and lamb. It also had to be said that the smell was alluring, and the taste was definitely unique.

"So, how was your first experience with authentic Persian food?" Lucius asked, surprising me that he genuinely seemed interested to know.

"Really good, I loved the…uh, what did you call it, the

crispy rice thing?" He gave me a warm smile that nearly made me breathless as he spoke the word with perfect pronunciation,

"Tahdig."

"Uh, yeah that," I said with a blush, making him hide a smirk behind his fingers as they tapped on his lips.

"What?" I asked, really wanting to know what it was he was thinking behind that hidden smile. But he shrugged one shoulder slightly and at the same time he raised his fingers from his lips in a silent gesture, one that told me he wasn't going to explain himself. No, instead he raised his hand so that Amir came rushing over.

"Do you like desserts?" Lucius suddenly asked me, and I nodded enthusiastically replying,

"I don't trust anyone who doesn't." This made him laugh again and I swear if this had been a real date, then I would have secretly been congratulating myself for it going so well. Which was why I had to bring myself back down to earth and remember that it wasn't. Far from it in fact, because coming back down to earth was one where Lucius and I were miles apart.

Miles apart and with an ocean of indifference in between. And what was I doing? I was drowning in it that's what. I was drowning in my own ocean called hope and he was happily sailing away on his boat called nonsensical. Because I was human, and he was a Vampire King who would live eternally.

And no matter how many times I made him laugh, it just didn't matter.

Nothing was building that bridge...

Across a supernatural ocean.

CHAPTER SIXTEEN

HOME, BITTER SWEET HOME

I shook off this inner battle that was sticking around the edges of my mind and creeping in like old cobwebs of doubt blowing in the wind. They just kept coming at me until just one thing was all it would take for them to come floating back.

"Sholeh Zard, Lotfan," Lucius said briefly looking to Amir and it was obvious that he was ordering something. I knew the word 'Lotfan' meant 'please' in Farsi, so it made sense. And I was right, because the next course to be put down in front of us was a dessert. It was a small bowl of something yellow and was set like a custard tart only without the pastry. It had a pretty little display on the top with what looked like some brown spice and slices of almonds.

I leant forward a little and took a sniff, looking back up at Lucius as if needing his guidance here. He chuckled and picked up my spoon, passing it to me before saying,

"Here, try this." I rolled my eyes at his sarcasm but did so without being able to suppress my grin completely, especially because he looked so good smiling, damn him! I dug my spoon in and took a bite and the second I did, I wished I hadn't. I held the spoonful in my mouth far too long and started looking around hoping that Amir couldn't see me. Meanwhile, Lucius burst out laughing and the second he did, I had no choice but to swallow, pulling a disgusted face like my features were melting off.

"Here." He offered in an amused tone as he passed me the water that he had ordered earlier, half of which I had already drank because he was right, I had needed it.

"Not a fan, I take it?" Lucius asked after I had stuck out my tongue a few times in hopes the air would help, damning ladylike behavior all to hell, a place ironically where this dessert must have been invented! Okay, so that was harsh but let's just say that I wasn't a fan of fragrant cold rice, rose water, saffron and cardamom all together with nuts on top.

"That would be a big fat no on that one…*what was that?"* I hissed behind my hand after looking to make sure I wasn't about to insult Amir.

"Their version of the traditional Persian dessert Sholeh Zard," Lucius told me before picking up his own spoon and taking a mouthful. Gods, even watching him eat was turning me on!

"Amir, please get the lady some ice cream, I am afraid the dessert is not to her taste, *she usually craves something sweeter,"* Lucius said calling out to the owner, making me first blush in shame and then the heat in my cheeks was there for another reason. As the way he said this last part was as though there was a sexual meaning hidden in plain sight.

Amir walked a few steps closer and asked what flavour I would like after giving me the options.

"Chocolate please."

"Chocolate." Lucius and I both answered, shocking me.

Amir smirked as if he could see something big was happening when it wasn't and no doubt getting the wrong impression. But then, was it any wonder considering how Lucius was acting. For starters during this whole meal he had been like a different person and I for one had never seen him looking so relaxed and at ease. He had laughed, teased, joked and conversed with me as if this had been…well, *an actual date.* As if not only an hour and half ago he hadn't run into the room and acted as a super human shield before then aiding in killing a guy, watching him melt as if someone had stuffed a lit firework up his butt.

But then again, was a day like this considered the norm for someone like Lucius?

Shortly after this Lucius was taking my jacket from Amir and helping me into it, creating a shiver that zip lined all the way up my spine the second he let his fingers graze across every bit of my body they could find. And I suddenly cursed the decision not to become a nudist when I first turned eighteen.

Then his hands lingered on my shoulders after my jacket was on, making me question why he hadn't yet let go. But then he turned his gaze to Amir and I guessed it was because he still had an act to portray that I was his girlfriend. But wait…why did he want to pretend that? Because, if there was one thing I definitely knew about Lucius, it was that he generally didn't do anything that he didn't want to.

"Khoda hafez, my friend," Lucius said nodding to his friend and in return Amir did the same. After this we left and again Lucius portrayed the perfect gentleman as he held open the door for me as he always seemed to do.

"What did that mean?" I asked him the second we were back in his chauffeured car that no doubt cost half of the flats in my building combined. Lucius turned to look at me before giving his answer to the window as we drove away from what I very much suspected was his favorite restaurant.

"It means 'May God protect you'," he said in a quiet voice and it was then that I finally understood why he acted this way. Let's just say that God and he weren't exactly on the best of terms and leave it at that.

After this, silence descended until I could stand it no longer, as it was one of my biggest weaknesses…*awkward silences.* But as it turned out that after I spoke, I quickly vowed it was one weakness I was now promising myself to be mastering, because then it would have stopped me from blurting out shit like,

"Why have you never taken a woman there before?" The second I asked I wanted to take it back and prayed so hard I felt a vein popping just for him not to have heard me. But this was Lucius we were talking about, so of course he bloody did!

"Why would I?" was his question back to me, which had me stumped.

"Uh…well, that is what someone usually does on a date." I reminded him making him scoff,

"I don't date, sweetheart." I would be lying if this little piece of information didn't make my heart sink a little, but then when he added to that last sentence, it didn't just sink, it thundered against the bottom of the bloody ocean floor. One so deep that the surface was merely a speck of a dot of light above me.

"I fuck, plain and simple." I swallowed hard and couldn't help but flinch at the sound of his harsh and unfeeling tone as if having a woman in his bed was a chosen commodity. I found I had no choice but to look out of my side window or I would have just ended up giving too much away the second I couldn't stop myself from asking one last question.

A question I knew I never should have voiced but what choice did I have? These last few days, seeing him this way, as more of a man than the King I had walked in on that day. The day I had stupidly stumbled into his kingdom and ran away from it leaving my heart behind.

Did he really have no idea what he had done to me?

Did he really have no idea what he was doing to me now?

So, no, as much as I hated to ask the question I knew that I had no choice but *to* ask him.

"Then why did you take me?" His answer was even more confusing than from the dark and dangerous root the fruit of where that question had grown from.

Crushing it in his hands the second he spoke.

A thing called *faith*...

"Because it's just you."

———

Lucius and I didn't speak again after this and for once, I let the awkward silence roll over me like a comfort blanket. This time knowing that at the very least it meant he wasn't hurting my soul with his words.

With regards to how Lucius was feeling or what he was even thinking, well like always that was anyone's guess because as usual he gave away nothing. I swear it was like looking at a different person to the man I had been sat opposite to back in the restaurant. He had been so at ease back then. As if he wasn't just letting you into a secret slice of his world, but also a small peek into the root of his soul. Jeez, but I was starting to sound like a hopeless romantic when in reality I was just plain hopeless.

No, all I needed was to go home, say goodbye to the day by drowning my sorrows in the rest of that bottle of Prosecco in a bath full of bubbles. All the while toasting the asshole in my life who was unfortunately, both the man of my dreams and of my nightmares.

But then, as I was planning the rest of my day ahead which of course included going to the toilet at some point, I suddenly shouted just as we were passing a Tesco Express (which was a smaller version of the large supermarket chain that was popular in the UK).

"Stop!" I actually made Lucius jerk in the seat next to me.

"I mean, you can just drop me off here," I added so that Lucius could stop looking at me as if I had lost the plot.

"No," Lucius said firmly, and the car continued on.

"That's fine, I will only end up walking back this way anyway," I said crossing my arms and making Lucius growl.

"Look, I know this might be a foreign concept for you, but us *humans* need little things called groceries and things like toilet rolls are kind of important to us," I said in a condescending tone because let's face it, it was needed. He looked at me and sighed, giving in and telling the driver to turn the car around.

Well, being chauffeur driven to Tesco was certainly a first for me. The car pulled up on the right side of the road so that I didn't have to try and cross the traffic. Which I was thankful for as getting run over by a car was really the way to go and top off a day like today, I thought rolling my eyes at myself.

"Okay, well I guess this is goodbye and…" I had started to say after turning around back to face him with my hand on the door frame, one I had to let go of as I paused mid-sentence.

"…Wait, what are you doing?" I asked the second he followed me out of my side. He ignored me and my question, instead going over to his driver's side window and telling him,

"Wait for us."

"Erm, I don't think he is allowed to park there," I warned but one look from Lucius told me that he didn't give a damn. I knew this when he said,

"Let them ticket me." This blasé attitude to breaking the law and parking in the way of people shouldn't have been surprising to me considering I had not long ago witnessed him nearly killing a man.

"But…but…what if the police come or…or…" I started to say making him pause a step before coming back to me. Then he hooked my chin with his gloved hand and tilted back my head in an affectionate way, that once again was playing havoc with my mind.

"Then we'd better be quick, had we not, before we get into trouble," he said in a teasing tone that told me the type of trouble he meant was the private moments like this that we shared. Alone in the world yet surrounded by the echoes of life.

I swallowed hard as was quickly becoming habit around him and his own habit in return was watching the second I did it. Then he tapped on my chin twice before letting go of me and saying,

"Come on, little rabbit, let's get you those much-needed human provisions you seem so passionate about." Then he actually winked at me before taking my hand in his to pull me into the shop. I didn't know what my mind was focusing on the most, the fact that he was going grocery shopping with me or the fact that he had winked at me?!

And also, I don't know why but the nickname 'little rabbit' was finally one I found cute and for once, not patronizing. However, now all I wanted to do was ask him why he called me it and wondering now, if he would again.

The automatic doors slid open and let us inside. I reached for a basket, one which Lucius quickly took out of my hand without saying a word. I wanted to tease him about being such a gentleman for a Vampire but admittedly I was too afraid to do so. I watched as he scanned the shop as if assessing it for a threat and I wanted to laugh. I didn't know exactly what threat he was looking for, but I suppose after today, then it was bound to put someone on edge.

But England wasn't usually a place where supermarket cashiers, banks or even petrol stations were held up at gun point and if it did ever happen then it was usually big news. Then again, I guess this wasn't very surprising considering there were practically no guns in the country. So, unless you were a farmer, then to get one was extremely difficult.

Don't get me wrong, crime still happened, just as it did in the rest of the world. But the difference being was that hospitals weren't usually dealing with gunshot wounds or accidental deaths where, Gods forbid, a child happened to get hold of their parent's gun.

I think everyone had the right to defend themselves, especially in their own home. However, if you knew when a home invasion happened that they weren't armed with a gun and your trusty baseball bat would be just fine, then those were injuries that people could usually survive…unless of course you had the swing of a once Viking king like Ragnar, my old colossal bodyguard who could barely flick you and make you fall over.

The sound of Lucius clearing his throat finally jarred me out of my thoughts and I mentally started to make a list of all the things I needed. So, I walked down the aisles like a woman on a mission grabbing things and putting them in the basket Lucius was holding. He didn't say anything but just watched me as if this was the first time he had ever seen a woman shopping before and he was curious.

Well, to be honest, I couldn't exactly imagine Lucius buying his own food as he had an army of minions to do that for him and I wondered just how far down that food scale did someone have to be to be put in charge of something like his laundry?

I knew that once my mum had moved in with my dad she

had soon made sure things had changed in that regard. Which was why I was used to seeing my mum cleaning and cooking and even on occasion making my dad do the same. I remember asking her once after hearing her muttering to herself about 'annoying cleaning day' why she didn't just let other people do it.

She looked up at me from the bathroom toilet she had been cleaning, put down her cleaning products and sat back on her legs. Then she told me that when she first met my dad that he was so lost and grown apart from humanity, that she felt it her mission to try and change this. I asked her why he had got that way and she told me that after years of living in a world as a king, whose only job it was to care and maintain a way of life for his people, well then, he had never known what it was like to care for himself.

He had never cleaned a day in his life unless it was wiping the blood from his weapons. He had never once cooked a meal for himself or washed an item of clothing. But then he met someone who started life as a human and little by little things began to change. His respect for human life started to grow the more he allowed himself to be around them and essentially to understand them. But what my mum had told me really changed him was when I had been born. Because here he was, the King of the Supernatural world with a human baby he utterly adored and rendering him for once in his life something other than a king...something greater.

A father.

So, as that new role started to take root, he then became just like any other parent. He would find himself getting his hands dirty with changing diapers, preparing bottles, bath time, getting me dressed and when I grew older, even learning how to braid my hair. Something my mother laughed at when he made her vow never to tell anyone, for he feared his enemies would no longer consider him as a feared warrior.

My mum even told me that once, after a particular bad explosion of baby poo, she found my father hunched over the sink in the bathroom scrubbing it out of my clothes. It was in that moment that she finally knew that her husband had most definitely found his humanity.

Because there was a time he would have just burnt it and declared he would just buy me a new one. But the reason he didn't, my mum learned, was because it was his favorite dress on me and he feared that to use his powers might damage it beyond repair, something he didn't want to risk at the time. So that day my mum taught me a valuable lesson. She taught me that no matter how much money we had or how many people there were who could do other things for us, that sometimes it is worth doing these things ourselves so that we may be thankful for what we have.

So that we may be thankful that we were alive. It was in that moment that I knew, without her even saying it, that at some point in her life she had truly believed she was going to die. She also quickly added,

"Besides, I wouldn't ever wish upon my worst enemy someone to have to clean this loo, especially after I just made your father's favorite, 'Kazzy's Demon Chicken'." After this we had both burst into a fit of giggles and still found ourselves chuckling as I picked up a cloth and helped her clean the rest of the bathroom, before then taking the cleaning stuff and doing my own.

After that day I had vowed to become more independent, which was when my mum taught me how to cook, do my own laundry and basically fend for myself...I had been ten years old at the time. Now, of course, I lived on my own so had no choice but to do these things, which included grocery shopping. But at least now, when I am washing or cleaning, I would always think back to that day and continue the chore with a smile on my face as I thought about my mother.

However, Lucius looked as though he had entered another realm where the strange monsters of the human world roamed...

The dreaded 'Shoppers!'

I smirked at the thought as I picked up a bag of tea bags and a jar of jam. I also picked up some bread, milk, ham, cheese, a pizza from the frozen section that I always had in my freezer in case I couldn't be bothered cooking, which during the weekdays was often. Then I grabbed the much-needed toilet rolls stuffing them under my arm because the basket was nearly full, and I knew I wanted a box of cereal so left room for it.

"Mmm, what to do?" I said to myself as I stared at the shelves.

"What seems to be the dilemma?" Lucius asked me, making me jump as it was said very close to my ear.

"They are all out of Crunchy Nut Chocolate Clusters Cereal," I said as if this was the worst thing ever, and well, it kind of was. Because I could have eaten a bowl of the stuff for my three meals of the day and still never get bored of it. In fact, I usually bought at least three boxes whenever I got my food delivered but well this week, what can I say, I had been a little preoccupied. I heard Lucius chuckling next to me and I looked up to see him looking highly amused.

"What?"

"It's nothing," he answered with a shake of his head, done not so much in way of an answer but more because it was as if he didn't know what to do with me.

"No, go on, what's so funny?" I asked again, determined to get it out of him.

"Alright, it's just that today you had three men show up and try to kill you. Then you were shot at, just before you had to watch as a man…how did you describe it…"

"Melted like a firework was stuffed up his butt?" I added this time making him throw his head back and laugh, causing every female within the immediate vicinity to pause whatever it was that they were doing and stare at the Godly sight before them. I swear I was surprised that none of them threw their panties at him like he was some sexy man on stage rocking it out with a Fender in his hands.

"Yes, that. Then, you are forced to hand over a puzzling artifact that is obviously in your nature to crack and yet they don't have your favorite cereal and you look as though you are close to tears," Lucius told me, making me fight a blush. In the end I grabbed a box of frosted flakes, dropped it into the basket and said,

"Well, good food is important to some, Mr Authentic Persian Cuisine." This comeback made him smile.

"Touché," he said warmly, making me grin.

After this I got in line at the checkout fully aware of the amount of people staring at us or should I say…*Lucius*. But then again, what wasn't there to stare at as Lucius didn't really give the female population a chance. Incredibly tall and built like an Olympic athlete who does body building on the side, meant that he looked like a living Adonis. With his sandy coloured hair in a messy style that just screamed that he didn't give a damn and got out the shower, rubbing a towel over it before it dried naturally that way. Or was it his chiseled jaw line and perfectly shaped lips that had women ready to sign over their ovaries and beg him to make babies with them like I was close to doing right alongside them?

Okay, so that was a bit much as I liked to think we as a species were blessed with a little more self-control than that. Even if it didn't stop a girl from fantasising. But then there were his eyes. Eyes that seemed to have the power to pierce your very soul, capturing it and only releasing it again when his gaze was no longer blessing you by being directed your way.

The silver grey with flecks of blue that looked like ice over water. The colour reminded me of a storm that was brewing, rolling in over clear blue skies and consuming them. Even the sandy blonde brows that slanted across his deep-set eyes gave him a dark angelic look that would have fooled anyone naive enough to believe that he was a man to be trusted with your life in his hands. But then, hadn't he had my own life in his hands twice now and each of them he had chosen to save it?

Lucius nudged me from behind and I looked up to see that a cashier was now free and waiting for me to approach.

"Oh, right," I mumbled before taking the basket from him, as I stepped forward and placing it down on the counter. Then I waited for the lady to ring up my stuff and noticed the way her eyes kept wandering to the man at my side, making me want to lean forward and say, 'I know, ridiculous how handsome he is isn't it, should be illegal if you ask me.' But thankfully, I squashed down the urge. Then it came to paying and just as I was still fishing out my card from my purse, Lucius had taken control. I looked up to hand it over to see Lucius already had his own fancy black card in the reader.

"Uh…what are you doing?" I asked, making the cashier smirk.

"What does it look like I am doing, paying for your goods with gold doubloons?" was his sarcastic response and I laughed, unable to help myself, something that stopped suddenly when I just caught in time him enter his pin number. I frowned the second I realised it was, unbelievably… *my birthday*.

Okay, so what were the chances of that, like ten thousand to one?

"Thank you, have a nice day," the lady said, prompting me

to reach for my bags, ones that were quickly grabbed by Lucius first. I watched him nod to the lady in thanks and I mumbled a thank you before following Lucius out of the shop with my mind doing the bloody hopscotch, bouncing all over the place!

"Hey, why did you do that?" I asked, catching up with him and grabbing his sleeve jacket to hold him back.

"Do what?" he asked like it was no big deal and therefore *I shouldn't be making a big deal out of it.*

"Why did you pay for my stuff?" I demanded to know instead of saying what I really wanted to know, which was how come my birthday was his pin number? Of course, I didn't because of how potentially embarrassing his answer could be, which would mostly like be, 'Oh is it, that's a coincidence but hey wait, you didn't think it was intentional or anything did you? Because why would I do that when I don't care for you'… you know, that type of mortal embarrassment.

"Why do you think, naturally to hurry things along, which I believe is the opposite to this," he said looking down at where I still held on to him, preventing him from moving unless he yanked out of my hold.

"Oh." I said disappointed, letting my hand slip from its hold, shamefully thinking his reason seemed logical enough. Then he nodded to the car, no doubt trying to get me to hurry up, which I decided right now was for the best, as the sooner we got back to my flat, then the quicker it was that I could get back to my life, one where Lucius didn't feature in it.

To be honest though, I didn't actually know how I felt about this because no matter what I knew was best for me, it didn't mean that I didn't want what was clearly bad for me. But it was like having an addiction you knew was bad for you, rotting away at your core like the way smoke does to your lungs.

So, after getting back into the car and soon pulling up outside my building, I had mentally prepared myself for saying goodbye and forcing myself this time to move on. And who knew, this may even mean that Peter and I would have a chance to take things further with the hopes that deeper feelings would grow.

If I were being honest with myself, then really with claiming that my heart belonged to Lucius, I was setting myself up for a fall. Because then I would have to admit that there was never a chance for me to find happiness with another person. Now was this really something I was prepared to give up on finding for the rest of my life? What if true love was out there waiting for me and I don't mean the type found only in Disney movies. The ones where all it seemed to take was a stroll through the forest, singing at woodland animals to make a guy declare that he was madly in love with you.

Again, my thoughts were interrupted the second we arrived, and I noticed Lucius getting out of the car. I followed his lead and did the same, but before I could reach for my bags, he beat me to it. Again, I wanted to comment but it just seemed like the time for teasing was long gone and now all he wanted to do was say goodbye and have done with this little 'London Mess'. Which meant that we were both silent all the way to my flat door and as I reached to take the bags from him he nodded to the door for me to open it. Wow, talk about efficient, he wasn't kidding around when it came to doing a job.

"It's okay, I can take it from here," I told him, not knowing how I felt about him being inside my tidy little private space that was, up until now, a Lucius neutral zone. The last thing I wanted was to live in a place with the memory of him lingering around like a ghost of time, haunting my mind. I just wanted to unlock the door, scream bye bye now, in a barefaced lying kind of 'it was nice knowing you' sort of way and slam the door in his handsome face.

But then he frowned down at me and ordered,

"Open the door, Amelia." The way he said my name again made me want to shudder. So much so, that instead of being able to argue against him, I had to turn away just so that he wouldn't see how much the sound of my name coming from his lips affected me. I swear that I would still be hearing that voice of his whispering it in my ear this time next year.

I shuddered at the thought before doing as he asked.

But then, as I unlocked the door and opened it, the sound of Lucius' voice was the least of my problems.

Because the moment I walked inside there was only one thing that happened.

I screamed as…

My world had been invaded.

CHAPTER SEVENTEEN

HOME INVASION

I screamed first in shock and then in anger the second I walked inside my once perfect space only to see that it had been trashed. Someone had broken in and totally smashed up the place. Lucius suddenly acted on impulse turning into dominant protector mode. He dropped the bags, grabbed my arm and spun me so that he was suddenly pressing me up against the door. I swear it was almost worth the home invasion for that single moment alone.

"Stay here and don't move, do you understand?" he growled down at me and I tried to swallow down the hard lump which wasn't going down quick enough for me to answer.

"I mean it, Amelia, I want your back against this door and you don't move it until I say so, now is that understood?" He said more determinedly this time. I nodded, thinking this was the best course of action with an angry Vampire stood over me looking like some coiled white tiger ready to pounce at the first sight of danger.

"Good girl," he said tapping me under the chin with a curled finger before he pushed himself back off the door. Then he did a walk-through of my flat making sure no one was still in there. Needless to say, it didn't take long as he only had my bedroom and bathroom to check. Just the idea of Lucius in my bedroom meant that by the time he came out my cheeks were red and hot. Thankfully though, I had just been broken into, so any smart person would put it down to this and not having lust induced hot flushes.

"It's clear," Lucius said as he scanned the floor where it looked like most of my possessions were scattered.

"And not as secure as someone likes to think," he then muttered to himself making me frown and question what he had meant by that. But then I took one look around the place and the comment was quickly lost to overwhelming misery.

"Who would do this?" I asked as I too now looked around feeling heartbroken at seeing everything they had done. All the cupboards in my kitchen were open, some of which were barely hanging on their hinges where someone had just swept their contents to the floor. I knew this because beneath the open doors lay dinted tins, broken jars, cooking sauces splattered on broken tiles with rice and pasta sprinkled on top. Then, next to that were smashed plates, cups, bowls and even my beautiful cake stand that I had bought on sale in one of the country manor house gift shops. I shook my head as I took in the state of my kitchen seeing that even the contents of the fridge were on the floor and I was only thankful that I had been due a food shop or it could have been a lot messier with sour milk added to the top.

"I think it's safe to say they are part of the same group of people that attacked you today," Lucius said.

"Yes, but why, if they already knew I had the box on me?" I asked suddenly remembering the suspicious van parked across the street the night of the gala. Had they been watching me?

Lucius was about to answer me when suddenly I looked to my living room and screamed,

"NO! No, no, no!" I then ran over to my beautiful sofa and picked up the slashed cushions, holding the now unrepairable pieces to me as if this would help. Lucius watched my desperate actions with a frown and what looked like a clenched fist at his side in frustration. He looked very much like he wanted to kill someone.

"Oh no, this is awful! Those bastards! How could they do this!" I ranted making Lucius take a step towards me and saying in a soft tone,

"It's just a sofa, sweetheart, it can be replaced." Now this being said was sweet enough, especially after he had chosen the right time to use an endearment like sweetheart. But unfortunately, I was too lost to my rage. So, I looked up at him, held out my cushion and said,

"No, it's not! Its more than that, Lucius! Me, Ben and Wendy had to heave this bugger up here and then it took me hours to…" I paused midsentence as from the look on his face he just didn't get it.

So, I took a deep breath and told him,

"Look, I am not expecting you to understand here, but this is something I made! I bought it secondhand and then spent hours lovingly re-covering it…Hell, I spent hours washing the bloody thing just to get the old lady smell out of it…and now look at it!" I said in a sad voice looking down at the pinstripe material I loved and threw it aside in my anger.

Lucius looked as though he wanted to say something, but I wasn't finished and for once, I wasn't taking notice of him. Because if I had been then I would have noticed the tender look he had been giving me from the start. But the reason I didn't was that I was scanning for more damage and when I found it I freaked…my precious nerd collection.

"Oh, Gods no!" I shouted before storming over to my shelf and looking down at all the pieces on the floor. Then I bent down and picked up pieces of Lego that quickly crumbled between my fingers to the floor. I felt like crying.

"Just look at this! Do you know how long I spent building this?!" I said as if speaking to myself as it suddenly occurred to me that Lucius had no idea what Lego was or how important it was to a geek like me.

"Whatever it was, it's in a lot of pieces now," he commented making me snap my head up and almost growl at him.

"This is a Lego Death Star that had 4016 pieces! It took me over twenty-four hours to build and now look at it, blood of the Gods but I will be lucky if I even find half of them! And look, they even ripped the head off my Chewbacca." I said shaking my head in sorrow.

"What kind of demon is a Chowbacca?"

"Chew, not Chow…and he's not a demon, Chewbacca is a Wookie," I corrected making him frown.

"And what in Hell's depths is a Wookie?" At this point I stopped trying to get Chewie's head back on and looked at Lucius as if he was the one missing the head. Or should I say that he had five heads and none of them knew what Star Wars was.

"Are you joking?" I asked making him frown.

"Seriously, how is it you have lived this long yet you do not know of the greatest movie franchise ever created?" I asked him in an incredulous tone.

"How about ruling over thousands of Vampires, saving the world a few times, including your troublesome mother's ass, running a business empire and oh, let's not forget doing the few favours here and there whenever your father feels like making me one of his fucking lackies, that's how," Lucius snapped, and I don't know why but it was in that moment that I looked around the room and really felt like crying. Not because of the stupid ass in front of me who had zero tact in this situation when being around an emotional woman who'd just lost everything in her world. But mainly because my beautiful little flat was in ruins.

A shuddered breath escaped me, and I looked down at the floor as my shoulders slumped, meaning Chewie's head and body rolled out of my hands. I heard Lucius sigh before saying,

"Look at me, Sweet" At first, I shook my head, knowing that if I did I wouldn't be able to stop the tears from coming. Then he asked me again and this time when I did I could feel the tears already fill my eyes and one blink was all it would take to make them overflow. He homed in on my eyes just before I looked down again but not before I caught his frown and the sight of him raking a hand angrily through his hair. Then I heard him hissing two words,

"Fuck it!" the second before I was in his arms. I gasped when I felt them wrap around me, pulling me to him and placing a gentle hand to the back of my head so that he could pull me tenderly to his chest. I didn't know what to do at first and kind of just froze solid in his hold, being in too much shock to even breathe.

"Relax, sweetheart, I won't hurt you," he whispered gently down at me and it sounded so sincere I would have sealed it away in my heart as a promise. Then he purred his next command.

"Now take a breath for me." I did as I was told and the second I did it broke the damn flood gates, drowning me with emotions that had built up over the last two days.

It was seeing Lucius again that night of the gala. It was the confusing emotions he stirred up in me yet again. The flirting and teasing that quickly turned to annoyance and irritation. The irrational behavior that was jealousy and over protectiveness.

The lies he told and the gentlemanly actions he bestowed. Then there was being attacked and nearly shot to death, going on a date to a place Lucius had never taken a girl and now standing here in his arms after he just snapped at me. And now being surrounded by the life I had created in ruins, and I didn't just mean my possessions…but more like the vault I had built back up around my heart against this man.

It took me a moment to realise that because of all this I was quietly sobbing in his arms and he was simply holding me close and letting me. I wouldn't have been able to tell you how long this lasted for, but I know that when I heard him utter my name on a barely heard whisper, I knew he was saying it to himself and not to me.

"Oh, Amelia."

"I'm…I'm sorry, I guess it's…well, it's just been a…" I started to say pulling back slightly, so that I could look at him and I was surprised to find that he didn't let me go as I thought he would have.

"Bad day?" he finished off for me making me sniff a laugh, saying,

"Yeah, something like that." Then I reached my arm up in between us and rubbed my nose, making sure it wasn't running. He tilted his head to the side a little as if trying to get a read on me but yet again, he still hadn't let me go. I didn't know what to think in that moment but if I thought just being in his arms was confusing then what he did next blew me away. He let go of my neck where he had let one hand rest the second I had pulled back to look at him. Then he raised it up to my face and tipped my head back so that I was looking up at him before he captured my fallen tears, wiping them away with the pad of his thumb.

Then he spoke,

"Your eyes are always beautiful but when you cry…" he

paused a moment and closed his own eyes as he hissed a curse before continuing,

"Fuck me...they are breathtaking," he told me with such a fervor of lust and emotion in his voice that I didn't know what to do. Didn't know what to think, how to act, how to even breathe again! I was just frozen like time for me had stopped and the world was no longer spinning...it was *paralyzed.*

Because that was the power of Lucius. The feeling that in that moment he had the power to turn back time and heal the fractures he had inflicted upon my heart. And I wanted to hate him for it, but all I could do was love him even more for not breaking it completely, for surely if he had, then I wouldn't be feeling this way now?

This blinding love I felt towards him that was ready to sacrifice the depth of my soul just for one night. Just for one single moment where he made me his and branded himself in my small forever as the one who took my virginity. The first man to claim me, even if the memory of it was only a drop of water in the turbulent waves that was his long eternal life. But for me...

It would forever be my ocean.

However, even after this admission, the kiss I had been desperately praying for never came, as I could see it the second he felt himself going too far. I felt his hands relax their hold before his body followed. He took a step back from me and I couldn't help but notice the way his chest rose and fell in a heavy rhythm. But then again, maybe he also noticed the way I then wrapped my arms around myself to replace his. Did he know it was so that I could keep the feeling of warmth and comfort he had given me for just that moment longer? Fooling my body and mind into believing his touch still lingered, if even for a mere few seconds longer...it was worth a try.

Then his voice shattered everything, and it did so in the weirdest way when he asked,

"This Wendy, how long have you known her?" I frowned at his question before saying,

"For years, why?"

"So, you trust her?" he asked in an assuming tone.

"Yes, with my life," I replied watching as he walked over to my handbag where I had unconsciously dropped it on the floor the second I saw what had happened to my flat. Then he dug out my phone and handed it to me at the same time issuing his orders.

"Good, then call her and ask if you can stay the night," he told me, and I took the phone but argued,

"But my flat, I have to…" This was when he decided big bossy Vampire King was back in play and he growled the next demand at me,

"Just do as you're told." He saw my face drop and must have felt guilty about it or something, because he lowered his stern tone and actually said,

"Please, Amelia, just this once, do as you're told… yeah?" And because of this I nodded and tapped on her number making him sigh in what looked like relief.

"Yo Smock, you get laid yet?" she asked making me blush when I saw Lucius raise an eyebrow at me in question. I turned away from him and hissed down at the phone,

"No! Gods Kirky, so not the time!"

"Oh Christ, what's happened now, did you fall off the toilet whilst painting your toe nails and break your coccyx again?" I groaned aloud knowing again that Lucius could hear her, and I was just thankful that I was never going to get these two in a room together seeing as embarrassing me was like her second job!

"I didn't break it…it was…it was just sprained," I argued

hissing at her making her chuckle.

"Uh, not sure you can sprain your tailbone, sweetie, and I was with you remember…oooh, do you remember the sexy doctor that was totally flirting with you and asked you about grabbing a coffee…man, why, oh why doesn't shit like that ever happen to me?" I rolled my eyes knowing that Lucius could still hear all of this and I looked over my shoulder at him to see that he was looking more than pissed off with his arms crossed.

"Firstly, you're not clumsy, not even in the ridiculous heels you wear, so no chance of doctors asking you out and secondly, he wasn't that sexy and it was unprofessional of him to ask me out," I said still whispering, although with Lucius only a few feet away it was pretty pointless. However, it was enough for Wendy to pick up on.

"Why are we whispering?" she asked mimicking me.

"Because I am not alone, that's why," I told her making her squeal down the phone and I held it away from my ear giving Lucius a shrug of my shoulders and a nervous little chuckle.

"Oh my God, you hussy! You did it, didn't you!? Oh praise the lord above she is now a…"

"Kirky! Just shut up a second okay!" I said seriously before she blurted out the embarrassing truth that I was a twenty-seven-year-old virgin to the man of my dreams and the very one who I had been saving it for all this time, like some hopeless romantic in some period drama waiting for her soldier to come back from war or something.

Man, I was pathetic! To the point I would have shaken my head at myself had he not been in the room.

"Why, what's wrong?" she finally asked, getting a hint on my panicked voice and becoming the good friend I knew I could rely on.

"Okay, so don't freak out but someone broke into my flat and…"

"Holy shit! Are you okay? Were you there? Are you alright, are you okay? Jesus, Emmie, talk to me!" she said repeating herself in a high-pitched tone of panic.

"It's okay, I'm fine, just my place is trashed and I just wanted to know if I could sleep with you tonight?"

"Yes, of course! You know you don't even need to ask," she replied making me release a sigh of relief seeing as I didn't really fancy a night on my own tonight. Then I turned around to face Lucius and nodded yes, that she would, when really, I didn't need to because he could hear it for himself.

"Great, I will grab some stuff and head over in a bit." After this I said goodbye and hung up only to find Lucius on the phone, this time giving orders to someone else.

"I want that surveillance footage with me in the next ten minutes, everything in the building and within a two-mile radius." Lucius listened to who was on the other line and suddenly shot me a look before saying,

"What no, not Caspian, he will scare the shit out of her! No send me Ruto and tell him to bring D, I want everyone on this and I want these fuckers caught yesterday, do you understand?!" he snapped, pausing to listen again before snarling a deadly promise, one that made me shiver.

"Your only job is to keep them alive long enough for me to deal with them and deal with them I will." I swear seeing Lucius this way should have had me running for my life not turning me on as it was doing. Okay, so it was official, I needed therapy!

"Take them to the warehouse, I will be there this evening…I have a few things to deal with here first," Lucius said looking to me once more as I was currently picking up any of the figures that managed to survive the attack and looking as though I was not listening, which I certainly was doing.

"And get Liessa to call me." The second I heard him utter

the other woman's name I swear my heart skipped a beat and the Star Trek original communicator I got three Christmas's ago snapped shut from the pressure I applied with my tense fingers. Who was Liessa? Oh, Gods please don't say that she was his girlfriend. I don't think I could cope with that on top of everything else. But how was I to find out? It wasn't as if I could just casually drop in the conversation, 'So are you seeing anyone recently?' Oh yeah, just been broken into and this was what I was focusing on…okay, so note to self, google therapists in my area the second I was alone.

"You need to pack a bag," Lucius said making me realise that he had finished on the phone and was now talking to me. I nodded getting up from my knees now noticing my slashed rug and thinking that another trip to Ikea would be happening in my immediate future. Then, as if on auto pilot, I walked into my room and hunted around for my bag, wanting to suddenly cry again when I saw that even most of my clothes had been slashed.

Well, even if I didn't scream like I felt like doing, I must have made a noise of distress of some kind because Lucius was suddenly in the doorway and found me sat slumped on the bed, with my beautiful bedding in shreds as well.

"What is it?" Lucius asked with his hands on either side of the door frame looking ready to turn the wood to pulp, he was that tense. I looked down at the heap of cut material in my lap and said in a small voice,

"I don't have anything left to pack." Lucius followed where my gaze was focused, and I heard the wood splinter like before, only this time he didn't even bother to fix it, and why would he…look at the place, what was the point! I hated the idea that I might have to use my father's credit card because, realistically, there was no way my meagre savings were going to cover all this!

"Alright, Sweet forget packing, let's just get you to your friend's place," Lucius said after obviously needing a minute to compose his anger. But after that minute when I didn't move, I jerked the second I felt his hands come to mine and I looked up to see him crouched down in front of me, trying to pry my hands from one of the funny T shirts I had been bought years ago.

It had a picture of a toothbrush and a toilet roll talking with each other. The toothbrush said in a speech bubble, 'I hate my job' and the toilet roll's pissed off reply was in another speech bubble that just said, 'Seriously?'

"My Aunty Pip gave me this T-shirt," I told him for no particular reason other than the fact it was as if I needed to tell someone, before it was lost in some bin somewhere.

"Figures," Lucius said with a chuckle as he saw it for himself with the way I was still trying to hold the two pieces it was cut into back together. That's when I remembered that he knew Pip well, as she and her husband Adam used to work for him back before my mum and dad got married.

"Come on sweetheart, let's get you out of here," he said gently, taking my hands and pulling me up to stand in front of him.

"But what about my clothes?" I asked looking around and trying to see something that I could take…even my damn underwear had been cut up!

"Let me worry about that," he said pulling me from the room and I had to look down to check I wouldn't trip up on anything as my stuff was scattered everywhere.

"But, but I…" He cut me off by stepping closer to me and placing a leather covered thumb across my lips as he gently ran his fingers down my cheek. Then he looked down at me and asked me only one thing,

"Do you trust me?" I thought about my answer for what

seemed like an age but in reality, must have been only a minute. I knew this because I am pretty sure Lucius was the type of man who didn't like waiting for anything, let alone my answer. But no matter how long it *did* take me, I couldn't help but really think about the full depth of that question.

Did I trust Lucius?

Well, I think that after today and what happened many years ago then I could safely say that I trusted him with my life. He had proved himself back then and today after placing himself in front of me and taking I don't know how many bullets for me.

"Amelia, I asked you a question," Lucius said again, obviously getting impatient and making me realise he had been waiting what must have been a minute too long. Which was when I noticed that for some reason this seemed important to Lucius and now, along with everything else, I was asking myself why?

So, in the end this was why I nodded a 'yes', not trusting myself to speak in that moment from fear of what I might blurt out if given the chance. To ask him why he cared if I trusted him or not. To question why in fact, he hadn't taken one look at my flat and said, 'nope that's it, I'm out, my job is done, I have the box now have a nice life and good luck cleaning this shit up'.

But he was still here.

So, in the end, the answer that I had given him had been a 'yes', I did trust him but even as I nodded my head and gave him the answer he was looking for, I knew deep down that it was only half true.

As there was still one big part of me that didn't trust Lucius.

Because the truth was, I didn't trust him…

With my heart.

CHAPTER EIGHTEEN

TEXT ME A TORMENT

"Okay, so explain to me again why it is we have a bodyguard outside our door," Wendy said after handing me a much-needed glass of wine before she joined me on her couch. Her apartment was also in Twickenham as she'd moved closer to me a few years ago. As, in her words, she was sick of catching one taxi, one bus and then the underground just to get back to her old apartment after seeing me and to be honest, I had felt the same. At one point, we had even talked about moving in together, but she couldn't yet get a mortgage for her half of the flat we would buy, so she was saving up for a deposit. I told her I didn't mind but she refused, saying she needed to pay her own way and as I already owned my flat, we decided to wait. Unless of course one of us just so happened to get married first, but two years on from this discussion and that was still yet to happen.

So instead, she found herself a cute one bed place that we had lovingly painted and scrubbed within an inch of its plasterboard thanks to the previous tenant having an attachment to weed. It wasn't only the smell that gave this away but mainly the big cannabis leaf that was painted on one wall in what would be Wendy's bedroom. I remember her showing it to me for the first time and we both just stood in the doorway staring at it. I said the first thing that came to mind,

'Now, I am not an expert here, but I am guessing that would be a big mood killer in the bedroom?' Of course, I wasn't just referring to the homage to the plant but more the slogan that had been written beneath it in spray paint, which read…

'Me Biatches be getting high'

'I know right, I mean you would have thought he would have at least spelled bitches right, the dumbass!' Wendy had replied making me say,

'What do you expect, this fine fellow and obviously upstanding pillar of society was too busy getting himself and his 'biatches' high…give him a break would yah.' We both burst out laughing and spent the rest of the day feeling sorry for the poor people that used cannabis for actual medicinal uses, spoiling it for everyone else.

But now there wasn't a gang sign, drug sign or biatch in sight and the only rude words were in the many erotic romance novels that were sat on her shelf.

No, instead her flat was as bright and as girly as you could get. It was true to say that Wendy liked bold colours and her favorite theme was 70's pin-up girl. Her walls were mainly cream, with one painted hot pink and all the skirting boards, covings and door frames were painted turquoise blue. Then on the pink wall she had a huge canvas of a black and white pin-up girl lay back on a piano sipping on a cocktail and looking seductive.

On the opposite wall above her black and white patterned

couch she had twenty plus pin-up pictures all in different frames and different sizes. A fluffy white rug and pink painted coffee table I had helped her carry back from some overpriced high street shop sat at the centre.

The rest of the theme carried on in her entire flat and I swear there was so much pink that if a guy ever did want to come in for a nightcap, he would take one look at the place and his balls would probably shrivel up to the size of raisins before dropping off...yes, it was that feminine.

"I mean not that I mind, because bloody Nora, but could that guy be any hotter?!" Wendy said fanning herself as she sipped her wine, stopping it from overflowing. She was, of course, referring to the 'bodyguard' that Lucius had assigned to watch me for the evening, making sure the assholes that trashed my flat didn't come back. I had only found this out the second Lucius took my hand and lowered me into the car. But then my mind had still been spinning from his goodbye, as he was leaning down between the open door resting all his weight on the frame as he kissed my cheek.

Then he said,

"It's been fun, Sweet but do me a favour and try to stay out of trouble." I had been about to say something witty in return when he whispered against my skin this time what sounded like a promise,

"Until next time."

After this he shut the door but not before giving a nod to someone I'd only just noticed was sat in the car with me. His name was Dante, to which Wendy had blurted out the question after I introduced them,

'Like the inferno?' making him clear his throat once as it was clear he didn't know how to respond to that. Thankfully, I saved him by nudging her inside before the drooling commenced, which I had to agree, was definitely not an overreaction. It turned out that Dante was a seriously good-looking guy, that was if you were into the Jason Statham look and swapped the British accent for a southern American one. And if I hadn't been so obsessed with Lucius, then I would have added that he was totally dreamy and sexy as hell to that list. But in the end, I hadn't needed to for Wendy happily did this for me after only getting a quick glimpse of the guy through a crack opening in her door.

However, there was a little more to Dante than meets the eye, or should I say, a lot of something. Because there was something Wendy didn't know and that was that the dreamy, hot guy wasn't human.

Dante was what was known as a Drude, which was known as a malevolent, nocturnal demon whose specialty was the creation of nightmares. They had a strong influence over a person's dreams when their victims were asleep, and they could tap into that lucid state and take control. Of course, the nice ones would often prevent nightmares too and favour a more sexual experience from their 'feeding'. You see most Demons and Angels fed from the emotions of others and it wasn't just as clear cut that all Angels were good and all Demons were bad. Not like a library full of history books would have you believe anyway. And Drudes were no exception for they fed from the emotions invoked by dreams, but more often than not a sexual high was just as strong as a fear induced one, or so I was told.

Which made me wonder what type of Drude Dante was?

They were also known as expert hunters and could smell the presence of witchcraft from ten miles away, which was another reason I suspected Dante had been a good choice as a protector, seeing as we knew someone was casting Hexes.

Dante was as tall as Lucius and built like a brick shithouse, although to be honest, I am not entirely sure where that phrase originated from considering there was nothing shit about the man. He had a deep yet surprising softly spoken voice for such a large man. It was in a smooth sexy way that said, 'I can lure you to sleep with a single story' and added to that, my southern charm. I had heard that this had been like all Drudes as it was part of their gift. To be able to send people to sleep, even other supernatural beings, with just a few whispered words.

Dante was also bald with a full black beard cut close to his face and his thick neck joined even thicker muscles. But his main feature were his eyes and like most handsome men, they were startling. Although granted, they weren't as mesmerizing as Lucius' were, but they were certainly ones that would cause you to look twice.

They were a light olive green colour with a burst of hazel around the pupil that sometimes, when he spoke to you and smiled, looked like flecks of illuminating honey. And smile was something he did often as I had only been with him in the car for about fifteen minutes and he had made easy conversation and when he did this, he did so smiling.

But I wasn't as fooled as another may be around him, as for one, I knew what he was and two, he worked for Lucius so he was bound to be a badass and no doubt one of the most powerful of his kind.

You see, Lucius was known as somewhat of a collector of powerful beings. Asking them to join him by offering Lucius their complete loyalty in return for, well… kind of an upgrade. He would turn them into Vampires creating hybrids of sorts that would mean their original powers would be increased fifty times over. But in doing so, you were also tying yourself to Lucius as not only your King but also your soul's master. He had complete control over these beings and let's just say, after over two thousand years of collecting, he didn't just have an army, he had his own kingdom!

This was what made Lucius such a badass King and one

most definitely to be feared because he was one that once you accepted his blood, then you were in essence binding your life to his and paying for that upgrade of power with your very soul. For he owned you and your soul for the rest of your eternity...*or his.* Because it was said that if he ever died, then so did a whole nation of Vampire hybrids...

My mother included.

Which also no doubt meant that Dante was the same. A 'Blood convert' as it was often referred to in supernatural slang. I had heard the term growing up, but it took me a while to find someone who would actually tell me what it meant. See, considering I had grown up surrounded by some of the most powerful angels and demons the world had ever known, I had led a surprisingly sheltered life, thanks no doubt to my overbearingly overprotective father.

Which meant that it had taken me years of digging to gain all this information and thus became the reason for my love of books. My one source of knowledge and let's just say that Afterlife had one hell of a big ass library!

"Yes, he's hot," I replied after she obviously wanted me to confirm this.

"So, like I said, you are so going to have to explain this to me again, because I am seriously at a loss here... which is crazy given that my imagination is coming up with everything from Mob Boss' daughter, to someone in witness protection program and your real name is Betty Miller from Jacksonville!" I laughed and asked,

"And what do you know about Jacksonville, North Carolina, um?"

"Okay, so I heard Ryan Adams sing about it in some of his songs once, but that is so beside the point here." I laughed at her before taking a much-needed sip of my wine.

"Come on Emmie, you have to give me something here,"

she pleaded, and she was right, as much as there was that I *couldn't* say, there was also equal amounts that I could.

"Alright, so you met my dad."

"Mr Hottie of the Year, yeah kinda hard to miss that one," she responded sarcastically, laughing when I scrunched my nose up.

"You know it's gross to know that you fancy my dad, right?" I told her making her shrug her shoulders and drink back her wine.

"Okay, so let's just say that he's influential, rich and has a business in just about everything."

"And he's married you say?" Wendy asked with a raised brow, making me throw a spotty cushion at her the second she put down her wine glass.

"Kidding, kidding...and yes I know you have said before, madly in love with your mother, the love of his life...Jeez, touchy much." I rolled my eyes and said,

"Anyway, that day my dad came to visit me he brought me something to look at, an artifact," I told her.

"Oooh, and here comes the juicy bit," she commented, making me groan as she was forever the journalist.

"So, it turned out that some people want it."

"What type of people?" she asked with her beautiful big eyes growing even bigger.

"Bad people, Kirky, very bad people," I replied, hoping now that she would take it seriously.

"Jesus, so what, they turned up at your flat trying to find it?"

"Well, yeah, but after they turned up at my work first," I told her, no doubt already saying too much. Now her beautiful green eyes bulged slightly, and she reached for my arm.

"Oh my god, Emmie, are you okay, did they hurt you? Jesus, but this is serious shit here...have you called the police?"

"Wendy, calm down, it's fine and I am fine," I told her quickly before her mind could run away with her.

"I mean look at me, don't I look fine?" I asked, now making her give me a sceptical eye.

"Yeah, actually you look great, but how is that possible after everything you have been through today?" she asked, frowning.

"Well…I kind of had help and well, he's…"

"He? Oh my god, it's him isn't it? Mr Mystery sexy voice himself?" My blush and coy look said it all.

"It so is! Oh, please tell me that he flew in and saved the day like some kick ass action hero we drool over. Oooh, like that Thor guy we fancy," she said making me smirk, thinking oh just you wait, as Thor has nothing on Lucius. For one he didn't need a big hammer when he had hands that could do just as much damage, if not more. But, then again, I had no idea what he was packing in the downstairs department as that could have been classed as his 'big hammer', I thought with a smirk.

"Oh lordy, he's even hotter isn't he? I can tell by that look that you think he is. Jesus, why can't some drug lord come after me when Mr Inferno is outside my door to save me?" Wendy said, making me chuckle as she had a habit of calling all men a 'Mr' nickname and I had a feeling that Mr Inferno was going to stick.

"Oh, you have it bad for him, don't you?" I questioned as she gazed at the front door in that dreamy way. Her head snapped back up and she blushed, something Wendy hardly ever did.

"Maybe," she confessed in a coy tone.

"Then why don't we invite him in?" I asked, making her suddenly look panicked.

"We can't do that!" I laughed, never seeing her like this about a guy because she usually had this, 'I could eat that man for dinner' type of attitude whenever she was hit on. Although, in her defense, she was never approached by the big muscly types that she was attracted to. She was a sucker for a big guy who could throw her curvy frame over his shoulder without breaking a sweat. Well, Dante certainly fit the bill on that one.

"Why not?" I asked, chuckling.

"Well, for one, he is working," she argued, which again was unlike her and the second I saw her ringing her hands on her skirt I knew it was because she was nervous.

"Yes, and I would say keeping us safe was just as easy to do in the same room as us than it would with a door in between." I made the obvious point, making her smirk.

"Alright, but first things first, pits, hair and makeup," she said grabbing my hand and pulling me up, making me nearly spill my drink. I quickly placed my glass down before she pulled me to the bathroom which looked like a place you would go to pay homage to being a girl. Yep, it was that girly and it was clear that Kirky had a consumer addiction when it came to beauty products. I sat down on her toilet (after putting the fluffy pink lid down) and picked up one of her many creams from the shelf behind.

"What the hell does this do anyway?"

"I don't know, what's it called?" she asked raising her arm and giving her armpit a swipe with her roll on anti-perspirant.

"Vitamin C Glow Boost," I read out.

"I think it's supposed to make you look ten years younger or some shit like that," she said with a wave of her hand.

"So, you want to look fifteen again?" I asked smirking, seeing as she was only twenty-five, a little factor she was clearly forgetting.

"Oh, hell no! Are you kidding me, who would want that… no Jesus, going back to being a spotty teenager with braces on my teeth…no thank you," she said, making me laugh. Which is when she turned to me and noticed something,

"Hey, you're not wearing your glasses today, any reason for that?" she asked making me suck in my lips and shake my head before saying an unconvincing,

"Nope" She gave me a pointed look and I added,

"What? I just fancied the change, okay."

"I think doth protest too much," she said chuckling and hitting a nerve because the truth was, I doubted that Lucius even knew that I did wear glasses, seeing as every time he had seen me I had been wearing contacts. A pair I might add, that I had stupidly slept in last night. But hey, a few drops of solution and they seemed good for another day.

"So, whilst I try and make myself look naturally irresistible, you can tell me everything that has happened, and you can start from the very second you found yourself with a hot date last night, who thankfully for you, wasn't your dad," Wendy said, making me release a big sigh before I took another deep breath and told her all that I could.

Not surprisingly, it took up all the time she was getting ready.

After about an hour of watching Wendy getting ready and spending half of it trying to convince her that a swing, polka dot dress wasn't classed as at home casual. And she couldn't exactly class it as the 'just slipped into something more comfortable' category, she finally changed into something else. She now wore a pair of three-quarter length jeans with a thick red belt and a T shirt that was horizontal black and white stripes that also had an anchor on the front entwined with roses. She had the longer part of her pixie cut pinned back on one side with a red bow attached. She looked so pretty and cute all at the same time and her red glossy lips were ones that could tempt any man to kiss them.

Which was a shame that when we opened the door and I invited Dante in, his answer had been a stern,

"No." I frowned up at him and then asked,

"Why not?"

"I'm sorry, little Miss, but I have my orders," he replied in a less grumpy way this time and I wasn't sure I was feeling the 'little Miss' nickname. Meanwhile, I shot a look to Wendy behind the door who was looking very disappointed. I smiled at him and said,

"Okay, leave it with me," making him frown in confusion before I closed the door again.

"Well, that was a waste of my good perfume," she said in a deflated tone.

"The night's not yet over, my friend," I said going to my bag and retrieving my phone. Then I brought up the number for Lucius and typed out a text message, holding my breath when I clicked send.

It simply said,

'Hello'

I thought I would start off simple to see whether or not he took the bait. For starters, I wasn't even sure I was allowed to text him, so I thought it best to test the waters first. Then I waited, thankfully not having long before my phone buzzed.

"Is that him?" Wendy asked now coming to sit down next to where I was curled up on the couch feeling like a bloody teenager and this was a crush I had at school who was messaging me for the first time. Well, to be fair, I had never felt like that because it wasn't as though I had dated much in school. Not with my dad being the scariest most intimidating man in town that was for damn sure! I think most of the people in the small town I grew up in had thought my mum had sold her soul to the Devil when they heard the two of them were together. It had been big news and the main source of gossip for years later.

Of course, with one look at Wendy and her eager expression, then I would have to say that this was her own bit of juicy gossip. I couldn't really blame her as she had known me for years and in all that time nothing exciting had ever really happened to me. Except, of course, clumsy falls and trips to the Emergency room, like the 'tailbone' nail painting disaster.

'Hello, Princess, how may I be of assistance this evening?' was his reply, making me both want to growl and smirk at the same time…damn sexy Vampire. Of course, this was another little factor I had wisely left out.

'I thought I told you not to call me that' was my reply, but his was even more shocking. To the point once again by habit, my mouth actually dropped open.

"What? What is it?" Wendy asked as my face must have said it all.

"He sent back a winky face!" Wendy burst out laughing and then said,

"So?"

"Well, let's just say that Lucius is not the emoji using type of guy," I replied making her say over the rim of her glass,

"Well, clearly he is." Then my phone buzzed again, and I swear my heart felt like it was going to beat its way out of my chest. I felt bloody giddy!

'Ask your question, Sweet' The second I read it I swear that I could almost hear his voice asking me right by my ear and making me shiver.

"Oh my god, you have got it so bad!" Wendy said making me shoot her a look.

"What makes you say that?" I asked, trying to play dumb and innocent all at the same time.

"Uh, because you have read that same one line four times now…oh, and the sappy loved up grin on your face is kinda screaming it to the world."

"A little over dramatic, but yes I will admit, I might like him a little more than I originally let on." Wendy laughed at my reply and said,

"Oh, you think?! Anyway, you're acting skills are utter shit so it's not like I'm shocked here." My phone buzzed again, and I jumped, nearly dropping it and making Wendy mutter into her drink,

"Yep, totally smitten." I rolled my eyes before unlocking my phone to read yet another message.

'I am still waiting' was his silent warning. So, I typed back,

'Does Dante have a girlfriend?' I asked making Wendy screech,

"You can't send that?! Are you crazy?"

"Why not?" I asked, frowning.

"Because he will get the wrong idea. Just ask if he can come in because you have a single friend, but for the love of God, don't just send that on its own without explaining." I could see her point, but then again, Lucius wasn't interested in me in that way…was he?

Well, that was the million-dollar question wasn't it, one of many I seemed to be asking myself lately. But Wendy was right, that was a little too blunt even for me to blurt out. So, I started to try and delete it but ended up tapping the wrong button.

"Ooops," I muttered before the true horror of my mistake set in.

"Oh no, what did you do?"

"I might have accidently sent it," I replied with a grimace, then I winced the second I felt it buzz again.

"Oh dear…what was his reply?" This was when I looked down and read,

'That depends' he sent back, making me frown.

'On what?' was my reply, just because I was curious. Of course, what I received back made my heartbeat work double time.

'On if you want his death on your hands?' My mouth unsurprisingly this time really dropped as I re-read it over and over again. Did this mean Lucius was jealous? No, surely not.

"What did he say?" Wendy asked getting excited and before I could stop her she grabbed the phone off me. Then she read it and released a dreamy sigh,

"Oh boy, looks like you're not the only one who has it bad," she told me.

"No…surely not? Do you think?" I asked trying not to get carried away here. But she just popped her gum and said,

"Oh yeah," in an over exaggerated way before taking a sip of her drink. So, before I could ruin it or get poor Dante a one-way ticket down to Hell, I texted back.

'It's not for me! It's for my friend, she thinks he's hot' was my response in hopes he hadn't already been trying to find me a replacement.

'Is this friend of yours suicidal?' I laughed, and this time held my phone to my chest to stop her from grabbing it out of my hand.

"Oi, no fair!" she complained before getting up to refill our glasses. I stuck my tongue out at her and went back to replying.

'Not suicidal but perhaps a little crazy'

'She would have to be, Dante is dangerous' he replied, making me roll my eyes before wondering if I shouldn't be a little daring in my reply here? In the end I typed out my reply four times before closing my eyes and tapping send so that there was no way of going back.

'Some women like a bad boy' Then I swear I was on tenterhooks as I waited for his reply.

And then when it finally came, there was only one way for me to take it as it was as clear as day.

It was a warning.

A warning for me to stay away…

'And those who do usually end up getting hurt'

CHAPTER NINETEEN

INTIMIDATING INFERNO

A *nd those that do usually end up getting hurt'* When his warning came back in answer, it spelled out a clear message and one that made my heart sink into a pit of misery. In fact, I was just typing out my goodbye text when another message came through,

'Unless of course they're the type of woman who can snap human bones and win in knife fights ;)' I swear his reply nearly made me drop the phone! Was he actually saying what I thought he was saying? Or was it just a harmless bit of flirting? At first, I had no idea how to respond to that and had to take a moment to down a large gulp of wine just to steady my nerves. And he wasn't even in the same room as me!

'So, what you're saying, is that some men want a woman who can kick their ass?' was my brave and cocky reply. I swear I couldn't keep my face straight as I waited impatiently for his reply.

"I take it by that look you're still flirting and haven't even got to the reason you text him?" Wendy asked, making me smirk and say,

"Pretty much." Then I jumped again the second his reply came in.

'More like a woman who can take a firm hand' Now what the hell he meant by that one I didn't know, but I blushed all the same as I knew how I personally took it.

'Now for the real reason you messaged me' He sent directly after and I had to say I was a little disappointed to know he no longer had time for me. But then again, I had definitely received more from him that I ever would have thought, so I couldn't be too unhappy.

'I asked Dante if he wanted to come inside and join us so that Wendy could talk to him, but he said he wasn't allowed' Even to me, once I re-read it, I realised that it sounded childish and now I was regretting it.

'I am glad to hear that he can follow orders' was his curt reply.

'But I don't see why not, he can protect us just as well from inside' I complained sending one back quickly before I chickened out. The reply however was not the outcome I had been hoping for.

'This isn't a fucking dating service. He's there to do a job!' I sighed and let my shoulders slump, feeling as though I had been told off for being a naughty girl.

"Well, any luck?" Wendy asked, and I shook my head.

"Afraid not, sorry."

"Oh well, I guess I will just have to go ahead and stare at the back of his fine bald head out of my peephole for the rest of the night." I laughed at this but seconds later I couldn't help but find myself looking down at my phone and re-reading through all the messages. It was a shame it ended on a sour note. I had been enjoying our flirty sparring.

Then, just as I was releasing another disappointed sigh, there was a knock at the door. Wendy and I both looked at it as if it was a foreign concept. Then we both launched off the sofa and ran to the door, stopping to compose ourselves just before we opened it.

"Lucius said that I was to guard you from inside," Dante said, looking surprised himself as he was still holding his phone as though he questioned if he really had received that message or not, one that was still lit up on his phone. I stepped back and let him in and the second he did his eyes automatically went to Wendy. She blushed from the heated look Dante was giving her and looked visibly shaken by the sight of him. She even turned her back as it was obvious that she needed a minute to get herself together enough to form words. So, I decided to help her.

"Uh, welcome I guess...so would you like anything to drink, I think there is a beer in the fridge?" I asked, knowing that there was from the last time Ben had been here. He sometimes tagged along, having met Wendy a few times and fallen madly in love with her (not in a romantic way of course, on account of the gay girly friendly thing) so it wasn't surprising that we all hung out together on a regular basis. And well, this was one night he would no doubt be gutted to have missed out, considering the sight of the man candy that just walked through the door.

"Thanks," he said nodding and unbelievably the first words out of Wendy's mouth were,

"Drinking on the job, that's not very professional of you." I shot her a look behind his back the second he turned to face her, that silently screamed 'what the hell?!' But then I watched as Dante gave her a deadly grin and openly looked her up and down and from the look of things, he definitely liked what he saw.

"Don't worry sugar, I can handle it, don't you go worrying your pretty little head over it," Dante replied giving her a wink and then turning around to take the beer from my hand. Meanwhile, Wendy looked as if she was going to have a heart attack or at the very least, need some smelling salts as clearly, she was having palpitations.

"Uh, Emmie, a word please," Wendy said all of a sudden in a tense tone and I followed her retreating frame into the bathroom, unable to miss the smirk Dante had, as if he knew he had knocked her for six…or shit, even twelve!

"I think we made a mistake," she hissed, making me frown.

"What do you mean, nothing has even happened yet, other than him putting you in your place for once," I told her, making her give me a pointed look.

"I just don't think it's a good idea him being here that's all," she said, now making me wonder what was really going on. Did she know something about who he truly was? I didn't know how she would, but maybe she just sensed something. So now I felt duty bound to push her on it hoping for her sake that she *didn't* know.

"But why, I mean he seemed nice enough to me and he is here to protect us?"

"You, he is here to protect *you.* Me, I could be collateral damage and it wouldn't matter." I rolled my eyes and said,

"Come on, do you really think that big massive guy out there would let anything happen to either of us and besides, did you see the way he looked at you…man alive, it looked as though he wanted to eat you!"

"So not helping here!" she hissed.

"What, I mean it in a good way!" I hissed back.

"I don't know…I just, well I just…"

"What Kirky? Just tell me," I pleaded, now getting worried as I had never seen her acting this way before.

"He just scares me, okay?" she admitted and after the shock of her admission we both released a sigh.

"Look, I know he is a big guy, but trust me on this, some of the biggest guys out there are just big teddy bears at heart." She gave me a disbelieving 'really?' look that said it all.

"It's not because he is so big that scares me, or even the fact that he looks badass enough that he chews nails for breakfast," she admitted, and I placed a hand on her arm and asked,

"Then what is it?" She took a deep breath and then whispered what I was utterly shocked to hear, especially as she had only spent five minutes with the guy and said one thing to him.

"What scares me is that I really like him…as in…*really like him.*"

"Oh…*Oh, I see,*" I said repeating myself the second her eyes told me how serious she was. Now, the thing about Kirky was that I had never known her to act like this…*around anyone*. She was usually the most confident person in a room. But around this guy, then I guess for the first time in her life she didn't know how to act and that in itself scared the shit out of her. And to be quite honest, I could relate because there was only one person out there who had that type of power over me and his name was Lucius.

"Well, if that is the case, don't you think it's a better plan to go out there and try to make conversation instead of hiding in here for the rest of the night?"

"Uh…do I have to answer that?" Wendy said, making me laugh.

"Actually, I was thinking about calling it an early night," she said, this time making me put a hand on my hip and say,

"Really, what, have you got school tomorrow or something?" When she gave me a questioning look, I explained,

"Kirky, it's seven 'o clock." She scrunched up her face before admitting defeat.

"Okay, fine, just don't…don't…"

"Don't what?" I asked in confusion.

"Embarrass me, okay?" Now this did make me laugh.

"Oh, you mean how you do to me all the time?" I questioned, surprised when she admitted.

"Yeah, just like that." I released a sigh and said,

"Fine, I will try not act like you."

"It's all I ask," she replied, giving me a hug and making me chuckle.

After this we went back out there and did what all girls did when coming back from the toilet together, acted as if we hadn't spent the entire time talking about a guy we were now going to face. Dante nodded to me making me smile back in return, but man alive the look he then gave Kirky was one that could melt panties right off the skin. Jeez, no wonder she was all hot and bothered around him and talk about intimidating... I could totally see it now.

He smirked at her as she went past, muttering her little,

"Hey," and in response he answered,

"Darlin'," making her blush scarlet. I decided to get out my phone and text back to Lucius, just because I couldn't help myself.

'You're right, she can't handle a bad boy, but thanks anyway' I said finishing it off in a way that he didn't need to text back if he was busy or just plain didn't want to. Of course, I felt my heart lift the second he did.

'Not all woman can, but you're welcome all the same' Oh boy, was I in trouble if a single message as basic as that one could make me swoon. But it didn't end there because of the next text I got seconds later and all it said was a playful,

'Ps… and he is single'

I smiled to myself which in the end wasn't as private as I thought it was as Kirky sat down next to me and said,

"There's that look again." So, I decided to play her at her own game and nodded to Dante who was currently sat at her little breakfast bar on one of her crown shaped stools managing to even own the space around him and not make him in anyway less manly. He had just swigged back some of his beer and his eyes strayed straight over to Kirky.

"And there's that look again," I whispered, nudging her arm and making her shoot me a 'don't you dare, you promised' type of look in return. So, I decided to get up and refill my drink and in the process try to be sociable in the hope that Kirky might loosen up and follow by example.

"So, Dante, how long have you been working for Lucius?" I asked, hoping he didn't forget himself and say something like the last five hundred years. I watched his lips twitch, noticing that they were large but not in a weird way, as they suited the rest of his features. But it did mean that when he smiled, he smiled big...which I kind of liked.

"Just started," he said in that deep baritone voice of his.

"So, you're not a qualified bodyguard then?" Wendy asked now getting in on the action and once again questioning his ability to do his job. However, Dante simply looked more amused at her comment than affronted and he rose to his full height which, in her flat, fluffy slippers (because even I managed to convince her that heels when you're going for the 'chillin' in my own home look' didn't exactly scream comfort) meant he towered over her. Then he purposely moved in her path so she ended up taking a step back into the breakfast bar with nowhere to go. Then he leaned in close and said,

"Don't worry, Darlin', I can handle anyone that might walk in this room..." he said pushing off the side and giving her the space to breathe, however I didn't then miss how when he threw his empty bottle in the bin he added to that statement.

"...or those who are already in it." Then he winked at me after looking back over his shoulder at Wendy who looked as though she was a missed breath away from passing out.

"In truth, I owed Lucius a favour so here I am, paying that debt," he said mainly to me as Wendy wasn't exactly being her usual friendly self.

"Oh, well I for one am happy you're here protecting us... aren't you Kirky?" He smiled at me and then tilted his head a little as if wondering to himself why I called her this.

"Kirky?" I said again, more forcefully this time.

"Oh yeah, I mean you gotta get experience some way, right?" This was her nonchalant reply that could have been taken as sarcastic. But again, Dante just seemed amused by it, as if he hadn't ever experienced this type of response from a woman before. And well, if a little curvy, blunt ice queen, with gorgeous green eyes and strawberry blonde hair was his type, then Wendy was definitely in there. In fact, it looked like an obsession was quickly building in his eyes as they kept giving away little signals that were subtle enough that Wendy couldn't see. But I could, and let's just say that lust was playing a big part in them whenever he looked at her.

I was just about to speak in his defense when suddenly his phone rang. He answered it with a manly,

"Yeah?" A few seconds later what followed was a knock at the front door. Wendy yelped in surprise as I gasped, but the difference between the two was that little miss ice queen suddenly decided to trust in the abilities of who she classed as 'Bodyguard in training'. She rushed over to him and stood behind him, making him look down over his shoulder at her as if wondering to himself where she had just come from.

"Right, they just turned up," he said making Wendy even

more fearful as she grabbed onto his canvas khaki jacket as if he was her saviour. Then he ended the call and grinned down at her as if enjoying the contact. He turned side on, before taking her chin between his meaty fingers and tilting her head back before saying,

"Don't worry sugar, it's not the bad guys." Then she blinked her big eyes a few times as if trying to escape from the trance she was being put in, only it was all in vain as he was still touching her. Another knock at the door was what broke their moment and it suddenly made me realise that maybe this hadn't been such a good idea. To encourage this type of connection between a demon and a human was a recipe for disaster, considering it was breaking the rules in a huge way. But from the look of things, then I would say that Dante didn't give a damn for rules. As it was now clear that he had his sights set on a curvy strawberry blonde bombshell.

Now, exactly how Wendy would feel about having a massive, badass scary demon as a stalker was anyone's guess but from the look of her right now, still holding onto his jacket as if it was her lifeline, then I would reckon she could grow to live with it. Oh dear, and I had harmlessly thought this would just be a night of innocent flirting.

"Stay here, the both of you," Dante said, now having to step away from her after first being as gentle as possible, which was surprising for such a big guy, when he peeled her fingers from his jacket. Then we watched as he walked to the door, looked out the peephole, which he had to bend a little to do, unlike Wendy as unless she was wearing heels, then she obviously struggled.

Then, because it was safe to do so, he opened the door and was handed a large suitcase by a man we couldn't really see properly, on account of Dante being so large. After this he closed the door and carried in the case before setting it down in front of me.

"For you," he told me, nodding down at it when I didn't respond.

"What do you mean?" I finally asked in confusion.

"Oh, maybe Lucius found some clothes and stuff for you in your flat that wasn't damaged," Wendy said, looking down at it too.

"Maybe," I muttered before getting down on my knees to open it and find out. I unzipped it and flipped the top over gasping the second I did.

"Or maybe not," Wendy said, seeing for herself a case full of brand-new clothes all with the expensive tags on show. I looked up to Dante in question, making him hold his hands up in a defensive way, telling me,

"Don't look at me, sugar, I'm just doing as I am told for once." Wendy made a scoffed sound but one pointed look from Dante and she lowered her eyes submissively and I couldn't say that I blamed her. I went back to the contents to see it was all stuff in my style and size that I would have bought if I'd had the money to do so. But, considering they were all designer then they were definitely out of my budget.

"But why…I…why would he…?" I started to stammer.

"My guess is that you needed them," Dante said just like that and with a shrug of his shoulders went back to sitting on one of the kitchen stools like this was no biggy.

"Wow, it's gotta be said, but the guy has great taste," Wendy said picking up a beautiful crimson silk scarf that when worn around my neck would look like blood floating in water. Oh yeah, he had great taste I thought with a grimace knowing why he had bought that scarf, being a blood sucking Vampire after all.

"Hey look, there is all your favorite beauty products in here too and even the shoes are in your size…cool huh…okay, not so cool for some unknown reason," Wendy said after seeing my frowning face and ending that sentence in a sarcastic tone.

"Why has he done this?" I questioned.

"Well, duh, my guess it's because he cares," she replied patting me on the back.

"But…but…" But nothing really as I was utterly stumped on this one. Which was why I got up and grabbed my phone, knowing there was only one person I would get my answers from.

Lucius.

'Your suitcase arrived' I sent him this message and I swear I stared at the phone so hard waiting for his reply that I started to get a headache.

'I think you will find it's your case, sweetheart' The endearment at the end didn't go unmissed.

'Although it's true I suit most things, even I have to draw the line somewhere and pink panties and stilettos are a hard limit for me' he added in another message directly after, and my mouth dropped at the fact he was joking with me so easily. So, I couldn't help but send one back saying,

'That's a shame, I bet you would have looked hot' I said, adding a wink emoji at the end and shaking my head at myself for flirting when really, I should have been asking him why.

'Behave, kitten, or you will make me blush' was his shocking reply and like this, anyone could have been fooled into believing we were actually a couple. And I had to admit, I much preferred kitten to princess. So, I decided to be as forward as he was right now and follow his lead by being daring enough to tell him so.

'I'll take kitten over princess any day' Then I started biting the tips of my fingers as I waited for his reply. I smiled the second I didn't have to wait long for it.

'Good to know'

'You had another question for me, Sweet' I smirked at his first text but then his second made me frown, as it was starting to look as if he knew me too well. So, it was time to be honest.

'Why did you send me those new clothes?' I finished typing and sent it, only to wait on tenterhooks for his equally honest reply. Because this was Lucius we were talking about...he didn't deal in bullshit.

'Because society today deems it necessary that we cover our nakedness in public and correct me if I am wrong, but you do still work in a public building, do you not?' This was his sarcastic reply and I couldn't help but laugh, even though I was pretty sure that if he'd had been here I would have just rolled my eyes at him.

'Yes of course I do, but why did YOU buy me the clothes?' I asked this time, making my point with the handy use of shouty CAPS. This time he must have been giving some careful thought to his answer as I didn't receive one for at least five minutes. Enough time for Wendy to have made me a cup of tea (as evidently, we were out of wine) and a coffee for both her and Dante, who amazingly had started talking in the kitchen together.

'Because I do as I please and what pleased me was the knowledge that you weren't burdened with the chore' I frowned at this as it sounded both sweet, kind and also some of it the BS I convincingly thought Lucius was beyond. But I didn't say this, no instead I kept it lighthearted and replied with,

'A chore...you do get that I am a girl, right? Shopping for us is never a chore but more like written into our DNA'

'Yes Amelia, I very much 'get' that you're a girl and haven't missed the obvious fact' was his strange response.

'And I believe society would also dictate that the right

response you are looking for when receiving a gift is, Thank You' I laughed again and typed back,

'Ha! Since when do you care to conform to society?'

'Since I pay my taxes every year like a good little Vamp, instead of just eating the Taxman like I want to' At this I nearly sprayed my tea everywhere as I laughed into my mug.

"Something funny?" Wendy asked with a smug look before saying,

"Oh yeah, it looks like you're giving him hell over buying you a whole new wardrobe." Of course, she had no clue that when she said this, there was a deeper meaning hidden in the Hell part of that statement and Dante had to hide his smirk under his hand as he looked at me and winked when she wasn't looking. Because we both knew that you couldn't 'give' hell to someone when they were actually created there by the Devil himself.

'Then in that case, may I say that I am impressed by your restraint, even if I don't agree with your decision as I personally feel he deserves to be eaten' I replied, yet again adding another wink on the end. Then I wondered what his reaction reading that would be? Would he laugh or just smirk and shake his head like he sometimes did, with an expression that said he didn't know what to do with me.

'Then I might consider it the next time I get my bill...now that I have your blessing of course'

'It's all I ask' was my witty response and again I wondered if he was smiling reading it?

'Besides, then I may be moved enough to actually thank you in person' I added, blushing at just all the ways I would actually like to thank him and none of them were with words, but all were with the use of my lips.

'Also, good to know, funny girl' Okay, so if I thought reading his replies had made me smile before then none of them

compared to this one…*I was beaming.* I didn't want this night to end because then I would have to go back to a time that this didn't exist. This playful flirting between us that even though it was new ground, it strangely felt familiar. As if this was the real way that we should have been together, and we had finally found our place in each other's world. Because I was pretty sure that I wasn't the only one who felt the sexual tension sizzling between us. As it was like he said, he does what he pleases, which meant that if it pleased him to be with me then he would have surely done that by now?

So, I guess the only place this left me was firmly in the friend's zone. And if I were honest with myself, then I would take all that I could get. I knew the smart thing would have been to save me the heartache and walk away and before these last few days then I might have been strong enough to do that. But now? Well, now I knew that it wasn't an option for me any longer.

So, friends it was I decided, even if it was always going to be a one-sided boat and one day I would find myself drowning because of it.

I gave myself a mental shake, trying to rid myself of all the ways that this could go wrong and instead focused back on my phone, wondering what it was I could say now, when in the end he was the one that said it for me.

'Goodnight Kitten, and you're welcome for the clothes' I smirked even though this clearly meant the end of our conversation. But just the fact that he had called me kitten again told me that he was at least doing so because he knew I liked it.

'I haven't thanked you…yet' I replied wondering if he would read in between the lines on this one.

'No, but you will' Now this sounded like a promise if ever I heard one. But no, remember Emmie, this is the friend's zone,

so don't get too carried away here. Well, that was until his next message came through,

'Oh, and Princess…' Okay so this might not have started out so good making me growl at back to being called princess, but then the end of the message came through and it was about as far away from the friend's zone as you could get.

Even further than my own personal hell…

'…I had fun picking out your underwear ;)'

CHAPTER TWENTY

A FLY AWAY WEEK

Aweek later and I would have liked to have said things were back to normal. But the truth was that Lucius had destroyed all chances at normal ever returning home to me. One of the reasons for this was that my home, now felt more like *him*.

But let me start from the very beginning, and this was when my first order came from Dante that Lucius thought it best if I was to stay with Wendy for a few more days just to be sure. Of course, this also meant that Dante too became a more permanent fixture. Not that Wendy complained at this, for I think she was ready to buy a manlier couch if it just meant that he could stay longer, as it was where he had been sleeping. Wendy and I had bunked together, something Dante smirked at knowing. But even if she was secretly happy about this, (about Dante staying not sharing a bed with me) she was still playing the ice queen role to its Oscar worthy performance which Dante, most of the time, just seemed amused by.

However, I hadn't heard another word from Lucius in the

time that I stayed with her and I swear my fingers had itched to text him again. But, in the end my pride won, that and the fear of rejection playing heavily on my mind, for I remembered what it had the power to do to me the first time…*crush me, that was what.*

Thankfully, at least I had work to contend with for I went back on Monday to find the room exactly as it was, as if nothing had happened there only forty-eight hours before. So, I resumed my earlier work before my dad had showed up with that box and my life went from mundane and regular to, as my aunty Pip would say, bat-shit crazy in a heartbeat.

But then, after everything that had happened, I had found my mind constantly going back to the box. In the end, I was glad to hear that on Tuesday night I was allowed to go back to my apartment with the hope of finding that the pictures I had taken of it were still there. Unfortunately, everything had happened so quickly that I hadn't had the time to check before Lucius had ushered me out of the room and sent me on my way, even going as far as packing for me.

Every time I looked down at my new suitcase full of clothes I was reminded of him. I had so desperately wanted to keep just one part of me safe, but now I couldn't even be in my own home without seeing him right there amongst all the chaos.

I quickly felt the safe cocoon I had spent years building around my life had piece by piece been peeled away. And in this I wasn't only referring to Lucius, but the lies my father had also told me. And it all started four days ago when I had first been allowed to go back home.

I had decided to take Wendy with me, knowing that I would need that mental support just to see it again. Oh and of course, help in clearing it out and pretty much starting over again. I had decided that no matter how long it would take me I still wouldn't use my father's credit card to buy stuff. So, even if I had to sit on folding deck chairs and eat at a plastic table for a few months, then I would. Or so I thought I would.

"Okay, so I have to warn you, it's bad, okay." I said to her as Dante had already been inside to check that it was safe before leaving for good…or so I had assumed.

"It will be alright, Emmie, we will go through it together, a bit at a time," Wendy said, holding my hand and giving it a squeeze. Then I had taken a deep breath, turned the key and opened the door. The second we had walked in my mouth fell open and Wendy whistled.

"Wow, what type of burglars were these guys, the interior decorating kind, or just Santa's elves and if so, did they leave their card?" she said, looking around in surprise like I was. Because walking in here I had expected to find it the way it was before I had left. In fact, it was what I had been preparing myself for all day. But what I got was my original flat only better…*much, much better.*

"But I…I…don't understand," I stammered in astonishment. It had not only been cleaned, repainted, and refurnished in all top end new pieces but they had also been ones chosen with a particular mind set and this was to try and replicate what had been here originally.

"Oh my God, you even have a new kitchen and that leaky tap you keep bitching about has gone! Holy shit, even your cupboards are full of food and your fridge!" Wendy said getting excited and now going on a hunt of what else was new. Just in the kitchen alone she found all new, top of the range appliances, and a new expensive dining set in Stoneware Imperial blue that was in a country style I loved. All new cooking tools and gadgets, the best pots and pans, stunning glasses all in a matching set, along with mugs matching the plates, bowls and side dishes. Even the bloody cutlery was fancy and now divided in its own drawer instead of just being grouped together in the old milk jug I had on the side to free up drawer space.

And Kirky had been right, the cupboards had enough dry food in them to last me an apocalyptic event. Okay, that might have been a slight over exaggeration but still, it was a lot of food, which like she said, included the fridge. Hell, it was so full that most of it would no doubt go out of date before I had chance to eat it all, that was unless I had a dinner party for ten guests. But thankfully, I had a snazzy new freezer along with my fridge, both hidden away behind one of my new cupboard doors. So most of it could be stored away in there and saved for a rainy 'I have no food in the house' day.

But even this wasn't the most shocking part. No, what was really shocking was the ideas that had gone into my living space and obvious thoughtfulness behind it. Because it hadn't just been redecorated without personal thought, which even if it had been, would have still been a blessing I would have been forever grateful for.

However, it was the fact that the couch had been picked so that the material from my old couch would match because with what had survived had been made into cute scatter cushions. Even my old rug had been used to cover a new footstool in a hexagon shape. But none of this had been what I had screamed over, as I ran towards my pink Star Fleet cushion my aunty had given me, which was now sat pride of place in my new love chair by the window.

"Oh, hold the papers, Emmie, have you seen your geek shelf?" Wendy said making me look back at her to see her now outstretched arm pointing to what I hadn't yet discovered. My head snapped back around and I gasped before covering the lower part of my face with my trembling hands.

"It's like the holy grail, Em," she said again as I took a few steps towards it and she was right, it was. There was everything that I had on there before, including my precious Death Star that had been made whole again. But now it also had a Millennium Falcon, Yoda's Jedi Starfighter, an X-Wing Fighter and a Tie Fighter. Even Chewie's head was back on his body and was now stood next to a figure of Han Solo.

Then, there was my Star Trek shelf that held the most expensive models of the different ships, including the original Enterprise NCC-1701, and the Enterprise NCC-1701 D from the Next Generation. Along with the collectors' must haves like the Klingon Bird of Prey, the USS Excelsior NCC-2000 from the original movies that Lieutenant Sulu lusted after before one day becoming its captain. There were also other pieces that had been on my Christmas list in like, forever, which were now sitting on my shelf. Some of which were the Borg Cube, a Deep Space Nine Space station along with a USS Defiant. Then there was also a Romulan Warbird, known as the badass evil version of Vulcans. Even my precious signed posters of Spock were there on the wall, taking pride of place.

"Seriously, what did they do, rob a comic book store or just drag the biggest geek off the street that they could find and basically look inside his brain?" Wendy asked, as she was right, it was every science fiction geek's wet dream. There were a few other favorites of mine dotted around, like the Alien vs Predator figures, or the Terminator head, but most of which were my clear favorites on their own shelf.

"Wow, you wanna check out your bedroom!" Wendy suddenly shouted only now making me realise that she had gone exploring. I followed in her footsteps and found that the shock just kept on coming.

"Okay, so now its official, I want to marry your boyfriend," she said making me jerk my head to the side to look at her.

"Wait, you think he did this?!" She started laughing and then stopped, saying,

"Oh, you're seriously asking me that…well yeah, I mean, duh, who else would?" I frowned wondering if she was right and this wasn't all just down to my dad after all. I mean he had been the most logical choice considering he knew my likes and dislikes. But then again, spending twenty minutes in here even when it was wrecked would have told you what my hobbies and passions were.

"I thought it might have been my dad but now you mention it, maybe it was Lucius."

"Well, kinda makes sense seeing as he was the one to set up you coming to stay with me and with Captain Inferno as your bodyguard but also packing you a bag full of brand-new clothes…" Then she looked round and opened the closet that was now full of new clothes too, making me gasp.

"Seems highly likely don't you think?" she said sarcastically seeing as all evidence was pointing towards it being Lucius. I couldn't help but slump down on the bed, whilst running my fingers along my new handmade comforter at the end of my bed that actually brought a tear to my eye. It had been made out of all the collection of funny t shirts I had been given over the years and where Lucius had watched me trying in vain to hold the two pieces together he could obviously tell that this stuff had meant a lot to me.

"Oh, honey," Wendy had said when seeing me getting upset and she sat down next to me so that she could comfort me with an arm around my shoulder.

"I just don't understand why…why would he do all this for me?" I asked in a small voice that felt as though it had echoed off my fragile soul.

"I think that's obvious, Emmie," she replied in a soft voice.

But that was the problem I was having. *It wasn't obvious.* Because this was Lucius we were talking about here, which meant obvious would have been him taking me in his arms and telling me that he wanted me. It would have been him staying in London and being in my flat right now to show all of this to me himself. But instead, he had gone back to Germany with his new puzzle box in hand and he'd done so without me seeing him again before he left. There had been no more funny, flirty messages between us and no more hints at seeing each other again in the future.

So, needless to say, I really didn't know what or how to feel about this overwhelmingly grand gesture. Only that I wanted to run into his arms and kiss him, telling him how much I appreciated everything that he had done in saving not only my life but also everything in my little world. But then the other half of me wanted to get on a plane, fly to Germany and demand he explain himself. Explain what was going on and why would he ever go to such lengths for securing my happiness and wellbeing. Unless, of course, it was the biggest question of all and the most heartbreaking,

What if it wasn't for me at all…

What if it had all been for my mother?

To say that this question plagued me would have been a huge understatement as the rest of the night I couldn't sleep. I would just have dreams of Lucius standing watch over me and hushing me back to sleep with a gentle touch to my face, before covering me with a blanket from fear that I would be too cold. It was a sweet and tender side to Lucius I had never yet seen in real life and to be honest I wasn't sure it was one he possessed. But in my dreams, he was as tender and gentle as he was hard and stern.

He was like he had once referred to himself… *my Puppet Master.* And this was no more so than in my dreams where I was powerless to stop him. I was his willing servant to obey his every command, never stopping once to ask myself why. Why he controlled my dreams the way he did. Not that he would have any idea that he consumed these thoughts of mine and rendered me his willing slave in all of them. I would find myself sometimes even going to bed early just in the hope of having another one. Because in them, I don't know, but it was like the only time that I could be free. To let myself be taken care of by someone I could trust with my life and my every decision to be made with my best interests and wellbeing in mind.

But at the very top of all these reasons there was only one constant and a truth that remained no matter what the dream world held for me.

In every single one of them…

He loved me.

Not surprisingly on that first night, I'd woken up and found myself sat at my window, first seeing my reflection in the night sky until seeing myself just slowly fading away in the morning light. I had my phone nestled in my lap just in case, as I found myself doing every night since that first message. I had obsessively re-read every single one trying to painstakingly decipher each of their hidden meanings and in the end finding myself with more questions than answers and almost all of them ended or started with *why?*

Of course, this confusion didn't help when I opened my door the next morning before leaving for work to find I had a housewarming gift. I had no idea who had put it there for him as I had it on good authority that he had left for Germany. Which made me ask myself what the person he'd had deliver it must have thought? Well, it was clear he wouldn't have given a damn what was thought of him because there I was, now staring at a box of my favorite cereal with a blood red bow tied around it.

I picked it up and read the card, unable to help myself from grinning like an idiot the second I read it.

TRANSFUSION

You're welcome
Lucius

Now, if I thought my week couldn't have gotten any weirder then I would have been wrong. Oh, so wrong in fact, as the first thing to happen had been much later that day, when I had arrived back home to find extra security cameras being installed in the building. I had thought at first that Lucius might have forced the hand of the landlord who owned the building, as there were only a few flats that had been bought, like mine and Ben's. I had thought this was weird at first and only knew it because of overhearing some people arguing about rent and it being cheap for a reason.

Well, this time I was overhearing a strange conversation and it was between the two men that were installing the new security. They had been talking about being paid double time for getting this stuff installed today as the owner wanted them focused mainly on the front door and on my floor.

Now, this would have been a logical reason if Lucius had made this request to the owner, but then how would that have accounted for what I heard the next day. The day which finally ended up solving a few puzzles, one of which had been Lucius' strange comments about the building. Ones mentioning that 'he had been right, she hadn't been as independent as she first thought'.

I had just been about to leave for work yet again when I forgot my phone on the counter, so left my door slightly ajar, meaning that when I went to open it, I heard a voice coming from the staircase below. Now, I wouldn't have normally stopped to eavesdrop, but the second I heard that respectful greeting I had grown up hearing, well then, I froze.

"My Lord."

259

As quietly as I could I opened the door a little more and placed my ear to the open gap to listen.

"I can assure you, my Lord, that I have been keeping my eye on her as we all have, but as was agreed years ago, this was only when she was to be in the building and that day she was not." I sucked in a sharp breath and found myself slamming the door before I heard more because I didn't need to. It was clear that my father had been spying on me ever since I moved in here and doing so without telling me!

I was outraged!

So, when I went to work that morning and one of my spying neighbors was still on the phone to my dad, the second he saw me he made a shitty job of pretending that he was on to his friend talking of all things, about the weather.

"Yeah, lovely weather we have been having uh… dude." Well, it was the only opportunity he would ever have to call my father 'dude' that was for damn sure. Especially after he was going to be out of a job as my dad's personal spy in about three seconds, because I couldn't help myself as when I walked past I said,

"Say hi to my dad for me, as I most certainly won't be speaking to him for a while." Then, just as I grabbed the front door to open it, I turned, seeing now that he had his mouth open in shock and looked as though he was trying desperately for something to say to salvage this. Something that he soon discovered was pointless the second I said,

"Oh, and it's raining out, genius." Then I let the door swing shut and by the time I got to my bus stop my phone was ringing. I looked down at the screen knowing whose name I would see flashing up. I answered it only the once, vowing not to do so again.

"Save it, dad, because I don't want to hear it this time." Then I cut him off just as he was saying my name. After this, I turned off my phone, something I hadn't ever done before and definitely not now in case it was Lucius texting me. But this time I just didn't care.

I was seething.

So much so that it was lunch time and I still hadn't turned it back on, something I was trying really hard not to feel guilty about. But damn it, I was a grown woman and all this time he had been watching me as if I had been a bloody teenager he didn't trust. And where had it gotten him? I had still been attacked and my flat had still been broken into.

But then I started to notice something just as I was in the queue to grab a subway when it looked as though someone was watching me. This, of course, didn't look good for me considering what had been happening in the past week, so it went without saying that I freaked. But then freaking out on the inside and trying to seem calm on the outside were two different things. Because, although I could handle myself against an attacker, that advantage I might have once held over an enemy that was a little thing called 'assumption' was now long gone. So, for all I knew, the two watching me across the way could have been carrying guns.

"Salad?" The person behind the counter asked me and I nodded telling them what I wanted but still trying to keep a watchful eye over my shoulder. But then, by the time I had been handed my bag, I still didn't know what to do. I would have eaten inside but it was too busy and all the tables were taken, which meant that they would know that I was on to them if I stayed inside much longer.

So, I decided that I had no choice but to try and make it back to the museum without them catching up to me, as at least there I had the security team to fall back on. This was when I put the meatball sub in my bag and waited for the right moment which was when a group of lads all left at once. I used this to my advantage, trying to use them to shield myself. It worked quite well until I looked back at them and saw that the tallest of the two recognized me and nudged the other guy before nodding back at me. Oh yeah, I was their target alright and this was when I started to really move it.

I weaved in and out of the busy street full of people, but it was when I got stuck behind some Chinese tourists that I really started to panic as this gave them a chance to gain on me. In the end I shouted a sorry and barged my way through just before I decided to start running. Now, seeing a woman in panic running down a street you would have thought was cause for some alarm. But seeing someone running in London was like watching someone running for their flight in an airport. It was one of the busiest cities in the world and a day didn't go by when you didn't see at least one person running to catch a bus, taxi or underground tube.

However, the hardest thing about running around the city wasn't just trying to get through the mass of people but the busy traffic. So, just as I ran past a Hilton hotel called the Double Tree I knew that I would need to cross over and the second I saw the lights turning red on the pedestrian crossing, I legged it. I continued along that straight road, passing a small park and looking back in time to see them both getting caught up by the same road. Finally, this at least gave me enough time I needed to make it to the museum as it was just continuing straight, and I would be there at the gates.

I was going to make it…

Or so I thought.

That was if a massive van hadn't shown up and stopped directly in my path. The doors then swung open and I quickly found myself being grabbed from behind. I was about to cause a massive ruckus so that people would notice that a woman was being kidnapped in the middle of the street.

But this didn't happen.

And another thing that didn't happen was the second I made a break to get away, the move was counter blocked to prevent me from escaping. I then noticed that four big guys all closed in around me and there was suddenly a man at my back who had covered my mouth to capture my screams for help. They did this of course so that no one could see the woman at the center who was currently trying to fight for her life. They had created a barrier of flesh around me so that no one would see anything but a group of guys all stood around a van.

Then, I was picked off my feet as I found myself in a bear hug by someone immensely strong meaning I had no hope of trying to escape. Which was when the side door was slid back and I found myself gasping in panic as I found the darkness inside coming closer and closer.

I couldn't believe that after everything I had gone through the last five days that this was how it was all going to end!

I felt so stupid! So helpless and totally moronic knowing now that I should never have switched off my phone. That way then either Lucius or my father may have been able to track me.

And I knew that once I was inside that thing, then the chances of me getting back out of it again were slim to none. Especially when I was put in the van and the first face I saw was one I knew.

Mr Inferno...

Dante.

CHAPTER TWENTY-ONE

SPY ME A RIVER

The second the van door slid shut Dante released a frustrated sigh behind me and then warned,

"Now, I am going to let you go, so please don't try anything that would only end up getting me killed." I frowned wondering what he meant by this.

"You gonna be good, yeah?" he confirmed making me nod considering my lips were still covered by his big beefy hand. Then he released me, and I quickly scrambled to the bench seat opposite. I realised now that we were the only two in the back of what looked like a surveillance van, as there were screens and computers framing either side.

"Wwwhat's going on?" I asked wide-eyed looking from him to the screens, one of which showed the front door of my flat and another of the front of my building.

"I'm sorry, sugar, but I am not the one who can answer that," Dante said before his phone started to ring. I watched as he answered it and said,

"Yeah, we got your wildcat." I didn't know whether to be

insulted or class it as a compliment. Then he passed me the phone and when I didn't automatically take it, he nodded reassuringly down at it in his hand. So, I took it and put it to my ear where my shock became complete.

"I thought I told you to stay out of trouble."

It was Lucius.

"Lucius?! What the Hell, you had me kidnapped!?" I shouted making him growl back at me.

"You are free to go, Sweet not my fucking prisoner, although it would be a lot fucking simpler if you were, then you might do as you're told for once," he snapped, sarcastically.

"Then why have men following me and then Dante grab me?" I shouted before the truth of my situation came to light, and it did this in the form of one pissed off Vampire telling me so.

"Because those two men following you weren't my men and Dante and his men got to you before they did!"

"Oh...Oh!" I said first in a deflated tone, before then realizing what he meant.

"You had me saved...again?" I asked, making Lucius sigh as if this was all very frustrating.

"It would seem that way wouldn't it?" he replied, once again being sarcastic.

"But why are they still after me if they know that you have the box?" I asked, confused.

"I thought that was one question you could answer," he told me in a sceptical tone as if I was keeping something from him.

"I don't know!" I defended, but then even after I said it I was doubting myself because I was starting to replay my actions over the last five days.

"Don't you?" Lucius asked in a sarcastic tone, as if he could hear for himself my thoughts playing out on rewind. Which was when an idea came to my mind.

"Do we know when they trashed my flat?" I asked him.

"They somehow managed to tamper with the surveillance footage in your building, so we don't know who they are but a vehicle we suspect they were driving was seen near there at twelve forty."

"Which means they trashed my flat after the attack," I mused aloud before asking,

"You said there were men that you heard asking about me, acting as a diversion…what happened to them?"

"Are you asking me if I killed them, Sweet" he asked in that controlling way that meant he was acting calmer than what he felt. Don't ask me how I knew this, I just did.

"Yes Lucius, that's what I am asking," I snapped, and I swear I could almost see his grin for myself.

"No, I left them both unconscious in a cleaning closet, one more broken than the other, which is how I found out what they had planned for you," he told me, and I couldn't help but wonder what he must have been feeling in that moment when he raced to my aid. How he must have thought when opening the door and seeing me about to get shot. Did he panic?

"And were they both still in there after the attack?" His growl told me what his words only confirmed,

"No, my men only found one, who we still have in our custody."

"So, it is possible that he told whoever he worked for that you now had possession of the box," I said, talking aloud.

"If not obvious, yes," Lucius replied in such a way that I would have rolled my eyes if I hadn't been currently too occupied freaking out.

"Meaning that they went to my flat after it," I muttered which was when it hit me why. Unfortunately, it was too late as I had already led Lucius to the same line of questioning.

"Which leaves the biggest question of all…why would

they do that, Amelia?" he asked in such a way as if he knew I was keeping something from him and of course *I was*. Because there was only one reason why they would have broken in...

I still had something they wanted.

"I don't know," I said, making Lucius growl his displeasure...*he knew I was lying.* I knew then when he issued me a warning,

"Don't lie to me, Sweet, you won't like where it gets you." This was when I hit my limit on being threatened. So, like any normal person insane enough to piss off a Vampire, I bit back.

"Well, lucky for me you're in Germany aren't you, so unless you're going to ask Dante to spank me for being a naughty girl, then I really don't see what you can do about it!" I snapped back and if I thought he was pissed off before then, now I knew I'd just made him enraged. I heard his roar of anger and then the sound of something smashing in the background along with a few shocked and startled screams.

Needless to say, this made me quickly hang up the phone and hand it back to Dante as if it was a bomb about to go off.

"Uh, not a wise move that, Darlin'," Dante said in an unsure voice. But what's done was done and there was no going back. Now, if someone told me that the first time I would speak to Lucius, after all he'd done for me in my flat, was going to be an argument, then I would have been shocked. But right now, all I wanted to do was go home and look at the reason they had broken into my flat.

"What sign is on the side of this van?" I asked making Dante frown before answering me.

"Telecommunications, why?" So, it wasn't a plumbing company like the other had been.

"Has it always been that?"

"Why are you asking these types of questions?" he asked

me, folding his arms across his chest and it looked like a mighty feat with them being so big.

"Has it?" I pushed before letting him know anything.

"Yes, in a city based on the backbone of its global communications then trust me, no one blinks an eye when they see this van," he told me, sounding proud and I smirked guessing something about him.

"This is your business isn't it, you're a spy for sale?" His lips twitched in what looked like amusement and respect before he answered,

"Among other things."

"You mean like kicking ass, beating men to a pulp and doing all of this in their sleep, those type of things?" I asked with a raised brow, being the one to now cross my own arms.

"Clever little Daddy's girl," he mocked, making me shrug my shoulders even if the comment pissed me off.

"Let's just say that I have a unique skill set and leave it at that," he told me.

"And the fact you're a Vampire," I added on a guess and making him frown before saying,

"Fuck no, I am pure breed first hierarchy Drude!" he declared, proudly. I gave him an impressed look as they were pretty rare and also more powerful regardless of being turned into a Vamp. But then, if this was the case, what was this guy doing topside? Well, there was one thing for sure, there was definitely no way I was letting him near my friend again, as Lucius had been right, this guy was beyond dangerous.

"So, you're a Royal then?" I asked knowing that I was close to pushing my luck.

"Careful, Sugar, you speak of things you don't understand." Yep, definitely pushing my luck.

"Fair enough," I said with a respectful head nod, especially now I knew who I was dealing with.

"Can you take me home, please?" I asked, knowing there was no way I was finishing out my work day now.

"Sure," he said before banging a hand on the cab side of the van that was enclosed, and shouted,

"Back to the apartment!"

"So, just how long have you been watching me then?" I asked needing to know if it was what I expected. Had my dad put Lucius up to protecting me all this time?

"I am afraid that's my client's private business and therefore I am not at liberty to say."

"Spoken like a true businessman," I replied with a coy grin and gaining a respectful head nod for it.

"And just how long has Lucius been your client for?" I asked in my best innocent 'trust me I am just a girl' voice. But damn him the smirk he gave me told me he saw right through it.

"I wouldn't give a very good service if I went and gave the person I have been asked to spy on information like that now, would I?"

"No, but you are a spy, so it wouldn't be like it's not expected…after all, isn't spilling secrets kinda like what you do for a living?" I teased, thankfully making him laugh and not get offended.

"Nice try, Darlin', but no cigar, besides, that boyfriend of yours isn't someone I wanna mess with any time soon, if ya get me." I frowned and then argued,

"He isn't my boyfriend." At this he chuckled once and then said,

"Oh okay, if you say so." I crossed my arms again and asked,

"And just what is that supposed to mean?"

"Only this, why don't you ask yourself why it is *I am* still here, under his orders, not just my usual men," he said, making me now think about the depth of his words.

"You don't normally do this yourself?"

"Bingo! Now that's the right type of question to ask."

"Then why are *you* here?" I asked as he had led me to and making sure to put enough emphasis on the 'you' part of that question.

"Because, Sugar, I am the best and for you, he wanted the best, plain and simple," he said, shocking me to silence.

"There you go, you just let that sink in there and then tell me that he ain't your boyfriend." To this I had no come back as I could see now why he would think the way he did. Hell, anyone would, but he didn't know our past and therefore didn't know Lucius' hidden reasons for acting the way he did. I mean, even I didn't fully understand them myself, but I just knew that deep down it had something to do with a promise he might have made to my mother. One that was perhaps to keep me safe.

I hated this idea and to say that it left a sour taste in my mouth was an understatement. But what could I do about it? Because any other reason to focus on and it would just stupidly give me hope and that was even more dangerous than anything else right now.

I was so lost in my own thoughts I hadn't realised Dante was now on the phone and we were soon pulling up outside my flat.

"Yeah, it's all good, we just arrived and one of my guys is coming out now, giving me the all clear," Dante said holding another hand to his free ear as if he could hear 'his guy' saying this. It was also obvious that he was talking to Lucius and I wondered if he had calmed down yet?

"No, I will tell her now," Dante replied to him, making me wonder what it was he wanted me to know this time. I tried not to let myself get carried away, as it wasn't like I expected to hear a sorry for being a dick on the phone, as come on, this *was* Lucius we were talking about.

The sliding door opened, and I shuffled along the middle aisle of the van in between all the expensive looking tech. Dante got out first and after giving the sidewalk a once over, he reached out to hold my hand as I jumped down. I could see now it was a pretty big van, much bigger than the one that had been parked across the street. But then again, in the midst of my blind panic, it was easy to mistake it for being the same.

"Thanks," I said once I was out and steady on my feet.

"What does Lucius want to tell me?" I asked as I took my handbag off him wondering if my meatball sub had survived? Dante smirked down at me and said,

"He wanted me to tell you…" Dante paused mid-sentence and then after listening for a few seconds told me,

"To turn on your fucking phone."

CHAPTER TWENTY-TWO

FLOORBOARD SECRETS

The second I got inside my heart was yet again pounding and it was doing it for the usual reason… *Lucius.*

So, I put down my bag, fished out my now cold sub and my switched off lifeless phone and sat down at my new kitchen island that, like Kirky's, had stools tucked underneath. Then I plated up my sub deciding to eat it cold as I switched on my phone wondering what I was going to find. I found about twenty missed calls from my dad and about another ten from my mum. Even ones from my aunties, but I ignored everything other than the one message I knew would be waiting for me.

The one from Lucius.

And it was shocking! So shocking that it took me a few times to read it just to make sure it actually said what I thought it said.

'Word of warning, Princess, you ever refer to another man spanking you again and next time I will break someone's bones instead of my dining table…are we clear?' Uhh…I would say

that was a big fat 'no' on how clear that statement was! Which was why I sent back this reply,

'Are you insane?' I couldn't help myself because if he wasn't then it most certainly meant that I was.

'Push me again, sweetheart, and you will soon find out'

"He is insane," I said after taking a big bite of my sub and talking with my mouth full. This was when I decided that enough was enough and come out and say how I felt, first starting with what I thought was a very important question,

'Are you bipolar?' and I swear this wasn't a joke, seeing as it would make a bit of sense, considering his mood seemed to change like the British weather. This question must have had him stumped because it took him longer to reply. Well, it was that or he was too busy playing at being Master of his universe.

'I don't know, can someone annoy you enough to turn you bipolar?' This was his sarcastic reply and I couldn't help but laugh. It had to be said, he was pretty funny when he wanted to be.

'Nope, I don't think so. Why, do you have another pesky stalker girlfriend on your tail again?' This was what I typed out first but then thought better of it and deleted it before just going with the safer,

'Nope, not unless she's the coolest nerd in the world with an awesome new Sci-fi collection and has super powers that include turning people crazy…know anyone like that?' Then I tapped on send before I could change my mind. Another two bites later and I had my reply.

'Only one equally cute and annoying person comes to mind that makes my palm twitch in preparation.' I burst out laughing at this and nearly ended up painting my counter with bits of food. Thankfully, I swallowed, then grabbed a soda out of the fridge as I typed my reply,

'You should get that looked at, it sounds like a medical

condition' Then I sent it and instantly thought of something else to say, so quickly asked,

'Say, do Vampires ever get man flu?' Then I giggled to myself as I waited for his reply.

'No, but if we did, we wouldn't bitch about it like human males do, perhaps like ones named Peter who no doubt would.' Okay, now this was a shocking response as I hadn't heard him mention Peter before now and wondered if this was because it had been reported to him that I had been seen chatting to him on the phone the other day when he had called me? It was on my lunch break when I just managed to nip out and grab something at the cafe and now knowing that Dante was still out there watching me, then he most likely had relayed this information to Lucius. It would make sense as to why he was mentioning his name now. Making me wonder what would happen when I did meet up with him again? Would Lucius intervene in some way?

I decided to pull Lucius up on this and my next message was to use his own words against him,

'You know you sound a little jealous there...but surely the mighty Vampire King would have no reason to be, not for a cute yet annoying spoilt princess we shall not name?' Then after this one I waited with bated breath until my reply, wondering what he could possibly have to say about this.

It was disappointing.

'Tell me about this van that has been watching you' I frowned the second I read it, knowing now that he must have asked Dante what I had talked to him about on the way home. Wow, talk about obsessive behaviour.

'Well, surely you should know all about that shouldn't you, as there seems to be a club I don't know about...tell me, do you guys all get together for a monthly meeting and compare notes?' I sent back hoping he could gauge the pissed off tone of the text I was going for.

'*Enough fooling around now, Amelia, and answer my question*' Lucius' demand rang through loud and clear, so much so that I took a deep breath and placed my phone down on the counter just staring at it. Then I pushed the rest of my food away, no longer hungry. The more I thought about it, the angrier I got. I had made some good points, whether the tone of them could have been taken for the humorous kind or not, it didn't matter because there was truth at their core.

'*I am still waiting*' was another text I received, and I swallowed hard, pushing it further away as if this would help. Then I got up and leant back against my kitchen countertop, holding myself around my waist and staring at the breakfast bar as if any minute now it would start screaming at me.

How did this happen? How did I manage to lose control of my life so quickly? It vibrated again making me jump and before I even read it, I sent one back and said,

'*Why not ask my father, you both seem to know more about my life than even I do!*' Then I sent one more, vowing it to be my last, once more ignoring all his demands, caring little for my name shouting at me in capital letters.

It simply said…

'*Goodbye, Lucius.*'

Then, after sending all my contact numbers I had stored to my email address, I walked into my bathroom, opened up the toilet lid and dropped my phone in the bowl before giving it a flush for good measure. Then I walked into my bedroom, hooked up the loose floorboards and fished out the reason they had come into my flat and trashed the place.

Because they had been watching me that night and must have seen me taking pictures of the box through the window. And now they were the next best thing to cracking it, seeing as Lucius now had the box in his possession. And what had I stupidly done for them: left my purse with my keys inside, right in the open for them to take. In a place where all eyes had been on me and not at the end of the room where I had left them, easy for the picking.

Gods, but it would have been like child's play getting in here, that was once they had figured a way to cut the feed on the security. I wondered then why they didn't just get the box when we were still at the gala…unless they got interrupted?

"Oh, Gods no!" I shouted suddenly, stuffing the printouts back in their safe place, one they obviously hadn't found the first time round and then I scrambled to my feet and ran towards my front door. I wrenched it open and across the hall to Ben's, grabbing my keys as I went.

I had received only a single text off of him since that night, telling me that he had gone out of town and would let me know when he would be back. I hadn't thought anything of it at the time, as this wasn't unusual for him but now, well, what if he had been the one to catch them about to break in. What if they had to deal with him first and then ran out of time? They could easily have taken his phone and sent me that message pretending to be him.

Oh Gods, but if anything had happened to him then I would never forgive myself!

I found his spare key on my set that we had swapped in case of emergencies. In the end it took me three attempts to get the key in place as my hands were shaking so much. I swear the multicolored patterns he had painted on it even started to swirl around, I was feeling that light headed in the height of my panic. Finally, I unlocked the door and after taking a deep breath, I walked inside.

"Oh Hell…" I muttered covering half my face with my bent arm as the putrid smell wafted up my nostrils and stuck there. It hit me in a wave so strong I had to take a step back, almost staggering and struggling to stay on my feet. But I had to move, as I had to be sure if the smell was what I thought it was. I could feel myself sweating and my lip quivering in fear under my sleeve. My breathing became laboured and half of me wanted to turn around, slam the door and run out of the building to try and scream for help.

To scream for Dante.

But I couldn't do that. Not yet. Because Ben was my friend and therefore, he was my responsibility…dead or alive. Of course, in my heart I wanted so badly for him to be okay and the second I found where that rotting smell was coming from, to just find it to be some dead animal or something that accidently got trapped and died in here. Just anything other than what I feared the most.

So, I carried on, stepping carefully into his space and flinching whenever the bare wooden floor would creak. I remember helping him when ripping up the carpet, as he said he wanted it to be as natural a space as it could be. As he only wanted his art work to shine through against the bare walls and floor. Of course, that had been years ago and, as I now took careful steps, watching my feet so as not to knock anything over in case this was in fact a crime scene, then I now noticed even this had his artwork stamped all over it. Splats of paint in big clumps surrounded by tiny droplets were obviously where he had moved one wet painting after another. There were even lines made up of what looked like fine blue dust where he had obviously been using spray cans and not covered the floor properly.

I used to tease him about the mess but he would just shrug it off and call it 'it's what living in the mind of a creative genius looks like'. Now, as I took in the messy New York loft style he had going on, then I couldn't help the tears that were flooding my eyes.

Even the sight of those old coffee jars filled with mud

coloured water each holding a number of brushes had me tearing my eyes away for they were too painful. I remember my mum having a window sill full of them, reminding me at the time of an artist's natural bouquet, with flowerless dead stems sticking out of a pot where the brushes sat.

Then the morbid thought flashed before my eyes, wondering how many flowers would soon fill this room when all his friends and family knew that he was gone. And all because he opened the door to see me and no doubt ask me about my night.

No! Stop it, just stop it! You don't know…

"You don't know…you…don't…know". I ended up whispering this to myself all the way up to the bathroom where the smell was at its worst. Then I reached for the door knob and my hand froze. What was that sound? I swear I could hear something inside. Something like a gurgling, sloppy sound as if someone was slurping or lapping up something on the floor. Could it be possible that a dog or some wild animal had really gotten inside? Maybe a cat was currently finishing the meal it had just made out of some unsuspecting bird or something?

But then surely something like that couldn't account for the smell. I even started to create any excuse, like his toilet might be blocked up or worst, flooding out all over his floor. But then where was the water, wouldn't it have been coming from underneath the door?

I would have chosen any of these for what I knew deep down had really happened. Because, I may not have been an expert and I might have not known the smell of a rotting body when behind a closed door, but there was one thing I definitely knew the smell of and that was…I knew the smell of blood.

Lots and lots of blood.

So, I finally turned the door knob, knowing that I couldn't put it off any longer. And in doing so I finally let go of my tears, freeing them to finally overflow, as I knew now that there was no going back from this point. There would forever be whatever image lay behind this door imprinted on my brain. Now, all that was left was to see what image that was and pray to every God I knew existed, that it wasn't that of my friend lying dead in a bath like I suspected.

So, I closed my eyes and whispered,

"Please." Before then opening the door and gasping the second I saw it,

A room of death.

And who was at the centre of it all…

But Ben.

CHAPTER TWENTY-THREE

DEATH SCREAMS LIKE A GIRL

I *screamed!*

I screamed the way anyone would when faced with so much death.

However, I wasn't the only one.

Ben started screaming the second he saw me, and we were both locked in some kind of screaming match, seeing who could make the most horrific sound the longest.

"Oh shit!" Ben finally said as I just continued to scream the second I saw what *he* was doing. My friend, my once kind and innocent little artist friend who I'd spent time with, watched movies with and cooked my pasta bake for with homemade garlic tear and share…I had fucking eaten a meal with this guy and now I find out he is a bloody zombie!

I watched in pure disgust as the bloody forearm he had been chewing on slipped from his decaying fingers just before his bloody lips said,

"This isn't what it looks like." At this I seemed frozen to the spot and asked myself if I was some extra in a dark comedy horror movie I didn't know about, because all I wanted to do was cock my hip and say, 'Oh no, because it looked like you'd massacred a couple of people, chopped them up into small manageable pieces before you had yourself an all you can eat human buffet!' But instead I went with my instincts and just started freaking out the good old-fashioned way.

"Oh, my Gods…Oh my Gods, no! Oh my…Fuck!" I screamed, backing away to try and get away from him, but doing so in a way that I thought he might pounce.

"No! Oh Gods, Emmie it's not what it looks like! Emmie please!" He started shouting after me, but I ran from the bathroom and back into the living space. Then I looked over my shoulder to check that he wasn't following me and the second I took my eyes off where I was going, I barreled straight into someone.

"Dante!" I shouted, throwing myself into his arms, knowing that he would keep me safe now. Safe from the monster that I had once thought of as my friend. Because I had seen demons, hundreds of them over my time, but nothing could have ever prepared me for the horrors that lay hidden inside that room.

That room of death, decay and for Ben, what had looked disgustingly like a…*a feast.*

I would have liked to have believed that zombies weren't real and as far as I knew I had never heard of demons that looked and acted like a zombie, so for all I knew Ben could have been the first. This sent my mind into a panicked overload asking myself everything from, secret government experiments to infected diseased monkeys that were going around biting people!

Was Ben infected? Could he infect others? Was there a cure for such a creature?

"Alright, darlin, it's okay, you're safe now. Just calm that little human heart for me, yeah." Dante said in that soothing voice of his. But then I heard Ben emerging from the bathroom and the second I looked over my shoulder at him, covered in blood and still with a piece of dead flesh hanging from his cheek, I screamed again.

"For fuck sake, shifter, you're gonna give her a fucking heart attack!" Dante shouted at him and I frowned before looking up at him, asking myself what the hell was going on here?

Did he just say a shifter? But far worse than that, Dante knew him, knew all along what lived opposite me?! Knew that any minute he could have just unlocked my door and helped himself to a midnight snack…say, on my freakin' leg!

"No…No, no, no, it can't be…it…let me go!" I screamed again as I tried to fight my way from Dante's arms, because now it was clear that Dante knew not only who Ben was, but more importantly *what* he was.

"Calm down, fuck, calm down now okay, we won't hurt you, we just want to…"

"NO! LET ME GO!" I roared up in his face as his arms tightened around me. Then he looked down at me with a regret before he said,

"Very well, but remember, Princess, you left me no choice." I paused in his hold wondering what he meant by that and now asking myself what choice he spoke of that I had taken from him. Well, I was soon to find out as he suddenly placed his large hand over my eyes and the second he spoke my entire body froze.

I was suddenly plunged backwards as his hand pushed on my forehead and I heard him quickly whisper,

"Take a breath."

I did as he said and just before I landed painfully with my back on the floor, I crashed through water. I felt my whole body floating backwards so slowly that when I opened my eyes I saw a world of nothing all around me. Then, as I continued to fall with my feet rooted to the spot, it felt as though the whole world was tipping on its axis, meaning that my feet were soon above me. I was suspended there, totally losing all sense of direction as to what was up and what was down. I took a careful step forward and the second I did the world flipped and I was suddenly upright again. It was as though I had been forced into a different dimension or was it worse...was this the realm of nightmares?

I had heard it being rumoured that such a place existed but seeing that most people who woke from a Drude's touch didn't remember a thing afterwards, then there was never any proof. Drudes never confirmed or denied such a place so again, it simply became a rumour. One that I had to wonder how it even started, for surely there was at least one person to have remembered or how would such a place even begin to exist if only in people's imagination?

So, the question remained, was this the secret to the Drudes' power and if so, just how many people over the years had they left down here in this abyss to feed from. Was this where all the people in comas were trapped?

For some reason, I knew that even having these questions was unheard of in a place like this, for the lack of conscious thoughts down here were no doubt the reason no one ever remembered. But questioning why, how and where was the very root of conscious thought, so what did that make me down here then?

Suddenly a small white light shone and the second I saw it a voice from all around me started to speak in soft and hushed tones.

"Follow the rabbit down the hole, darlin'...*deep...deep down she goes...follow her down...*" From the very first moment he started speaking, my world became dominated by that single voice. As though I needed to obey it at all costs. I saw the small light in front of me where, surprisingly, a small white rabbit started to glow. Then it started to hop away, meaning that if I didn't chase it I would be left standing in the dark. I looked around for a brief second and saw that it was so black that it could have been a brick wall surrounding me or an eternal abyss of dead space. I just didn't know but I was too scared to find out, so I took a step towards the rabbit and then another.

That's when I heard his voice once more, echoing around me.

"Follow her and she will take care of you…deep down there…you see her, she needs you to follow or you will be lost… that's it…keep going…" and I did. I continued to follow her like he said and then once I finished running I saw her sat at the edge of a large hole looking down. I started to question what she was waiting for when the voice spoke again and told me.

"Go on, she is waiting for you…that's it…just a little more…" I frowned thinking that I didn't want this. I didn't like the look of that hole, with its broken and cracked stone wall only two bricks high. It looked like a broken old well or something. But more importantly, what exactly was down there?

No, I wanted out of this place! I didn't want to go down there, not now or not ever. Why had I been forced here to begin with? I couldn't remember. No, I didn't want to follow the rabbit…I didn't want to go deep down there with it. I… I…

"Why isn't it working…she should be gone by now?" I heard the faint whisper behind me, next to me…all around me as if we were in a vast open room and it wasn't just echoing off the walls, but it was being repeated over and over, but with hundreds of them all in the same room as me.

"Silence!" Suddenly, a roar of command snapped the cord

on that echo and instead it boomed all around me, taking place of the once hushed tones.

"Follow the rabbit, Amelia…go and follow him…" Him? But I thought it was a she? I looked the second I heard the mistake being made, for I don't know how I knew, I just did. This was proved when the rabbit turned its head to look at me and I saw its eyes.

Burning olive green that started to cloud over to glowing white so bright that it pierced the night and cut two lines straight through the darkness.

"She won't go." The calmer voice of the two said again and this time there was no echo that followed.

"YES. SHE. WILL." The voice suddenly boomed and suddenly this dark chasm started to cave in around me and the rabbit suddenly started to grow bigger and bigger, morphing into something hideous. It rose up on two back legs after it first grew to the size of a child before then rising up further into that of a man…*and then beyond.*

Now a great white beast stood in place of the rabbit and it looked as if someone had elongated a bear, with arms that touched the floor and feet ten times that of a man. It wasn't looking my way, but I just knew that when it did, I would be utterly terrified. Long white fur grew and started to twist into clumped spikes that dripped with some kind of dark liquid as if the monster was secreting it from its skin. Long yellow talons grew and curled round in on themselves. Then, as a heavy demonic paw landed by the hole, the deadly claws left deep gouges on the small stone wall that surrounded the hole, telling me how easily those same claws could tear through a person's flesh.

Oh yes, now I was truly terrified.

"No…please…please…bring back that rabbit…I will go with her…not with him…anything but him," I said in a terrified whisper and the second I did, the creature threw back its head and let loose a mighty demonic howl, showing me the half face of a monster and the half face of a *man?*

I questioned this and couldn't help but gasp into my hand as the face was covered in hair that was parted in the middle. The top part was pulled back taut and came to two points at the top of his head which I now realised were wrapped around a pair of antlers. Then the bottom half was pulled down by his chin making it look like the creature had a long beard. A pair of ears like you would see on an elf were pulled back with the tips elongated and curled enough to reach the top of its head. But even though the face of the creature wasn't human, it also had enough distinguishable features for me to be able to see now that the beast in front of me was also a man.

It was…

Dante.

Then suddenly, after granting me a swift look, his white eyes started to fade back into olive green and he then started to retract back in on himself. He threw his head back and roared once as if in pain before he bent over double, curling inward and rocking forward before he started to get smaller and smaller until soon the small rabbit was back in his place.

Had I really just seen the true image of a Drude?

They were extremely secretive by nature, which is most likely why no one had ever seen one before or seen one and remembered, which begged the question…*would I?*

"Now, keep your promise…deep, deep further down she goes…your time to follow is now…one chance…or he will take you!" I swallowed hard and knew that now it was as he said, I had no choice. I knew what this was. This was the difference between a nightmare and a good dream and here Dante, the royal Drude was God. So, I looked back at the darkness and

suddenly as if all I needed was a push I was shown the very thing I had been running from in the first place.

I screamed just as Ben's blood covered hand reached out for me. That dead man's flesh still hanging off him as if he was shedding his skin and the old had to first decay before it fell. But then it was his face, his demonic face, that had been feasting at the centre of a massacre. Human lambs brought to the slaughter for a flesh-eating demon to feed. That was what I had seen the moment I opened that bathroom door. A room full of blood as limbs had been torn from torso, as arteries slashed open and sprayed outwards like the paint had on the floor from his cans. This was his real art work.

The crimson art of death and carnage.

A creation I quickly started to run from.

So, I ran and jumped down into the hole, looking back up only to see that the rabbit hadn't followed like he said it would. No, now instead it simply stared at me, with its little white face growing smaller and smaller the further I fell.

"Finally, she falls." I heard the voice speak behind me as Ben spoke like a zombie with the memory of his own voice.

"That's it...run, little darlin,' down you fall..."

"...Fall deep down and finally sleep."

CHAPTER TWENTY-FOUR

SLEEPING BEAUTY PACKS A PUNCH

"Will she ever wake? It's been forty-eight hours straight!" I heard a worried sounding Ben asking and my mind felt lost to the fog of a deep sleep. I vaguely thought about work and going through the motions of asking myself if my alarm had worked or not. Then I asked myself why had I dreamt of hearing Ben's voice?

"I had to send her deep," a gruff voice said that sounded less than happy. Seriously, what were these men doing in my bedroom and what was that one talking about?

"But…but is that even possible with a human, for them to go that deep and find their way out again…can't you help her?" Ben asked, again sounding dire.

"Relax shifter, she is still in there, she's just been sleeping sound is all."

"Yes, but for forty-eight bloody hours! I may not be an expert on you Drudes, but even I know that isn't usually possible!" Ben argued, making someone growl in response.

"What do you want me to say, that I have never heard of it,

so I'm fucked if I know why that is…or what exactly she is for that matter! Is that what you want me to say?" An angry and clearly frustrated voice said and now I was starting to recognise it as one I knew.

Dante.

I could hear his voice and in it, heard an equal amount of worry and aggravation in his words before he expelled a deep sigh. Ben then said a word that I had no problem in bringing me closer to home.

"We should have told him…we should have told the King."

"Oh yeah, and what do you think he would have done? Do you think if he knew this was half your fault that he would let you live as well as me… uh?" Dante said sounding equally threatening as he did annoyed with himself.

"Yeah, well don't pretend it's only my skin you're protecting, as what do you think he would say knowing you sent his Princess down so deep into her own mind that she is practically in a coma…huh, give you a bonus?" Ben snarled back before the noise of something like a chair being knocked back on the floor sounded and seconds later gargled spluttering for breath could be heard.

"Remember who you speak to, flesh eater, for I could quite easily send you down just as deep and fucking keep you there for a millennia without breaking a sweat." A threatening voice snarled back and even in sleep I flinched. After this he must have let Ben go as he started coughing and trying to test his voice again.

"Besides, the King just believes the girl is too angry to speak to him and I have assured him she is continuing on as usual."

"Yes, and how long before he grows impatient enough to visit again, like the last time…you know he can't go long before he sees her and his trust in people grows thinner with each passing year?" Ben asked now with a croaky voice.

"She will wake soon, I feel it…her mind is becoming her own once more…you shall see, for this little lamb will find her way home soon, won't you, darlin'?" A now kind and gentle version of that gruff voice spoke to me and I felt a slight touch along my cheek as if someone was giving me an affectionate caress.

"But what I want to know is how she even managed to fight you for so long…how is that possible? I thought she was human, it's what we were told…what he told us…" Ben asked in confusion and at first I wondered who they were talking about now, but then that thought seemed to fade away just as quickly as the time it took for me to hear it.

I could feel the darkness seeping in again and the last thing I heard this time before the emptiness that was this dark wakeless realm consumed me once more was,

"I don't know, but no human has that type of power…*no human alive.*" And the very last question I asked myself…

Which King had they been talking about?

———

The next time I felt my mind coming back to me was when I heard my name being whispered from above. It was Lucius and he was whispering a demand…

"Wake now…wake for me, my princess…my Amelia."

"Lucius!" I shouted as I bolted upright, reaching out with my hand as if I could grab on to him to stop him from leaving. But there was nothing there but the closet opposite my bed and the mirrored door that only showed my confusing image reaching for myself.

"Emmie!" Ben shouted my name and rushed into my room.

I threw my arms around him and held him to me before I even asked myself why he was here.

"Oh Ben, I had the weirdest of dreams, a nightmare really! It was terrible, and you were there but you were someone else and…and…Ben?" I stopped the second I felt him tense in my hold and I pulled back to say his name in question as I knew that there was something he wasn't telling me.

"Ben?" I said his name again and he lowered his head as if he couldn't look at me any longer. Then he rose from the bed and stepped back, looking utterly ashamed. His big blue eyes were actually filled with tears, a few he swiped at with the back of his hand before he finally said,

"I am so sorry, Emmie…but it happened…*it all really happened,*" he said softly, making me frown first before I shook my head as the ghost of an image in my mind started to form. Making me then argue,

"But…no, it couldn't be…you were a zombie, Ben," I said making him scoff and then a booming laugh was heard behind him as Dante walked inside my room. The height difference between them was a little comical as Ben was about my height making Dante look huge next to my podgy little friend. A friend who was now trying to tell me that he was actually a flesh-eating demon.

Dante slapped him on the back making him fall forward a step before righting himself with a wince.

"Ah, don't be too hard on this guy, Sugar, he was only doing his job," Dante said before shifting around him to come over to the side of the bed.

"What do you mean doing his job and what happened…you, I saw you, I dreamt of you?" I asked, feeling like I was groggy after too much sleep. I watched as Dante shifted uncomfortably for a second and then asked,

"You dreamt of me you say?" I frowned before closing my

eyes a second as I recalled it. I remembered the black room, then the white light. A voice wanting me to follow it…but no, not a light…something else.

"A white rabbit," I muttered before confirming,

"You were the rabbit." This time I heard the gasp from Ben by the door and Dante shot him a knowing look before asking,

"What else?" This was said in a tense tone as if me remembering him wasn't a good thing, but he needed it confirming all the same. So, I let my memory find the dream with ease and hissed through my teeth the second I saw him… saw what he became.

"You changed." This was all I needed to say for Dante to hang his head in what looked like defeat.

"But that's impossible, isn't it…she shouldn't have remembered?" Ben said in astonishment and again Dante gave him a pointed look as if trying to tell him something without words.

"I don't understand, what is going on? How did this even happen?" I asked which seemed to make Dante relax a little now that my questioning had changed direction.

"Ah well, your friend over there might have gotten a little carried away with his meal and you unfortunately picked the wrong time to walk in on him." I frowned in question and Dante decided I needed more than just that.

"Your friend is what is known as a Manushya-Rakshasi demon, a shapeshifter of sorts, if that helps," Dante said making me look at him in shock before turning my stunned gaze on my friend. Ben gave me an awkward little wave and said,

"I am so sorry, Emmie. Gods girl, but I would never have wanted you to see me like that. But the truth is I hadn't fed in a such a long time and well I needed to regenerate before I got sick and the feeding lust just took hold and…well, it all got a bit messy," he said screwing his face up as if even he found it all too yucky but couldn't have helped it. I thought about all he'd just told me and the first question out of my mouth surprised me, as it was one that I never believed I would have found myself having no choice but to ask a friend.

"Did you kill them?" Ben looked upset a moment, obviously knowing the reasons why I would have to ask something so bad. He shook his head a little as if his voice couldn't be trusted not to break.

"No, he didn't… *but I did,*" Dante said, totally unashamed of the fact. I now shifted my shocked gaze to him and asked,

"But why and who were they?"

"They were about to break in to your flat, Emmie, so I hit them over the head with a cricket bat," Ben told me making me raise a brow at him in question, making him shrug and correct himself,

"Well okay, so it's Owen's bat but still, I couldn't let them break in. But then you came back with the King and I got scared I would get in trouble, so I just hid them in my flat," he told me as if this was his confessional and I was his damn priest. Ha, well I couldn't have gotten further enough away from that role now could I, not if my upbringing was anything to go by.

"He called me the next day and I found the assholes hogtied in the bathtub. So, I tortured one who, the second he started to speak, a Hex took hold. Knowing the other would be just as useless I snapped his neck and not being the wasteful type, I let your friend have his meal," Dante finished for Ben. It was at this point the memory came back to me of Ben in the middle of some horror film gorge fest and I had to be honest I started to feel slightly sick, although now no longer terrified as I had been.

"I should probably mention now that my kind only eat the flesh of the dead, although the fresher the better but hey, we will often take what we can get." I wrinkled my nose a little making Dante laugh and say,

"I have a friend at the morgue if you're wondering." I wasn't but no doubt I would have been later.

"Can I have some water?" I asked feeling suddenly a little queasy and now I knew it wasn't just down to Ben.

"I have been trying to keep you hydrated as Dante had been influencing you to drink." Ben told me before running into my kitchen and obviously getting me a bottle from the fridge.

"Influence me, so you did make me sleep?" I asked confirming it had all happened just as I was starting to remember it. Then, just as Ben came back, they both exchanged a few wary looks with each other before Ben handed Dante the bottle.

"What? What is it, come on guys?" Dante handed me the drink and after running a hand over his shaved head said,

"Alright, sugar, now don't freak out but when you saw our little friend over there in…well, shall we say…"

"Looking like a zombie?" I added making him complain,

"Hey, I resent that…*what, it's insulting, okay."* Ben said muttering this last part at Dante and the look he gave him.

"Well, you freaked out darlin' and I thought the best thing was for you to have a little nap but…well…" he paused to hand me the bottle and I took a good long gulp before asking,

"Well, just how long have I been asleep for…a few hours I guess as it's still light outside." Their faces said it all.

"Three days," Dante said making me sit up quickly and squirt a fountain out of my water bottle.

"WHAT!?"

"Something went a little wrong and…" Ben started to say when I noticed Dante give him a look and shake his head a little, promptly shutting him up.

"Wrong? What went wrong? I thought you guys could just

send people to sleep and then wake them up whenever you wanted to?" I questioned feeling as though there was something big they weren't telling me.

"Look don't w…"

"I swear if you say don't worry about it after what I have been through this last week, then I will flip my lid and I will do it screaming, so start talking, Drude boy!" I snapped, making him flinch back as if something I did just wasn't right.

"Did you see…?" Ben started to ask and Dante shot him another look before coming back to me.

Now what had that been about?

"Alright, Sugar, this is what I know. Yes, I tried to get you to go under, but you fought me."

"But I didn't think that was possible?" I questioned as everything I had heard about the Drudes was that they were pretty powerful beings and that was without being of royal blood like Dante claimed to be.

"It's not…wasn't…Shit I don't know okay, the truth is I have never encountered it before so let's just say that when I finally got you under, I just didn't realise how deep it was you fell," Dante admitted, now looking uncomfortable about it.

"And it took me three days to come back out of it?" I asked, making sure.

"Yeah, look I am sorry but if…" At this point I held up my hand stopping him.

"Look, no offense, but I think I just hit a limit or something, so all I really want to do now is get a much-needed shower, brush what feels like fur off my teeth and eat the biggest meal of my life…yeah?" I said looking first to Dante and then to Ben who now smiled and said,

"You shower, I will order us pizza." I nodded and then got up out of bed, feeling a little queasy the second I did but thankfully Dante held me up.

"I'll help you to the bathroom," he said, looking guilty as hell.

"Okay, but I'm warning you guys, by the time I am out of the shower and sat in there with the biggest ass pizza EVER, you are both then going to explain to me what the hell is going on and why it is I am living across the hall from a flesh-eating demon…no offence." Ben shrugged his shoulders and said,

"Meh, it is what it is, so watcha gonna do?" Then he left to go and order me food. I looked up at Dante and said,

"Go make sure he orders two pizzas, I really don't think I can stomach sharing food with that guy for a while."

"You got it, darlin'," Dante said with a chuckle.

A little time later, after I had scrubbed my teeth within an inch of their enamel and I had consumed over half a large pizza, I was ready to talk. I now found myself sat opposite Dante and Ben on the couch looking like naughty children. Well, Ben did and Dante well, he just looked like the school bully who had been pulled into the principal's office for like the thousandth time that year. The bully and the nerd, so what did that now make me?

The victim.

"Right, you can start talking now and begin with telling me how long you have been working for my father?" I asked remembering them talking about the King and after overhearing one of my neighbors, well it wasn't hard to guess. Dante and Ben gave each other a look but didn't say anything.

"Look guys, I already know my father has been spying on me, I overheard the neighbor from upstairs giving him a recap, so all I wanna know is how long and how many?"

"How long and how many what?" Ben asked interrupting before Dante could speak.

"Oh, come on, Ben, just how stupid do you think I am? Christ, I am just surprised that he doesn't own the building and fill the place with…" I paused the second I saw Ben's face giving it away and it turned out that, unbelievably, this day could in fact get worse.

"Oh, by the Gods…please don't tell me he owns the building…he does, doesn't he?" I asked them both and I did this with my head down, eyes closed and my finger and thumb running along my forehead as if a headache was on its way. Then, when no one answered, I looked up and saw Ben shrug his shoulders and add a little,

"Uh…*maybe.*" This was when my rage exploded!

"Oh no! No, no, no!" I shouted getting up and nearly knocking over my pizza, which thankfully Dante saved, or it would have been yet another rug to buy and honestly, just how many rugs could one girl get through in the space of a few years?

I stomped a few feet away before whipping back round to face them both.

"Are you telling me that I bought this flat off my father cheap because I was conned by a nice old lady on the subway because she was planted there?!" I snapped making Ben nod his head a little and I wondered in that moment who he was most afraid of, me or my father now that the demonic cat was out of the bag.

"And just how many people that live here are of your kind, um?" I asked putting a hand on my hip when really I was angry enough to stamp my foot and roar at the ceiling.

"Oh well, there is only one of…oh you mean like our kind as a whole, oh well there is…um…*all of them,*" he said in the tone of a question and wincing as though he knew that this wasn't going to help with my mounting rage. This was where Dante stepped in as he obviously didn't mind 'raging Emmie'.

"The whole building is full of people loyal to the King, sweetheart," Dante finished off before Ben could continue to make a list.

"Oh, by the Gods, it's official he...*he is insane!"* I muttered as I staggered back a step holding my hand behind me until I found the kitchen counter.

"And how did I not know about any of this...? I can see my father's kind and...ah, but of course, Rue did something, didn't she?" I asked referring to Afterlife's resident witch, Vamp and demon all rolled into one. She could have easily placed a casting over the building and its inhabitants. Which meant I would never have known had it not been for seeing Ben in his true form when feeding. But then, that alone caused a painful thought to take root. I cast my gaze to Ben and he flinched seeing the hurt now there and knowing why seconds later when I asked him,

"And you...were you just told to be my friend? To help me that day and start pretending? Was this all an act for you, a job you had to do for your king, uh?" But of course, send the unassuming cute teddy bear, gay friend as a safe choice...Gods, but I was such a fool!

"No! Well, I mean yes, but it wasn't like that, Emmie, I swear." I felt the tears rolling down my cheeks and swiped them away angrily before saying to both of them,

"Get out."

"Oh, Emmie, please don't..."

"I said GET OUT! Both of you, leave now!" I shouted tensing my fists by my side and even Dante looked as though he felt sorry for me as the tears were running freely, dripping from my chin and to the floor.

"But...But, Em..." Ben tried again, clearly getting upset himself.

"Come on, Shifter, let's give her some space, yeah?" Dante said patting Ben on the back and I tore my face away from the sight of Ben looking so heartbroken. I didn't want to feel guilty right now, I wanted to feel my anger. So, I held on to it, not looking at them again but instead placing my palms on the counter and leaning my head down. I didn't look up again until I heard my door close and the second I did, I grabbed the closest thing to me and threw it at the front door as I screamed!

Whatever it was smashed, shattering glass everywhere, but I didn't care. I was so angry I couldn't think, couldn't do anything but slump down to the floor and cry.

It had all been a lie.

My whole adult life.

The one I was so proud of myself for building had all been a lie. Every single aspect of it, right down to my friend. I had people who had been watching every single move I made and then reporting it back to my father. I felt like I was part of the Truman show, trapped in a prison with no bars but surrounded by wardens. I wasn't my own person like I thought...

I was back to being that fucking princess locked in a pretty tower!

And now I knew, there was only one road for me left to take...

Time to escape this life.

In the end I don't know how long I had sat there fuming over all I had learnt, but all I knew was that I needed to get away. I needed to run as far as I could and for once, live in a world where no one knew where I was. I needed to take control back!

And to do that, the first thing I needed to do was buy a new phone. Of course, I also needed a few other things, so I grabbed what I had and stuffed them in the biggest handbag I owned, which included the pictures of the box I had printed out. Of course, this would have been so much easier had I not accidently deleted them from my phone after printing them, as then I could have just emailed them to myself. But unfortunately, my clumsiness wasn't just confined to the physical type. So, without the real thing, this was all I had left, and I gathered the bad guys knew it too or they would have just tried to steal my phone already. For all I knew they had looked and seen this for themselves, hence breaking into my flat for the only evidence of the box they could get their hands on.

After I had what I needed, I grabbed my jacket, heaved up my bag and swiped my keys off the counter before crunching the glass under my boots, no longer caring about a flat that I now knew was never truly my own.

I slammed the door and saw Ben open his a crack before asking me where I was going in a panicked tone.

"To Tahiti where no fucker will find me!" I shouted back over my shoulder, not caring even a little that I was being a bitch. I was too hurt for that.

"Wait! Emmie, please," Ben shouted, throwing himself against the banister so that I stopped on the staircase going down, pausing long enough to ask in a strained tone that spoke volumes to my vulnerable state of mind,

"Was any of it real?" I whispered, knowing he would hear me. But of course, he would, he was just like the rest of them. The ones I could now feel were all around me, like someone had snapped their fingers and all supernatural life became known. But my voice sounded so frail, so hurt and fragile because I didn't care about the rest, not like I cared for Ben.

My fake friend.

"Oh Emmie, please believe me when I say that it was real, it was real for me, even if it didn't start out that way," he told me in a pleading tone that tore at my heart.

"I am so, so sorry," he added, and I finally looked back at him with tears streaming down my face before saying,

"So am I, Ben...*so am I."* I said this for so much more than he would ever know. Then I dropped the sunglasses down from my head and over my red puffy eyes before I continued on with my plan.

See, when I was slumped over, cradling my body and crying my hopelessness out for good, I finally made the decision to get out of Dodge. I didn't know what had happened with my job, but even that now seemed like it had all been orchestrated and for all I knew Daddy dearest had forced his will on that too.

Deep down a little voice told me that he did it all out of love for me and that may be so, but it was no excuse for what he lacked having for me...which was respect! Respect for my life, for my decisions, for my bloody privacy! I was twenty-seven for Gods' sake, not twelve!

"Oh shit, okay boss, Princess is on the move." I heard, the second I spotted a guy dressed in black making me want to roll my eyes at him. He had been speaking into his earpiece and seconds later Dante turned up and started walking in step with me to my bus stop.

"Hey darlin', want a ride somewhere?" I ignored the offer and said,

"You know if you want your guys to fit in then I would try moving away from the Sopranos extras look and maybe on to Men in Black." My sarcastic reply was simply met by a raised brow and a smirk.

"Nice to see you're back on form, Darlin', but how about making life easy for me and letting me drive you wherever it is that you need to go?" he said, and I stopped, folded my arms seeing as I had three minutes until my bus showed and said,

"Am I under house arrest?" He jerked his head back a little and said,

"No, but I just…"

"And do you have the authority to pick me up bodily and man handle me into a car *or Van* and force me somewhere?" I asked, knowing this had happened once.

"Well no, but again I…"

"Then I am doing nothing but wasting my time and yours… good day Mr Spyman, no doubt I will be seeing you around," I said, turning my back on him and walking to my bus stop where I could see it in the traffic not too far away. Then, after I scanned my card, I found a seat and waved at Dante and his men as they got themselves in a car so that they could follow the bus. Thanks to traffic and them not being prepared for my abrupt departure, it didn't take long for them to get left behind, so the second I couldn't see them following, I raised my hood and got off at the next stop before slipping inside the nearest shop.

It turned out to be a corner shop selling newspapers and a few London tourist gifts, so I hid behind the T shirt stand and waited until I saw them go past, still following the bus.

Then, after a sigh of relief that so far, my plan was working, I bought what I needed. I picked up a black winter wooly hat with a big fluffy ball on top and an 'I love London' hooded sweatshirt two sizes too big for me to change into. Then I stuffed my jacket and sunglasses inside my large bag and fished out a pair of my everyday glasses to replace them with so that I could see. After this, I pulled down the purple hoodie and tucked my longish hair in a twist before tucking it inside the hat. The guy behind the counter watched as I did all this, so I said,

"Stalker ex…whatcha gonna do, eh?" Then I walked out of there to catch the next bus back to Wendy's, but first I needed to make one more stop. So, I caught the next bus that I knew took me to the shops I needed so that I could buy a new unlocked phone that no one could trace. For starters, no one would know I had it and secondly my old one was still learning how to swim in my toilet bowl.

Next, I bought a pad of paper, some pens and lastly nipped into a shoe shop going straight to the best pair I knew would fit the outfit I had in mind. They were red leather covered toe shoes with an ankle strap fastening that came down in a T-shape in white leather. It gave it that vintage rockabilly style I was looking for as the white leather continued down the front of the shoe and finished in a little bow.

They were a great pair of shoes and really, if I was going to get out of here and was going on the run, then the least I could do was…

Escape in style.

CHAPTER TWENTY-FIVE

PIN-UP PLAN

A fter my little shopping trip, I now had everything I needed before jumping back on another bus, this time using the journey to start the cogs of my escape plan in motion. Now, all I could hope for was that if Dante couldn't find me, then neither could anyone else out there, which meant I had a good chance here at outrunning everyone...*even the bad guys.*

So, after first writing down the things I needed on my new pad, I made an important phone call. This was to my boss, with the expectation of getting an earful for not being in touch and then having to tell him I needed time off... well, let's just say I really hadn't expected it to go well. Especially when my boss told me to hold on as someone wanted to talk to me and it turned out to be the Chairman himself.

"Oh, my dear, my sweet girl, how thankful we were for your little tour but more so with the gentleman you brought with you," Sir Allerton said with such enthusiasm I was dumbfounded as to why.

"I'm sorry, Sir, but…"

"Oh, no need to play coy my dear, but surely you must know." I frowned at first in reply before telling him the truth.

"No, I am sorry, Sir, but I don't, has something happened?" He started chuckling and then whispered to my boss, something about the sweet charms of a lady before retuning back to me and shocking me to the core.

"That gentleman you brought with you contacted me a few days ago and told me that he was so impressed with your work and your personal knowledge and clear passion for history, that he felt moved enough to make a donation…a very *considerable* donation," he said, stretching out the word considerable to emphasize just how substantial a donation it was.

"He did?!" I shouted, making him laugh.

"Oh yes, and as I said, quite a large donation at that, over twenty times what we needed to fund the dig, along with many others to come, as his only stipulation was that you were to head each one and have a say in future digs, for that is all the money is to be spent on. So, well done, my dear, and as for your time off, I would say that you have certainly earned it, so take all the time you need." After this I thanked him and ended the call in a stunned state. Lucius had made a huge donation, millions in fact, going from what Sir Allerton had said. And Lucius had made it sound as if I deserved all the credit.

I was in so much shock and still trying to process it all that I nearly missed my stop. I didn't know what to think other than asking myself why? Why would he do that? Because there was one thing turning up and saving my life, or acting out a favour to my parents, but this…what was this for? Who gained from it other than me and why would he spend all that money on something he knew I was most passionate about in the world if only for my gain? Who does that for someone they think of as a job?

Or someone they don't care about?

I had no answers. None whatsoever. Because deep down there were only two possibilities left and only one of them I wished for…that he actually cared more for me than he led me to believe.

The other one was…well, that he cared more for someone else than he led *her* to believe. This thought was just as heartbreaking as it had been all that time ago.

But no! I couldn't think of that now. I still had a job to do and for that I needed Wendy…the only person in this world I could trust. So, as I got off the bus I had my pad in my bag at the ready.

I checked my surroundings as subtly as I possibly could and smirked to myself the second I realised that it was as I thought, there was someone watching Wendy's flat. Which meant that my plan just might work like I thought it would. I could even see the way the guy across the street started touching his ear and speaking in that obvious way. I swear this spy game didn't look half as cool as it did in the Bond movies. I wanted to go over there and tell him to stop touching his ear the way Daniel Craig did in Casino Royale just before the epic free runner chase through a building site.

I made a show of pulling my hat down hoping he was at least smart enough to take note of what I was wearing as this would end up playing a main part of this plan of mine.

I buzzed Wendy's flat at the front door of her building, lucky that I knew she often worked from home and according to her google diary we had synced up long ago, I knew that today she was working from home again.

"Hey hun, can you let me in?" I said before I knew what was coming.

"Holy Christ where have you been, I have been out of my mind with worry and Ben said something…"

"Look I will explain, just let me in okay." I said, this time in a more serious tone, one she understood the second I heard the buzz of the door. I then made my way up to her flat wondering just how many people were also planted here to keep an eye on me when I was at her place? I would have liked to have said I was being paranoid but really, after everything I had learned today, then I knew if anything, I wasn't being paranoid enough!

I decided to take her stairs instead of the lift, that way hoping no one would see me as I took the notepad I had written on whilst on the bus out of my bag, ready for this moment. Then, when I reached her door, I knocked and the second she opened it I held up the pad for her to read.

It said

'Follow my lead, they are listening!' Then I spoke.

"Hey honey, sorry I didn't call but I am really upset, can I come in and stay with you for a bit," I said in a dire tone that I hoped was believable. Wendy gave me a look of shock before schooling her features quite quickly and nodding her head telling me she understood before saying,

"Oh Emmie, yeah of course...I have been so worried about you!" It had to be said her acting was a heck of a lot better than mine that was for damn sure. I walked in and closed the door behind me and just hoped that the one flaw in this plan could be that the place wasn't just bugged, but it also had cameras in here too. Which meant this plan of mine would be over before it really even took shape.

But the idea came to me when I remembered seeing Dante one morning with his hand reaching up by her lampshade, thinking it weird at the time but shrugging it off as the excuse he gave me. He noticed it flickering the night before and was just checking the connection.

Of course, after everything I had learned since then, I now

started to question it and I knew I was right the second I walked over to it. Wendy mouthed the words,

'What you doing?' at me so I flipped over the next page and she read the answer I already had planned.

'Your place is bugged'. It read and her mouth dropped open in shock. I rolled my hand as if to get her to start talking normally. Thankfully, she soon got the hint and said,

"So, what happened to you, 'cause I got a text off Ben that said you were feeling poorly and just wanted to sleep it off, was that true?" I quickly showed her the small black dot I found attached to the inside of the shade and then took a step back before answering her.

"Yeah, something like that, but don't worry about that now, I just needed to get away from that place," I said only half acting. Then I showed her another page that said,

'Answer is: Make yourself at home, I was just about to have a bath but chill out if you want.'

"I just needed somewhere to think, I've called in sick at work, just needed to take a week off you know, after everything that's happened. Do you mind if I stay the night and we just do something normal like watch a movie and order a takeout or something?" I said before giving her big eyes and a nod of my head for her to do her thing.

"Yeah, of course, that sounds great, but I was just about to have a bath, so why don't you order something and chill out for a bit, I think Next Gen in already in the DVD player," she said with a shrug of her shoulders obviously silently asking if that was all right and I gave her two thumbs up for the show.

"Cool thanks hun, I owe you big time." Then I grabbed the remote and pressed play on the DVD player, turning it up loud enough so as not to be ridiculous but be loud at the same time. Then I nodded towards her bathroom and once inside I turned on the taps full blast.

"Alright, we should be fine in here."

"Seriously Emmie, I am starting to think you lead a double life here," Wendy joked, and I felt like saying, 'you have no idea'.

"Okay, so I am going to take a not so wild stab in the dark here and point the end of my blade at Mr Inferno being the one who planted that bug in my apartment," she said crossing her arms and looking less than impressed.

"Yeah, that would be a good guess, as in the type where it's not actually a guess but more of an obvious…oh, anyway you get the idea, look I wasn't kidding when I said I needed to get away," I said, making her nod as she had no doubt gathered as much.

"Alright Smock, I am your Kirky, what do you need me to do?" I gave her a smirk and said,

"Easy…*I just need you to be me.*"

After this bombshell drop of a plan I then told her a heavily edited version of the last few days and then told her my plan, all in the time it took for the bath to fill. Then that was it, our time was up. We had to keep up with the act, so we ordered Chinese food and I made a show of shouting to Wendy telling her it would be with us in forty minutes. She stayed in her room as I told her to, so that she wouldn't be seen as her curtains were already closed.

Thankfully, unlike my place, you couldn't see anyone in the living room, so they wouldn't be able to see that I wasn't actually watching Star Trek the Next Generation at all but instead was joining Wendy in her bedroom. Which meant we had forty minutes to do this whilst technically Wendy was in the bath.

*"Okay, so we have to try and do this as quietly as we can...
you ready to become me?"* I whispered, and she replied,

"Ready when you are."

We then spent the next forty minutes transforming ourselves
into each other and we started by swapping clothes. I undressed,
giving her my hat and sweater, after finding a pair of jeans of
hers that would match in colour. Then we added a pair of high
heeled boots underneath, so they made up for the extra height.

Her hair was short, so tucking it in the woolly hat wasn't a
problem. Thankfully, it was cold outside, so it was the weather
for it because if this had been summer and a sunny day outside,
then we would have been so screwed.

But it was winter so by the time she added my jacket, one
Dante had also seen me wearing, she definitely looked the part,
especially after putting on my sunglasses that I had purposely
shown them I had with me today, on account of hiding the tears.

"Your turn," she whispered, picking out one of her swing
style dresses that was black. We picked it as it was too tight on
her so should in theory just about fit me fine. I smirked when
she mouthed the word 'Bitch' to me when it actually turned out
to fit me like a glove.

It had a sweetheart neckline and a red underskirt giving the
skirt volume. It also was a halter neck with red ribbon that tied
at the back of my neck and was keeping up half of the dress. To
this she added a matching red sweater so I wouldn't get too cold
and the biggest jacket she owned.

"No I can't, you love this jacket," I protested on a whisper,
placing my hands on it to stop her. I knew it was her favorite
and one she had saved up to buy for ages.

*"Then make sure you bring it back in one piece and I don't
just mean the jacket,"* she warned with a worried smile and I
grabbed her to me and hugged her tight.

"I will, I promise."

So, after hanging the heavy jacket over my arm ready for later, we walked out of the bedroom looking good enough that it gave us both hope that we would fool everyone. But first, we had an act to put on. And it started the moment after our takeaway turned up.

"Oh, damn it, I totally forgot!" Wendy said winking at me.

"What's up?"

"I forgot that I have to meet that contact tonight for drinks...shit!" She said acting it out perfectly. So, I tried to do the same and sound disappointed.

"Oh, well that's alright…"

"No, no, I will cancel…I wonder if Roger could go in my place and do the interview," she mused to herself, making me mouth the question, 'Who is Roger?' She shrugged her shoulders and mouthed back, 'Hell, if I know', making me want to giggle.

"It sounds important, honestly I don't mind staying here by myself, in fact whilst you do that I could do with going home and grabbing some stuff anyway…that is if you still don't mind me staying here," I said, making Wendy smirk at me as if we had rehearsed this a million times and it was now perfect.

"Yeah, I already said you could stay as long as you want but I agree, you at least need your PJ's if your gonna share a bed with me, don't want me turning the other way for real now, do you?" she said obviously improvising and my mouth dropped before I burst out laughing mouthing 'What was that?' making her reply, 'I don't know!'

"Well, I have been known to have that power to turn people to the boobie side of lust." At this we both laughed again as if this was some weird game called 'who could say the weirdest shit to the hidden microphone and get away with it'.

"But you're right, I need to pack some stuff."

"Then it's settled, take my keys and let yourself back in, I warn you though, I might be back late," Wendy said.

"Why, where are you meeting this contact?" I asked knowing that this part of our story was key in case they decided to follow Wendy, which would actually be me.

"At the airport."

"That's a weird place for a date." I smirked when she frowned at me.

"It's not a date! Look, the guy is some businessman who can only meet me in between his flights, he's got some big corruption story on his boss, who naturally I can't name at this time, but who knows, the story could win me a prize, that or a cheap bottle of perfume at duty free." I laughed, and we continued to make small talk, like the way I 'convinced her the black dress with the red coat was a winner' just to fully cement our story. Then, after putting on the shoes I'd bought that day, knowing that would have been the only flaw in our plan considering we had different sized shoes, we were ready.

So, I put on the jacket she loved, that hung down the full length of the skirt showing just my black tights underneath and high heel red shoes, hoping they wouldn't notice the biggest different between us, *our height.* One of the reasons I didn't pick a massive heel and had Wendy pick a pair that were some of her highest, yet ones she could still hide under a pair of jeans. Plus, how many men really noticed a woman's shoes, um? Well, knowing my luck then Dante would have a foot fetish and zone straight on Wendy's feet which, thinking about it, would have been mine. Man, I was confused already, and we hadn't even stepped foot outside yet.

"I have to say, this look really suits you," she whispered as way of goodbye then she added,

"Good luck."

"You too." Then after putting up the hood and grabbing the

swapped bags that now had the printouts in and everything else I would need, like my passport, I nodded to her.

"See you later…oh and have a nice date," I said, playing the part and holding up my hand to tell her to wait five minutes like we had planned. She nodded and said,

"I told you, it's not a date! Now don't forget my keys like you usually do" she said, and like me playing the part but giving me the thumbs up as well.

Then I left, holding my head down and letting the massive fur lined jacket cover most of my face. It was quite a gothic style being red and black brocade that was double breasted with big black buttons that matched the fake fur cuffs and edging round the hood that was currently tickling my nose. It was a long heavy jacket of thick material that corseted in at the back and flared out around the skirt. One of the reasons she chose it, was because it was adjustable in size so I could get away with making it looking bigger than it was, so I appeared to have Wendy's curvy bottom half.

I would pull it in once I was in the clear so that it fit better. But for now, I walked out into the night, pulling the hood further over my face and thanking the fates for rain so that this made sense. Then I hailed a cab and got in telling him to take me to the airport. I had already checked the time of the flights but still had no clue as to where I was going, knowing that I only had enough cash on me to get me so far. I couldn't risk paying on my card, knowing that was easy to track, so I managed to get out a little over a thousand pounds over three different cards. It wouldn't last me long, but it would be enough to figure it out when I got to where ever it was I was going.

Maybe Ireland would be good, as far as I knew my father didn't have any property there. Well, at least I had the coat for cold weather I thought, tugging all the layers back a little as it was roasting in the back of the car. But I didn't want to chance being seen in case Wendy was being followed.

I don't know how long it took to get to Gatwick airport as I lost time just by playing my plan over and over again in my mind. See I had it in my head that if they didn't know where I was, then maybe they would finally get the hint that I valued my private life. That way, if they ever wanted me to come back, then things were going to have to change and big time because what Lucius and my father had done had only made me feel one way...*Violated.*

Well, no more.

I paid for the cab or should I say, taxi as they say here. Then I walked into arrivals with my handbag firmly over my shoulder. I still had a part to play so just hoped that no one was going to go as far as following Wendy inside or it would look odd that I made my way back to departures. Then I paused to look up at the outgoing flights on the screen. I decided that Dublin must have been fated, because there was one leaving in two hours' time. Now all I had to do was hope that Wendy didn't get discovered before then and we were all good.

So, after I purchased my ticket, I made my way to security and finally felt it safe enough to take off my jacket, placing it on the belt along with my bag and phone. Then I walked through the metal detector getting some strange looks for being dressed the way I was, making me blush a little. After all, it was a little late in the day to say I was heading to a wedding.

As it turned out my bag was picked randomly to be one that was checked so I walked over to one of the security officers. She asked if it was my bag and if I packed it myself. I nodded, and she started emptying the contents, frowning down at all the rolled-up printouts.

"Can you show me these, please." I wanted to sigh, but thought that may look a little weird, especially if I suddenly blurted out about how much more trouble were these papers going to get me in?

"Sure," I said pulling the elastic hair bobble I had placed round them and showed her.

"What is this?" she asked in curiosity, not because she had to as let's face it, they hadn't exactly been blue prints of the airport or schematics of the plane I would shortly be boarding.

"I am an archeologist and they are pictures of an artifact I am working on," I told her.

"Oh wow, like that boy king, what was his name Tuk or something…found in…" the second she started talking I stopped listening as something she said suddenly clicked at the same time I looked at the images. I frowned down at one of the squares that had a hieroglyph on it that represented a King or a God as they were both very similar. But it wasn't one that was in a cartouche, like it should have been. It was also a king I hadn't heard of before and therefore its name had been hard to decipher. I remembered getting frustrated before the gala, and the short time I'd had to look at the actual thing in the flesh.

But now I was looking at it in a whole new way because the way I had taken this particular picture was at an angle. It was one at the time I classed as a bad picture and thought of as pretty useless. But now it was showing me something completely different. I could read the real meaning and it was one that had me quickly freaking out.

"Miss…miss, are you okay?" My head snapped up and I looked at her a second before shaking off my horror enough to respond.

"Yeah, I mean I just realised I have to change my flight, it's really important, can I go back through and do that?"

"Yes, alright, here are your things…oh and good luck," she said making me frown. Had she seen the horror in my face?

"With what?" I asked making her laugh, before nodding

down at the pictures I had now stuffed under my arm, along with my jacket.

"With your papers and figuring them out…it looks complicated," she said, my only dry response was a mumbled,

"Oh, you have no idea."

Then I started to run just in case I was out of time. Getting past the queue of people all now looking at me like I was a crazy person running for a flight in the wrong direction. But I just prayed that there was a flight to catch as it wasn't as if time was on my side. And when I say time, I didn't just mean having Dante and his crew on my tail in the foreseeable future. Or of course the unknown group of bad guys that were trying to kill me for these damn papers. But then now, after what I had just discovered, at least I knew why and let's just say that death was certainly on their minds.

I finally made it back to the information desk and after having a quick look at the flights to check there was one, I asked for a new ticket.

"Okay, let's see what we can do for you…where did you say the destination was?" Well, now after what I had just discovered, there was only one answer to that…

"Munich, Germany, please."

CHAPTER TWENTY-SIX

MAKING NEW FRIENDS

As it turned out I only just made it in time for my flight as check-in was closing five minutes after I purchased my ticket. Meaning, I only just had enough time to get to my gate to board the plane. This also meant that I was the last on board and therefore received some glares as it looked as though they had been waiting on me. However, I had more important things on my mind so paid them no attention. The plane was half empty anyway which was good as it meant I had a whole three seats to myself.

Flying didn't bother me, as I was used to it. Not only from travelling in my parent's private jet, joining them whenever they had to travel, but also because I got to see it being flown when my dad would pilot them. I used to love standing behind in the cockpit watching with itchy fingers, just desperate to press all those buttons. Of course, it was also kind of hard to be scared of heights or flying, when your dad had wings. Now spiders on the other hand scared the living shit out of me!

So, even as the plane was about to take off, I had those

pictures out in my lap going over every inch of them. But no matter how many ways I looked at it now, all I could see was that warning. The warning of what the box actually contained and what it had the power to do.

And no one knew but me. Which meant that I had to put my own personal feelings behind me. All the hurt and frustration, everything I had in my mind just evaporated into dust in the single moment that I looked down at that image. Because, without me, then they would all be lost. Not because no one else knew hieroglyphics like me, but because no one else knew what it was they were really looking at.

The box had been made as a puzzle, yes, but everyone thought that it was a puzzle set to open it. But that was just what its maker wanted you to think. No, the real riddle was far bigger and what lay inside it just aided the key in opening a much larger box, one to an eternal puzzle.

But the problem was time. Because someone else was after this box and if what the symbols meant were true, then this was far bigger than any of us could have ever imagined. So, Lucius had to be warned. He just had to be before it was too late. However, my biggest problem now wouldn't be how to escape those watching me, it would be how to reach Lucius without those watching him. Because if he had the box then there was no doubt that he would be their next target. Just like they had been watching me.

So, the key lay in these pictures and soon in the box itself. But for now, then this was all I had, and time wasn't on my hands. So, I had two hours until I landed and then I had to figure out a way to…

Well, to sneak into Lucius' domain…

To break into the formidable, *Transfusion.*

By the time we landed I was no closer to deciphering the hardest part which was cracking the code to opening it. It was like a keycode and all I had to do was figure out which numbers were pressed first. Only instead of numbers, I was actually looking at symbols of world history all centered around Ancient Egypt.

I decided it was best to put back on my heavy jacket and bring up the hood just in case they had people watching the airports, as I very well might have been discovered missing by now. I couldn't help but wonder if Lucius would have been informed and if so, how would he have reacted to the news?

No! I needed to focus and now was not the time to lose my head over my idiotic heart on this. I had a job to do and so many people unknowingly depended on it.

But first I needed to get these printouts somewhere safe, just in case we ever needed them again. I don't know why the impulse came over me as strong as it did, but the second I was off the plane I was asking an airport worker if they had any lockers there. He pointed off to where I would find them and after going to the Luggage Storage Service Center they helped me out in getting a long-term locker.

Then, I made my way out of the airport and the second I did, I noticed some suspicious looking guys dressed like Dante's men getting out of a massive blacked out Land Rover. Now, just because they were dressed the same as a couple of bad action movie extras, it didn't mean they worked for him. Not when the other guys sent to attack me looked just like them as well.

I swear these guys needed a new look, like maybe get a map, camera or at least a fanny pack and actually try looking like a tourist would, then that might fool me. They could even go the extra mile and add a Mickey Mouse T shirt from Disneyland Paris and really play the part. But what really would have made my life a lot easier was if they would have, at the very least, worn a badge or something with 'We're the Bad Guys' written on, then at least I would have some clue who I was running from.

I was suddenly glad that it was dark outside, hoping not to be seen. Then I quickly turned in the opposite direction but then jinxed my good fortune as unfortunately I wasn't quick enough.

Because, of course, they saw me.

In my panicked state I looked up and down the length of cars all picking people up and saw the sign for taxis so I ran. Thankfully, when I looked behind me, they'd got themselves caught behind a large family all wheeling luggage on three trollies in front of them. They started swearing at them in German throwing their arms up and down in frustration. This would have given me the advantage I had been looking for. That was if I hadn't then fallen over someone else's trolley because I had been too busy looking behind me at them.

I crashed into the load and fell over the top of it landing hard on my elbow on the other side.

"Shit!" I hissed in pain, grabbing it and at the same time scrambling to get up as they were now gaining on me.

"Es tut uns leid, Es tut uns leid" I repeated the word for sorry in German to the poor couple whose luggage had also taken an unfortunate nose dive. I could see them now, only a few metres away from being within grabbing distance, so I quickly turned, running into the road just as a car came to a screeching halt. Then, just as I thought that was it, it was all over, a woman stuck her head out of the window and shouted,

"Quick, get in!" Well, I didn't need telling twice. She had reached back and opened the door for me so all I needed to do was dive in the back before she slammed her foot to the floor. We drove off on screeching tires and the smell of burnt rubber was all we left behind. I quickly sat up and slammed the door shut before looking through the back window to see the men now getting in their own car, ready to make chase.

"They are following us!"

"I know," she said calmly, looking in the rearview herself as she changed gear before hammering it forward in fifth gear. Then she swerved around some parked cars, not slowing down in anyway, making me grab onto the back of the seat just to stop myself from being thrown down on my side.

Then the second there was a large enough gap in the road ahead she overtook a small VW that definitely let us know they didn't appreciate our driving or the mystery woman beeping her horn at them. Then she went speeding past the shaking fist through the window of the small car with a laugh. As we shot ahead I saw the Land Rover coming out of nowhere, sideswiping another car in its way. And the chase was on and all that was left for me to do was hang on for dear life whilst a person I had never met tried to get me out of this mess.

"Who the hell are you, lady?" I asked, making her chuckle before she quickly turned down one of the side streets making the Land Rover have to slam on their brakes and reverse to follow us.

"Call me Bess Athis." I frowned thinking that was a weird last name,

"Bess Athis?"

"Yeah, as in the Best at this, now hold on!" she said as we started driving towards a set of steps and I freaked,

"Oh shit!" I shouted, bracing myself with a foot on the door and my hand on the holder above. But then, just before we went off the edge careening down the side, she tugged up her handbrake making the brakes lock on the rear, causing the wheels to scream sideways as she spun it round. Then she dropped the handbrake again and off we went at killing speeds once more. The Land Rover wasn't so lucky not having the same maneuverability as the BMW we were currently pushing to the limit. I say us, what I meant was the crazy blonde lady I had never met before.

It slammed into a post caving in one side of the passenger door on impact. However, it kept on coming, meaning we kept going and I wondered for how much longer I would last without throwing up. Let's just say that there wasn't much need or room for that matter for high speed chases in London, so I had to say this was my first.

"Oh shit, we won't fit!" I shouted slapping a hand to the seat in front of me as if this would help in stopping the car before we went speeding down the narrow pavement only meant for pedestrians.

"Oh yes we will, we just need to…oh, there you go!" she said adding this last part when we had mounted a curb and were currently driving side on down the long street with our wheels only half on the road. I looked behind and saw that the Land Rover knew it couldn't get down here so backed up, obviously knowing another way.

"We lost them" I said, releasing a held breath.

"Yeah, but not for long," she warned and a minute later she was right as they were at the end of the road waiting for us. Then the second they saw us coming they floored it, coming at us head on the moment the road widened up and there was room for them.

"Oh look, hello fellers," she said laughing and obviously letting me know she was insane.

"Oh, oh, oh shiiiiittttt!" I shouted the second she did another handbrake turn, snapping the car around and down into another narrow street before they could hit us in that deadly game of chicken.

"Jesus lady, who taught you to drive?!" I asked before we

went over some bumps in the road at speed and making me hold a hand to the roof so that I wouldn't bash my head.

"Well, it wasn't him that's for damn sure, now hold on, this is gonna be tight!" she said, first referring to Jesus not being her mentally unstable driving instructor and then to the intersection we were just about to fly through. I screamed and covered my head with my hands as I saw the red light and moving lanes of traffic we were about to suicidally drive into.

"AAAAAHHHH!" I swear they say your life flashes before your eyes, but for me all I could see was the red light we were driving through, even after I closed my eyes.

"You can stop screaming now, we survived," she said calmly reminding me that she was right, if I was screaming then I wasn't dead...*yet*. But then she had no choice but to join traffic and the second she swerved around one car, there was another one on the other side for us to try and miss.

In fact, this was when I shouted in pain as a lorry locked its brakes and its load jackknifed coming towards us and ended up passing its own cab and driver, without anything able to stop it.

"Oh goodie, this will do nicely," she said in that crazy cool tone before she barely missed it, by I swear what looked like an inch! Locking up the brakes once more, she only just managed to get us down another alleyway. But the move knocked me clean on my side and my head hit the door frame with a crunch. Then she stopped the car and looked behind her with an arm on her seat as if waiting to see what would happen next.

She shrugged her shoulders at me, not looking too concerned but then again, she was more occupied currently and I too looked up to watch. The Land Rover went crashing into the oncoming lorry and I thought this was it, they were definitely not walking away from that one.

But then I was wrong.

As it turned out there was at least one of the people in that car that must have been a supernatural. I knew this for certain when the car suddenly erupted into blue flames and the second they touched the lorry's load, it then burst into a cloud of ash. As if one touch from a forked flame and it literally was incinerated.

"Ah, damn it!" the woman said, losing her cool and slapping a hand down on the back of her seat before putting the car back into first and driving off at killing speeds once more.

"Oh dear, that is unfortunate. Pesky little men, you got their baby," she said weirdly, and I had to admit I had no clue what she was talking about or to whom in fact, as I swear it was as if she had even forgotten that I was back here. And now, with what I could feel was blood trickling down the side of my face, well let's just say I was asking myself if I should be worried about this woman's state of mind.

We continued on and when I looked back, for once I couldn't see the bad guys following us.

"I think we lost them for good this time," I said, making her chuckle again and say,

"Time to be sure." Then she pulled into an underground parking garage, swiping some kind of card and then parked the car before turning off the engine and killing the lights.

"What now?" I asked, whispering for some reason and it made her smirk.

"Now we wait a minute and if no one comes to kill us, then I think it means we are good to go," she said as though the idea of someone coming to kill us didn't bother her one little bit. But in fact, was more of a fun thought to play around with in her mind. If there was one word to describe this lady, then that would definitely be 'unhinged'.

But then again, it had to be said that she had mad crazy driving skills that certainly came in handy in my first official car chase. And well, she had most likely saved my life, so big plus and thumbs up from me on that one. Which prompted me to say,

"Not that I don't feel eternally grateful here, but why did you save me and who are you?"

"Eternally grateful, now I will have to remember that one," she said smirking again. Then she stuck her hand in between the seats for me to shake and said,

"Honestly, my real name is Bess, Bess Shaw and I came here to save you." I took her hand and gave it a shake and said,

"I guess that means you know who I am then." She smiled and then said,

"Oh, I know who you are, everyone in my world does. I have been dying to meet you, to meet the girl who has got a certain Vampire King's panties in a twist...so tell me, girl to girl, how did you manage that, uh?" she asked, making me jerk my head back in surprise.

"Uhh, I am not sure what you mean." She scoffed at my vague answer, one I gave her because, one I was surprised by her question and also because I couldn't get a read on what she was. She definitely wasn't human, but she wasn't coming through as an Angel or Demon either. Of course, I only understood this after I asked the question,

"So, who sent you?"

"No one sent me," she answered bluntly, making me frown.

"Then why and who and..." She started laughing again, which I had to admit, sounded a little cackled and any minute now I kind of expected her to start rubbing her hands together or something. But then she stunned me by saying,

"No one sent me because, *I am the new oracle.*"

After my new friend Bess dropped this colossal sized bombshell on me, I first sat in silence too shocked to know what to say. Then she declared I was still bleeding and got out of the car. I followed her and just as I walked round to her side she threw a scarf at me, telling me to use it. So, I held it to the cut on my head and followed her from the parking garage up onto the street level.

"So, what now?"

"Now we walk, come on, it's not far from here," she said before crossing the road and zipping up her tight biker jacket. It was now that I finally had chance to take the rest of her in.

"I have to say, you're not what I had in mind for an oracle," I told her, as in truth she was far from it.

"Yeah well, that chick Pythia was some tough boots to follow," she said referring to the original and oldest oracle and a now good friend of my mother's. Not that she got to see her much anymore, as let's just say, where she lived now wasn't exactly what you would call easy to get to.

But, as for this new one, well let's just say, blonde, beautiful and also wearing the tightest clothes you could get on a person without them being classed as an extra layer of skin, hadn't been it. But it had to be said that she definitely drove like a badass, so it wasn't surprising that she then looked like one!

Knee high, spiked leather boots clicked along the pavement as she strutted along like a pro. She certainly couldn't be classed as clumsy that was for sure as there wasn't a scratch on her, unlike me. No, I had a cut just in my hairline and no doubt a nicely mottled bruise brewing under my skin just ready to scream angrily at me tomorrow every time I twisted my torso. I could already feel the skin getting tighter as the pain was setting in and walking in heels wasn't helping. This had been both from where I had been thrown around in the car and also when I fell over the luggage at the airport. That, along with the pain throbbing in my elbow, then let's just say that tomorrow was going to be fun when getting my first look at myself in the mirror.

But, I followed Bess because really, what else could I do? It obviously wasn't safe to be out here alone, which made me wonder if she had seen all this? So, I decided to ask her.

"So, you saw all this happening?"

"Something like that, it's why I had the garage plan and this," she said, holding up a card with a small chip in it, making it look like a credit card.

"What's that?"

"A way to get in," she replied with a grin over her shoulder at me.

"A way to get in where?" I asked feeling in some way as though she was enjoying playing with me. But then again, from what I heard of Oracles, well then in a word, they didn't usually get out much.

"In there," she nodded ahead of her and now I could see it for myself. It was a huge five story building made of black brick and was framed by a thick light grey stonework all around the windows and doors. The building itself was set at an angle, so that the front door was situated at the corner.

Then, running down the sides, were ten sets of windows reaching high up to the top of the building. However, like on the Land Rover that had been determined to get to us, each of the windows was blacked out. This just made the building look eerie and even more intimidating, like a giant insect staring at you with a hundred black eyes. All apart from the very top row that were from the inside framed by red velvet curtains as if this was someone's home.

It certainly set the scene for a gothic nightclub that was for sure, especially with all the twisted wrought iron that framed each window's stone arch above. Below them, however, were wilting metal flowers the size of bedside tables that looked worn and rusted on purpose. It gave the place a steampunk, industrial vibe. They had been made into lamps that made the street below glow red from the crimson bulbs, as it bathed the long line of people waiting to get inside in a blood coloured hue.

However, the most unusual part was the metal vine that had been embedded into the ground where it started before it then grew upwards attaching itself to the side of the building. It was there in certain points that massive bloody spikes, the size of a person's head, looked to have attacked the building, by latching its thorns into the brick.

So many people were still stood in line just waiting for their chance at getting inside before the night was over and I suddenly wondered what the time was. Well, it looked like it was far from closing anytime soon so at least that was a plus.

The very last aspect of the place for me to take in was the name above the door. A gothic script of calligraphy in red and black metalwork was hung over the entrance, spelling out the club's name with the F in the middle dragged further down the rest of the letters. This was done for a single purpose as a metal droplet dripped down and hung from the razor tipped edge.

I shuddered, not only at the sight of the single blood droplet, but also at the name and the memory it invoked from the very first time I had seen it, doing as I did now as if that memory was trying to drag its way back…

My lips then formed the name and I knew in that moment, unlike what I had vowed that day, then it wouldn't be the last time I saw it as I had hoped.

But it most definitely sent me back to the first…

"Transfusion."

CHAPTER TWENTY-SEVEN

KING OF CARNAL LUST

S eeing Transfusion again was like receiving a bullet to the heart to the point that I couldn't help but place a hand there. It was as if I just had to check that there wasn't a mortal wound there I was bleeding from.

Because now here I was again, looking up at the building as I had once done that night, only feeling so very different than I did back then. Because now I knew…I knew what to expect and what horrors lay behind those walls and at the front of it all was a cruel, heartless King who thought nothing of crushing a young girl's hopes under his boot and right along with it…

A fragile and bleeding heart.

I tore my gaze away from the place, now stood across the street knowing that I had no choice but to go inside. I don't know why the place affected me so much.

Well, that wasn't true, I knew why, and well… it all started…

SEVEN YEARS AGO

"This is a bad idea," I said to myself out loud as I looked up at the imposing building that I swear was one second trying to draw me closer, whilst at the same time trying to warn me away. And why was I here, because I let my cousin Ella talk me into it that's why! Go tame the wolf she said, yeah like that was even possible around someone like Lucius. But then again, I didn't know how much longer I could go on the way I was.

I had tried to get a hold on this obsession. By Gods in Heaven and Hell, they all knew that I had, but it was all in vain. Because here I was, after creating an excuse that would eventually land me in Germany. I had decided that studying here might be as good a place as any to start my dream of becoming an archaeologist and with LMU university in the heart of Munich, I thought it might have been perfect. Okay, so it was true that I was hoping for another reason for me to find perfection here and I thought that if I was a regular enough face in someone's life then maybe something more could grow from it.

I was twenty years old and I wasn't a kid anymore. I was an adult so maybe, just maybe he would finally start to view me as one. I mean, it wasn't as if I had grown up seeing him or that would have just been weird. But then again, didn't these guys have a massive age difference with anyone they dated...look at my dad and mum for example, he had been thousands of years old and my mum had only been twenty-three when they met.

Alright, so from what I heard there had been that one time when he saw me as a baby, but since then the first time I remembered ever seeing him was when I was at the tender age of sixteen. That had been the first time I had ever spoken to him in person but the second I saw him I couldn't believe my eyes.

To find the man I had been dreaming about since I was seven years old had been like being plunged into my dream world and imprisoned there with him as my personal jailor.

At first the dreams had just been of a man watching over me, but I never saw a face until much later on. It was as if the older I became the more, little by little, parts of his image would start to emerge. So, by the time I was sixteen I finally had a face to go with years of an intimidating shadow.

However, there was never anything sexual about these dreams, but just a few stolen touches to my cheek as if he had been checking to see if I was hot or cold. There would be a caring spark in his intense grey eyes that I couldn't look away from. But then, after that first moment I met him, my dreams did change, now taking on a more heated element that had me both waking up gasping for air and experiencing my first orgasm on the night of my seventeenth birthday. I swear it was the best present I could have ever received, and his touches hadn't even been real.

But since then I'd had three more years to cope with, as those dreams only intensified. Those dominant hands that would control my body along with the state of my mind. Hands that I knew were as dangerous even when they were adoring my skin. It was as though I belonged to him, and every touch granted was just another brand to my soul for me to collect. I often asked myself, wondering how long it would be, how many brands would it take, for him to consume me whole. For there to be nothing left that belonged to me but in fact to find that he had taken it all and I had been powerless to stop him.

This was why I was so obsessed.

And it was the sole reason for me to be here now.

I had been in Germany a week, seen the university and spoken with people at the Faculty for the Study of Culture, which I learned was a course that comprised a variety of disciplines, ones which were based on philological, archaeological, anthropological, ethnological, and sociological methodologies and each and every one of them was a mouthful. But, so long as it combined my passion for learning history and cracked the secrets of the past, along with being placed in his path, then that was all I wanted.

Of course, all I needed to do now was get up the courage to actually step inside. But what if he turned me away, or I wasn't even allowed past the front doors? But surely not, I mean he knew my parents, was friends with them even, so why wouldn't he meet with their daughter? What reason would he have not to?

No, I was at least confident that he would see me, and I had everything I was going to say all planned out. I would simply tell him how my father thought it was a good idea we meet, considering I was going to be living in his city and he thought it best that I have some protection.

This part actually wasn't something I had made up just as an excuse...okay, so when I had been trying to sell the idea to my father and he'd been about to refuse, I simply reminded him that the college in Evergreen didn't do my course. I also asked the question, didn't he have a good friend in Munich who could be there for me if I needed help, even watch out for me?

I couldn't understand why my dad had scoffed at this, but good old mum came to my rescue, declaring it a wonderful idea. She then helped me convince my dad and the next thing I knew I was on a plane heading for Germany with my best dress secretly packed away ready and waiting for this night. I knew it was naive to hope that he would fall madly in love with me on first sight, now getting that chance to see me as a grown young woman. But I just knew that it must have been what was going to happen…surely? Because there was only one reason for all these years' worth of dreams and that was simple…

He was my Chosen One.

He was to me what my dad was to my mum, I was sure of it. And my mum always spoke fondly of him, encouraging me one day to meet him. When I had hit my teens, I tried to do as much research on him as possible but could only find his history going back a few hundred years and nothing before. I didn't know his background story even though I had a feeling everyone else did around me. I would ask my mum and she would just tell me, that it wasn't her story to tell.

So yes, in essence all I knew was that he was King of the Vampires, so sired my mother at some point, but this was yet another story I didn't know. I also knew that he used to be my father's righthand man until again, something happened that I didn't know the story behind. So, all in all, other than knowing him to be a pretty powerful being and the most handsome man I had ever seen, then I was in the dark when it came to what the man himself was like as a person. Which I know didn't exactly set the foundations for a loving relationship, considering the guy could just be…well, *a dick*. But then once again, if this was the case and we weren't meant to be together, then why all the dreams? Why did this obsession even start to flower?

So, didn't it all mean that it was time to put this obsession to the test?

I took a deep breath and told myself it was time to be brave. To cut the cords from my safe world that was Afterlife and step into what could be my future…

Into Transfusion.

After this thought process took root, I stepped into the line, waiting my turn and pulling nervously at my jacket, wondering if my dress was too short beneath it. I had bought it because worn with jeans or leggings it just looked like an overly long strappy top. But then lose the bottoms and add the thick black belt I had tied around my waist and presto! I had a sexy dress that showed enough leg that I think my father would have made it a record for the first supernatural to have popped a vein.

I matched it with a pair of strappy black heels which had ribbon that wrapped around my ankles and tied in a pretty bow at the side. I had done my hair in a twist with curls cascading down around my face and worn my contacts lenses that I was still getting used to. I had done my make up a little heavier than I ever had before, but I think it suited me, with the darker shades making my eyes look bigger. The dark plum lipstick managing to give me a slight gothic edge which, considering it was a gothic nightclub, I thought was best. After all, I didn't want to stand out by looking preppy. Besides, I kind of had in my head that this was a look he would like or go for in a woman.

I saw that I was next in line to be admitted and my nerves started to double.

"Halt," the doorman said and placed his hand out to prevent me from going in.

"Wie alt sind Sie?" he said, and I had to think back to my German lessons to try and piece together what he'd asked, something about age I think.

"Um, twenty, oh I mean… siebzehn, oh no wait that's not right, I mean zwanzig?" I said getting my numbers mixed up and first telling him that I was seventeen by mistake. He raised an eyebrow in question and looked slightly amused by my mumbling. I just hoped he didn't think I was as young as seventeen as I knew that I had always looked younger than the age I actually was. Well, at least over here you didn't have to be twenty-one to have a drink like in the states.

"Englisch?" he asked, and I nodded, thankful he was at least being nice to me.

"Passport?" he asked me, and I frowned first wondering why he would need to see my passport when it suddenly occurred to me that he wanted to see proof of my age.

"Oh, I didn't bring it, I am sorry…I didn't know that…"

"Then no inside, lady," he said in broken English.

"But…but wait…" I said the second he tried to get me to move along whilst the next couple took my place. I decided I had no choice but to say the words that suddenly started spilling from my lips,

"I know the owner…Lucius, I know Lucius, he will let me in." This made him stop and the look he gave me was one of pure shock before then one of…*was that pity?*

"Are you sure…sure you wish this of yourself?" he asked in a low tone, bending his head slightly to look in my eyes and I knew what it was…

A warning.

I swallowed hard and nodded, trying to lift my head a little. Because I may not be able to account for the other mortals in the club but for me at least, then I knew he wouldn't hurt me. If only because of who my parents were. Surely this would be enough…*wouldn't it?* The guy sighed and nodded in acceptance but looking dejected all the same.

Then I listened as he spoke to someone on his radio before waiting a moment to see.

"Name lady?" he asked as the people on the other end obviously wanted to know.

"Amelia, Amelia Draven," I said leaving out my middle name and for once using my first name, strangely one I never used. I had always been Faith or Fae, to everyone, so why change now? Was it to sound more grown up? I held my breath as I waited, not sure whether I would find myself pleased or disappointed not to be let in. Either way, nerves were all I felt the second he nodded and let me inside. It even turned out that I didn't have to pay as I stepped up to the booth the door man waved me off,

"Nein, keine Zahlung," he said to the lady who was collecting and stamping. I gathered it meant that I could go on in, which I did.

There was a staircase straight ahead that obviously led up to the upper levels, but I thought it best to go into the main level first. Although, if this was anything like Afterlife, then I knew where I would most likely find Lucius and that was in his own VIP at the very top.

But I decided to go inside the main room first and I couldn't help but gasp as I looked all around the massive space, including up at its tall ceilings. The main room was a huge open space with a heavy industrial vibe that looked in parts very steampunk.

It looked as if it once could have been an old warehouse of sorts, that had been converted into a nightclub. On the side of the building where I had been queueing was, on the inside, a long bar that ran nearly the full length of the large room, covered in elaborate twisted metal work.

The nightclub looked to be on many levels as the open space was framed by a series of metal staircases and wide balconies that framed the entire circumference of the room. Each space was filled with so many bodies dancing to the heavy rock band that played on stage, it was hard to make each person out as a singular entity as they all seemed to merge into one.

The stage area was on the level above the ground floor I was stood on and it curved outwards over the room in a half moon shape, which was mirrored above. It had great metal columns reaching the full length of the building from floor all the way to the roof either side of it as a main feature. The dance floor was below it and fanned out, spreading outwards not far from the bar area where I was stood.

It was hard to see all of its details with the hundreds of bodies dancing and jumping around, moving as one with everyone singing in German, joining in with the band's main singer.

But from what I could see, then I would say that it had a mixture of old-world elegance combined with a harsher industrial grunge. The lighting seemed to play havoc on my eyes as strobe lights bounced all around the space, reflecting off the people below in streams of green and red beams. The only lights not dancing around were the ones attached to the balcony railings that were like dulled red floodlights. Above the bar were unique just like the ones outside. They were wilted thorn covered roses that lined above the bar so that the bar staff could actually see what drinks they were mixing.

I walked further in, trying not to get crushed in the masses and made my way to the bar area first as I thought a drink was a good start. I ignored any stares I received, putting my head down and once again asking myself if this had been a good idea? Maybe I could just get one drink, call it a baby step taken and then go home to try again another night.

I swear by the time I made it to the bar I had to place my hands down on the counter and close my eyes a second.

"You can do this," I whispered to myself.

"Are you sure about that, Princess?" The second I heard his voice I whipped around expecting to find him stood there behind me. I swear it had sounded as if it had been whispered directly into my ear. I looked all around and saw no one and everyone at the same time. But I was only looking for one person. Did this mean he knew I was here? Could he see me right now...*was he watching me?*

Did the beast know when a willing victim had walked into

his domain? Deep down I knew that he did. But before I could follow through with my plan I needed a drink, so I got the barman's attention and ordered a diet coke and rum. Then I took a big long gulp and made the decision to see if I could get his attention another way.

So, I decided to be brave and after I swallowed down a hard lump of nerves, I slowly unzipped my jacket making sure that if he was looking that he could see...*all of me.*

My back was to the bar and what faced me were three rows of balconies, being the one at the very top that was mainly cast in the shadows. It was also the one I was most interested in.

But wait, was that a figure I could see stood there at the centre looking down? Was it the king of the castle? I didn't know but I continued anyway, peeling away my jacket and revealing my tight short dress, hoping it was as sexy as I hoped. But the second my shoulders were bare and I was letting it slip from my hands, I jumped when I heard a bottle smash behind me. I turned and nearly dropped my jacket when someone caught it for me.

"Sorgfältige Dame" the guy said, telling me to be careful.

"Oh, thanks." I muttered to the stranger.

"Ah, you're English," the guy said with a German accent. I turned to look at him fully to see that he wasn't a bad looking guy, but there was something in his face I didn't trust. As if he was acting.

"Yeah I..."

"You will tell him you are with someone, do it now!" Lucius' demand suddenly spoke in my mind and I wondered how it was he was doing it. I looked up and all around the balcony, but the shadow had gone.

"You were saying?" the guy asked with a grin that didn't reach his eyes. He had sharp features, with a thin nose and dark eyes that were slightly shadowed as though he never managed to get enough sleep.

"I'm sorry, I...I'm with someone," I told him, and the guy then made a show of looking around as if he didn't believe me and I soon found out why.

"I don't see anyone, and besides, I saw you come in alone," he challenged, making me frown and wonder if this guy knew how to get the hint when a girl wasn't interested.

"I am waiting for him, he owns the place," I said, adding this last part and hoping he would take me more seriously...*he didn't.* No instead that asshole just started laughing making me frown.

"What's so funny about that?" I asked with a slice of attitude.

"No one sees the owner or if they do, then they don't remember it...he is a Geist, a phantom, the how you say, Boogieman... one second you see him and then POOF, he is gone!" the guy said, trying to be dramatic and scare me. Ha! Well that was funny considering this guy had no clue why it was I wouldn't ever scare easily.

"Yeah, alright then...look, thanks for catching my jacket and everything but if you could just give that back before he turns up then...hey, what are you...?" I stopped mid-sentence when he stepped into me and placed his hand behind me at the bar, then he leaned in close and warned,

"Demons are real, little girl, so watch yourself in the dark, for they are waiting for you." I gasped the second he issued this warning and went back a step when he winked at me. Then someone who looked like security, started making their way through the crowd shouting,

"Du da, komm her!" Which I knew meant 'you there, come here'. The guy saw this and after granting me a last sadistic grin he left, ducking in and out of the crowd and getting lost. I picked my jacket off the floor from where he had dropped it and then turned around to take a large gulp of my drink. Could that have been any weirder? How did he know that demons were real? He was definitely human, that was for sure, but then how did he know unless of course he was just trying to scare me?

"Excuse me, miss can you please come with me?" A man said approaching me, who definitely was security and one that wasn't German for he had an American accent.

"I didn't have anything to do with that man, he just approached me and…"

"Yes, we know," he answered in a stern voice looking off to his side and in the direction the man disappeared to.

"The boss wants to see you, come this way please," he said, and my heart did a sudden back flip. Lucius wanted to see me?!

I quickly turned around, took my drink and downed it in one, knowing that I needed it. Well, there was no going back now, I had come all this way to see him and after so long of planning it then this was the final step before hopefully my new life would begin.

Would he know about the dreams…? Was it possible that he had been having them too? I know that's how it happened between my mum and dad. All the things she described before they got together, well, I never said anything, but I just knew that it could only mean that Lucius was my fated one too.

For what other reason could there be?

The security guard gave me a head nod telling me without words to follow him. I thought we were going to go back the way I had come in and up the staircase I had seen near the entrance. But instead he started to lead me the opposite way to the furthest end of the room. It took us a while to get through the crowd of people and when one guy bumped into me, I turned and swore I could see him looking back at me with crimson blood red eyes flashing the second the strobe light fell on him.

I frowned, wondering if that meant that his kind were allowed down on this level to mingle amongst the humans? And if so wasn't that a bit of a risk? I shook it off, deciding now was not the time to focus on what was humanly right in his nightclub. So, I followed the guy in front of me, but once again I swear I caught sight of another one in the corner looking directly at me. It was starting to freak me out, so I quickened my step making sure not to be left too far behind.

The guy was just approaching a set of doors at the back that was guarded by two massive guys that looked to spend all their free time at the gym or making protein shakes. The security guy that I had been following gave them each a nod and then swiped a card by a reader at the door. Then he looked back to see if I was close. I finally managed to squeeze past a tight group of people just as the doors opened and revealed it to be an elevator.

"Ready?" the guy asked me when I finally made it inside and was now next to him. I frowned in question and wanted to ask him, 'ready for what?' when instead he just closed the doors with another swipe of his card and we shot up the three floors to the top.

Then the doors opened and he answered my silent question...

"For this," he said nodding ahead as the doors opened into an entirely different room and definitely not any type of VIP I had ever seen before. No, this was one of pure salacious behavior and debauchery. It was sinful with a supernatural twist and I felt my cheeks getting hot the second my wide surprised eyes took in the room.

But most shocking of all wasn't the utter erotic events that were occurring, no it what was centred in the very middle of them.

The King of his dark, twisted and carnal world…

Lucius.

My Chosen One.

CHAPTER TWENTY-EIGHT

THE GRASS IS BLACK AND DEAD ON THIS SIDE

The moment I saw him I froze, I couldn't even take that first step needed to get me into the room. I had dreamt of this moment for so long and now the man I had been obsessed with was right there. I felt myself going crazy the longer I went without seeing him in the flesh and now this was it. Here I was and I couldn't even take one bloody step!

But he finally turned in his seat and the second those burning silver eyes of his made contact with mine, I was trapped. Locked inside his personal spell and I could do nothing I wanted to do, for now all I seemed to want to do was *run*. I suddenly realised the mistake I had made but I had no choice now. I needed to see this through and hope that just more than my heart would survive.

Because, how could I tell a man I loved him when he didn't even know me? Hell, but it sounded impossible just thinking it! But I couldn't help it. It was as though I was born to love him, cursed even. But like I said, he didn't know me and what I knew of him was hard and cold and brutal. Was I really the one in this world meant to tame such a bloodthirsty beast? Was this really what the Fates had in store for me?

Well, there was only one way to find out because now there he was and I was caught in his sights. I knew this when he started beckoning me forward with a simple flick of a couple of fingers.

So, I took a deep breath and stepped out of the elevator, noticing how the room widened into a much larger area than you would have thought.

The large space on the top floor narrowed back towards a staircase, meaning I must have come up by a private elevator. Next to these doors I noticed another pair of doors that looked far more intimidating and I wondered if, like in Afterlife's VIP, this was the entrance to his private home?

The rest of the upstairs was set out like a playground for an X-rated club, where all that was on the menu was sex and blood. Vampires and demons alike all fed freely along with indulging in the acts of the flesh. But that wasn't where the weird ended but seemingly only where the normal began, for everything after that just got weirder and weirder.

Like the woman in the centre of the narrow room who was dancing round and doing a sexy routine inside a giant old-fashioned champagne glass that was filled with what I could only assume was blood. She was splashing and teasing her audience with it as at least thirty people all sat round watching her blood tease. The whole of her face was hidden under a lace mask with only blood red lips showing through.

Then there were two white haired twins that were dressed like broken dolls, only let's just say that it didn't look like it was part of their costumes where their skin had been sewn together. It started at their hands where someone had joined by sewing each of their fingers together using a crude crisscross pattern. One that had been done with a thick needle that impaled their skin and which was still hanging down in between them by the red thread. It swung like a pendulum dripping with the blood that slowly trickled down the pierced flesh.

They also had crosses on their faces along with sewn circles around one eye each. Then, these thick crude stitches of red cord, tied in the shape of hearts over naked breasts and exactly where their actual hearts were buried beneath tortured twisted flesh. They were simply skipping back and to, obviously holding hands and letting their large attributes swing and sway freely.

There was also a line of cages that had inside what looked like willing humans all dressed in barely seen underwear. Each had messages written on their bodies with words and phrases trying to entice a buyer, for a group of people all sat waiting their turn to be called up and chosen. I watched horrified as some placed five euro notes into one of the cages like it was a change machine. It ate up the small amount of money and the door swung free, and an excitable girl jumped out into a man's arms. Seriously, were all these people drugged?!

How could he have all of this happening in his club? What kind of man was he? I swear was it me or was the air in here getting thick and making it hard to breathe?

I glanced back to Lucius, knowing that I was walking towards him painfully slow, as I took it all in and he seemed amused by the sight. Was it my face, was I giving away too much of the horrors of this place and what I thought.

Alright, so for someone who had zero sexual experience other than a self-induced orgasm, then I confess I was seriously naive about all of this…this…well the kinky side of sex. But then this, well this must have been something else entirely because it wasn't your simple whips and handcuffs type of gig. No, this was a sexual deviant's playground!

Which begged the biggest question of all…what did that make its owner…*what did that make Lucius?*

I continued on, tearing my eyes from the scene as best as I could, and I winced when I heard the chuckles of people that I passed knowing I was the source of their amusement.

This part of the room was much larger and, thankfully, somewhat tamer than at the back. It spread out at the center in an arc that curved over the floors below, meaning you could see everything but the parts below it, like the band. The middle section was framed with the same huge metal columns that were attached to the stage below and in between the steel frame work was frosted glass panels that I guess prevented anyone from taking a nose dive three stories down.

It was decorated with a black tribal pattern like a gothic thorn that was thicker at the bottom, creeping its way up to the top. I couldn't help but steal a glance as I was prompted further into the room by the guy behind me. Like I said, you could see everything from up here, especially the bar area and where I had been stood.

The centre of this wide space was taken up with a huge sofa that curved round and could easily have fit up to ten people upon it. Covered in a black velvet material with blood red piping around the edges it certainly stood out against the wooden flooring. Even the base of it was of a gothic nature, being made from thick dark oak and its feet were carved into large dragon's feet with deadly talons that were actually embedded in the floorboards.

And at the centre of that imposing gothic setting was its King.

"Lucius." His name slipped from my lips on a barely heard whisper only I knew that he hadn't missed it. His eyes told me as much when they burned brighter for a second. I had seen many of my dad's kind do this and it was once described to me

as a sign that someone's other side, their demon or their angel, was showing through. It was as though a piece of themselves was permanently on lockdown but every so often it would act up and try to push itself through, fighting for dominance or control over their host.

"Ah, but to what do we owe to this, such a royal presence, to grace my humble little establishment?" Lucius' voice rang out in a taunting way, as he leant back against the couch, resting one out-stretched arm along it's back. He looked like such a powerful figure and far more intimidating than he ever looked in my dreams, that was for damn sure!

He wore a tight pair of fitted black trousers that were tucked into a pair of laced grey boots that looked as if he couldn't be bothered to tie all the way up. Meaning the tops of them were peeled back at the sides and buckled to the rest of the straps on his boot. With this he wore a black shirt that was rolled up at the cuffs and was open at his neck, unbuttoned all the way down to the start of his waistcoat. This meant that you could see the defined chest muscles just peeking through and he looked utterly solid.

He looked casual smart without a jacket and the unconventional biker boots with his expensive looking suit. One that was without a doubt made to measure, as it was molded to his large frame perfectly. He was dressed entirely in dark shades other than the blood red stitching against the dark grey tweed material on his waistcoat.

He was officially the sexiest being I had ever seen in my entire life and for that reason, along with many others, I couldn't seem to find my voice. That and the stunning blondes that were sat either side of him, one of which he had obviously been feeding from if the two bloody puncture marks on her chest were anything to go by. If anything, it looked like blood on tap with them still bleeding that way. Of course, the pain of seeing this and making me suffer was one I hadn't been expecting or prepared for. In fact, I just wanted to excuse myself and run home as fast as I could, hoping and praying that this was the end of his hold on me and my heart.

But of course, I had come too far now and he wouldn't let me go that easily without first doing what he looked as though he did best...*playing the puppet master.*

"Well, does this royal visit come with a voice?" he asked in such a way it made the others around him snigger and I swallowed hard.

"I...my father thought it best that I..." I started to say when his laughter cut me off.

"Oh, I doubt greatly that daddy knows where his precious little girl is right now, for I think I would find myself with a few more unexpected guests to accommodate, instead of just this lost little lamb I see before me now," Lucius replied, making me tense my hands and hating the way he ridiculed me for nothing more than who he thought I was.

"I am not lost," I stated bravely, straightening my back and showing him that I had some courage. He raised his brows in feigned surprise and then grinned before slapping his hands to his knees and making me flinch as he rose to his full height. I don't know why but I couldn't help but take a step back and I didn't know why I let him intimidate me so much. Not considering I had grown up surrounded by tall, well defined men that were much bigger than me.

Was it because I knew how dangerous he was? How powerful? Or was it because deep down I knew what he was to me, what I was to him that certain Fates had deemed so? But from the looks of him now and the way he walked slowly towards me with indifference clearly written there to see, then did he not know what I knew? I would have said not.

"You're not lost, you say?" he asked, tapping two fingers on his slightly blood-stained lips as if toying with me and I so badly wanted to put my fingers to my mouth and nibble on the ends. I shook my head in the end as I didn't know what to say to him to stop him from mocking me the way he seemed to enjoy.

"Then enlighten me, whatever drove such an innocent little doe into the wolf's den?" he asked, pausing his motions before taking a step towards me and frightening me enough that I took a sudden step back. I banged into the glass panel making it vibrate and I gasped.

"I…I…" I started to stutter out my words as he continued to get closer until soon he rested an outstretched arm over my head with the gloved palm against the glass. I so badly wanted to ask about that hand as I still didn't know. It was the same at the first time I had seen him as he always seemed to have it covered. Why? Just what was he hiding from the world?

"You…you…you were saying?" he taunted, drumming his leather covered fingers against the glass as a clear sign that he was waiting for his answer. The sound felt like it was beating in time with my pounding heart, as from this close I could see, smell and hear everything.

I could smell the intoxicating scent of his aftershave, a sandalwood and leather, with some spice I couldn't place. Then there were the small lines near the corners of his stunning eyes, that I wondered if they creased deeper when he smiled or laughed? There were the flecks of blue ice bursting outwards in his eyes and the long lashes that framed them. The chiseled jawline that just begged for a pair of soft fingertips to trace along. There was even the small sound he made like an impatient hum to himself, like a habit even he didn't realise he had.

He was finally real to me.

And my heart couldn't cope.

"I came here to…" I stumbled on my words again and this

time the grin he gave me was one that totally belonged to a sadist.

"To? Come on Princess, for I will be in my coffin before long," he teased as I knew he didn't sleep in a coffin like the story books would have you believe. Seriously, who did he think I was, some Vampire groupie that had no clue they were real? I decided to hold on to my anger at the way he was viewing me and said this time with less of a trembling voice,

"I am here to tell you that I will be moving here." At this he raised a brow in question before saying,

"Oh, will you now? Then tell me, Sweet do I at least have time to pack my bags before royalty evicts me?" he taunted again, and I scoffed before saying,

"Well, obviously not here, here…"

"Obviously," he mocked, doing so in the same tone and nodding his head condescendingly. Then he raised a hand up and started to touch me, making me flinch and suck in a startled breath the second he made contact. It was like feeling a supernatural current dancing along my skin. He paused a moment as if he too had experienced it, that or he was giving me time to adjust to the feel of his touch.

"And this pretty little black dress, was it for my benefit?" He purred the question as he started to run his fingers under the thin straps and downwards until they were getting closer and closer to the curve of my breast. I held my breath and even found myself unable to keep my eyes open at the feeling of my dream man touching me for real this time.

"I asked you a question, Princess," he reminded me sternly and my eyes snapped open at the sound of his authority being revealed.

"I thought I would… that you would…" I found I couldn't finish that sentence as I felt far too exposed doing so.

"Find you ripe for the picking?" he finished, and I suddenly blurted out,

"No! No, I didn't think that," I told him making him smile this time and for once it wasn't one done to mock.

"You do not wish to entice me then, as the others do?" he asked, suddenly frowning and I was surprised by his question. So, I shook my head telling him no and surprising him again. But then it was his turn to shock me as the second my gaze wandered to the blondes he had referred to as the 'others', he suddenly slammed a hand against the glass in a moment of anger. Then, at the same time, his lips were suddenly snarling dangerously at my neck. I screamed in shock and froze, feeling as though any moment a chunk of my neck would be missing and thinking it was quite an important piece to lose.

But, instead of feeling the pain I just felt the fear. That blinding fear that had my heart trying to save itself by pounding its way out of my chest like a Captain jumping from a sinking ship. I waited, not knowing what to expect next when suddenly I felt his lips against my neck, not so much in a kiss but more a grin against my skin. Then I flinched the second I felt a cold set of fangs extending against my tender flesh.

The second I moved even the slightest bit his free hand came to my side to hold me still. I swear his hand was so large it spanned half of my belly as he pushed me back flush against the glass.

"Now hold still whilst I play with my new toy," he warned, making me suck in a startled breath at being referred to as his play thing. I don't know how that made me feel as it was conflicting and confusing to be both outraged and turned on from it at the same time. Then I felt him run his extended fangs up the length of my neck, making me shudder against him. I felt his fingers flex at my side as if he was holding himself back from doing what he wanted.

"Now answer the fucking question," he growled low by my ear and I was suddenly reminded that we weren't alone as this felt we should be. I couldn't help my gaze from glancing over his head and he pulled back as though he felt my actions for himself.

"Eyes! Give me your fucking eyes, girl!" he barked, making me snap my gaze back to his as if he had just flipped a switch.

"Now, I will not ask again but instead will remind you in other ways, when I tear this scrap of material from your body, baring you to all." At this my mouth dropped before I uttered,

"You…you wouldn't dare?" I asked in shock making him smirk down at me before the hand on my side suddenly fisted a handful of my dress making it become so tight, it did indeed feel as though one simple tug and it would tear from it seams and render me naked.

"Try pushing me and see where it gets this sweet little body of yours," he warned on a growl and my hand acted on impulse and went to his fist to hold it tight in my palm. I don't know why but the second I touched him his eyes flashed a completely different colour, one of burning amber. And for a single moment it was like looking directly into the flames and hoping that they didn't have the power to burn you.

So, I decided to answer him quickly as I took every threat he issued me as a serious one.

"Yes…*I wore this for you,"* I admitted on a breathy confession. This genuinely seemed to please him and his hold on my dress relaxed and because I didn't want to push my luck I, in turn, released my hold on his hand. Then he started to smooth that abused part of my dress out with his palm flat to my skin, making sweeping motions that ran from just under my breasts and down to the top of my thigh. I swear this time his touch had such power behind it I could feel it driving my sexual urge higher and higher to the point I thought I would come if only he asked it of me.

"That's my good girl, so honest, so innocent…just look at all this untouched virgin skin on show, just ready to be tasted… *to be fucked."* He snarled this last part as a whisper by my ear and at the same time his hand spanned my ribs just under my bra as he pushed me further against the glass, pressing his body into me.

I shuddered and sucked in a shocked breath through clenched teeth for I was so close, I could feel myself building without him even touching that part of me. I was both terrified and elevated to the idea of just one fingertip finding my core as I knew that I would have only begged him for more. I could feel myself getting so lost in him, the way he played me, teased me, mocked me, it was all just a cruel game to him, one I was desperate to win.

But then, just as I felt his lips kiss my neck and his mouth open ready to take their first taste, their first bite in making me his, if only for one long pull of my blood and binding me to him if only for a short time…he pulled away and snarled the horrifying truth in my ear,

"A shame then that I am not into corrupting pretty little virgins with no experience….*as I can smell your innocence and it reeks."* My eyes snapped open and the spell was broken. I tried to pull away from his hold, confused when he was the one who wouldn't let me go. Not until it was that he had delivered his final blow.

"Run on home to your castle, little girl, for you're on the wrong side of that safe world you grew up in." This was when he placed a finger to my painted lips and then ran his thumb down the center, smudging the shade down my chin. I felt like crying at his harsh and humiliating treatment, so I turned my face away, making him run the backs of his fingers down my cheek, telling me,

"For I can assure you, Princess, it is far from greener on this side, for this isn't Afterlife ... this is the gates of Hell I own and here… *I show no fucking mercy!"* he warned on a growl and snapped his teeth at my cheek making me flinch back. Then he sealed my shame and mortification when he tugged me roughly into his arms and whispered down at me,

"Not even to fresh little virgins who nearly cum before I have even uttered their name." Then he grabbed my chin in a bruising hold, held me still and kissed my lips in the very last way I ever thought our first kiss would have been. It was just another way for him to make a mockery out of me in front of all his people and I couldn't help my reaction, I yanked myself out of his hold and before I could stop myself I drew back and went to slap him.

However, his lightning fast reflexes meant that he caught my hand by the wrist before it could touch him with the leather on his palm slapping against my skin.

Then he warned dangerously,

"Not. Wise." He said this in a deadly calm that was far scarier than if he had screamed it at me. Then he spun me around and gave me a little push so that I stumbled a step towards the staircase at the back of the VIP.

"Now run along, Princess, for you have wasted enough of my fucking time on these silly little games of yours…time for a real drink!" he said as he let himself fall back on the sofa before putting his arm behind one of the girls and making her giggle. Then he grabbed the other one by the neck before yanking her hard towards his waiting mouth. Making this a fitting end to the most humiliating moment in my life.

I couldn't help the gasp of pain that escaped as I turned around and started running towards the staircase, having first to try and make my way through the crowd of people. It was the ultimate walk of shame and he and I both knew it. It was, after all, why it had been done. He could have just let me go back down in the lift but this way, it only managed to add that extra slice of cruelty to the act. He wanted me to hate him, now the question was why?

Well, if he wanted me to despise him then he had just got his fucking wish!

So, I didn't care that people were laughing and sneering at me as all I could feel was the pain. Even as the hot fat tears continued to fall down my cheeks, I no longer cared. Let them laugh, let them amuse themselves with the sight of my torment. I just wanted to run as far away from this Hellhole as I could get. However, the amused crowd was prolonging my agony in being here, which was when I heard Lucius one last time roar out a command in German.

"Lass sie durch und fass sie nicht an!" I tried to figure out in my mind what it meant, something about not touching her…this was proven right when suddenly the room parted like the Red Sea for Moses as I was now free to run through the room without being held back. But then I felt my head begin to spin as I felt myself start to feel foggy. Like that moment when you first realise you're drunk, only that was impossible after only one drink?

I reached out to the side, thankfully finding someone's table to lean on whilst I shook my head to try and get my focus. I put a hand to my head as if this would help in clearing the fog and when it finally passed I briefly looked back at Lucius. This left me wondering in my insanity should I tell him that something was wrong with me? But when I saw him look over his shoulder at me frowning and sniffing the air as if he was looking for something, I decided then that I would get nothing but more humiliation from him. Something no doubt this time about my lack of ability to hold down a drink. I even saw him motion for the guard that had brought me up in the elevator to come forward, no doubt asking him to make sure I was removed from his club and quickly. I knew this when I saw him speak into his radio whilst still looking at me.

This was when, after staggering a little, I ran for it. I got to the staircase, nearly throwing myself around the corner holding on to the banister so as not to fall and break my neck. I must have lost my jacket and my purse at some point because by the time I ran through the front doors of the club, I had nothing on me.

The doorman shouted something at me, trying to get me to stop but I just ignored him and carried on running. I just needed to get as far away from this place as possible! How could I have been so stupid! How could I have let myself believe in such a man, such a being! He was just a cruel cold bastard who obviously got his kicks by hurting people. He really was the heartless Vampire King that they said he was.

I finally stopped running and had no clue where I was, but the second I stopped, unfortunately for me the world didn't as my mind became so lost now that it spun and spun and spun until everything was falling around me. It was only when pain exploded at the back of my head that I realised it hadn't been the world falling... *but it was me.*

For a moment I just lay there looking up at the night sky that kept fading in and out every time I closed my eyes slowly. Part of me couldn't understand what was happening and the other half of me just didn't care.

He had crushed me.

But then, as I lay there on the cold hard floor, I heard something approaching me. However, when I tried to lift up my head to see, pain exploded in my head. My eyes refused to focus as I felt as though I had consumed a whole bottle of vodka. Or like that time aunty Pip let me drink too much champagne and she ended up holding my hair back as I puked whilst she sang the Gummy Bears theme tune like it was a lullaby. But I couldn't understand, I had only had the one drink, unless…

This was when a figure suddenly approached and the second they leant down, getting into focus, I opened my mouth to scream when a hand quickly clamped down over my mouth. For there, above me, was the most hideous creature with rubber textured skin stretched out into a face. Beady unblinking eyes stared down at me and a mouth full of fangs that remained wide open like it was going to bite me but didn't close even when it spoke.

Even when its smug voice didn't fit the snarling mouth of a demon as it reminded me…

"See, I told you demons are real."

CHAPTER TWENTY-NINE

THE REAL MONSTER

"Just hurry up and grab her would you!" I heard a frustrated voice say in an American accent as I felt my body being moved around. But it was strange, as though I was only sort of semi-conscious to what was happening around me. But I still couldn't seem to move my body as for some reason it just wasn't working.

"Well, I thought we would jump her on her way home." A boy said, with a German accent this time and when I finally opened my eyes I saw again that demonic face, but now at an odd angle as it was now on top of his head instead on…well, *his face*. I couldn't understand it as it seemed just frozen in that one facial expression looking as if it was about to take a chunk out of you.

"The van isn't far, then we can have our fun with her just like the rest and then dump her somewhere, she will wake up tomorrow without remembering a thing other than being fucked by two demons!" The American said chuckling and that's when I realised he was also helping to carry me, but I couldn't make out where. It was like a fog was stopping me from getting my body to do as it was being told. which was when I started questioning if I had somehow been drugged?

I felt myself being heaved into something after I heard a door being unlocked and slammed. Then I felt hands on me and I frowned not liking it.

"Oh, looks like we have a fighter on our hands this time," the American said in a pleased tone.

"Oh, good I like it when they...*wait, what was that?"* he stopped and started whispering as I felt the hands on me stop moving as well. I looked up and saw the German pull his face down making me realise now, even in my drugged state, that it must have been a mask.

"Never mind, its nothing, let's cut this fucking dress off her, I want to see those big tits," the American said and even if I wasn't fully aware of what was happening, I knew that was a bad thing. I heard the snip of something by my ear and felt myself being man handled up a little, until suddenly I had the biggest urge to scream.

In the end, I don't know how I managed it but I opened my mouth and let go of all the energy I had left,

"LUCIUS!" I screamed his name so loud even my own ears hurt and suddenly I felt pain explode over the side of my face where I must have been punched. To be honest, it probably should have hurt a lot more than it did but a second after it happened, I didn't feel a thing. What I did feel, however, was when the van started to rock and suddenly what sounded like a door being ripped clean off its hinges. I managed to open my eyes and get them to work for a short time and this time there really was a demon knocking at the door.

And he was without a doubt, the most terrifying creature I had ever seen. It was Lucius, but not as I had ever seen him, even if my mind was showing me a clouded version of him.

There were two crimson glowing eyes that looked like the Devil himself had gifted him his own. Two mighty wings stood at his back and they morphed between that of a demonic bat and a flaming phoenix. But I couldn't make out any of his features as there seemed to be a black shadowed aura that floated around him like Hell's essence was clinging to his form.

Then came the scariest sound I had ever heard in all my twenty years alive, all of which had been lived with the knowledge of demons. But this was something else! It was a demonic roar so deep that it sounded as if a beast from Hell had just broken loose and was now on the rampage right outside this van. Then I saw a black hand slap to the top of the last remaining door before it was slowly peeled back as if it had been made from tinfoil.

The sound of screams followed less than a second later and I closed my eyes as one started to sound as if it was dragged out of the van. I then opened my eyes just in time to see the petrified face of one of my attackers getting smaller before he disappeared altogether. Then, in the distance, I heard one last blood curdling scream before a wet slashing and tearing sound followed. After that the only screams left were the ones belonging to the last man standing and he was still in the van with me.

I knew that even without looking as he was currently trying to scramble past my numb body. Then the shadow emerged once more and even though I couldn't focus, I could now see that it was a figure bathed in crimson.

"So, you like to play dress up, drug young girls and pretend to be a demon, do you?" I didn't recognise the demon's voice, but this time I most certainly knew it was the real thing and that it belonged to the deadliest one of all…

Lucius.

The guy next to me started begging for his life, which was a pitiful sound and the strong smell of urine soon filled the small space around me.

"Then, it's time I introduce you to the real thing, after all... you will be seeing a lot of them in the place I am sending you..." This part was said with eerie calm for such a monster. Then his shadow was gone from the end of the van where he had torn off the doors and dragged the other guy out. The German was looking all around for him in panic and then cried out when the side door was suddenly punched through, telling me that it must have been locked. Then I watched in fascination as a strong demonic hand emerged through the punched hole and calmly unlocked the door by flicking off the lock with a curled razor sharp, black claw.

The guy scrambled back further away from the door on my side, stepping on my hand and making me cry out. This was when the door was quickly yanked open. It was done so hard that in the end it came clean off its runners and I saw it through the back as it went skidding down the street creating sparks along the floor with the force. Lucius now stood panting like a wild beast in the opening and I could see the two massive horns emerging from his back as his demon side took over completely.

"FUCK NOOO! Please...oh fuck, please man, look just take the bitch and... AHHH NO!" The guy started to say, but then the second he said 'bitch' the movement came as a blur of colour as Lucius was inside the van. I could only just make out that Lucius' body had been outside one second and the next he was right there. Then, as I looked up and back over my head, I could just make out the single stretched arm above me. One that had now cut the guy's screams off by pinning him to the inside of the van. I could hear the dying gargling sound and saw the blood trickling down his neck from where Lucius had his talons embedded in his flesh, looking ready to rip his throat out.

"What did you call her?" Lucius' threatening question must have made me flinch and he didn't miss the slight movement, because in that moment Lucius' burning crimson eyes looked down at me and their Hellish stare, that was one still filled with blood lust, now strangely took on a softer side as they gazed at me. Then, with his free hand, and as if compelled in this strange horror fueled moment a tender second passed between us, he ran a single finger just under my eyes as I still looked up at him from where I lay.

"Close those pretty eyes for me, Sweet I don't want you to see as I rip him to pieces for you." I swallowed hard, unable to nod or move other than to do what he asked. I was so terrified in that moment that my eyes snapped shut as I took his threat as seriously as death itself.

So, as I closed my eyes for him, what followed swiftly after was a quick breath of movement, as if something extremely fast had moved past me. Then, after a quick scream, a very angry demon finished his threat in the scariest voice I had ever heard spoken…

"Enjoy Hell…after I tear you, limb from fucking limb first!" Then I felt a spray of something wet hit the side of my face and even behind closed eyes I saw a crimson mist before I finally passed out and I did so to the distinct sounds of…

Torture and death.

"Ssshh its alright, it's alright…I have you and you're safe now." I heard the calm tender sound of a man whispering by my ear as I shifted as if something was holding me still. That's when I realised I must have been in someone's arms as it felt as though my body was weightless.

I decided to test my single thought of who it could be, but

even then asking myself why it would be him, when I whispered his name,

"Lucius?" I heard the shuddered breath in return before it was confirmed,

"It's me, sweetheart." I don't know if I was imagining it, but in those three words alone it sounded like it held a weight of emotions that were like a ticking time bomb about to erupt. They were on a fine edge…or was that just my own?

"I don't care which, just get me a fucking car here now and do it fast!" Lucius snarled making me tense in his hold as I could now feel some of the movement coming back to me, even though my head still felt lost and fuzzy. At least I seemed to have more of my eyesight back as the second I opened my eyes I was looking up at him. But wait what was that across his face…?

Blood.

He couldn't see me looking up at him as he was too busy on the phone, snarling into it with every order he issued.

"Just do it and bring the team," Lucius snapped and once again I flinched, making him hold on to me tighter in a reassuring way as if it was an impulse.

"I need clean up, two bodies and lots of parts, so tell them to get their asses here quickly before someone notices a van pissing blood!" he shouted this time before ending the call. I don't know why but I tried to get away from the angry sound and started squirming in his hold.

"Ssshh, calm yourself little one, calm for me now. I will not hurt you… nothing can hurt you now," he told me in a soothing voice when I couldn't stop my lips from moving, wondering if the sound ever made it out of them for I couldn't tell,

"You already did." The only indication in the fog of lies that was my mind was the feeling of someone inhaling a quick, sharp breath before pulling me tighter to their chest. And again,

I couldn't be sure, but I could have sworn that the answer to this had been a whispered,

"I know… as intended." After this I must have fallen unconscious again or at least in and out of consciousness as I would pick up bits here and there, asking myself what was real and what was a dream.

The first of which was the feeling of being in someone's arms and them sitting down with me nestled in their lap. Then I felt a hand smooth back my hair before cradling my head against a very hard chest, one's whose breathing sent me to sleep with the steady rise and fall.

"What is to happen now, my Lord?" I heard someone ask and it was a voice I didn't recognise but sounded strangely as if it belonged to a young lad. Lucius didn't answer right away, but instead I felt a hand come to my face as if examining it, as though there was a bruise there or something.

"My Lord?" the unknown person prompted making Lucius release a sigh.

"Get the Imp here, she will know what is to be done," was Lucius' reply and I frowned in response. Then, I felt the pad of his thumb smooth out my frown before he cooed down at me,

"Ssshh now and sleep, my girl." Then just as the other person started to speak Lucius interrupted,

"We will speak of what is to be done later for she is restless *and listening…isn't that right, my little royal Šemšā?"* Lucius whispered down at me, humming the foreign word I didn't understand. I released a sigh and then after long moments of silence, this time when I found sleep I stayed there. And I stayed there to the feel of Lucius' gentle hand stroking my hair and him holding my hand.

I don't know how long it was after this that I woke up, but when I did I knew that I did so in his bed for it smelled like him and the comfort I felt knowing that made me want to stay here forever. I was about to open my eyes in curiosity, wanting to know what it would look like in his bedroom, but the second I heard voices nearing, I remained still and clung to the sleepy state I was still in.

"Oh gosh, just look at her!" I tried not to frown or make a move to give away the fact I was awake or the fact that I had just recognised my Aunty Pip's voice. But what was she doing here? Unless of course, Lucius had called her to come and escort me home? That was a depressing thought.

"Was she hurt?" Pip asked in a tender and worried tone that nearly broke my heart to hear.

"You mean other than being fucking drugged in *my* club and nearly fucking raped after I'd just let her walk out of here?!" The sound of Lucius' snarled response made me clench my fists under the covers.

"This wasn't your fault, Luc," Pip said reassuringly in a soft voice.

"It was, just not as it intended to be." This was his strange and confusing response in return.

"How long has she been asleep?" Pip asked, obviously thinking it best to change the subject.

"Sixteen hours but it will take longer before it fully leaves her system," Lucius stated in a stern voice that sounded less than pleased.

"Any other injuries?" Pip once again asked.

"A bump to the head, no doubt from when she first passed out and a punch to the face, which she received after she screamed my name for help," Lucius said and again, it sounded as if his jaw was that tight, he could have chewed through nails.

"I heard you made them pay," Pip said sounding happy about this and Lucius growled,

"Not nearly enough for touching her," Lucius said like a sworn vow and again I wanted to frown in confusion as to why he felt so protective over me. Was it just because he felt responsible for it all? Pip laughed at this and said,

"Luc, you tore one guy to pieces and ripped the other guy's genitals out before slashing his throat, I am pretty sure that wasn't fun for them." Lucius grunted and said,

"It should have lasted longer." This made Pip laugh and reply,

"Spoken like the true badass, killer assassin we all know and love." Lucius growled but there was no malice in it as it was done more playfully as he warned,

"Careful, little imp, you and your husband are still on loan to the Dravens, for I will be asking for you back before long and then once I do, your punishment will be of your husband's choosing." Pip laughed and clapped her hands a few times before saying in a genuine tone,

"Oh goodie!"

"How is my right hand these days, bored I imagine?" Lucius asked Pip as I knew they had once worked for Lucius back before my parents were together.

"I must admit, he is eager to come back, but I... well, you know I will miss my Toots," Pip said referring to my mum who was often like a sister to her, being as they were best friends. Hell, but I had never known an Afterlife without Pip in it.

"You have time yet, I am sure," Lucius replied making Pip sigh dramatically.

"What about you, when is your time, Luc?" Pip asked making me wonder what she meant.

"It is foolish to believe there will ever be one, but you know this," Lucius replied and again I really wished I knew what they were really talking about.

"Then what now, are you really just going to send her home after everything…oh no, what did you do?" Pip asked, obviously after something in Lucius' expression gave him away.

"I did what I had to do for the girl's own good," he snapped.

"Oh no, Luc… please, oh please tell me you didn't end up telling her about being in love with…" The second Pip's words were out I swear I felt my heart stop beating for a time but then Lucius replied, interrupting her before she could finish her sentence.

And in the end, I really wished that he hadn't.

"No, Pip, what did you think I did, just take one look at her and then tell her to go home…That I…" He paused a second as if he was frustratingly dragging a hand through his dark sandy coloured hair and couldn't form the right words. As if they were too painful for him and I didn't have to ask myself why for long.

Because unfortunately for me he didn't stop. He didn't stop speaking, for if he had then I would have gone home, yes, but I would have done so at the very least with some of my heart still intact…before of course, he utterly destroyed it…

"You think that I would send her home knowing something like that…to actually tell her that I love her fucking mother!" The second I heard those devastating words I couldn't help my silent gasp as my eyes snapped open to see that Lucius was facing Pip. He was in the middle of his frustrated rant, one focused on having to deal with me. So much so in fact, that he didn't realise that Pip was now staring at me with nothing but horror and sorrow in her beautiful forest green eyes.

"Uh…" she mumbled trying to break through, but Lucius carried on and said,

"Who thought that was a good idea, because yes, I want to push her away and I am a cruel bastard granted, but I am not that fucking…" This time he finally stopped, and he did this the second Pip grabbed his shirt and looked back to me before telling him…

"Uh…Luc, *I think you just did.*"

My mouth dropped open as I sat up, staring at him with our gazes locked. His was in shock and mine, well mine was as if he'd just shot me in the heart and was still holding the smoking gun.

"Amelia, I…" This was the first time I'd heard him saying my name and I wanted to tear my gaze from his but couldn't. No, instead as I felt the tears pouring down my face, I could only find the strength to say one thing to him.

It was as if I needed it confirmed. Needed it said and out in the world just to know that I wasn't, in fact, just locked inside a new nightmare, one far more horrific than what the last twenty-four hours had given me. For that pain would fade along with my bruises.

But this pain, this *sheer agony*…the one he'd just inflicted would stay with me for the rest of my life.

And he knew this.

He knew this when I uttered in disbelief the last words I vowed to ever say to him…

"You're in love with my mother."

CHAPTER THIRTY

BROKEN VOWS TRAPPED IN STEEL

That was seven years ago, and I would have liked to be able to say that the pain he inflicted that day had faded...*but it hadn't.* No, instead it had just become a dull ache that I simply spent years learning how to ignore. That was until the night he turned up, standing behind me at a gala. The night my heart started to beat again for the first time in seven years. And yet here I was once again, where that heartbreak all began.

Even now when I think back to how naive I was, standing in this same spot and looking up at the building, believing that I would be good enough to tempt a man like Lucius. Ha! And to even think I thought someone like me could have tamed the beast. I wanted to laugh at myself, but unfortunately all I could do was shake my head in pity.

Oh, but to have the chance just to go back to that time and save myself all that pain. My advice would have been simple...*run.* Run as fast as you can, run home and start living your life. Ignore your dreams for the Fates have played a cruel trick on you. There is no such thing as a Chosen One for anyone other than your mother and father who were lucky enough to have finally found each other. But Lucius wasn't a man who needed to be found or have a heart that needed to be claimed.

He was a man to be feared and nothing more. Because, after that day, I knew that he was only capable of ever being more than that with only one person and it wasn't me.

It had been my mother.

I remember the numb state I felt once I heard those words. Words I couldn't have run away from even if I had wanted to. Because they were already free. They were out there and could never be words unheard. So, there it was. The man I was cursed to love was also cursed by loving my mother. A woman who was eternally in love with a man she was destined to be with. So, you see, there was only one happy ever after in that story and unfortunately, it wasn't ever going to be mine.

And nor was it to be Lucius'.

I knew that, as I had spent the last seven years resigning myself to that fact. Another reason I had vowed never to come back to this place. Yet, here I was and this time *I wasn't just here for Lucius.*

So, I looked down at my hand and the same key card that I had once seen being used on that private elevator of his. I didn't ask how Bess had gotten hold of one or how she knew of an unguarded elevator at the back of the club that could only be accessed by a back door. I also didn't know how she had come to find out the key code to this one either. But to be honest, the second I had seen this place again, then there wasn't much that I *had* asked her. I had just stood there across the street and found myself staring at the place as I listened to her plan. All the while just asking myself was he in there? Would I walk through those doors into that VIP of his, that sexual playground, and find him as I had before? Surrounded by blonde beauties to feed on, that painfully made me spend a full year asking myself, had he done this to remind him of my mother?

Needless to say, that for a while, this had made my relationship with my mum a difficult one, especially as I knew none of it was her fault. But she didn't know, and I kept it that way. As far as I knew she just believed I was going through some difficult life questions and gave me the space that I needed. It had been a blessing she gave me that, so she would never know the full extent of the problem. At first, I wanted to hate her for what she had unknowingly taken away from me. But in truth, I could never hate her, she was my mum and she... well, *she was wonderful.*

So, after about six months of not knowing what to do with myself and finding myself sat for long hours on the rooftop gardens of Afterlife just looking out to the world and asking myself why, I came to a decision. I decided to throw myself into my only other passion in life...and it had worked. I worked my ass off and instead of spending my youth at parties and singles nights out flirting with strangers, I had studied. I had burnt the midnight oil and passed all my exams with the highest grades anyone could get. A historical genius, one lecturer had claimed and boasted to my parents at my graduation, but in truth I had felt like a fraud. Because what was the truth, that I had used it as therapy to get over the biggest heartbreak in my life so far? That every time he had plagued my thoughts, I found the only way to drive him back out again was to pick up my books and study.

To simply swap one obsession for another.

And it had worked.

I had made it my life and up until a little over a week ago, I had been happy. I had my simple little life, which included my small group of friends, a warm and cozy little flat, one I had been so proud of owning and most of all, *my independence.*

And now, one by one they had all been taken away from me, the blindfolds removed from each element and it had left me naked to the truth.

My life was just a lie.

It was a smokescreen for what I really wanted, for what I could never have and by the Gods how I wanted it back! But first, I had a job to do and one that was far more important than what I wanted. So, it was time to crack on then really, wasn't it, I said to myself.

I had already turned around ready to say goodbye to my new friend only to find her gone. This had been about ten minutes ago and since then I had been in some kind of trance, just staring at the place and convincing myself that I could do this.

You see, when she had first told me of her plan for me to get inside I had asked the obvious questions, as to why I couldn't just do as I did last time and announce that Lucius knew who I was and would therefore just let me in. But she had convinced me that this wouldn't have been the case. That, in fact, she had it on good authority that there were orders to ship me back off to Afterlife no matter what I said or did, for it was for my father to deal with me.

Gods, but I felt like a bloody, naughty child!

She also told me that Lucius had planned to ship the box off to someone in Egypt to look at, where it was rumored that plans were in place to try and take it during transit. Something I knew I couldn't let happen. Bess told me that my only hope was to try and get to the box without him knowing and try and open it before this happened, so that the box was empty when it was stolen.

This all made sense other than the fact I wasn't A: James Bond, B: A Ninja or C: A jewel thief... or even a member of Ocean's Eleven which would have also been handy right about now. No, instead I reminded her that she was dealing with a bookworm who collected toys, went to Star Trek conventions wearing fake Spock ears and whose idea of a crazy night was ordering extra jalapenos on my pizza. Or even breaking out the wasabi when drunk and seeing between me and Wendy, who could eat the most of the stuff without breaking into a sweat and pulling a disgusted face first. Hence, all these perfectly good reasons as to why I was the biggest flaw in this plan of hers. Plus, not to mention the clumsy aspect to all of this as that was enough of a reason all on its own.

But my only reply to all this was her yanking her now bloodied scarf out of my hand, patting me on the back and saying,

"You will be fine." Then I had unknowingly talked to myself for about three minutes before realising that she was long gone, still feeling like an idiot even though no one was around to witness it.

So, with all that in mind and without one shred of confidence in me achieving even half of what was needed, I crossed the road after raising up my hood. I walked around the back, to where she had pointed to, telling me there was a side door the staff used to get rid of rubbish. But it was the fence at the back that she told me would be left unlocked ready for me to go through. That way I could then go to the back of the building where I would soon discover was where all the vehicles were parked and was how Lucius and his people entered the building.

So, I did as she said and made my way back there, soon seeing for myself her idea of it being 'unlocked' was actually a hole cut in the fence with bolt cutters.

"Nice," I muttered sarcastically as I took off my jacket and rolled it up into a ball so I didn't snag it on the fence, but instead fed it through and placed it on top of my bag that I had

fed through there first. Then I gave it all a little push out of the way before pulling the interlocking metal links back as far as they would go and scooting in there myself.

"Okay, so that's step one down, only forty other impossible steps to take," I grumbled out loud to myself after putting my coat back on and tucking my bag strap diagonally across my shoulder to free up my hands. Then I continued round, trying to stay out of view of the cameras and stay in the blind spots Bess had told me about. I think I held my breath the entire time and looked up at those security lights as if I expected them not only to turn on, but also start screaming at me like a police siren.

Then I looked across the lot and saw that lines of parked, shiny new cars filled the open space with only a few that looked like something my dad would drool over. Expensive, sleek supercars that took pride of place and were parked closest to the door. I looked up and noticed now the high brick wall that surrounded the car park with large heavy metal gates at the entrance.

A gulp later at the security of the place and I turned to face where I needed to get to without those damn lights coming on. But, thankfully, it also seemed that this was another successful step to tick off the list as I made it to the door and after entering the four-digit code she gave me, I could then tick off my third. Wow, I was on a roll!

I slipped inside and again, as with the floodlights, I kind of expected some kind of alarm to go off, so froze for a moment as if waiting for it. But again, when nothing happened I thanked my lucky stars and carried on.

The lobby was an elaborate one and definitely one suited to the private entrance of its rich owner. But other than it being a room with luxurious black and red wallpaper and it having a glass table at the centre, then that was it. Well, that wasn't strictly true as it officially had one of the strangest sculptures I had ever seen, sat in the middle of it. The piece was made from carved wood that had been charred black and was of a pair of demonic hands with their fingers interlinked at the top, with claws embedded in their own flesh. And at its centre, nestled safely inside the hands, was a bleeding heart made of red glass.

I don't know why, but I found myself staring at it as though it held some inner meaning I couldn't figure out. Then I finally tore my eyes away from it as I walked round to the double doors at the centre. There were two other doors either side that I gathered took you straight into the main floor of the club, but it was the elevator I stood opposite now that held my interest. So, I took a deep breath and took the card out of my pocket and slapped it to the scanner saying,

"Well, here goes nothing." I don't know why but I found myself only half happy that they actually opened, and the card had worked. Because now that meant I had no excuse to get myself out of this crazy situation. No, instead, I stepped inside and pressed the button to the top floor. Bess had told me where Lucius' personal vault was as he had a false wall in his apartment and assured me that at this time of night it would be empty.

I had wanted to scoff at this almost asking what if he got lucky, but in the end, the very thought of it stopped me in my tracks, finding that the words were just kind of stuck there, too painful a thought to speak aloud.

By the time the doors opened again I had once more convinced myself that it was behind this door surely that I would be faced with a guard of some kind. But there was no one. So, after giving it a quick glance both ways and after sticking my head out in what no doubt looked a comical way, I stepped out into another lobby of sorts.

This one had a number of doors around its centre table and this time the sculpture was like the one downstairs only in reverse. It was a carved wooden heart that was charred black, opening up as if the two glass hands inside were trying to break free, splitting the heart from within. The difference in the hands was that they weren't just made of red glass but this time, they were a pair of woman's hands. I wondered once more what it meant and if it was symbolic or personal to Lucius?

"No, it's just a rich man's art," I whispered to myself before getting on with what needed to be done. I looked from left to right wondering which door it was. Then I looked to the biggest set of doors straight ahead of the elevator and knew the second I saw them that this was Lucius' apartment.

I remembered it now. The day I ran from those doors shortly after hearing his secret confession. Pip had tried to stop me, but he only ended up stopping her, telling her to let me go. I had found my way downstairs somehow and into the waiting car ready to drive me directly back to the airstrip, where one of my father's planes was fueled and ready to take me home.

I may not have remembered much after he said those words, but I remembered those doors. Doors I had needed to brace myself against as at the time I had placed a fist in my mouth and cried around it so that he wouldn't hear me. I didn't want him to see my tears or hear my pain, for he didn't deserve them.

I don't know why I was feeling this way now? Why not when I was back in London... was it because he was in my domain? Or was it just because being back here after so long and seeing the place again, just brought up painful memories and nothing more?

Back in London he had been different. I had finally got to see him as a person not just the cruel king of his kingdom. Not just the brutal killer I had barely witnessed that night. I would often wake screaming in the night for him, just as I had done when inside that van. But because of the drugs in my system I often asked myself what had been real and what had just been a warped memory?

Because, as much as I remembered seeing a tender side to Lucius when he found me, I couldn't trust in any of it being real. Not after piecing together everything that had happened as a whole. The humiliation he put me through in front of all his people shortly before the attack…I shook my head just thinking about it and unconsciously was surprised when I found that, just like when I woke, I was doing the same thing. With a hand to his door holding my body steady as the memories assaulted me. But unlike then, this time I couldn't run. Not until I had finished this mission.

So, with this in mind, I slapped both hands to the double doors and pushed hard, no longer caring who could have been in there, because let's face it, if they were there, then I would be a goner anyway. So, I walked inside and got my first glimpse of Lucius' private world. And what I did discover didn't shock me…

Lucius' world was cold.

I frowned as I walked further into the space that opened out into a spacious living room, asking myself where the life in this room was. Oh, there was the personality of some control freak minimalist who wasn't into his creature comforts. Like a decent couch for that matter as it wasn't exactly one for putting your feet up and watching TV relaxing at night. No, it was functional and that was it. As if he had called a designer and said, here is the money, now do anything you want but the only colour I like is blood red and nothing more.

Because the whole place was in different shades of grey and black, with the smallest amount of red accents dotted around the place. One full wall was like bare grey concrete that held a few grouped pictures where each section made up a piece of the image. But it was one you would have to stand back to see.

However, from what I could see just walking past then it looked like sections of the same tree.

This was hung over a large L shaped couch that was dark grey and looked about as comfy to sit on as a park bench. It was low, wide and hard looking. The only saving grace to it was the few big blood red cushions placed along it. The rug in front of it was a lighter grey and was mostly covered by a glass coffee table the shape of a kite only arched at its rough edges. It was a strange design and looking at it from a different angle you could have said it was a broken cross.

I tore my gaze from it and took in a few other aspects of the room, like the way it seemed to be sectioned off. There was a small bar area that was all glass and chrome. The floors were cold slate with panels of dark grey hardwood to help section off the rooms. There was even a large dining table the further around you walked, that was a slab of what looked like black glass. But on closer inspection I realised it was highly polished granite. I wondered briefly if this had been what he had broken when on the phone to me and he had fused it back together or just had the whole thing replaced?

I also couldn't help wondering had it looked like this when my mother had been here? Or had he had it changed since then? Well, I can imagine you would certainly redecorate a place and it had been twenty-seven years at least. Another painful thought that I ended up having to shake off as I continued on. I had to keep my mind on the end game in all this and that was the box, nothing more.

So, I purposely walked into his bedroom and tried to ignore the space, looking right away for his walk-in closet that Bess had told me about. I had to wonder again how she knew all this stuff, but then again, she was an Oracle. But no matter how much I tried I couldn't help but slap a hand to the entrance of the closet and lower my head, letting my shoulders slump. I just wasn't strong enough. I had to look. I had to see if it was the same bed I had woken up in that day or had he changed it?

I didn't know how I would feel either way so what was the point, I argued with myself and then lost, as I turned my head.

It was the same.

The second I saw it I knew my mistake as it brought back a flash of memory. It flooded back to me with such force I felt my hand tighten around the wooden frame just to keep me still standing. It was of him standing there with Pip, holding himself so still, so steady at the end of the bed as he gazed down at my misery. His eyes, the way they tracked my tears as each one fell as if counting them and saving the memory of them for later.

He had not long ago told me that my eyes were beautiful, but when crying they were *breathtaking.* Had he first thought this that day? Had he taken one look at my heartbreak and thought it beautiful?

So, the bed was the same, so what…what did that mean…? Nothing, that's what!

"Get a grip Emm, time is wasting," I told myself and walked inside the closet trying to ignore the smell of Lucius that surrounded me from all of his clothes, making me wince with my eyes closing tight for a few seconds as if this would help with the way he assaulted my senses. Then I walked over to the elaborate gold cross on the wall I knew would be there and shook my head when I did. Well, so far Bess had been right about everything, but now this was the main test. Was she right about this? So, I did as she told me to and grabbed hold of the cross and turned it until it was facing upside down, now making the sign of the Antichrist.

"Cute," I scoffed aloud then watched as a code panel appeared. Now, this was when things got tricky as she said she didn't know the code. Which had me questioning how she knew everything else but this last part? I had asked her how I was supposed to get inside it and her answer hadn't exactly been a confidence booster because it was a simple…

"Wing it." And unsurprisingly just repeating these two words in question and a slightly high-pitched tone didn't get me any other answer but a shrug. So now here I was, faced with 10,000 possible combinations to choose from, meaning it would most likely take me well into my thirties before I got it right.

But then again…

"Could it be?" I asked myself before giving it a try as really, at this point, what did I have to lose? I punched in the number I thought it could be and I was right,

It was my birthday.

Just like the pin number for his card. Now what the hell did that mean?!

Suddenly a heavy lock sounded to be moving and a false wall clicked open so that now I could push it open and the second I did, I gasped. The room was a brightly lit space that was filled with, well everything you would expect from a man like Lucius.

A wall to my left was full of weapons, that held everything from swords, hammers, maces and daggers to guns in all sizes. It was like a weapons collection of the ages, all behind glass cabinets and with what looked like a fingerprint recognition pad for them to open. Well, I just hoped that the box wasn't behind something like that or I was screwed. Not unless I could wait until he fell asleep, bang him over the head before dragging his big ass in here.

"Yeah, well that's not happening," I said mocking myself before turning around to take in the rest of his treasures. There were your typical locked boxes like you find in a bank vault covering the wall opposite, making me wonder what lay inside. A small giggle escaped me when I wondered if it was his stamp collection or something equally as geeky.

But then I stopped dead and my mouth dropped as I took in the centre of the room. For there stood a huge sword held in its own glass case. I knew instantly what sword it was so the historian in me gasped, and my hands flew to my face in shock.

"No...could it be, *Caliburnus?*" I muttered its old name that was Latin for the better known, Excalibur. It would make sense considering the setting for the sword was sat in a feminine stone hand that was reaching up through blue glass to represent the water, making it a piece of art in its own right. See, a lot of people would question this and ask themselves why not an anvil, which is the better-known legend, but there was another one. The true one, if supernatural belief was to be believed.

Excalibur was said to have been given to Arthur by the Lady of the Lake sometime after he began his reign. She told him that the sword was named Caliburnus, meaning the King's sword, and held great magic. The Lancelot-Grail, in which this legend takes place and is a major source of Arthurian legend that was written in French, is a series of five volumes that not only tell the story of the quest for the Holy Grail but the more romantic element of the tale which was the famous romance of Lancelot and Guinevere.

Now, in these volumes it is told that Arthur was at the brink of death and so orders Griflet, one of his Knights of the Round Table, to throw the sword into the enchanted lake. But after two failed attempts, failed because he simply believed that such a great sword should not be thrown away, Griflet finally complies with the wounded king's request. So, this time when he actually threw the sword into the lake a hand emerged from the water to catch it.

The supernatural element to this story isn't the hand in the lake however, it is who it was said to be fated for next and who was to be next in line for such greatness.

And here it was.

I was utterly astonished by such a find, knowing that if ever something like this was discovered it would be one of the marvels of the modern world. That was, if it could be proven to be real. The historian in me was desperate to forget the damn box, hunt him down and demand he tell me all about it! I wasn't sure how he would have felt about that, however.

I finally tore my eyes from the sword and looked towards the other side of the room on my right. Hoping to then see what other secrets it held. The whole wall was sectioned off into box shelving and each place held some kind of artifact, meaning that it was obvious that Lucius and I had something in common. As it looked as though I wasn't the only one who held a passion for history, not if that collection was anything to go by.

The huge difference between his collection and what you would find in any museum was that his all looked brand new and made only yesterday. Making me realise that these weren't just pieces he had picked up at some rich man's auction or something found on the internet by some private buyer. But these were actual possessions only ever owned by one person, the one who no doubt commissioned them...*Lucius.*

This was when I realised that out there in that apartment was just a cold hard front of a shell of the man he portrayed himself to be. But in here, surrounded by a man's long life and the things he owned, the things he treasured enough to keep safe...then this right here was the real side of him. This was the man he kept hidden from the world...

A secret world I'd just broken into.

This thought suddenly filled me with dread and I couldn't help but look over my shoulder at the door, wondering if I shouldn't just make a run for it whilst I still could. I played out every other scenario that didn't include stealing that box, but every one ended with the possible death I would then forever have on my hands.

No, I couldn't do it.

So, I needed to hurry, grab this damn box and run for it. So, after scanning the wall for less than a second, I found it sat in the middle as if it had been placed there ready for me. It was even at my height being eye level and therefore impossible for me to miss.

Looking at it now I couldn't help but reach for it, feeling as though it was calling out to me, but at the same time warning me away. I even thought about Indiana Jones and wondered if I would need a bag of sand to swap it with or something.

Then I shook off that silly thought and finally reached out for it. But the second I did, it was starting to look as if that sand bag idea hadn't been so silly after all. As now I must have unknowingly triggered some kind of alarm. I had barely even grazed it with my fingertips when an alarm was ringing out making me step back.

I looked all around me as massive metal doors all started crashing down at speed. They came from the ceiling and down the front of the walls making me jump in fright when they slammed into the floor locking in place. It started with the glass cabinets full of weapons and I screamed once it continued all around the room with metal coming down all around me. The wall of lock boxes was next and then quickly after it the wall of artifacts in front of me.

I took another staggered step back then turned the second I heard a noise behind me. I was just in time to see that even the glass box around the sword and its sculpture was now being quickly encased in steel that had risen up from the floor.

It was clear that the room was going on lock down and the second I realised this my eyes shot to the door. This was when my panic really started to set in as I saw the heavy metal door now swinging inwards making me scream first in fright and then at my stupidity.

"NO!" I shouted after I pointlessly ran for it just in time for it to swing shut in my face and sealing me inside for good.

"Shit, shit, shit!" I shouted, banging a palm on the inside of the vault door, but it was useless. It was locked and unless I was Bruce Banner and had unknowingly become the Hulk in the last five minutes then there was no way I was getting out.

I was trapped.

But worse than that, for now he must have known what I did.

Which meant only one thing…

Lucius had caught me.

CHAPTER THIRTY-ONE

HEART CAPTURED

Well, that most certainly wasn't how I expected it to go, that was for damn sure! I don't know how long I had been waiting by the time they opened the door, but it must have been at least twenty minutes. Twenty bloody minutes of being sat on the floor panicking and freaking out. I swear there must have been a hidden camera in here somewhere and he was doing this to me on purpose and no doubt, for his damn amusement!

For why else would he have left me in here for so long? Because he must have known there had been someone breaking in and it was on lock down. This was confirmed when I finally did something that I should have done when I first walked in the place and that was to look up and see if there were any cameras in there, and as it turned out, there were.

I felt like slapping my forehead in a true 'Duh' moment. But instead I wanted to prove my theory of him watching me, so I raised my hand and promptly gave him the middle finger. Needless to say, that the doors opened two minutes after this. I half expected to see Lucius himself, stood there behind the door as it opened but no, it was just his lackies. They gave me a nod, with no need to say anything as I knew the drill, which was why I quietly and without fuss followed them back to their master.

So, this was it. My time had come to face judgement. Hell, but it was punishment enough just from being made to go back into that room. Back into the VIP, only to replay my humiliation out like the remake of some sadistic theatre. I twisted my features into a grimace the closer to those doors we got, as I knew where they would take me. It was one thing stepping foot back in his club but quite another stepping foot back in that playroom of his.

But what choice did I have? I guess I could run and see how far I would get. The elevator doors were still open, could I still make it?

"He told us to tell you that if you run, you will only make it fun for him when he gets to hunt you down." One of his men said making me shudder. He must have seen me looking longingly at the doors.

"But of course," I muttered sarcastically making the guy chuckle before opening the club doors for me, so that I could enter the very last place I ever wanted to go. But once again, what choice did I have? None, zero and absolutely nothing left in me. Because for once I had to stop running and face my demons…Or should I say,

Just the one.

Because I wasn't that naive twenty-year-old princess who believed in 'happy ever afters' and fairy tales spun by the Fates of prophesied Chosen Ones. I wasn't walking in there unprepared for what it was he had the power to do. I knew what he was and what he was capable of. So, I would make this my weapon. The weapon of knowledge so that I may prepare myself for what was to come.

However, no matter how much I tried to tell myself this, the second I saw him as I did that night, sat there master of his domain, I couldn't help my foot faltering a step. It was as if the very sight of him made it hard to breathe. Made it hard to move any closer.

It was like looking directly into the eyes of a stunning predator that utterly captivated you with its dangerous beauty. But it was free. It wasn't confined by anything in between you and it. It was just there getting ready to pounce any second, like a tightly coiled and concealed rage just waiting under a false veil of calm, ready to erupt any second.

He saw this. He saw the fear in my eyes and for a single moment it looked as though for once it didn't please him to see it. Not like the last time where my fear had amused him. No, now his dark stare softened as he recreated the moment when beckoning me forward with two fingers. The guy next to me nodded down at me and whispered,

"We aren't authorized to touch you, so please, just make my life easier and keep walking…yeah." I frowned looking up at him in surprise. The guy was asking me nicely not to do anything that would get him in trouble, as if I had that power. I decided it wasn't worth the two of us getting into any more shit than I already was on my own, so I gave him a break and took a deep breath.

I am not that girl, I am not that girl, I am not that girl, I repeated in my mind trying to hold on to the fact that I had stupidly dreamt of a moment like this. To be dressed sexy, walk in here and slap him before walking out again. Well, from the looks of things I think if I tried to do that then all that would happen was my hand swiftly captured in his palm and then this night's recreation really would be complete.

So, I walked and watched him as he in turn watched me. However, when I did it, I did so with a fake expression of indifference. But when Lucius did it, he did it as though he was watching his dinner coming closer and he liked what he saw.

Also, like that night, I noticed that he was wearing a suit, only this time it was all black and consuming every thought I had. Just the sight of him looked so dominating, so powerful and forbiddingly handsome, it was hard to think of little else. Every inch of him screamed of control and a dark force to be reckoned with. From his trousers, to his shirt and waistcoat all of it black and like before, he wore it the same way, without a jacket and with his sleeves rolled up his strong forearms. One black leather glove on show and, like back then, it was one that didn't stop at the wrist but continued up under his shirt.

You would have thought the sight would have looked odd or even feminine but boy, you would be wrong. If anything, it only managed to add a dangerous element to his look, as if it was a hand so powerful that part of it needed to be contained. I always saw it and wondered what lay hidden beneath those worn straps of leather? Today's choice was one that looked like something that would have been worn to a boxing match only with all the fingers covered.

His hair was, as it always was, in that natural fall that looked barely tamed. Just the type you wanted to run your fingers through just to see if it felt as soft as it looked. Did it feel like the rough sands of his past it's colour resembled?

"Ah, but here is my little thief," he said with a smirk as I came to stand in front of him and it was only now that I realised there was a startling difference than before. A difference that, thankfully, made me breathe a little easier, for this time the only people who had joined him on the couch were who I imagined his council members to be, with not a blonde beauty in sight.

"Lucius," I said in greeting and doing so with a steady voice unlike before. His grin grew further up on one side before he nodded to the seat next to him and offered,

"Won't you take a seat." I swear that the spark of mischief in his eyes told me he enjoyed being able to throw me off centre, seeing that this also hadn't happened last time. He watched me frown in confusion and then obviously figured it out for himself where my thoughts must be…stuck in the past. But I couldn't trust this. I couldn't trust him, and he knew this when I gave him my answer.

"I think I will stand, thank you." The second I replied he raised a brow in question and then said,

"Very well then." Then he stood himself, pulling his waistcoat down with a pronounced tug. Now, like last time, the moment he did this my natural reaction kicked in and I took a step back…a step back through time.

And this was where it began and he knew it too. He knew that to get me past this memory, he would first have to rewrite the old one…rewrite it with something new.

"I must say that I'm impressed to see that you made it as far as you did," he told me, stopping in front of me and giving me enough space to at least breathe easy. Oh yeah, two metres away was a good start but I wished it was further, as I had a feeling that it wouldn't stay this way for long.

"Your little switch worked just long enough for you to catch that flight," Lucius continued when I didn't respond, letting me know that he had been monitoring my progress. Then he walked closer and as if this was a dance we knew well, I took my step back.

"Clever girl that you are," he praised making me swallow down this new lump called lust, especially when his same gloved hand came to rest just slightly above my head. Then he looked me up and down slowly and said,

"Well, looks like we have been here before, haven't we, Sweet?" he said cutting through any bullshit this time. I found myself only able to nod, hating that I wasn't strong enough to snap a witty reply back at him. But instead, I gave him insight to the emotions that I was feeling. Letting him know exactly what this was doing to me and letting him in.

"Then let's make it complete, shall we?" he said before his free hand came to the buttons of my jacket and I couldn't help my reaction as I covered his hand to stop him.

"Wh…what are you doing?" I stammered. His reply first came in the form of a bad boy grin before he told me,

"Well, if I remember correctly, then under this heavy wrapping, I should find the gift of a pretty dress worn especially for me," he told me in a smooth tone that was coated in confidence and lust. This was when I told him,

"It wasn't worn for you…not…" I took a deep shuddered breath and continued with a whispered reply,

"…Not this time." Lucius nodded his understanding before saying,

"No, I suppose not. But I wish to see it all the same," he said and then slipped my buttons free one by one, even as my hand was still held tense over his. And each one he freed with his skilled fingers, he watched me, his stunning grey blue eyes never once moving from my own, making me want to ask what it was he was searching for in them.

This was when I uttered without thinking…

"I am not that girl anymore." The look he gave me was first one of surprise and then one of challenge.

"Oh, but I think you are, I think you are still that scared little girl running lost, until found by the wolves she was trying to escape from," he told me, and I wanted to snap back at him but in the end didn't trust myself to speak, so I bit my lip and shook my head no. But then his knowing grin made me feel a little braver, so I said,

"You mean wolf," I corrected.

"Perhaps," he hummed as he tapped on the glass with his fingers.

"But let's see, should we?" he said before peeling back the sides of my jacket and letting it drop from my shoulders into a heavy heap of material on the floor. Then shamefully, Lucius took a step back to admire me and the second I tried to cover myself, he didn't like it. He didn't like how I held my arms around myself. I knew this when he stepped back into me and took my hand by the wrist. Then he pulled my arm out straight and looked down at me.

"Tut, tut, my little Sweet, you have done enough hiding from me these last few days, don't you think," he said, letting me know that he had been searching for me all along. I shook my head at him and tore my gaze away, looking off to one side at the floor, for I couldn't do it this time. I couldn't be a part of his games.

"What do you want from me, Lucius?" I asked as I tried to pull my hand from his hold on my wrist, a freedom he wouldn't grant me. So instead he captured my arm between our bodies as he placed himself close once more and I was unable to make eye contact. Another thing that he didn't like as I soon felt his hand come to my chin to force my gaze once more to his. I felt enough pressure there so that I was forced to lift my head back to look at him.

"Isn't it obvious?" he said making me frown, before saying,

"With you? It never is." He smirked at my confession before running the back of all four fingers down my cheek. But this was all the reply I was to receive as his attention went back to what I was wearing, and the hand that first trailed down my cheek now continued further this time. He let his touch graze just over the swell of my breasts, making me suck in a surprised breath, one he grinned at seeing. Then his hand dipped lower down my side before coming to rest at my waist.

"I think I like this one better, for it suits you," he told me, giving me a compliment that for once wasn't attached to an insult of some kind.

"I...I..."

"I am starting to think that the words 'thank you' don't come easy to you, for I believe I am owed quite a few of them by now and in person like you promised," he teased referring to our flirty text messages. Well, this was certainly going differently than last time that was for sure and I couldn't say that I was complaining. But then what if this was just all part of his game?

Although by now I had to finally ask myself...just what game was that exactly?

"Why do you do this to me?" I found myself asking before I could talk myself out of it. This was when Lucius released a sigh as if now was the time for something and I half expected that to be for him, for him to just walk away. But then instead of coming right out and saying it, he obviously decided to answer my question with a question.

"Why did you come back here, after all this time...? What took you so long?" His question had me dumbfounded! Had he wanted me to come back? The way he worded that question sounded as if he had been waiting for me to. But why? Why on earth after last time would I?

"You have to be welcome, Lucius, to want to go back somewhere," I told him, this time without a single waver in my voice. Lucius laughed once and then grabbed me tighter and yanked me close,

"Does this not feel like a welcome to you," he growled with lust and I swear he must have heard my heartbeat going wild, for he looked down and glanced at my heaving chest, one now brushing against his own every time I took a breath.

"I don't understand...what...why?" I couldn't fully form

that sentence. Then I felt his hand slipping down, slowing starting to gather up my skirt and making me shoot a panicked glance at the rest of the room behind him, one I hadn't fully taken in until now.

"I warned you before, now give me your fucking eyes!" he snapped, making me look back to him and his commanding presence that was drowning me.

"Please, Lucius, I…" I started to say but stopped when he groaned, making a guttural sound as if in pain for a second.

"Mmm, I must say how I like the sound of that coming from your lips," he teased sexually, and I jumped a little in his hold the second his fingertips lightly grazed my thighs, but this obviously wasn't enough for him as he uttered to himself,

"Skin." This was my only warning when I felt his claws start to grow from the end of his fingertips making me flinch.

"Be still," he warned, humming the warning by my ear before I felt him curl those deadly talons ever so slightly, enough that I felt the sudden pull and tug of my tights. Then I felt it ping back the second the material found it's limit and tore, as he shredded five long slashes the length of my thigh. I jerked against him but then his claws retracted and in its place were four fingertips and a thumb starting to caress up my leg in the holes he'd just made. It was done so softly, it was shocking to feel, considering where it came from.

I swear, just the feel of him touching me this way and so close to that place, the one I had been close to begging him to touch the last time then, as before I was close to coming undone. But just like that the moment was broken, as I remembered the pain from last time he played with me, his new toy.

"Lucius please, don't do this here…don't humiliate me like this again, if only to stop and taunt me for being so close…" I stopped myself before I revealed too much. But it worked for his hand did stop and he froze next to me as if my words had inflicted more upon him than he would ever let on.

"You think I wish to humiliate you?" he asked on a hiss, as if shocked. I nodded, not trusting my voice right now, then he must have replayed my words back again.

"Go on, finish that sentence." I shook my head telling him no when he snarled down at me.

"Finish it!"

"Please, don't make me," I asked him in a pleading tone and for once he must have heard the desperation in my voice and instead of gaining pleasure from it, he considered the root of it.

"Alright, Sweet, but know that what I do now is not to humiliate you, for if I wanted, I could command every last person in this room to drop to the floor and place their foreheads to the ground, and stay that way for hours," he said and when I looked at him in disbelief he clicked his fingers causing a wave of movement behind him. He then turned slightly so that I could now see that he hadn't been joking. But instead of everyone being on the floor like ancient servants in sight of their king, he had simply frozen the room. Every single person in his VIP had turned into a statue of flesh.

Then he suddenly bent down slightly and swept my legs from under me, catching me in his arms before standing.

"What are you doing?!" I asked in shock but more so when I received his reply.

"Righting a wrong," he said then clicked his fingers again, bringing everyone back. I cried in shock and I automatically held onto him as he started to carry me out of the room. Then, unbelievably, he told the room,

"We are not to be disturbed!" Meanwhile I was left in a state of utter bewilderment as he continued to walk through the VIP doors straight towards his personal rooms. It was all happening so fast, I never even saw it coming. I knew where he was taking me, of course, but why was he? That was the biggest question. In fact, it was the question for so many things. Why was he acting this way? Why wasn't he having me removed from his club or sending me back to my father like last time? But most of all…

Why did it feel so right here in his arms?

But I didn't ask him any of these things. But simply remained in stunned silence until he finally made it inside and then unfortunately, letting my legs slip slowly from his hold. Then he held me steady until he was confident that I wouldn't fall.

I couldn't help in that moment but look up at him with big beseeching eyes, hoping now he would finally let me in. Finally release me of the mental chains he had wound tightly around my heart, ones that he continually tugged on the end of every time I saw him.

I wanted freedom to breathe, to speak, to shout, to scream when finally, I yanked myself free and almost ran from him when in the end I only made it to his dining table. He watched me retreat calmly as if this wasn't an unexpected reaction for me to have towards him.

"I…I…don't understand," I told him after first turning around and placing my palms on the cold stone, looking down and seeing a shadow of my reflection in the polished surface.

I did look lost.

Then, after long agonizing moments of silence, I turned back to face him when he spoke.

"What don't you understand?" he asked in a soft tender tone that only managed to mess with me even more.

"You don't even like me!" I threw back at him and this time he laughed once, only it was without humor but done more so as if a cruel punishing joke was being played on himself.

"I can assure you that your statement couldn't be further

from the truth," he said dryly, making me hold on to the back of the table just to steady myself. Was what he was saying really true?

"But then why, if that is true, why treat me…" I started to question when he quickly admitted,

"I'm not proud of how I treated you before, but it was a necessary evil at the time…one I find I can no longer inflict," he said confusing me.

"What are you saying?" I asked shaking my head a little.

"What I am saying is that this time… I want you here." Hearing this I sucked in a sharp breath hoping, no, praying that I had heard him right and this wasn't just the Fates playing some cruel cosmic joke on me, ready this time to push me fully over the edge.

So, I tested it.

"You…you lie," I said, now realising that I had tears falling down my cheeks, knowing now the full extent of his power. Because if I thought that he had the power before to crush me, then now, I knew for certain that he had the power to do much more than that…

The power to kill me.

But instead of the cruel laughter or the sarcastic remark, he took a step towards me and said,

"No, I. Am. Not." There was such strength and finality in his tone that it was hard not to believe him.

"Yes…yes, you have to be, this…this can't be real," I stammered again, this time forcing my words through a sob as my voice caught on the emotion. I swiped at my chin where tears had gathered and with just that slight motion, by the time I looked up again I gasped, for he was right there in front of me, taking my hand in his and lifting it to his lips.

"By the Gods you're so beautiful…painfully so," he whispered before tasting my gathered tears from the crook of my finger. I shuddered as the next set of tears fell the second I had to close my eyes as the overload of emotions assaulted me.

"I did lie," he said making my heart stop and my eyes snap open, thinking this is it, here it comes. The point where he tells me it wasn't real…none of this is real.

But what came was the opposite.

"But no more," he vowed and then before I knew what was happening he took my face in his hands, and a leather covered thumb swiped away my tears like last time.

"There is only now…" he vowed in promise.

"…My Amelia." Then he lowered his lips to mine and finally my world exploded into pure bliss of the likes I had never known. He kissed me, and I couldn't help myself as I opened up for him almost instantly as I cried out in surprise. He took advantage of this and swept in there to take his first taste, moaning the second he did…or had that been my own sound made? I couldn't tell, for time just stood still. This was what first kisses were meant to be. To feel yourself soaring just because of the way he made me feel. The way his hands held me locked to him from fear that I would pull away. But then why would I, when my hands held fistfuls of his shirt as I clung on. I never wanted this moment to end.

This beautiful, perfect moment.

For I knew that even when it did eventually end, that in my heart it would remain forever, replacing all other moments of cruelty…the lies he inflicted. I didn't know why he lied but right now I didn't care. Not when his lips were consuming my own as he dominated the kiss. Then his arms wrapped around me and he growled over them, giving me a moment to breathe before crushing them to me again, this time biting me a little to prompt me to open up once more for him.

And I complied.

But of course, I did, for I wanted more just as he did.

Because in this perfect moment I knew that if I was to die right there, if he was to suddenly produce a blade and plunge it into my heart, then I would still cling on to him for just a second longer.

That was how much I loved him.

But this was when I realised it wasn't me he was killing…

It would only be himself.

For I remembered now why it was I was here. It was the box.

The box that held the key to something everyone thought was impossible.

For all of eternity nothing had been strong enough until now.

The key inside that box was …

How to kill a Vampire King.

And in doing so…

The Death of my Mother.

To be continued

ABOUT THE AUTHOR

Stephanie Hudson has dreamed of being a writer ever since her obsession with reading books at an early age. What first became a quest to overcome the boundaries set against her in the form of dyslexia has turned into a life's dream. She first started writing in the form of poetry and soon found a taste for horror and romance. Afterlife is her first book in the series of twelve, with the story of Keira and Draven becoming ever more complicated in a world that sets them miles apart.

When not writing, Stephanie enjoys spending time with her loving family and friends, chatting for hours with her biggest fan, her sister Cathy who is utterly obsessed with one gorgeous Dominic Draven. And of course, spending as much time with her supportive partner and personal muse, Blake who is there for her no matter what.

Author's words.

My love and devotion is to all my wonderful fans that keep me going into the wee hours of the night but foremost to my wonderful daughter Ava...who yes, is named after a cool, kick-ass, Demonic bird and my sons, Jack, who is a little hero and Baby Halen, who yes, keeps me up at night but it's okay because he is named after a Guitar legend!

Keep updated with all new release news & more on my website
www.afterlifesaga.com
Never miss out, sign up to the
mailing list at the website.

Also, please feel free to join myself and other Dravenites on my Facebook group
Afterlife Saga Official Fan
Interact with me and other fans. Can't wait to see you there!

facebook.com/AfterlifeSaga

twitter.com/afterlifesaga

instagram.com/theafterlifesaga

ACKNOWLEDGEMENTS

Well first and foremost my love goes out to all the people who deserve the most thanks and are the wonderful people that keep me going day to day. But most importantly they are the ones that allow me to continue living out my dreams and keep writing my stories for the world to hopefully enjoy… These people are of course YOU! Words will never be able to express the full amount of love I have for you guys. Your support is never ending. Your trust in me and the story is never failing. But more than that, your love for me and all who you consider your 'Afterlife family' is to be commended, treasured and admired. Thank you just doesn't seem enough, so one day I hope to meet you all and buy you all a drink! ;)

To my family… To my amazing mother, who has believed in me from the very beginning and doesn't believe that something great should be hidden from the world. I would like to thank you for all the hard work you put into my books and the endless hours spent caring about my words and making sure it is the best it can be for everyone to enjoy. You make Afterlife shine. To my wonderful crazy father who is and always has been my hero in life. Your strength astonishes me, even to this day and the love and care you hold for your family is a gift you give to the Hudson name. And last but not least, to the man that I consider my soul mate. The man who taught me about real love and makes me not only want to be a better person but makes me feel I am too. The amount of support you have given me since we met has been incredible and the greatest feeling was finding out you wanted to spend the rest of your life with me when you asked me to marry you.

All my love to my dear husband and my own personal Draven… Mr Blake Hudson.

Another personal thank you goes to my dear friend Caroline Fairbairn and her wonderful family that have embraced my brand of crazy into their lives and given it a hug when most needed.

For their friendship I will forever be eternally grateful.

I would also like to mention Claire Boyle my wonderful PA, who without a doubt, keeps me sane and constantly smiling through all the chaos which is my life ;) And a loving mention goes to Lisa Jane for always giving me a giggle and scaring me to death with all her count down pictures lol ;)

Thank you for all your hard work and devotion to the saga and myself. And always going that extra mile, pushing Afterlife into the spotlight you think it deserves. Basically helping me achieve my secret goal of world domination one day…evil laugh time… Mwahaha! Joking of course ;)

As before, a big shout has to go to all my wonderful fans who make it their mission to spread the Afterlife word and always go the extra mile. I love you all x

ALSO BY STEPHANIE HUDSON

Afterlife Saga

A Brooding King, A Girl running from her past. What happens when the two collide?

Transfusion Saga

What happens when an ordinary human girl comes face to face with the cruel Vampire King who dismissed her seven years ago?

Transfusion - Book 1

Venom of God - Book 2

Blood of Kings - Book 3

Rise of Ashes - Book 4

Map of Sorrows - Book 5

Tree of Souls - Book 6

Kingdoms of Hell – Book 7

Eyes of Crimson - Book 8

Afterlife Chronicles: (Young Adult Series)

The Glass Dagger – Book 1

The Hells Ring – Book 2

Stephanie Hudson and Blake Hudson

The Devil in Me

OTHER WORKS
BY
HUDSON INDIE INK

Paranormal Romance/Urban Fantasy

Sloane Murphy

Xen Randell

C. L. Monaghan

Sci-fi/Fantasy

Brandon Ellis

Devin Hanson

Crime/Action

Blake Hudson

Mike Gomes

Contemporary Romance

Gemma Weir

Elodie Colt

Ann B. Harrison